Amanda Kyle W[illiams] ... the Atlanta Journal-Constitution and other local newspapers, owned a small business for thirteen years, is active in the humane community, and a founding director at Lifeline Animal Project in Avondale Estates, Georgia, a non-profit animal welfare organization.

In order to lend authenticity to her Keye Street series, she took courses geared to law enforcement in criminal profiling and serial homicide investigation under the tutelage of a well known criminologist and profiler and worked with a PI firm in Atlanta on surveillance operations. Amanda regularly consults with experts in bond and law enforcement from the Georgia Bureau of Investigation and the Atlanta Police Department.

Amanda Kyle williams lives near Atlanta, Georgia in the American South, which provides unending fodder for fiction.

Praise for Amanda Kyle Williams:

'This is one Street worth acquainting yourself with' *Sun*

'Smart, ironic and compelling, this 21st century heroine is certain to gather ever more fans as the series unfolds. She is too great a character not to last. Catch her before she becomes a household name' *Daily Mail*

'Keye Street immediately puts herself in the top echelon of suspense heroes. She's a mess of fascinating contradictions – effortlessly brilliant on a case, totally inept in managing her own life. She is brutally funny and powerfully human. Williams has created one of the most realistic protagonists in crime fiction that I've had the thrill to read' Tess Gerritsen

'An ex[
that t[

'An ex[
Karin[

By Amanda Kyle Williams and available from Headline

The Stranger You Seek
Stranger In The Room
Don't Talk To Strangers

AMANDA KYLE
WILLIAMS
DON'T TALK TO STRANGERS

headline

First published in 2014 by
HEADLINE PUBLISHING GROUP

First published in paperback in 2015 by
HEADLINE PUBLISHING GROUP

1

Cataloguing in Publication Data is available from the British Library

ISBN 978 0 7553 8426 6

Typeset in Century Schoolbook by Avon DataSet Ltd,
Bidford-on-Avon, Warwickshire

Printed and bound by CPI Group (UK) Ltd, Croydon, CR0 4YY

Headline's policy is to use papers that are natural, renewable and
recyclable products and made from wood grown in well-managed forests
and other controlled sources. The logging and manufacturing processes are
expected to conform to the environmental regulations of the country of
origin.

HEADLINE PUBLISHING GROUP
An Hachette UK Company
338 Euston Road
London NW1 3BH

www.headline.co.uk
www.hachette.co.uk

For Kate Miciak,
who took me to school

Prologue

She was going to make a lot of noise. He could tell by the way she moved, the attitude, the way she spoke to her friends, the way she carried herself. The ringleader. He could always spot them. Some guys, they liked the mousy ones, the ones with their little heads down. Not this guy. He liked them smart. He liked the struggle. And the fear. Not just theirs. *His.* The pounding drumbeat in his ears, the way time stretched like a piece of elastic, pulled until it snapped into a few astonishing seconds of utter terrifying pandemonium—fighting, biting, screaming, his skin under their sparkly nails. He liked that too. It was a way inside them.

He pulled out a brown bag and took a bite of the bologna-and-mustard sandwich he hadn't gotten around to at lunch, washed it down with a freezing-cold Coke, the kind in the green-glass bottles from the old machine in front of Smith's Hardware.

He leaned back into the bench—*bird-watching,* he liked to call it. And the little chicks were out today. Same time. Same route. Same chatter shooting up over the breeze as they crossed the park. Nothing he could make out, just the high-pitched peaks of female voices stabbing giddily at an otherwise serene day.

They would split off in twos soon, head for their own neighborhoods and families and homework and dinners. But she'd walk alone through a strip of woods and down a gravel lane to the ranch house with the white fences—a latchkey kid on a quiet stretch of road.

He finished his sandwich, dusted off his hands, and dropped the bag in the trash bin. He didn't hurry. There was plenty of time. Today it was about the dream—how it would go, what he'd say to her, the way her smile beaconed, *Take me, take me.*

1

I squinted through about a million tiny crystal-like dings as the late-day sun landed on my windshield. I'd been sitting here for an hour. Waiting. I do that a lot. I had an address and a hunch. That was about it. That's about it most of the time.

My name is Keye Street. I am a detective, private, a bail recovery agent, a process server, and a former criminal investigative analyst for the FBI. And when I say *former*, I mean fired. Capital *F*. The Bureau likes their profilers sober.

I dropped the doughnut in my hand into the green-and-white Krispy Kreme box on the passenger's seat and peered through the smoggy dusk of another hot August night. The house, like the others on the street, had been stamped out sometime in the 1960s with a builder's cookie-cutter eye, a starter home—one-story brick, two bedrooms, one bath, a thirty-six-inch picture window to the right of the front door, bedrooms on the left end, a quarter acre of grass with poured concrete driveways. The trees that must have been saplings when the neighborhood sprang to life now shaded the street and rooftops against the unyielding southern sun. But they didn't do anything to take the steam out of the air. Like most neighborhoods this time of year, the whir of condensing units fighting to push cool air through the ductwork was the background music.

I let the sun sink lower, slipped out, closed my car door quietly, and headed down the sidewalk. Four doors down, I veered left and worked my way along a driveway lined with droopy hydrangeas. They looked like they could use a drink. I know the feeling.

A light clicked on inside the house, and I saw him through the picture window. He was sitting in his living room, a Styrofoam box in his left hand, a remote control in the right, facing a television that was too big for the room. I edged closer to the house, saw him push back in his La-Z-Boy. On the big TV, the Braves were playing the Dodgers at Turner Field. There was a '69 Dodge Charger in the driveway, orange and black. The muffler needed a little work. He'd rumbled past me a few times this week. Hot vehicle, though, if you have an eye for muscle cars. I do. I'd grown up with them and the guys who drove them hard on Friday nights in Georgia.

I moved around to one of the bedroom windows. The house looked empty except for Jeremy Coleman. I was hoping his bail-jumping brother would be here. Ronald Coleman was charged with shooting a man while stealing his car in the parking lot of a Krystal hamburger joint. He then held up the drive-thru for five cheese Krystals and an order of fries while the car's owner staggered through the lot begging for help. Great guy, that Ronald Coleman. Coleman's court date must have slipped his mind. A little thing like aggravated assault with the intent to kill, armed robbery, and carjacking can do that. I'd been watching Jeremy on and off for the last week, hoping Ronald would show up. The family history told me the brothers were close. It was Jeremy Coleman who had pulled together ten percent of the $140K the state required for the bail money. Not easy for a working-class guy with a two-stall garage and a Monday-through-Friday classic auto restoration business. I was betting if anyone knew where Coleman was, it was his little brother Jeremy. About a week ago I would have bet the burger-eating creep would have shown up by now. So much for hunches.

I passed overgrown shrubs to a weedy backyard with grass tall enough to have gone to seed, the perfect environment for the mosquitoes to come out to play. Nice and dark and moist. I held on to a brick ledge and tiptoed to see inside the back bedroom. Jeremy slept in the front, I knew. If he had a guest, this would serve as the guest room. The bedroom door was open, and just enough light seeped in to let me know the room was empty. The bed was made. Everything looked exactly like it had the other five times I'd peeked inside. My hands and neck were stinging. Mosquitoes like dark clothes and dark hair too. I had both.

I headed back down the side of the house. The front door opened as I turned the corner. I stopped cold. Movement is what pops out at you at night. The eye catches it when it misses everything else. I stood dead-still in the shadows. Jeremy was on the front porch locking up with a fat, jingly key ring. He was still wearing his work clothes, navy-blue pants and shirt, mechanic-style with a name patch over the left breast pocket. I watched him get in his car. As soon as the engine started, I hightailed it through the yard and up the sidewalk to mine, a dingy Plymouth Neon with a dent in the hood—you don't want to spy on a guy who restores vehicles for a living in something flashy. So my white-on-white 1969 Impala convertible was at home in the parking garage. Missing me, I thought warmly. I'd had the car since high school. And my mother says I can't commit.

Jeremy was braking at the stop sign at the end of the block when I pulled out. I switched the headlights off until he turned. And then I kept my distance. An old orange-and-black Charger allows you that luxury. The taillights are distinctive—two long red bars. Also, this guy was about as unpredictable as the Golf Channel. Mostly he watched television in a recliner with a take-out carton in his lap he'd brought home after work. But tonight it looked like my diligence was going to pay off. He drove right past the liquor store on the corner, the bar up the street, and the grocery store—the only places he'd been all week other than work and his own living room.

I tailed him to a convenience store and watched him buy a carton of cigarettes. Jeremy didn't smoke. My hopes were high. I followed him down Ponce de Leon to a Wendy's on Scott Boulevard and watched him go through the drive-thru. Next stop: a motel off Church Street sandwiched between car dealerships. It was the kind of place the Bureau put their agents on assignment—stucco façade, two levels of crappy carpeting, and a great view of the parking lot. He got out with the cigarettes and a bag of fast food under his arm and climbed concrete steps at the corner of the building. He stopped at the fourth door. I picked up binoculars and checked the number. Two Twenty-Eight. Maybe I'd play that one in the lottery tonight.

I couldn't see who was behind the door when it opened, but I was feeling fairly confident it was Jeremy's fast-food-eating brother, Ronald. I slipped into a Kevlar vest and a lightweight black jacket that identified me as bond enforcement in big yellow letters and walked into the management office.

"My name's Keye Street. Bond enforcement." I slapped my identification on the counter. "Mind telling me who's in Two Twenty-Eight?"

"I don't want any trouble."

I smiled, took my ID back. "That makes two of us."

"We just renovated," the clerk told me.

"Understood," I said. We exchanged a long look. I waited him out. Finally, he fingered his keyboard.

"Coleman," he said. "Jeremy."

Just as I thought. Jeremy had gotten the room for his brother and now he was delivering food and cigarettes. A lot of cigarettes. Either Ronald was a chain smoker or he was about to take off. "When's he checking out?"

"Tomorrow," the clerk told me. "You're not going to shoot up the place, right?"

"Right," I said. I left the office, followed the concrete steps to the second level, and went down the breezeway to Room 228. I pressed my ear against the door. A noise from Room 232 got my attention. A tall, scrawny guy with a scruffy goatee came out. I hoped he'd go the other way, but some people just cannot mind their own business.

"Can I help you with something?" he asked.

"Bond enforcement," I whispered. "Keep moving." He hesitated. He was going to be trouble. "You been hanging out with Ron?"

"I don't know no Ron," he said. He was lying. Paranoid eyes darted from me to the parking lot.

I could hear the television inside, the occasional murmur of male voices. I reached for my Glock and made sure he got a good look at it. "Get him to the door."

He glanced at my gun, knocked lightly, raised an unsteady voice. "Hey, Ron, wanna hang out, man?"

"I'm busy," a voice yelled from inside. I gave him the signal to keep talking. "Um . . . Ron, man. It's kinda important," he said, talking into the closed door.

"Go fuck yourself," his pal Coleman yelled.

"Okay, just go," I told him and looked over my shoulder to make sure he was leaving, then tried the door. Locked. I knocked loudly.

"*Goddamnit,* Trevor!" Coleman yelled. I felt the vibration of heavy footsteps. The door swung open and Ronald Coleman stood there shirtless in jeans holding a half-eaten chicken sandwich.

"Bond enforcement, Mr. Coleman. Put your hands behind your head and step out of the room, please."

Coleman made a backward dive for the bed, rolled over a white paper sack that had a blob of ketchup and some oily fries spilled out like he'd been using it for a plate. But he held on to his sandwich. I heard him hit the floor with a thud on the other side. The bathroom door slammed.

Oh boy. I was clearly dealing with another genius. The chemical smell in the room was undeniable. I saw a tiny piece of foil with a crack rock about half the size of a marble on a table at the window. I looked at Jeremy. "He still carrying that thirty-eight he used in the carjacking?"

Jeremy shrugged.

I gestured at the drugs, the small brass pipe, and a cigarette lighter. "Are you smoking that shit too? You need to get a grip, Jeremy. Or you're going to lose more than the fourteen grand."

Jeremy's glassy eyes looked away.

"Get out," I told him. He didn't hesitate. He headed for the door while I moved slowly into the room and around the bed, weapon trained on the bathroom. The unpredictability factor is pretty high with these guys anyway, but when there's a crack pipe in the room, it goes into orbit. "Hey, Ronald, you missed your court date. We need to get this straightened out."

"Screw you," he yelled. *Sque woo.* He was actually finishing his sandwich while being pursued by a bail recovery agent. You have to admire that on some level.

I pressed into the wall on the other side of the door in case he wanted to do to me what he'd done to the guy in the Krystal parking lot, and double-checked my vest. "Open the door and kick the gun out. I want to see your hands on your head. I'll give you to three. *One . . .*"

"Leave me alone or I swear I'll fuck you up."

"Two . . ."

Bang. Ronald discharged his weapon. The bullet tore through the cheap hollow-core door and shattered the mirror over an oak veneer dresser. So much for the renovation.

"Still here," I told him.

Bang, bang, bang.

"Jesus." I pressed in hard against the wall. "You realize how stupid this is, right? You've trapped yourself in the bathroom. Now just come on out."

I heard fast shoes hitting the concrete breezeway, shouting. The manager/clerk showed up at the open door, red-faced and raving.

"You need to stay back," I ordered the manager loudly.

"I called the cops," he yelled. "You're gonna pay for the damage."

In that case, I aimed for the space between the bathroom doorknob and frame and fired. One solid crack and the door swung open. I pressed back into the wall and waited. The hotel manager glared at me like I'd just dropped his ice cream in the sand.

"You need to clear out," I told him again.

Bang. Shot number five was followed by a guttural yell, the kind you imagine coming out of someone who's just thrown himself off a cliff. Ronald Coleman came blasting out of the bathroom with his head down like a defensive lineman. He rushed right past me, leveled the manager at the door with one shoulder, and sailed over the balcony.

I rushed out the door and peered over the railing. Coleman was spread-eagled on the hood of a Buick, facedown. I leapt over the manager and took the steps two at a time. A Decatur police car was pulling into the lot. I holstered my weapon, grabbed Coleman's arms. He was groaning, trying to move. I cuffed him and ran a zip-tie through the cuffs to his belt loop.

The officer approached. I held up my ID. "Bond enforcement," I announced. "And this is Ronald Coleman. Jumped on aggravated assault with intent, armed robbery, and carjacking." I put my ID away and reached into my jacket for the paperwork. "I think we need an EMT."

The officer eyed me skeptically. "Ya think?" Cops don't like to see criminals get away. But they don't have a lot of affection for bail recovery agents either. At least not ones in their jurisdiction. He looked over the paperwork, then at Coleman, whose cheek was pushed into the hood of the car like it was a really soft pillow.

"He threw himself off," I said.

"Uh-huh."

"Seriously. He's high as a kite."

"You see drugs upstairs?"

I nodded. "Crack."

"Anyone with him?"

"Nope. Just Ron and the crack pipe," I lied, and glanced at the orange Charger sitting in the parking lot. I thought Jeremy must be behind the wheel, though it was too dark to know. Maybe he'd been waiting for his brother to make a run for it. Maybe he was ready to mire up even deeper in his brother's crash-and-burn life. Maybe he wanted to be sure Ronald was okay. Maybe he just needed to sober up before he drove. Whatever it was, I decided Jeremy had had enough trouble already. He'd veered off the path. Who hadn't? This is what happens when you watch someone for a few days. Empathy kicks in. You begin to feel their life. I'd seen Jeremy spend long days at work and come home with a take-out carton to an empty house. I'd been there. I'd watched him risk too much for family. I'd been there too.

2

Lieutenant Aaron Rauser was sitting at the kitchen bar with a toasted bagel, a tub of Italian cream cheese, and a jar of honey. I could smell coffee. Rauser likes it strong. Rauser's new dog, Hank, and my cat, White Trash, were sitting side by side looking up at him. When it comes to begging, dog and cat unite against their oppressors. White Trash actually seems to enjoy getting to know Hank. She preys on his weaknesses. Hank, bless his little heart, has a short memory. White Trash hides in shadowy places and waits for him to trot by, oblivious, leaps out on hind legs like a kangaroo, and scares the hell out of him. This terror is repeated daily.

Rauser leaned over and gave them mascarpone off his finger. This does nothing to improve their behavior but it is really cute. I gave him a kiss. His skin smelled like shaving cream. His thick black-and-silver hair was damp and raked back off his face. He was wearing a light blue dress shirt he hadn't gotten around to buttoning. A glimpse of tight abs and chest hair isn't a bad way to wake up.

Rauser had been sharing my loft for a little over a month now. An EF4 tornado had blown into town early in July, chewed up a path through Atlanta, then slammed Rauser's neighborhood full-force. About ten thousand pounds of pine tree sliced the house in two like an axe splitting wood. I remember it well. I was inside the house at the time. Rebuilding was supposed to take a couple of months. It now looked as if it might take six. We hadn't discussed this extension. Maybe we were both trying to figure out how we felt about it.

"You get any sleep?" I asked. I'd felt him climb into bed with me at about three. This was not unusual. Seems like the bad guys always come out at night. I reached down and gave Hank and White Trash a pat.

Rauser mumbled an answer at me. He was more like my father every day. I thought about that. Maybe he'd always been like my dad. Oh God. I did *not* want to be one of those women who look for a father in their partners. The idea pretty much makes me want to shove an ice pick in my eye.

Rauser got up, poured coffee into a mug, handed it to me, then re-filled his own. In certain light his gray eyes are flecked with gold. But this morning with the sun bleeding through the windows overlooking Peachtree Street, the flecks were green on a field of blue-gray. And boy, did he look grumpy.

"Want to talk about it?" I asked.

"Long night. A fatal stabbing. A security guard was shot and killed because some thugs wanted the copper pipes from a warehouse where he made rounds. And a drive-by. Nineteen-year-old victim. Gang tats. Couple thousand bucks in his pocket."

Murder was not an unusual topic for us over breakfast. It works for me. I don't need Care Bears and roses. "You have the best stories," I said sarcastically.

Rauser almost smiled. He'd gotten awake enough to remember he liked me. "Heard you brought in the shooter in that car theft and shooting last night." He said it casually. Depending on Rauser's mood, this could be a delicate subject. He didn't always approve of my bail recovery jobs. And I'm not open to discussing the work I take or the choices I make. Again, I don't need a daddy. So the tension usually just hangs there. "Heard there were shots fired," he added.

I took a sip of coffee, set the mug down. "What else did you hear?"

The skin crinkled at the corners of his eyes. "I heard there was a Ronald Coleman–size dent in the hood of a Buick."

I laughed. "The guy locked himself in the bathroom and then tried to shoot himself out. He was a total doofus."

"Criminals usually are." I reached for his bagel. An eyebrow came up. "You want one of your own?"

"No. I want a bite of yours," I said. He put another bagel in the oven while I took a moment to admire the way he wore his jeans. "Why are guys so weird about food sharing? It's a knuckle-dragger thing, isn't it? You want to take it to your cave and be alone with it?"

He closed the oven door and looked at me. "I know you don't wanna pick on me this morning."

"I kinda do," I told him. "I think it's your grumpy face."

He opened a kitchen drawer, pointed down at the contents. "Want to tell me why you felt the need to label the silverware?" He began to read the bright green sticky notes inside. "Knives, small forks, long forks, short spoons, long spoons. What the hell is that, Keye?"

So now we were getting to what was really wrong with his mood. I didn't say anything.

"Not only have you labeled the silverware drawer, you've dumbed it down. You think I don't know what a salad fork is?"

I tried unsuccessfully not to smile.

"This isn't a joke, Keye." He closed the drawer too hard.

"Okay," I said. "So what is it?"

"Exactly. What the hell is it? Because from where I stand some-body who feels they have to label the goddamn silverware drawer is not ready to share their space." He leaned across the counter and grabbed his bagel. I didn't move. I just sat there with my coffee and watched him walk out.

M y detective agency, Corporate Intelligence & Investigations (CI&I), sits in a row of refurbished warehouses off North High-land Avenue in Atlanta. The dock door was raised when I pulled into the parking lot. We can get away with this early in the day. But by noon the sun is as hot as an arsonist's match. Even our concrete offices won't stay cool. Atlanta's weather had been extreme again this year. Summer came out swinging, pummeled us with violent storms, then turned up the dial and took away the rain. Television meteorologists were so friggin' excited about tornadoes, then drought, they were practically huffing into paper bags, reporting new watering restrictions like they were brand-new commandments from God. I think they secretly hoped they'd have heatstrokes or deaths by dehydration to report, which was probably preferable to a television death by reporting gorgeous, hot weather every damn day.

My neighbors had their big doors up this morning too—the gay theater company, the hair studio two doors down, and the tattoo artist and piercing salon on the corner. The sounds from our businesses mingled like a scene from Hitchcock's *Rear Window*—show tunes rehearsed, customers chatting from high swivel chairs while haircutters buzzed around with scissors, a faint bass rhythm from the piercing guy, whose throbbing music distracts customers while he drills silver posts into their nostrils. I smelled the ovens from Highland Bakery as I came up the metal steps to the landing that had once served loading docks. Actors from the theater company were clustered outside around a tall metal ashtray, alternating sips of coffee with long hits off their cigarettes.

"Y'all are here early," I said, and smiled as I passed. I'd been here long enough to know that when actors show up for work before I do, it's the final week of rehearsals before the curtain goes up. Hell week, they call it, and the sheer terror of it wakes them up early. I'd married an actor once, which was probably why I was taking pleasure in their pain this morning.

I could hear my business partner, Neil Donovan, in the kitchen with our new and, well, our only employee. Latisha had been with us nearly a month. To give you some sense of Neil's priorities, he was training her on the espresso machine.

"Morning," I called out as I headed toward the fenced-in corner I call my office—the brainchild of the overly enthusiastic design firm I'd hired to bring our old warehouse into this century.

Latisha showed up in front of my desk. "Look what I made." She set down a cup with a foamy top. Her nails were lavender and so long they had a little curve at the end. I find this creepy. She apparently finds it attractive. Latisha is Tyrone's daughter. That's Tyrone Eckhart of Tyrone's Quikbail, a substantial contributor to my monthly income. I owed him a favor. Right now it was standing in my office in a too-short skirt that matched the color of her nails.

I took a sip and licked froth off my top lip. "Delicious," I said, then opened my briefcase, handed her a receipt from APD. "I got Ronald Coleman last night. Get it to your dad today so we can get paid. And I need you to stop by Nussbaum, Kaplan, Freed, and Slott. Bernie called my mobile last night. They've got divorce papers they want me to serve tomorrow morning."

Neil came in holding his coffee and slouched into one of my chairs. He hadn't combed his hair or shaved. Golden stubble covered his jawbone and chin. He was wearing a Cuban shirt and baggy white knee-length shorts, Vans slip-ons, plaid—the usual. His lids looked heavy.

"Hey, I get to visit the offices of Assbalm, Complain, Fried, and Snot today," Latisha told Neil. She had taken to changing the names of our clients when she felt underappreciated by them. Bernie Slott would forever be referred to as Mr. Snot after he was less than overjoyed about being left on hold one day.

"Miss Keye, you ready to go over your day planner?" Latisha wanted to know.

I wasn't. I was ready to drink coffee and stare. "Can you drop the *Miss* thing? I feel like I'm in a scene from *The Help*."

Latisha held up a palm. "Oh no you did not just go there. Don't even talk to me about that movie. And then they had the nerve to turn it into a book!"

"I think the book came first," Neil said. He was looking at his coffee mug, moving the frothy top around with his index finger.

"Whatever. I'm just trying to be professional when I address you." She sat down in one of the two chairs across from my desk and crossed long, muscular, nineteen-year-old legs. She was wearing white athletic shoes with girl-jock socks that had a little fuzzy ball at the heel—lavender to match her nails and the skirt that barely covered her ass. I reserved comment on how professional I felt that was. Truth is, Neil and I had never run a tight ship. Life is tough enough on the outside. Might as well have some fun. "Remember you told Fairy Chin, I mean Larry Quinn, you'd get on that slip-and-fall this week," Latisha told me. "He needs to know if she's for real. Between us, that silly ho did *not* slip on that milk."

Latisha might be right. I'd done some checking myself. The woman was recently divorced, two mortgage payments behind, and she'd had an injury claim pending against a former employer. "What else?" I asked.

"Half a dozen deposition subpoenas for that nasty-ass criminal attorney," Latisha informed me.

Latisha had taken over a lot of the routine duties that had clogged my day—my schedule, the filing, the endless trips to county courthouse clerk rooms, delivering the background reports Neil and I compiled for the head-hunting agencies and employment services on our client roster. She answered the phone and didn't mind running errands. But she had a mouth on her.

"I've got the Monday-night sweeps as usual," Neil said. "Plus the background reports for the headhunters." We'd recently invested in state-of-the-art bug-sweeping equipment. The money was great but we needed more business. The technology was constantly evolving, as was our investment in countermeasures equipment. I prayed paranoia would seize Atlanta's corporate giants so Neil could lug his equipment out every day. I was beginning to fantasize about a bank account so full and a business so functional I could have an actual vacation—the beach, naps, hot sweaty middle-of-the-day sex, chocolate cake for dinner, no alarms, no phones. But that's just crazy talk.

"Can you get me a look at the slip-and-fall lady's neighborhood?" I asked Neil.

He pushed himself up like an old man, made a little noise, half grunt, half sigh. He was mopey this morning. Neil's moody. He has a lot of drama in his romantic life. That's because he's a philandering scoundrel. He's also smart and funny and complicated, and just shaggy enough to look like he needs a mommy. It really plays with the chicks.

He ordered the smart system in our super-wired office to bring down the TV, and a silver, dungeon-like pulley system lowered the thin, flat screen smoothly from the rafters. It is hands-down the sexiest addition to come from the high-strung group of designers who swooped in a couple of years back. And because the television is usually stashed neatly fifteen feet above our heads, it had survived a thug who'd broken in and smashed up the place last month. The cops thought he'd probably used a bat or a tire tool. We'd had to replace almost all the electronics, including the ridiculously expensive panel that controlled the animation system Neil had installed and trained to understand our voice commands.

Latisha lowered herself into one of the soft leather chaise longues scattered around the office, stretched out, crossed her ankles. Neil's busy fingers tapped at his keyboard until a satellite image of Beecher Street SW appeared on screen. He took us on a virtual ride down the street that made me dizzy. On a computer it's fine. But on the big screen it's like a roller-coaster ride. I saw a few cars parked curbside, some good-size oak trees lining the street. It's a lot easier to hang out in neighborhoods with trees and cars without being spotted.

"There it is," he said, and we looked at a small frame house with a wide porch and a yard spotted with patches of Georgia red clay that hadn't seen grass seed in a few seasons.

"I know that neighborhood," Latisha said. "I got cousins on the next block. The West End gets a bad rap, but those little neighborhoods are nice. You go there on a pretty day and people are sitting on their porches. Not like those fancy neighborhoods where you never see nobody in the yard. You ever notice that about rich white people? They don't come outside." She looked at Neil. "What's wrong with white folks anyway?"

The office phone rang. Latisha answered in her sugary-sweet fake-nice voice. "C, I, and I. This is Latisha. How may I help you?" She listened. "May I say who's calling?" Another pause. "Hold, please."

"Well done," I said. She was getting better on the phone. The first couple of weeks were touch-and-go. Turns out Latisha can be a little bit of a German shepherd.

"It's a Sheriff Meltzer," she told me. "Seven-oh-six area code."

I had no idea who Sheriff Meltzer was. "Run that real quick, would you, Neil?"

Neil's fingers skipped lightly over his keyboard. He could do this blindfolded. He'd begun his hacking career in high school, a for-profit test preparation program, as he called it, which really just meant he hacked the teachers, got the tests in advance, and sold them. "Kenneth Meltzer. Hitchiti County sheriff. In his second term," he reported. "Central Georgia. Lot of buzz about speed traps. They're housing state prisoners at the County Jail." Neil kept reading, his blue eyes quickly sweeping over pages of information. "He's bringing in a lot of revenue. The department is beefed up. Website bio says Meltzer's the youngest sheriff to serve the county. Thirty-three when he was elected. Forty percent drop in crime since he took over."

"So what's he want with me?" I said, pressing the SPEAKER button on the conference table console. I had never been crazy about county sheriffs. I'd worked with a few at the Bureau. They're elected. It tends to skew their priorities. "I apologize for keeping you on hold, Sheriff Meltzer. This is Keye Street. What can I do for you?"

"Good morning, Dr. Street." His voice was smooth with a rich, deep rumble. I thought I caught a hint of the western United States in his accent. "Major Herman Hicks at APD Homicide referred me to you, said you've worked repeat violent offender cases with the FBI and with APD."

I thought about the day I'd been escorted to my old convertible with a special agent trailing behind me, the pathetic remains of my life at the National Center for the Analysis of Violent Crime in a cardboard box. I had pushed toward the Bureau's Behavioral Analysis Unit with single-minded ambition and aggressively pursued the education in psychology and criminology that would guarantee me notice there. And then I blew it all to hell. It wasn't the first time I had walked away from something with my tail between my legs. I was never good at endings. Or perhaps I'm really good at them. If you like drama, I mean.

"Do you have a minute to talk?" the sheriff asked.

"Of course." I found paper and pen and sat down.

"My department received a call about three weeks ago," the sheriff began. "A father and son fishing a creek up here noticed an article of clothing caught up on the bank. It's a fairly isolated spot, away from the developed tourist areas, and there's not a lot of trash. So it was obvious. They pulled it out and realized it was a blouse. We had a young woman disappear up here eight months ago. Word got around—"

"How young?" I interrupted.

"She was thirteen."

"And it was her shirt?"

"Yes. According to the state crime lab, the skin cells they recovered from the collar belonged to the victim," the sheriff said.

"Did you recover a body?"

"We combed the area for a couple of days and didn't see a thing, then went in with cadaver dogs. We found her body upstream a ways. We also found the skeletal remains of another victim. A forensic odontologist identified her as Tracy Davidson, also thirteen years old when she disappeared. They were found at the bottom of a natural embankment half a mile into the woods."

"Same school?"

"No. But both girls lived in my county. And neither town has its own police department. That makes it my problem. Tracy Davidson lived in Silas, twenty miles away from Melinda Cochran, our second victim, who lived here in Whisper."

I made a note. *2 victims. Female. 13. Silas, Whisper, 20 miles.* "They determine cause of death?"

"Blunt-force trauma to the skull on the first victim. Wounds are consistent with something like the blunt side of an axe."

Heavy with a good swing, I thought. Nice and quiet, nothing to disturb the serenity of a Georgia forest. "And the second?"

"Could have been the same weapon, but he used the sharp side. Almost took her head off."

"How can I help, Sheriff?"

"I have two people in Criminal Investigations and they have their hands full with meth labs and pot growers and robberies. We've never used a criminal consultant or anything like that. How does it work?

What exactly did you do for APD? I guess I'm asking what happens if I hired somebody like you."

"The primary goal would be to evaluate the nature of the forensic evidence, and the value of it. Interpret that evidence and behaviors at a crime scene in order to identify offender characteristics, help investigators gain some insight into the offender's motivations, fantasy life, state of mind, levels of planning, evidence of remorse, risk, method of approach and attack, analyze linkage in series crimes. It's all meant to assist with interview and investigative strategy and ultimately in the identification of the offender." I paused. "I want to stress the word *assist,* Sheriff. Criminal investigative analysts assist law enforcement. We're not psychics. We work from the evidence you provide."

"To be perfectly honest, Dr. Street, my investigators didn't make any headway when the second vic disappeared eight months ago," Sheriff Meltzer told me. "APD says you're a good investigator and a good profiler. I could use both right now. Can you take a few days? You'd be on our dime, of course."

"Would you mind holding while I check the schedule?" I hit the HOLD button. I didn't check the schedule. I didn't do anything but watch the vein in my wrist tick, tick, ticking. I was thinking about the kind of killer who would kidnap and murder young girls. I was thinking about the thing that frightens me and tugs at me, pulls me like a magnetic field—the calculating mind of a killer.

"What's the time line on the subpoenas?" I asked Latisha.

"The deposition is five weeks away."

"Okay, so I can get them out next week," I said.

"You have to," Latisha warned. "Folks have to be given a reasonable timeframe to prepare."

"There's nothing here we can't handle for a couple days, I guess," Neil said.

I released the HOLD button. "Sheriff, would you mind sending the lab reports and scene photos? I'd like to review them tonight and call you in the morning." I gave him my email address. "You didn't mention how long the first victim had been out there."

"About a decade, according to the forensic anthropologist."

"And the second girl for eight months?"

"Closer to sixty days."

I sat forward. "But she disappeared eight months ago? She was held for six months before she was murdered."

"The first victim disappeared a year before she was killed," the sheriff told me quietly. "Dr. Street, we're not bad cops down here, but we don't understand this kind of monster. And we don't understand how someone held these girls without detection."

"Speaking in broad terms, Sheriff, offenders who kidnap and imprison their victims tend to be sexual sadists. Their gratification comes in dehumanizing their victims. In children and young adults dependency on the captor is created fairly quickly. The offender is generally the only human contact the victim has. Every scrap of food, every drink of water, every glimpse of sunlight depends on the generosity of their jailer. Lot of power in that for someone who craves it. And prisoners don't always run away or scream when there's an opportunity. Sometimes it's about traumatic bonding. Usually the offender has made threats. They're told no one will believe them, that he will find them, that their family will die, their pets will be murdered. Neighbors don't always know what's going on. Look at what Ariel Castro did in Cleveland. It's twenty feet to the next house and he held three women in his homemade dungeon for a decade."

"Like I said, we don't understand this kind of monster," the sheriff said. "But we do realize we're dealing with the same suspect since we have the same disposal site, which is why I'm calling you."

"I assume you checked family members and local sex offenders?"

"It's the first place we looked. Brought in a few for questioning. Cleared the families. And in my experience it's not the registered offenders you have to worry about. They know they're the first ones we're going to shake when something happens. The system does work sometimes."

"And you haven't wanted to reach out to the Bureau. Why?"

"Whisper is a little outside the touristy areas around the lake. It's quiet. Hardworking, private people. Having the Feds around isn't going to do anything to put the community at ease."

"The Bureau makes a good partner, Sheriff. They have resources."

"This is our case," he told me, and even though I didn't know him, I knew he wasn't going to take my advice. "We want to see it through ourselves if we can."

Most cops feel that way. Especially in small towns. It's personal for them. I didn't think it was smart, but I understood it. "I'll go over the files and speak with you in the morning, Sheriff."

"Look forward to it, Dr. Street."

3

read the names on the email from a sheriff I didn't know in central Georgia. Tracy Anne Davidson. Melinda Jane Cochran. I tried to remember my life at thirteen. I thought about boys, sports, my friends, fitting in, kissing, what to wear. I was happily and completely absorbed by my own narrow teenage world. My brother Jimmy left school when the bell rang, so I walked home alone after practice. Nothing bad happens in good neighborhoods, right? How easy it would have been for someone to approach me, trick me, and snatch me out of my life, my parents' life. It's hard to even consider the kind of wreckage that would have left behind. Or the suffering the families of these two girls had endured, first having their children vanish and then coming to terms with the lost hope they would be found alive when their bodies turned up in some remote crater in Georgia's red clay earth.

I opened an attachment with copies of the reports from the Georgia Bureau of Investigation lab and sent them to the printer in the outer office. I followed with the photographs from the disposal site, and glanced up from my desk when Neil groaned in his desk chair. I carried my laptop to the conference table. "You have time to give me a hand?"

"Are you kidding? I'm so frigging bored I'm ready to assign sex offender ratings to the Super Nannies staff."

Super Nannies On Call was one of our regular clients. We ran thorough background checks on their applicants. It was a thousand or so a month that I very much wanted to keep. Neil's overdeveloped technological know-how and frequent bouts with boredom were a recipe for mischief. The combination had been his undoing in the past and nearly landed him in jail. "Actually, that's exactly where I want to start—registered sex offenders in Hitchiti County and the surrounding area, level two and three. They would have needed access to the area in the last eleven years. Let's also look at offenders who came back into the area in the last two years. Melinda disappeared a little over eight months ago so she was probably active on social media. Latisha, get Sheriff Meltzer back on the phone for me."

Latisha did as I asked and put the sheriff on speaker. "Sheriff Meltzer, sorry to bother you. Quick question. Have you checked to see if Melinda Cochran had social media sites?"

"She did," the sheriff told me. "But her parents don't know the password and our tech guy hasn't been able to get in. All we're able to see currently is her profile picture. We've started the warrants necessary to get admin privileges but it's not moving as fast as we'd like."

I glanced at Neil. He gave me a thumbs-up. Okay, so sometimes we walk a crooked line in regard to privacy. Welcome to the private sector. "Thanks for your time, Sheriff. I'll speak to you in the morning." I disconnected, looked at Neil. "Their suspect is local. I can almost guarantee it."

"Wonder where he held them," Neil said. "I mean it can't be that easy to hide a live girl."

"I don't like being around when y'all start talking about some guy in the basement making him a girl suit," Latisha said. "I done saw that movie."

"They made a book out of it too," Neil said, and winked at me.

Latisha rubbed her arms like she had a chill. "That man had a dog named Precious. Okay? I will never be able to forget that."

"Break down Melinda's Twitter follows and Facebook friends for me once you get in," I told Neil. "Kids, adults, family, locals, and out-of-towners. And get whatever contact info you can on them. We'll pass it on to the sheriff's department."

"You're sounding a lot like you're going to take the job," Neil said.

"If he looks anything like he sounds," Latisha said, "I'll take it."

"Whether I take it or not, let's contribute what we can," I told Neil. He looked at me. I knew what he was thinking. He didn't like the police consulting work. The last two jobs had turned sour. A serial murderer had nearly killed me last year, and Neil was still nursing a limp from a bullet that pinged off our concrete docks six weeks ago when the subject of an investigation wanted to warn me off.

"Okay," he said, finally, and swiveled around to face his computer. "Registered offenders and social media."

"Latisha, how about you go with me to check on Larry Quinn's slip-and-fall." Latisha brightened. Neil looked at me as if a cabbage had just popped out of my nose. "What?" I said. "She has to learn the ropes. She can handle it. If we don't get anything today, you can do a couple of shifts on your own tomorrow."

"Do I get to carry a gun?" Latisha asked.

I laughed. "Good Lord, no." I cleaned out the printer tray, put the sheriff's reports in a manila folder. My phone went off. Rauser's ringtone. Aerosmith's "Dude (Looks Like a Lady)."

"Miss me?" Rauser's gravelly voice had years of cheap bourbon and cigarettes in it. "I mean it's been four hours. You don't think the day-to-day is killing the romance, do you?"

"It depends," I said. "You still mad? Because I gotta tell you that's not exactly an aphrodisiac." Neil handed me a parabolic microphone and hung a camera on my shoulder.

"That was icy," Rauser said. "I just got a chill."

"Is there something I can do for you, Lieutenant?"

I heard phones ringing in the background, voices. The homicide room was hopping as usual. "Can you go home and give Hank a pee break?"

"Speaking of killing the romance," I said. Hank is a white miniature poodle who once belonged to a serial killer. I'm still deciding if this makes Rauser more or less attractive to me. A masculine guy who is kind to animals really tugs at my heart. Holding Hank up in the air and baby-talking him, well, not so much.

"I'm slammed," Rauser said. "I'll do it tomorrow. I promise."

"I think we need to hire that pet-sitter we interviewed last week," I told him. "She could give him a nice walk in the middle of the day. Maybe it will calm him down."

"You think she'll come back? He humped her leg during the entire interview."

"I think she liked it," I said, and Rauser chuckled. The vet had warned us it might take Hank a few weeks after being neutered to get over his, well, hormonal urges. He wasn't there yet. "I have to run by and switch cars anyway. I'll take him out. But call the sitter today, okay? I may need to go out of town."

"Sheriff Meltzer called you?"

"He did. You know him?"

"Nah. The major told me he'd referred you. What's it about?"

"Two dead girls," I answered. "Ten years apart. Same disposal site."

"Uh-oh," Rauser said. He understood the implications very well. A killer had been free in central Georgia for at least a decade. "So you're taking the job?"

"I want to look over the files tonight before I decide."

"Which means you're taking it." Rauser disconnected.

I pulled into the garage at the Georgian Terrace Hotel with the top down and Latisha in the passenger's seat. "I'm just going to put the equipment in the Neon and take Hank outside for a minute," I told her. "Then we can go. Come upstairs and wait inside. You're okay with animals, right?"

"I don't like it when they lick me. Will they lick me?"

"I don't know."

She looked at my dingy, banged-up white Plymouth. "We're gonna sit in that thing all day?"

"It's important to be inconspicuous."

"Ah," Latisha said as we pushed through the double doors at the Georgian Terrace and headed for the elevator. "Stealth."

"Exactly."

I heard Hank's toenails on my wood floor as soon as I opened the door to my tenth-floor loft. Hank is a dancer when he's excited. But he wasn't dancing today. He was limping. I swept the room for White Trash and saw her perched on the bar between the kitchen and living room. I knelt down to Hank. "Did you have another spat?" *Spat* is code for White Trash kicking his ass again. I inspected his paws and shoulders and face and could not find a mark on him. His eyes looked okay.

"Eeeww," Latisha said. She was standing over me. "His thing is out. Like all the way out."

I stood him up on his hind legs and looked under him. "*Wow.* I've actually never seen anything like that. That's not good."

"Ya think? No wonder the cat's up there like that. Look into her eyes, Keye. That cat has seen some shit here today."

I put Hank down. He hung his head. "I think he's in pain." I found the vet's number on a refrigerator magnet, held on until someone could get an overworked vet tech to the phone. I then awkwardly described the emergency. When I hung up, I told Latisha, "We need to get it unstuck."

"That's not in my job description."

"Well, at least pet him or something while I figure it out."

"I ain't touching that." She backed up.

"The vet tech said to use something cold or something that lubricates." I pulled a pair of surgical gloves from my scene kit and opened the refrigerator. Buttery spread. Oily and cold. Problem solved. I dipped in my gloved finger.

"Oh Lord," Latisha said, laughing.

"I have a surprise for you, Hank." I petted him, then rolled him over and applied Land O'Lakes to his privates. As it turns out, fake butter is a total turnoff. It worked fast. Hank lay on his back, exhausted. I peeled off the gloves, looked up at Latisha.

"I will never look at you the same way," she groaned.

"Yeah, well, we're never going to speak of this. Ever. Not if you want to keep your job."

"My boss giving a poodle a hand job is not something I plan on bragging about. Just sayin'."

I took poor Hank for a walk down Peachtree Street while Latisha watched TV and while White Trash watched Latisha watching TV. Hank appeared fully recovered, though he was not as bouncy as usual. I decided not to discuss today's drama with Rauser. Some things just shouldn't be shared with the person you love.

Forty minutes later we parked under one of the giant water oaks that overhung Beecher Street. Huge roots that probably came to the surface during the first drought a couple of years ago had pushed some of the sidewalk slabs up into peaks, cracked and strained them.

Latisha ducked so I could pull the boom over from the backseat. The Neon isn't exactly roomy. "This is a microphone. It has video and a digital voice recorder," I told her. "That saucer on the end magnifies the sound so it can record and we can hear what's being said. There's a place here to plug in our headphones." I gave Latisha a pair and slipped one on myself. They were small, the kind you see attached to iPods. "If she comes out, point it at her and press this button." I set the mike in Latisha's lap. It was about the size of a small megaphone.

She frowned. "Oh yeah, this will be inconspicuous."

"Well, don't hang out the door with it. Just prop it on the window. Gently. Try not to drop it. It cost a bazillion dollars."

"What if she doesn't come out?"

"We wait," I said, opening the file I'd brought with me. "There's a lot of waiting in this business. Staying awake is the trick."

Latisha eyed me. "Did you wash your hands?"

"Yes. I was also wearing gloves."

"You in your little crime-scene gloves." Latisha giggled. "That was some funny shit right there. CSI Atlanta. Boner Response Unit."

"The BRU," I said. We both laughed.

Latisha trained her sharp eyes on the frame house. I began flipping through photographs—shots of a wooded area around a disposal site in central Georgia, thick in leaves and foliage; shots from above the site at the top of the embankment where a killer had once stood; shots of Melinda Cochran's decomposing, debris-strewn body; photos taken as they'd carefully uncovered her; more photos of Tracy Davidson's skeletal remains positioned just slightly below Melinda's body. Melinda was on her right side, a position she might have assumed for eternity but for the sensitive nose of a dog. A large hunk of granite had stopped her descent of the hill. I read a handwritten report the sheriff had filed on the day of the discovery, brief, to the point—who, what, when, where. He noted that they had found no impressions in leaves or dirt, and the scene photos reflected that. If the killer was revisiting his disposal site to fulfill some psychological requirements, he was very careful or he hadn't done it recently enough to leave tracks. Perhaps he wasn't romantic about his work. Maybe he had returned only once to dispose of the second body. I wondered what had triggered him and why he killed them when he did. Because he was done, because they had fulfilled his needs? Or because they were no longer able to? Had he simply grown bored, tired of them?

"Why do you like to look at all that stuff, Keye?" Latisha's voice broke my concentration. She was looking at the scene photos in my lap. Her headphones were hanging around her neck. I removed mine.

"Because I'd want someone to do it for me," I answered. She glanced again at the photos, then turned back to the street.

A car pulled up in front of the house where Larry Quinn's slip-and-fall woman lived. A woman got out and walked around to the back door, gently lifted a baby out of a car seat. "Showtime," I told Latisha, then cringed as she awkwardly banged the mike on the door before she got it propped up on the rolled-down car window. I showed her again how to activate video and sound. We both put our headphones back on.

The front door opened and I saw the woman I recognized from the grocery store video. She was in her late sixties, slightly overweight. She walked off the porch stiffly, but with a smile. "Mama, you okay today?" asked the young woman holding the baby. "I know that look." They hugged. The baby reached out for the older woman.

"Grandma can't hold you today, baby doll. I'll have to love on you like this." She kissed his chubby face and neck until he giggled and waved his arms.

"You're hurting," the younger woman observed.

"I can't seem to get comfortable, that's all," the older woman replied. "They say it's a compressed disc. It's just going to take time."

"We're going to make sure those people make this right," the daughter told her.

Latisha looked over at me. "This is depressing."

"No shit." I tossed my headphones onto the seat. "Let's go. We'll upload it to Larry when we get back."

"That's it? What if she didn't get like that in the grocery store fall? What if she faked the whole thing 'cause she was already injured?"

"Larry Quinn wanted to know if she was hurt. She's hurt. Send him an invoice and let him decide what to do with her."

"Well, I don't trust it," Latisha grumbled. "That fall looked fake to me. I coulda faked a better than that."

"Yeah. I know." I took the microphone out of her hand and put it in the backseat. "I don't trust it either. But that's not our problem. Not today anyway. Today we take her at face value because that's what our client cares about."

"That sucks," Latisha said.

"Tell me about it."

4

I picked up a couple of dozen Krispy Kremes on the way to a meeting. It was my week. Lot of coffee and doughnuts go down at these things. I knew from experience not to show up without the sugar when it's my week.

I pulled up to a squat redbrick building about the size of my living room surrounded by the hulking silver towers from the Georgia Power station. A cloud of cigarette smoke burned my sinuses as I waded past a group of four hot-boxing cigarettes around the front door. Facing an hour without nicotine had put them in a spin. I don't judge. We all have our crutches. I was holding mine, warm and sugar-glazed in a green-and-white box of pure happiness. I've been sober a little over four years and back in the program for only about six weeks. It's a pain in the ass—AA. Seriously. Carving out the time, whining about the tricks my obsessive addict's brain plays on me, slashing a vein for an audience. Not crazy about any of it. Way out of my comfort zone. Fortunately, the program works without love. It only requires my commitment. And to be honest, there's something about the people, all of them so different, from every imaginable background, probably feeling as awkward and exposed and as vulnerable as I do standing up in front of a group of strangers and bleeding out weakness, guilt, shame, and secrets. Okay, so if the bloodletting goes on for too long, I tune out. Zero tolerance for complainers and me, me, me people. But when someone steps up there after their lives have been totally derailed by addiction and they're not hanging on by the fingernails, they're not complaining, they are kicking it in the ass, now that's something to be present for. And if I'm lucky, I can duck out before the praying and hand-holding start.

I didn't speak at the meeting. A white chip was handed out to a newbie and I sat in a folding gray metal chair and sipped coffee from a small Styrofoam cup and listened to his story. Our stories all have a common thread. They all end with our addiction taking a claw hammer to our lives. This is part of what these meetings do for me. They remind me. And next time I want a drink, I'll remember that man standing up there tonight, thirty years old and utterly terrified he's not strong enough to do what he knows he must do—stop or die.

I found Rauser at home with a Braves game on television, a baseball cap on backward, Hank lying next to him and White Trash in his lap. He was sipping bourbon on the rocks. "You hungry?" he asked. His eyes hadn't left the television. "I ordered Indian."

"Starved," I said, and filled a glass with crushed ice and Diet Pepsi. I know, I know. It's frowned on here. It's a *Coca-Cola* town. Atlanta will forgive you for a lot of things, but being disloyal to the brand is just over the line. I have to sneak out to the grocery store in the dark of night with a fake mustache and glasses to buy what is generally referred to in Atlanta as swill.

We propped up on the floor once the food arrived with our backs against the couch and our plates in our laps. We seldom had time to do this without someone's phone going off. Our schedules are like that. Inertia or frenzy. There is rarely middle ground. Tonight was blissfully quiet as we pulled off pieces of naan and raked it through spicy eggplant and lentils and mint chutney. Rauser kissed me and the bourbon was warm on his lips. I wanted a drink every time I smelled it. But I would have never admitted this to him.

After dinner, I found the reports from Sheriff Meltzer I hadn't had time to absorb in the car with Latisha. Rauser was glued to the television. I wouldn't have known he even noticed I'd moved to the couch behind him except that he leaned his head back against me. This is just one of the things I love about the man. He's not the least bit threatened when my attentions are diverted.

I began reading the reports from the crime lab on the case of two dead girls discovered at the bottom of an embankment in Hitchiti County. Both victims had bone injuries. A forensic anthropologist had determined that the significant bone injuries occurred in life, not after death. But when the injuries had occurred in their young lives was unknown. Tracy had chips and fractures in her wrists, ankles, and feet. Her arm had been broken. Melinda had sustained similar injuries to her ankles, plus several other fractures. Melinda's body hadn't been in that hole long enough to disguise superficial curiosity marks on her arms and face—the point of a knife. Not deep. The killer was experimenting, still inventing himself. I began making notes of things I'd need from the sheriff. Interviews with the parents were at the top of my list. They would know if and when their children had been injured. I'd need medical records, which would confirm the parents' statements. I wanted to know if domestic abuse reports had ever been filed on their residences. The sheriff had excluded the families as suspects. I wanted to know why. I had some ideas about the breaks and fractures, their severity or lack thereof, and the location of the injuries. I'd seen similar injuries to ankles and wrists in victims who had been restrained, beaten, handled, victims who had fought and struggled with their restraints. But I needed to know more about these girls' physical conditions at the time they were abducted in order to develop a clearer understanding of their environment while they were prisoners and of the person who abducted and murdered them.

I went over the photos from the disposal site again—Tracy's bony remains peeking though leaves, Melinda's nude corpse draped around the rock that had kept her from hitting bottom. The blouse the fisherman and his son pulled off the bank had been the only article of clothing found. Trace evidence, hair and fiber, can cling to clothing even after long-term exposure to the elements. And so can DNA, as evidenced by the skin cells still in the collar of the blouse. Semen had been found in the underpants of victims after months of exposure, and it had been used to convict offenders. Did our killer know this? Was he educated in evidence collection? I thought about where those girls had been held. Was it damp and dark? Or were they positioned so they could see the free world passing by? Wherever they were, their terror must be painted on those walls.

Rauser was standing over me when I opened my eyes. I'd fallen asleep in the second hour of reading and rereading. "Braves won," he said. "It's after midnight." He'd taken the reports I had in my lap and stacked them neatly on the table. He smiled, held up the new smartphone I'd given him for his birthday, and snapped a picture.

"I'm going to take that phone away from you."

He held out both his hands for me, pulled me to my feet. "Get your shoes on."

We walked under the Midtown streetlights, holding hands, talking about our day—his cases at APD Homicide and the reports I'd received from a small-town sheriff—with Hank straining against his leash, sniffing at everything, seemingly unaffected by his Viagra incident. We didn't talk about the silverware drawer or Rauser's anger this morning. We walked home and Rauser closed the bedroom door as I undressed. His arms came around me. He kissed my bare shoulders. I felt his breath in my ear, his hands brushing my nipples, running down my body, between my legs. He knelt and pulled me hard against him—my hands in his thick hair, his mouth hot and wet. When he stretched out and I slipped easily down on him, felt his hands holding on to my hips, saw the muscles flex in his shoulders and arms, we kissed and rocked and I rode him until I felt him pulsing inside me. And then we slept that heavenly, dreamy, connected, after-sex sleep that's so good once you've learned each other's bodies. Our movements, even in sleep, were perfectly synced now.

Just before sunrise, I left Rauser in bed and slipped out for a jog with my brother. We peeled off the concrete path at Piedmont Park and jogged up the hill toward 10th Street in the foggy predawn.

Dewy fescue glistened under the skyline and soaked my running shoes. Jimmy kept the pace next to me.

We turned right on 10th and eased into our cooldown, dodging branches from the young maples planted in little strips between sidewalk and street. This was our new routine, the quiet time we carved out three days a week since Jimmy had returned to Atlanta. We'd run together as kids too—Jimmy pushing me, encouraging me. He'd never had my competitive streak, but that didn't stop him from showing up at high school track meets and rooting me on. Jimmy had always been my greatest supporter. Even at home when I'd butted heads with our mother, Jimmy's even temper and cool thinking restored the peace. He had always balanced out our high-strung family nicely.

We stretched tight calves while holding on to the darkened balcony railings on a row of town houses. Across the street, a men's bar was closed up tight for the day. The FOR LEASE signs that had papered the windows at what was once Outwrite Books had come down and a new restaurant had taken the space in Midtown's ever-changing landscape. On the opposite corner The Flying Biscuit was gearing up for breakfast. And Caribou Coffee was calling my name.

We walked into the coffee shop to the usual mix of bleary-eyed customers dressed for work and those of us still hopped up on endorphins. Jimmy's roving eye slyly checked out a guy in red bicycle clothes that didn't leave a lot to the imagination. What's up with that anyway? I mean, just how far are you people willing to go in the name of aerodynamics? He looked like an extra-strength Tylenol with a bulge in the center.

"Stop staring at his junk," Jimmy whispered.

"You were staring at it. Besides, look at it. It's like there's a little face under there looking back."

We put in our orders and downed bottles of water while we waited—a double-shot, skim milk cappuccino for me and a caramel high rise for Jimmy, which appeared to be ninety percent whipped cream and caramel sauce. Our sweet tooths had been nurtured early as testers for Mother's kitchen creations. Jimmy had been a good student and became an accomplished cook himself. Me, I just learned how to eat. I'm really good at it. Fortunately, I have a metabolism that burns through food like a Colorado wildfire, something genetic, I thought, inherited from the biological parents I didn't remember—two drug addicts and one exotic dancer. They'd handed me off to my grandparents as an infant, thank goodness, and rushed off to pursue their dream of procuring, smoking, snorting, and shooting into their veins as many drugs as possible. The money stuffed into my mother's skimpy bra probably funded their binges. I remember my grandparents, though the sound of their voices and the gentleness in their faces has been eclipsed over the years by their murder.

Jimmy and I took a table near the window. This had become part of our routine too. I was seven when my parents adopted Jimmy. He was five. We had bonded instantly—a scrawny, geeky Chinese girl and an equally scrawny black boy. I'd been living with Howard and Emily Street almost two years at the time. I'd learned to trust them. My faith in their stability and the presence of another child in the house had helped give Jimmy a comfortable landing in his new home. Unfortunately, I wasn't able to protect my gentle brother from the bullying he'd take in the world. By high school, our population was more diverse. I didn't look so different from everyone else anymore. But my dark-skinned, light-eyed, soft-spoken brother didn't fit anyone's mold. And he didn't fight back when they pushed him around and called him a faggot. He begged me not to fight for him. But I did. Because that's who I am—cocked and ready to fire. Jimmy just wanted out. He left as soon as he graduated with a bitter taste he would always associate with the South.

"Any word from the agency?" I asked. After nine years together Jimmy and Paul had decided to have a child.

"We're flying to Boston next week. She's four months' pregnant." Jimmy looked out onto Piedmont Avenue. The sun was burning through, and the streetlights had clicked off. "We'll get to meet the father this time too. They seem like nice kids. They're just not ready to be parents and they don't care that we're gay or interracial."

"I hope it works out," I told him. I meant it. I thought they would make good parents.

"Me too," Jimmy said. "Because you know if it doesn't we'll end up adopting a pair of Chihuahuas and putting them in tiaras."

I nodded. "It just escalates from there. First a tiara, then a tutu."

"Ankle bracelets," Jimmy added. "Chihuahua playgroups."

"Slippery slope," I agreed.

He set his coffee on the table and studied me with striking pale eyes that always seemed bluer against his dark skin. "How is it with Aaron?"

"We're still in the honeymoon phase. Kind of. I'm trying to enjoy it while it lasts."

"Rose-colored glasses as usual," Jimmy said.

I smiled. "I'm cautiously optimistic. That's a step forward, isn't it?" I pushed my blueberry muffin over to him. "I have a meeting across the street. And I have a job out of town. You want the shitty muffin?"

"Not if it sucks." Jimmy sipped sugary foam off hot coffee. "How long you away?"

"I think I'm going to need a couple of days at least. Count me out on the next run."

"Sounds mysterious."

"It's a consulting job," I told him. I didn't offer details. This kind of case would bother Jimmy. "County sheriff wants some advice on a repeat offender case. Sounds like he needs someone to interpret the evidence, translate it in practical terms. And it sounds like he's short on detectives. I'm cheap. And apparently less intrusive than the Bureau."

"So it's a murder thing?"

I nodded. "Two bodies found in the woods. Thirteen years old."

Jimmy's eyebrows knotted up. "I don't understand how someone could hurt a child. Or an animal. I just don't."

"This kind of person, they're not like us, Jimmy. They don't think about the victim." We sat there a minute while that hung in the air. Jimmy pushed the shitty muffin back to me.

"You're going to a meeting like that?"

"I'm serving divorce papers. The guy has no idea. Thinks he's meeting his wife." I pulled up the leg of my sweatpants and peeled off the envelope I'd banded around my calf in a plastic bag so I wouldn't lose it while running. "He won't care what I'm wearing."

"Wow. Great way to start his day. You feel good about it?"

I dumped the envelope out and left the plastic bag and two thick rubber bands on the table, got up, kissed my brother's cheek. "Next time, I'll jump out of a cake. Make it fun for him."

I crossed the street to The Flying Biscuit on a blinking WALK light, holding the divorce papers Latisha had picked up for me yesterday.

The breakfast crowd was streaming in. Another half an hour and there would be a waiting list. The host, a young guy with longish hair and jeans, met me with a menu in his hand. "I'm meeting someone," I told him.

"Is that him in the corner?"

I recognized Edward Dabato from the photo in his file. "That's him. Thanks." I walked to a small table where he sat alone with a glass of orange juice and a cup of coffee. He was reading a menu. "Mr. Dabato?"

Flat brown eyes lifted to me. Suspicious eyes. Maybe he was expecting this after all. I pulled out a chair and sat down so we could keep it nice and quiet. "I'm afraid your wife isn't coming, sir." I pushed the envelope across the table. He picked it up and read the return address of the family lawyer who had hired me. I saw the moment when the veil came down, when his eyes showed something, when he realized a few things about his life and his wife he hadn't known before. Man, this is a shitty job sometimes. "You've been served. I'm sorry."

Dabato stood up very calmly, tucked the envelope with the divorce papers under his arm, hooked thick fingers under the edge of the table, then flipped it in a surprisingly violent, jerky movement. Everything on top came sliding at me. Orange juice splattered my lap. Hot coffee stung my thighs. The mug and glass hit the tile and shattered.

The restaurant went silent. A saltshaker rolled across the floor. Dabato gave me a last hard look and stalked out. I snatched a handful of napkins off the table next to me and blotted my sweatpants while the breakfast crowd, the host, the servers, all stared.

"What?" I huffed. "You people really need to think about cloth napkins."

I hobbled out with as much dignity as I could muster in wet sweatpants that made me look like a candidate for adult diapers. It was going to be a long walk home.

5

Rauser was blasting out the door when I came down my tenth-floor hall, shoulder holster over a white shirt, a blue blazer draped over his arm, and an electric shaver in his hand. I saw him take in my damp clothes and the yellow-brown coffee stain on the crotch of the sweatpants. An eyebrow came up. "Can't wait to hear this."

I gave him the short version. "I had a little spill."

He grinned. "I see that. You heading out to the boonies?" He knew the details—I'd explained last night while we walked Hank—the girls, both the same age, both of them disappearing on their way home from school, both of them held for months before the heavy swing of a narrow-headed object ended their lives.

"I want to at least check it out."

"It's bugging you, isn't it?" Rauser asked. "Because those girls were held somewhere and because there may be another one there right now. I knew you wouldn't be able to leave it alone."

"Professional curiosity," I said, smiling up at him. He bent and gave me a quick kiss while keeping his body as far away from me as possible. "It's coffee and orange juice," I said. "It's not toxic waste."

"Whatever it is I don't want any." He slipped past me sideways so his clothes couldn't brush mine and headed down the hall.

"Hey, don't forget to feed Hank and White Trash while I'm gone!" I called behind him.

He stepped into the elevator, pointed a finger at me. "I got this," he promised. The doors closed on his big, handsome smile.

An hour later I was showered and packed and on the way to my office with a suitcase in the backseat of the Impala. Neil was sitting at the kitchen table with an enormous bowl of cereal when I came in. Latisha was there too with her nose in a paperback. This was a first. It was quarter till nine. There was coffee in the French press. I poured a cup and leaned back against the counter.

"You have a chance to look at sex offenders in Hitchiti County?"

He looked up at me through blond lashes. "Good morning to you too." He was wearing the plaid shorts and Vans slip-ons he'd had on yesterday, but his hair was combed and his eyes were clear. "Do you mind if I finish my Lucky Charms?"

"Is that seriously what you're eating?" I asked. "Why don't you just lick the sugar bowl?"

"Oh really? You want to compare diets?" Neil asked me.

I looked at Latisha. She held up a palm. "I don't start work until nine. Besides, I cannot put this shit down." She used the slate-gray paperback she was reading to fan herself. "Know what I'm sayin'?"

Neil hunched over his Lucky Charms. His spoon hit the side of the bowl on every bite. I stood there for a minute, sipping my coffee, marveling once again at the turn my life had taken. Five years ago I would have bet good money I wasn't going to end up running a private detective business with an insubordinate pot-smoking former cyber-criminal and an insubordinate nineteen-year-old potty mouth.

Neil rinsed his bowl and put it in the dishwasher. "Okay, so here's the thing. There's two hundred and thirty-four registered sex offenders in Hitchiti County," he told me. "A hundred of them are homegrown and either still live there or came back during the right timeframe. *A hundred.* Out of the hundred and thirty-four transplants, only twelve of them would have been there when Tracy Davidson disappeared eleven years ago. So that's a hundred and twelve possibilities among registered offenders."

"Okay, let's narrow the pool to something manageable. Exclude everyone in apartment buildings, quadraplexes, or duplexes where holding a prisoner would be too risky," I said. I found the reports from the sheriff and looked for the name of the town where the first victim had lived. "Melinda Cochran was from Whisper, Georgia, and Tracy Davidson lived in Silas. The towns are twenty miles apart. Draw a circle around that area thirty miles out, see who's left. He dumped bodies in a remote area. There's ten years between the murders. He's working close to home. He knows the landscape. Let's focus on those offenders with the right kind of property—freestanding structures or fortifications—a barn, toolshed, garage, someplace that could be soundproofed. Or someplace with enough distance from the neighbors that he wouldn't need those things."

"A basement would work if it could be secured," Neil added. "And a lot tougher to spot. Sometimes you can tell on satellite, sometimes not. Might have to go to real estate records but it's doable."

Latisha pulled an iPod out of her drawer, plugged in earphones, and tuned us out. We took a moment to watch her turn her computer on and take the first pile of work out of her inbox.

"It's a long shot," I told Neil. "The sheriff was right. It's the non-registered offenders that pose the greatest threat. But it's worth a look." I wondered what had attracted the killer to Tracy Davidson and Melinda Cochran. A look? A word? Opportunity? Did he know them, their families? Was it simply that he had a type—white, female, and young? I showed Neil the sheriff's report with the name of the creek and coordinates. "Can you bring this up on satellite?"

His keys began to click. Hitchiti County came up on the screen, a small, pear-shaped county hugging the northeast edge of Lake Oconee. He zoomed in until we had an overhead view of Catawba Creek snaking through the Georgia woods. No residences close by. No roads. "Pull in as tight as you can in the area of the disposal site."

Neil followed instructions, and what we saw was thick woods. No landmarks. Trees and more trees with glimpses of a creek. "Okay, let's see," he said. "The disposal site is about half a mile from this eastern point of Lake Oconee. In the other direction another half mile there are a couple of farms, lots of pasture. Half mile north there's a small campground. South is just more forest. There's a little break in the trees here." He used his cursor to show me. "Coordinates are right. Must be the natural embankment the sheriff mentioned."

"Where they found the bodies," I said, studying the screen. It was a dense forest, yet the killer remembered where he'd left a body ten years earlier, and he'd delivered the second victim to that exact spot. If it weren't for a piece of rock blocking her fall, Melinda Cochran would have landed next to the skeletal remains of Tracy Davidson. Would a tourist or a trucker or someone who passed through now and then be able to find that location so precisely again? I didn't think so.

"How about names and addresses of Melinda's Facebook friends?" I asked Neil.

"You do understand how many resident histories I had to run on those sex offenders, right?" He looked at me as if I'd just slipped into tap shoes and performed a stirring rendition of "The Lollipop Guild." "Am I supposed to pull extra hours out of my ass so I don't have to eat or sleep?"

"Are they free when they come out of your ass like that or will you be taking your salary this month?"

"I hate you." He fought off a smile. "Go away."

"Get on it, okay?" I stopped at Latisha's desk and waited for her to remove the headphones. "Did you see your dad yesterday?"

"I did. And I have our check. Plus, we have more due in today so after the mail comes I'll make the bank deposit. I'm also sending invoices to Fairy Chin, I mean Larry Quinn, Mr. Snot, I mean Slott, Rapid Placement, Super Nannies On Call, and the bug-sweeping accounts. Tomorrow the payables are on the schedule. I'll need you to sign some checks before you go. 'Cause we all know you're going." Latisha had been taking a bookkeeping course a couple of nights a week and it was paying off.

Speechless in the face of flagrant efficiency, I went to my office and picked up the landline, pressed in the number for the Hitchiti County Sheriff's Department. A woman's voice answered, "Sheriff Meltzer's office." She had one of those nice, pleasant, middle-of-the-road voices, the kind your credit card company uses to direct you through their automated systems, the kind of voice that makes you feel good about the 24.99 percent APR. I asked for the sheriff. She wanted to know who was calling. I gave her my name and waited for Kenneth Meltzer to answer.

"Keye Street, Sheriff. I'd like to drive down today. I'll need to see the rest of your files on the two vics. And I'd like someone to show me to the disposal site. Is that possible?"

"Done deal," Meltzer answered without hesitation. "Glad to hear you're coming. Plan on hanging around?"

"I'll need a day or two," I said.

"We'll make arrangements for you, then. Nothing fancy but it will be clean."

"All I need is WiFi and a bed." And no bedbugs.

"I think we can arrange that, Dr. Street. We have running water down here too."

I smiled. "Good to know. I'll see you soon."

I was on the interstate by noon, sunglasses up, top down, a scarf to keep my hair out of my face. The sun was beating down, and the heat was rising up off the pavement like flaming charcoal. It was going to be one of those days in Georgia. Already it felt like I was wading through sweet sorghum syrup. I-20 east out of Atlanta is not a pretty drive. It knows nothing of the achingly lush beauty of the South, of the sweet, heavenly scent of Confederate jasmine, of peach trees so fat with fruit the branches bend toward the ground, of potted ferns swinging off wide front porches with spinning ceiling fans, blackberry cobbler and home-churned ice cream on soft, starry nights. What I-20 knows is chain restaurants, shopping malls, and truck stops, eighteen-wheelers, horse trailers, and high-powered pickups, and the gassy, chemical smell of exhaust. Traffic flies out here, really moves. Everyone's on the way to somewhere else.

Seventy miles out of Atlanta, I exited the interstate and headed south into the countryside. Green pastures were dotted with rolled hay and grazing cattle and the occasional lightning-struck tree sitting alone in the middle of mown fields. The air smelled like cut grass. I covered another few miles of Georgia farmland before billboards with smiling, copper-colored boaters began to pop up on the rolling fescue shoulder of the central Georgia highway halfway between Atlanta and Augusta—Jet Ski rentals, restaurants, hotels, bait shops, boat sales, signs for all things golf: courses, equipment, cottages.

Minutes later, I crossed a bridge over the silvery blue waters of Lake Oconee. The city limit sign was waiting at the other end. WELCOME TO WHISPER, GEORGIA. POPULATION 2,884.

I slowed when I saw two black-and-whites with red racks on top and gold emblems on the doors parked in a gravel lot. There were a couple of civilian cars and a black Police Interceptor utility vehicle with the word SHERIFF in giant white letters that stretched across almost the entire length of the vehicle. The door had the department's star and black lettering that said HITCHITI COUNTY SHERIFF'S DEPARTMENT—LAKE OCONEE PRECINCT. The office was a light gray Cape Cod with white trim, designed to fit in with the shoreline architecture of a county dependent on tourism.

I parked, got rid of the scarf, raised the top on my Impala, and grabbed my camera and laptop so they wouldn't fry in the heat. I heard a voice behind me just as I shoved my Glock under the seat. I recognized it. It wasn't the kind of voice you forget.

"Let me take that for you." The sheriff reached for the case hanging off my shoulder with my laptop and notebooks. He was wearing a ring on his right hand, gold with a ruby in the center. His hair was longish, sandy blond, parted down the center and tucked behind his ears. Brown eyes, and the perfect triangle-shaped dot of a goatee under his bottom lip. "I assume you want to see the crime scene first," he said.

"Please. I need to see what he saw," I answered. "Really helps with context."

"Understood." He was lean with a leathery tan. Not the salon tans I see in office buildings all over Atlanta. This one came from being outside. He was in jeans and a short-sleeved uniform shirt with his department's logo over the left pocket. No weapon, a badge on his belt. He looked young—too young to be a sheriff and much too young to be in his second term. He opened the door and the resort vibe faded quickly away. It was a plain, uninspired cop shop with big metal desks in the front room, heavy on efficiency, light on aesthetics. "The main station is a few miles down the road. It houses our uniformed patrol units, evidence rooms, admin clerks, the county and state prisoners under our watch, my deputies, the detention staff, and our crime labs. I have two people in my Criminal Investigations Department that work mostly out of this office. Both of them are out on a call. You'll meet them later."

A woman smiled at me from a desk. "This is my administrative assistant, Doris. The fabric of my life," Meltzer said.

Doris was somewhere in midlife with thick wavy blue-black hair that looked like she used big rollers. When I said hello she answered with the calm telephone voice I'd heard earlier. Conversation trickled down from up an oak-banistered staircase. I heard phones ringing.

"County call center upstairs," Meltzer explained. "Two operators per shift twenty-four hours a day."

"You do it all," I commented.

"Have to. We're just a tiny blip on the map but Hitchiti County has a lot of shoreline and a lot of highway. And four of our towns don't have their own police departments." He walked to a back office and took a shoulder harness off a coat rack. A couple of seconds later a Smith & Wesson M&P40 was hugging his ribs on the right side. He filled an ammo pouch attached to the left side of the holster.

"Is that standard issue down here?" I smiled.

"No, it's not," he said. "But it's what I've always used. Plus, well, I'm the sheriff." He smiled, too, and waved for me to follow him into the kitchen. I could see an expanse of ruffled blue water through the back windows, distant shores rimmed with maples and lime-green pines. He opened the refrigerator, took out a couple of bottles of water, handed me one. "We don't get a lot of homicides, Dr. Street. Not like this. We get the old-fashioned kind with motive you can understand—money or love, greed, passion. This is different."

The sheriff gave a nod in the direction of my water bottle. "Bring it with you. It gets hot out there. You can leave your things."

I set my case on one of the chairs and kept the camera. Meltzer opened the back door and I followed him out to a wooden dock and a boathouse with a tin roof and the sheriff's department star on the side. A boat with a T-top was bobbing at the dock, black and white with a star and the word SHERIFF running down the side.

Meltzer tugged on a thick rope and pulled the boat closer. The long vein in his tanned biceps bulged. He climbed in and held out a hand for me. I hesitated. "It's the quickest way," he said.

I took his hand and climbed over. He started the engine, unfolded a pair of wire-rimmed glasses from his shirt pocket, and hooked them over his ears with hands I'd imagine on a musician or artist, not a county sheriff. He eased the boat away from the dock, glanced back at me standing behind him. "Not a fan of the water, huh?"

"I'm accustomed to enjoying it from land," I said.

He did a bad job of disguising a smile. "Better hold on, then."

6

don't want a water death. Put me on the coast with sun and sand and salt air. Put me on one of Georgia's strikingly raw barrier islands and I feel like I'm being healed from the inside out. But for the love of God, do *not* put me on top of some huge body of water.

I fixed my eyes on the back of the seat I was white-knuckling. It was the only thing that wasn't bobbing and swaying. I took long, slow breaths in through my nose and out through my mouth as the Yamaha V6 skipped lightly over the lake. The wind felt good against my face. There was a chance I was going to make it without barfing all over the sheriff's boots. Then Meltzer made a sharp turn toward the shoreline and my stomach came all the way up to my eyeballs.

He pulled alongside a lopsided, weather-beaten dock, got out, anchored the boat. "You look a little green there, Dr. Street." His eyes narrowed like he might smile.

"Thanks for noticing," I said and climbed over the side. Even the half-rotted old dock felt good under my feet.

Meltzer sprayed his arms with mosquito repellent, then tossed me the can. We headed up an incline into the thick woods that bordered the lake. "It's a little bit of a hike to where we found the bodies no matter which direction you come from," he told me. "By water or highway. My department has to have a visible presence on the water just to keep the tourists from getting drunk and running over each other. We're committed to heavy marine and highway patrols. It's the bulk of the department. But the suspect obviously slipped by us. Twice."

I'd heard about Meltzer's patrols and the highly successful speed traps. I didn't mention it. "Which way presents the least risk?" I was thinking about rhythms. The rhythm of a place—when people fish and boat and camp, when cops make their rounds. All the things a killer has to think about.

"There's a campground half a mile from the site. My patrols can't see it from the road. A lantern out here on the lake at night is going to be seen. And you need a lantern. Water's as black as oil at night. But the woods are thick. Nobody would see a flashlight. Plus, the climb isn't as steep. If it was me and I was dealing with a dead body, that's how I'd come in."

"Is the creek accessible by smaller craft?" I asked. I felt perspiration gathering around my hairline. Even the shady cover of the woods couldn't take the humidity out of the tropical system hanging over us, so heavy a butter knife would have hung in the air. I took a band out of my pocket and pulled my hair back off my neck as we walked.

"Catawba is wide but it's shallow in places," the sheriff answered. "Good for trout and inner tubes. Around here, mostly what you get is fishermen and hunters. Season for firearms doesn't start up again until the end of September. I've been out here several times since we found the girls and so have my two investigators. None of us has run into a human once."

"You run into anything else?"

Meltzer stopped, looked at me, the light growing in his brown eyes. "Animals, you mean?" He laughed. It was a good laugh, easy and un-inhibited. "Not really the outdoorsy type, huh?"

I'd dressed for a hike through the woods. I'd prepared. I was wearing combat boots and cargo pants, for Christ's sake. I looked like a member of a SWAT team. What did this guy want from me? Okay, so I don't like being on water and I think about things like bears. It's not like I'd shown up in Christian Louboutins. I ignored him and kept walking. "What do you know about the parents of the victims?"

"I haven't met Tracy Davidson's parents. But Melinda's parents are good people. They're friends of mine." We stepped over a fallen tree trunk and pushed our way through brush. "Not a lot of education but hardworking," the sheriff added. "She's a waitress at the Silver Spoon and he runs the bowling alley in Whisper. Melinda was a nice kid." His voice wobbled. "Damn." He kicked at rock and dry leaves. "Hard to see people hurt the way they did when Melinda didn't come home."

"Do you mind if I have a look at the interviews you did with the parents after each victim disappeared?"

Meltzer shot me a look I wasn't sure about. Annoyance, perhaps. "They weren't interviews exactly. Not with Melinda's parents anyway. More like informing them we suspected foul play in the disappearance of their daughter and watching their hearts break. I'll never forget it. Or what it was like when we had to tell them we found her body."

He'd known one of the victims. He was emotionally involved and prickly about questions. I understood it. But I wasn't going to do my job on eggshells. "I need to learn as much as I can about Melinda and Tracy, Sheriff. It's where I usually start—with the victims. If you have interviews already, we won't need to go back to the families and reopen that wound. Have you spoken to the Davidson family yet? And do you have the initial reports from her disappearance?"

"Major Brolin, my head of Criminal Investigations, notified Mrs. Davidson yesterday after the lab reports came in with a positive ID. And I've asked her to assemble everything we have on both cases for you." The sheriff pointed to a thin trail weaving through thickets of privet and woody vines. "We're going up this way so you can see the dump site. Then we can walk around toward the campground."

"I think I'd like to drive over to it later, if you don't mind, then walk from there."

The sheriff uncapped his water bottle and took a long drink. I did the same. "You want to see what he saw if he came in from the road, is that it?"

I nodded. "Any insight into his thinking helps."

"I don't like looking through a predator's eyes." The sheriff said it flatly.

"You must have had to before in your career."

"Started as a beat cop in Boulder, Colorado, made detective two years before I came here. Narcotics. Different kind of predator. I never wanted to be in homicide. I don't like spending all my time thinking about killers."

"I've always been drawn to it," I said.

Meltzer stood above me on the hill with his open water bottle. He studied me for a few seconds. "Well, you seem perfectly normal."

"Do I?" I smiled. "That's reassuring. What brought you to Georgia, Sheriff?"

He screwed the top back on his half-empty bottle and started walking again. "My dad passed away. Mom was a southerner. She wanted to come back here."

"Your mother passed too?"

Ken Meltzer turned back and looked at me. "Why do you ask?"

"You said *was*. She *was* a southerner."

"God. That's so telling, isn't it? My mother developed Alzheimer's symptoms nine years ago. I guess sometimes it feels like she's already gone."

"I'm sorry. Is that why you came here?"

"She had relationships here. I thought moving her would add to her confusion. And I was young enough to start over. It made sense."

"That had to be tough," I said.

"Thanks. It was."

Neil's ringtone, Main Source's "Fakin' the Funk," throbbed through the woods and hushed the birds. I'd forgotten to silence my phone.

The sheriff looked at me. "My business partner," I told him. "You mind if I take it?"

"No problem," he said.

"What's up?" I answered.

"Jimmy's here," Neil told me. I watched the sheriff walk ahead. "He made zucchini bread for the office. Too bad you're not getting any. So what are the cops like? All gun racks and shit?"

I glanced at Ken Meltzer moving easily through the woods. "I haven't met the others but the sheriff is a little bit of a Boy Scout," I whispered. "He's also totally hot."

"Bradley Cooper hot or Channing Tatum hot?" my brother piped in.

"Keith Urban hot," I said.

"Ah," Jimmy cooed. "A rebel. A little too wild and uncombed for the city. But sensitive. Probably exfoliates."

"Exactly," I said. "Listen, I'm in the woods on the way to the scene. Can this wait?"

"I found eight registered offenders that meet your criteria," Neil said. "I figured you'd want to know. They're in the area we mapped out. The timeframe works and they have sheds, garages, barns, carports, or basements. I'm emailing you the particulars."

"Great. Everything okay at the office?"

"You've been gone three hours, Kiwi. I think we're okay." Neil used the nickname he'd hung around my neck a few weeks ago when he discovered my middle name was Lei and rhymed with my first name, Keye. Together they sounded to him like, well, Kiwi. "Be careful down there. Lot of history. Weird stuff."

"Like what?"

"For starters, and this should give you an idea of the vibe, the Koasati tribe had a word for that area. *At-pasha-shilha*. Know what it is?"

"How would I know that? I didn't even know there was a Koasati tribe." I trudged through leaves up the hill and tried to keep my footing. The path was clear now that we were deep into the woods. No thickets to maneuver through, just tall trees and leaves piled on a pine straw bed.

"How can you grow up Chinese and be so totally clueless about other cultures?" Neil huffed.

"I didn't grow up Chinese. I grew up southern."

"It means 'mean people,' Keye. You're in the mean people county. Spooky, huh?"

"Yeah. It is. Look, I gotta run." I disconnected, and jogged to catch up with the sheriff. He heard me and waited.

"We found the bodies just up there," he said when I got closer.

We topped the hill. I could hear the creek. "How do you remember the spot?" I asked.

"When you come straight up from the old dock and top this hill, you're looking right at those two old oaks growing together. It's thirty yards north from there. When you come in from the road, there's a big poplar wrapped in dead vines about the size of my arm where the path veers down to the lake. You go east and climb up the hill from there. I spent a lot of time hiking in Colorado. You learn to remember natural landmarks."

And so do killers, I thought, and snapped some pictures as we walked, including the double oak tree the sheriff used as a guidepost. We approached the edge of a slope. The dry dead leaves crinkled under our boots. I gazed down at a twenty-foot drop, a natural indentation in the earth that looked something like a sinkhole. I thought about the photographs—Melinda on her side stopped by a rock, Tracy's remains below her at the bottom. "Can you come in from any other direction?" I asked Meltzer.

"It wouldn't be easy. Farmhouses and dogs, private property. The distance would be greater. Nowhere to leave your transportation. And he'd have to cross the creek. I don't see that happening."

I looked back down at the drop-off and thought again about the scene photos. He'd removed their clothes. Was it MO, something to defeat efforts at evidence collection? Or was it signature, something that fulfilled a psychological need, something unnecessary to the commission of the crime? Perhaps it reinforced his dominance over the victims. Had he kept their clothes? "Those girls were alive when they got here," I told the sheriff. "He walked them out here, made them strip and turn their backs to him. He's carrying something he can use to dispose of their clothing, something that wouldn't look suspicious if he ran into someone in the woods. A backpack, maybe. He dropped Melinda's blouse accidentally on his way out." I backed up a few feet from the edge, turned, and pointed toward the creek. "He was close to the creek when he lost it or else it would have either washed down the slope to the lake or ended up in the depression where he disposed of the bodies. And he'd want them back far enough so he could hit them hard without knocking them off. He'd want to check their vitals. He's careful. He has to make sure they're not breathing." I backed up a couple more feet. "So he stands about here and swings his weapon." I glanced up at the sheriff. His wide brown eyes were fixed on me. "This isn't just a disposal site, Sheriff; it's your primary crime scene." I walked around, took some more pictures. Flashes of sunlight broke through the branches and danced off the creek. There was an enormous granite slab sticking out of the ground like a ledge—not unusual in Georgia, the home of Stone Mountain. The stuff is everywhere. "You collected soil and leaf samples from this area?"

Meltzer nodded. "A few. Lab hasn't found anything so far that isn't natural to the area. Lost a lot of evidence to the elements, I imagine. My investigators bagged a lot of debris around the bodies."

"ME's office get them out of the hole?"

"We did. On cots with pulleys and ropes. It was a mess. Hitchiti County doesn't have a medical examiner. We're on the coroner system. It's ridiculous. He's a goddamn real estate agent." The sheriff shook his head and chuckled, but there was real irritation in his voice.

"Any deals on waterfront property?"

"That's about all he's good for," Meltzer answered.

I went back to the edge and looked down at the piece of granite protruding from a sidewall, the one that had stopped Melinda Cochran's fall. "The first victim was positioned more toward the center." I pointed down in the hole. "She would have had to be thrown. But the second victim was rolled off. That's why she hit the rock. And that's not the only difference in the behaviors here from victim one to victim two. He used the sharp side of the axe on the second victim. And he left behind evidence. The victim's blouse."

"Maybe he's getting lazy," the sheriff suggested.

"Maybe." I took a deep breath, just let myself take in the scene—the drop-off where a killer had dumped his prey, the woods humming with katydids and birds and every kind of insect, the creek shimmering through the trees, the brown leaves covering the ground, seasons and seasons' worth, deep and decaying, the rich scents of earth and pine sap. I took more photos. Sometimes the camera sees what I can't. The Georgia woods have a lot to hide. I knew this too well. Not long ago I'd wandered upon a madman's mass graves in the wooded hills of North Georgia.

"When Melinda disappeared, was she sexually active?" I asked.

The midday sun was cutting streaks through heavy branches. He rubbed his eyes. I saw tiny creases, white like scar tissue, cut into tanned skin at the corners. "Not according to her friends."

"Both parents worked?"

He nodded. "Melinda spent afternoons with her mom at the diner when she worked second shift every other week. I've seen her doing her homework at the counter a hundred times, I guess. They didn't like her going home alone. Molly was home the day Melinda disappeared. But she vanished between school and home. They blame themselves for letting her walk. But it's that kind of town. It's safe. At least it was." He checked his watch. "I have an appointment this afternoon. Major Brolin is at your disposal if you need something. We have an empty desk at the office if you want to work there. Doris will tell you where to find your hotel. One thing we have plenty of is hotel rooms. I have to tell you, though: The nicer ones are up the road where all the golf courses and resorts are located. But I thought you'd want to stay in Whisper."

"Sounds good," I lied. Room service and a docking station would have sounded good. But I was on the sheriff's dime. And I knew I needed to stay. You can't drive in and out of a town and end up with any sense of it. You have to feel it as you're drifting off, wake to it, hear its voices, smell its smells. I pushed myself off the granite slab. "Mind if we walk along the creek awhile on the way back down?"

"I've never been opposed to walking along a creek, Dr. Street."

"It's okay to call me Keye."

"You don't like the title, do you?" Meltzer said, surprising me. "Why not? Most people would be proud of it."

"Long story," I said.

We walked for a couple of minutes. The creek was rocky and shallow, clear enough and still enough in places to see the tadpoles feeding near the bank, trout swimming by. "Why do you think he held those girls so long?" Meltzer asked quietly.

"He gets something from them. At least until he doesn't anymore."

"What?"

"Sex, a sense of power. Control. He'd keep them until they no longer fueled his fantasy life. Or until it became dangerous to continue holding them. More likely it's the former."

"And then he kills them," the sheriff said.

"It's the logical next step."

7

could hear the phones upstairs, and the calm monotones of the emergency operators. Doris answered a call now and then on the sheriff's direct line and carefully put messages in a spiral message pad. I unpacked my case, put my laptop and notebooks on the desk Sheriff Meltzer had offered me in the main room. Meltzer introduced me to his head of Criminal Investigations, Major Tina Brolin, and her detective, Robert Raymond, before he left. Everything had been going pretty well until then.

A couple of file folders landed on the metal desk in front of me followed by a thumb drive. It skidded across the desktop. I caught it before it fell off the edge. "Just so you know, this wasn't my idea," Major Brolin told me.

"Oookay," I said, and looked up at her. She had a slight overbite. I zeroed in on two tiny permanent impressions her front teeth had made in her bottom lip. It was hard to look at anything else after that. She was five-five and trim. Size did not inhibit her ability to put out some really crappy energy. I mean, I'm not exactly a spiritual giant but I kind of wanted to set some sage on fire and chant something cleansing. "If I want to see physical evidence, will I have access?"

"Sheriff says to give you what you want." Major Brolin's dark hair was pulled tight off her face. It looked like it hurt. "We can instruct the evidence room at the judicial center if you need something. An officer will have to be present, of course."

"Of course," I said, and glanced over her shoulder at Detective Raymond. "Can we talk after I have a little time with the files? I'd love to discuss the cases. With you both."

"You'd love to discuss the cases?" Brolin said. They exchanged an incredulous glance. "This is *our* case. *We* live here. *We* care about the people here. You don't know anything about this community."

"Exactly," I said. Brolin and Raymond stared at me for three seconds before I was looking at their backs. They disappeared into a rear office.

I glanced at Doris. "Guess I missed a memo."

"You have no idea," Doris said quietly. I realized for the first time just how unpopular the sheriff's decision to hire outside help had been. It was not what I had expected to walk into.

I opened my laptop and waited for it to blink on and give me the password bar. It didn't. I pressed the POWER button and it came quickly to life. It had been shut down. And I didn't do it. I'm vigilant about this. I power down every other night for maintenance purposes. I take care of my stuff. I clean my gun, I change the oil in my car, and I shut down my computer on a schedule.

I checked inside my computer case and saw the manila folders with crime-scene photos and the reports Meltzer had emailed me, the notes I'd begun on a legal pad when Meltzer had first called my office, a list of assignments I'd given Neil. Everything was in order. And then I saw my car keys in the long front pocket of the case. I had intentionally zipped them into an interior pocket. I glanced at my car in the lot out front, then at Doris working at her desk, then toward the back office. One of these people had looked through my things and tried to get into my computer after I walked out the back door with the sheriff.

I pushed in the flash drive, began to skim back over the reports I'd studied last night from the state crime lab. I then went through the file for Melinda Cochran and studied the statements taken after her disappearance. The sheriff was right. The interviews with Melinda's parents were bare bones. The cops knew them. They had excluded them quickly. Some effort was made to reconstruct Melinda's interaction with family in her final days. No big blowups or arguments. Melinda didn't seem particularly upset about anything, according to her parents, beyond the "usual ups and downs with friends" and the normal concerns of a thirteen-year-old who wanted to "fit in." There were no medical records either, nothing to explain the broken bones.

I jotted down names and addresses of Melinda's closest friends and read over their interviews carefully. None of them remembered seeing anyone unfamiliar in the area in the days and weeks prior to the abduction. They'd been talking, laughing, as they left school that day. There were people around—parents, kids, teachers, all familiar. Melinda and three of her friends walked home together every day. They lived a couple of blocks apart. Melinda walked the last two blocks alone. The police had scoured the area. They'd found her cell phone in the street, crushed by traffic. The pieces had been collected, checked for prints, and stored. No prints. Not even Melinda's. Not even a partial—wiped clean.

Eleven years ago, Tracy Davidson's friends had made similar statements. They'd seen Tracy in school but not on the school bus that afternoon. The interview with Tracy's parents and brother had been more extensive. Her father had served six years for armed robbery and assault with intent. Her brother, then eleven years old, had been home sick the day Tracy disappeared. I read over their statements carefully and the investigator's notes. Tracy's dad had been considered a prime suspect in the beginning. There were multiple domestic abuse calls from their home. Investigators had executed warrants and searched the premises thoroughly after Tracy had been missing for a week. Mr. Davidson had been hauled in twice more for follow-up statements. No evidence had been found to link the Davidsons to their daughter's disappearance. The case went cold. Tracy was listed simply as missing, and the notations in the file made it clear the investigators suspected she was a runaway. I couldn't fault them too much. They'd found absolutely no evidence of foul play. And it looked like Tracy Davidson had a lot to run away from.

I stood up, felt Doris's attention shift to me, walked to the back. If they'd used the floor plan as it was intended, both the back rooms would have been bedrooms. But they were offices instead, one clearly belonging to the sheriff. An antique oak desk held a nameplate with raised gold letters. His windows looked out on the water. The second office had two desks, metal like the one I'd been using in front, both piled with files and papers, the occasional candy wrapper and coffee ring. A box of doughnuts was open on Raymond's desk, half full. I wanted one, but no one was offering.

I tapped on the door. "Sorry to bother you, Major, but I need to know if Tracy Davidson and Melinda Cochran had broken bones and fractures prior to their disappearance. There's no medical records in the file, and it wasn't covered in the interviews." I was hoping she'd offer to help. She didn't. Not even a courtesy glance in my direction. I sharpened my tone a little. "I need the statements from the parents regarding the physical condition of both girls as soon as possible. And I need the medical records."

"You hear that, Major?" Raymond asked. "As soon as possible. Guess we better snap to."

"We're a little busy, as you can see," Tina Brolin told me.

"I don't give a damn how busy you are. This is a priority," I said, and their heads jerked up. I needed to put an end to this before Brolin and Raymond rolled over me completely. "I'm here to do a job with the full confidence of the sheriff. And since we're obviously not going to be friends, I will hang you and your shitty attitudes out to dry if you get in the way of my doing that. I hope that's clear."

Brolin held my eyes for a few seconds. "Make the calls," she instructed Raymond, then went back to the work on her desk.

I returned to my borrowed desk. Doris watched me silently. I heard Raymond's voice on the phone apologizing for the call, inquiring about any injuries Melinda might have had. "We will, Bryant. I promise you that," he was saying. I looked back at the reports. Bryant Cochran, Melinda's father. A sick feeling washed over me. Murder is a wrecking ball. After it slams into your life, everything feels like a betrayal. No one can give you enough support. No one can fill the canyon that has been dynamited into you. It's unfillable. Melinda's father was pushing them for answers. And he wasn't getting any. "Just give us a little more time," Raymond told him. "We're doing our best, Bryant."

I doubted they were doing their best. In fact it looked to me a lot like they'd all but given up. I heard Major Brolin answer her phone. She came out a minute later. Detective Raymond followed her, slipping into a shoulder holster. "Another robbery in the golf cottage district," Brolin told Doris. She didn't look at me before she walked out.

Detective Raymond stopped at my desk. He was a big, beefy guy in tan slacks with pleated fronts and a short-sleeved dress shirt that pooched out with his belly over the waistband. "Melinda's father says she never had a broken bone. The medical records should be here later."

"Okay, thanks. What about Tracy's parents?"

"No answer."

"Thanks for making the calls. Not easy, I'm sure."

"I know them. Everyone does."

"How about we talk about it later," I suggested. Might as well extend an olive branch and see if he'd grab on to it without his boss around. "And Tracy's case. I'll buy the coffee."

Raymond's thick lips curled a little. "I'm gonna be busy."

I watched him walk out, then glanced at Doris. "I think I'm growing on him," I said. She didn't look up. The sheriff's little lakeshore office was feeling a little too small at the moment. I loaded up my stuff and left Doris with my mobile number in case anyone gave a shit. The chances were pretty slim.

8

Miles of flat county blacktop ran alongside the thick green forest. I cut left on a back road, found a way to the highway, and circled the woods I'd walked through earlier with the sheriff. I drove about a mile before I saw a sign that said CATAWBA CREEK. I U-turned and took a dirt lane that peeled off the road just after the metal railing of a bridge. Fifty yards down, it curved and deadened at a campground. A sign mounted on a post and cemented into the ground read: OCONEE CAMPGROUND AND RV PARK. It wasn't much to look at. Three picnic tables down near the creek, a big dirt lot, a few hookups for RVs, a few water spigots. A travel trailer with its tow bar propped on a cement block was parked in a grassy area. It looked locked up tight. No vehicles, no one stirring. I checked the location services on my phone and made sure everything was turned on. I sent Neil a text with my location. If this means I'm not the outdoorsy type, as Meltzer suggested, so be it. But I wasn't walking into those woods alone without someone knowing where I was. I take my share of chances, but I try like hell not to be just plain stupid.

I sat there for a few minutes in the Impala. The top was down and it was shady in this little dug-in acre of grass and dirt surrounded by Georgia pines. I couldn't see the highway from here. And the highway couldn't see me—the ideal place to walk into the forest unseen. The sheriff was betting the killer had come in this way. It made sense.

A beaten-down trail ran along the creek and disappeared into the trees. I thought about the terror those two girls must have felt, wondered if they knew he was going to kill them. Had he tormented them with that threat? Maybe that was his thing. They must have tried to reason with him, pleaded. They would have seen the weapon in his hand. It was hard to come to terms with that kind of fear, with that long walk of terror they must have taken with their killer. Maybe he'd hidden the weapon in advance. Maybe he'd convinced them he was going to release them. That would say something about him too.

I reached under the seat for my Glock. I didn't feel it. I reached farther. No weapon. I got out and knelt down, peered under the seat. There it was. Another thing out of place. First my computer, then my keys, and now my gun. They'd searched my bag *and* my car while I was out with the sheriff. *Sonofabitch,* I muttered. I inspected the Glock, checked the magazine, grabbed an extra clip, pushed the flap on a duty holster down inside the back of my pants. I'm not the superstitious type, but there was something dark-hearted down here in Whisper. It was seeping out of those woods like sap. *Mean people.*

I headed into the woods, walked until the trail that was beaten down by tourists who stopped at the campground to hook up their campers and get out their fishing poles split to the right toward the lake's edge. Catawba Creek meandered out of sight to my left, but I knew where it was going. It would circle the incline that led to the crime scene. I stayed straight and looked for the tree Meltzer had described, the one with dead vines as big as his arms.

The forest was hushed but for chirping birds and insects. Squirrels scurried up trees, and chipmunks rustled the dead leaves at my approach. No breeze. It was late afternoon and the sun was low enough to light up the treetops above me. I slapped the mosquito on my arm and cursed at the smashed gray spot with its splat of my blood. It itched already. There's no escaping the relentless barrage of hungry mosquitoes in Georgia's swampy heat unless you're slathered in chemicals. I could still smell deet on my skin from the spray the sheriff had given me earlier, gamy and oily. I guess smelling is all it's good for after a few hours because the mosquitoes were not deterred.

I took my time, paid attention to the trees, the shrubs, looked for landmarks, markers, something carved in bark, anything he might have used to mark his path. I snapped a few pictures. How had he remembered the spot where he'd first marched a girl ten years earlier and swung his weapon? Had he memorized these thin paths and dark trees? They all looked alike to me.

I could feel my quads starting to work. The incline was beginning—a leaf-covered mountain of earth in the middle of the hilly forest, climbing up toward the disposal site. I spotted the big poplar tree Meltzer used as his landmark, wrapped in thick, woody brown vines. I studied it for a minute, walked around it, photographed it from different angles. Was this the killer's landmark too?

I followed the sheriff's directions, moving to the left and climbing east up toward the crime scene. The leaves didn't make for great footing, and the brush and foliage nearer the lake had all but disappeared. There was nothing to grab on to if you slipped. I thought again about a killer pushing a teenage girl through these woods, knowing all along how it would end, where he would take her, how he would murder her.

I reached the top and heard water in the distance, trickling lightly over rock. I saw the twin oaks Sheriff Meltzer used as his guidepost when he came in by boat. I could barely detect a hint of kicked-up earth from our earlier visit. I thought about the soil samples they'd taken weeks after Melinda's murder. The evidence, if there was ever evidence, had spent as much as sixty days in the elements—and the slightest puff of air can dislodge traces. But the samples could be matched to a suspect's shoes or automobile in order to place him at the scene. Killers don't always leave evidence that investigators can detect, but they almost always carry something of the scene home with them.

I walked until I found the place where the earth sucked in like a crater. I peered down at the granite boulder that had stopped Melinda Cochran's fall, closed my eyes, and remembered the scene photos.

Had Tracy Davidson and Melinda Cochran been his only victims? If so, why? Why them? Why a decade apart?

The sound of shoes crushing leaves on the forest bed got my attention, heavy and undisguised. I reached for my Glock.

"Put away your weapon, Dr. Street."

I didn't put it away. I liked it just fine where it was at my side. "Detective Raymond, what brings you out here?" I asked cheerfully. "Rethinking that cup of coffee?"

"Saw your car." He was winded from the climb. His face was sweaty and his cheeks spattered with color. He came up on my left side and stood beside me. He was a bull of a man, the kind of guy who had played college ball and let his body get flabby. He couldn't have spotted my car from the highway. He would have had to drive down into the campground. Had he followed me? I turned my attention back to the hollow.

Raymond stepped forward and looked down into the hole too. "Didn't you come up here with Meltzer already?"

I nodded. "I wanted to come in from the campground, get a feel for the walk."

"Personally, I think the suspect came in from somewhere along the lake." I could smell beer on his breath, and I wondered why he'd gone for a beer instead of investigating a robbery at some golf cottage with Major Brolin. Maybe she'd sent him.

"The sheriff thinks he would have been spotted if he came in that way," I said. "Plus it's a steep climb."

"It's not that bad," Raymond said. "And all he'd need is a little rowboat. He could have pulled the boat up on shore and hid it between marine patrols. No sweat."

"The suspect has to be someone familiar with the area."

"No shit." The muscle in his jaw and the dismissive tone told me he was aching for a fight. "That why they call you doctor?"

"You have something on your mind, Detective?"

"Nobody wants you here."

I glanced over at him. "I'm starting to get that."

"We saw all those stories about you being some kind of big serial hunter," he said.

"I'm flattered you went to the trouble," I said.

"The sheriff may believe that shit but the way it looks to the major and me is that you just found a way to repackage yourself when the FBI kicked you out."

"Gotta make a living, Detective," I said. "And for the record, I was fired because I was a drunk. Not because I'm a shitty analyst." Though his view was simplistic, he was right. I had repackaged myself. And here I stood, unofficial to the world. No badge. No security pass. Hell, I didn't even have a wedding ring anymore. My past would always trail me—those failures, those lapses, the consequences of some spectacularly bad decisions.

Raymond took a pack of Marlboros from his pocket, lit one with thick, steady hands, pulled smoke deep into his lungs. He looked completely comfortable standing there—justified, confident, accustomed to confrontation the way cops are. "Major Brolin and me, we both started out in uniform," he told me. It was almost conversational. He might have been discussing the drought. He blew out a plume of smoke that hung like a cloud in the heavy air. "We worked hard. She's one step away from chief deputy and she might be the next sheriff if things go right these next couple of years. Wouldn't want anything interfering with that."

"You're saying I'm interfering?"

"The major's track record will be important at election time. You prance in here and get the glory for closing cases the whole county knows about—hell, the whole state for that matter."

"That's what this is about? Glory?"

"Don't be stupid. It's all politics. You think Meltzer is in a second term because he's a good lawman? It's because he's a charming sonofabitch who knows what asses to kiss. And we got a county full of little old rich, retired ladies who like their asses kissed."

"Well, in that case, the major is going to have to sharpen her people skills." I looked back down into the bowl-shaped depression that had been a killer's landfill. "There's a predator out there who forced two innocent girls to live through a nightmare, Detective. That's what I'm thinking about right now. That's all I'm thinking about. Politics don't interest me. And neither do your ambitions. Or the major's."

He cleared his throat and spat on the ground, dropped his cigarette, crushed it under the sole of a cheap brown dress shoe. He stepped close enough so that his arm was brushing mine and I was looking up at tiny red veins that had burst under his cheeks over the years. Hard years, I guessed. With a lot of drinking. "Watch yourself," he whispered. His eyes were flat. "These woods can be dangerous."

I returned the Glock at my side to the holster as Raymond stalked away, let out a breath. You could have bounced a quarter off the muscles in my neck. I watched him start down the hill. He slid in his slick-soled shoes and almost went down. I smiled. I hoped he fell on his fat ass.

I walked toward the creek, thought about the blouse found with Melinda Cochran's skin cells around the collar. The killer would have had to come this way. Otherwise the blouse would have ended up hidden in debris at the bottom of the embankment. A fisherman would have never seen it, reported it. But why was the killer near the creek at all? If he'd walked from the campground, he'd have no reason to come this far. Maybe Raymond was right. Maybe he'd come up from the lake and followed the creek, dropped the shirt on his way back to his boat. It mattered to me, not because it was a trail that would necessarily lead to the killer—the area was too wide, with acres and acres of lake, accessible by thousands of tourists and part-time residents. But it would say something about the way he thought and lived, his level of fitness, his precautionary actions, and whether he was comfortable with boats and perhaps owned one. I stood there on the bank watching shallow water trickle over the rocks. Was it some kind of ritual? Perhaps he'd tossed her shirt in the water—a good-bye, closure—believing water would wash away evidence as it usually does. But the blouse had snagged on a branch on the way downstream, and the folds and creases had protected the DNA inside the collar. Everything else had been lost to the elements: the trace evidence that might have told us where she'd been held, the fibers that would have revealed something about his home and automobile, if he had cats or dogs.

I thought about how they'd died. He'd stood behind them. He'd swung his weapon hard. Melinda had been hit with a heavy sharp weapon consistent with an axe. I pictured him double-clutching that handle like a baseball bat, swinging, the weapon slicing into her neck.

Spatter. That was it. He'd come to the creek to rinse off Melinda Cochran's blood. He didn't want to walk out of the woods and drive away with blood on his face and hands. And that's when he'd dropped the blouse. Had he come in the night and worked his way up tangled paths with a flashlight and a weeping girl? Or was he comfortable enough to come in daylight? How bold was this killer? Did he know the area and the routines so well that he could walk out here just like I had? He'd made mistakes last time. He'd dropped the blouse and as a result a crime scene I didn't think he ever wanted exposed was un-covered. Maybe we'd discover he'd made other mistakes too. But he wasn't stupid. That much I knew.

I knelt down, cupped my hands in the clear, cool water, splashed it on my face, raked my hair back with wet fingers. I imagined his hands rinsing off Melinda's blood in this creek, him splashing his own heated face, the evidence tinting the water and trickling downstream. I closed my eyes and breathed in the mossy banks, let myself feel it, feel the serenity of this place falling down around me like rain, feel him kneeling here as I was now, his knees pressing into the soft soil at water's edge. My ticking pulse, the blast of adrenaline that shoots through me when I'm learning a killer, was as welcome and familiar to me as this place must be to him. It felt good. I don't know how else to explain that moment when you know you've understood something about a scene, something intimate about the dark, veiled movements of a psychopath. All those tiny moments, all those little actions—they add up, one stacked on top of another, building a tower that would sooner or later come tumbling down.

I'd been here at least an hour. I pushed away from the creek and brushed sandy soil off my knees, walked back to the crime scene and took another look. Raymond's crushed cigarette butt near the edge of the embankment irritated me, reminded me of his visit, the not-so-veiled warning he'd left me with. *Fucker.*

I started back down in the direction of the campground where my car was parked, sliding down slick leaves until I got to the poplar tree with the dead vines, Meltzer's landmark. The trail began to even out there and thicken with privet and vines. I knew I was getting close. And then I smelled it. Smoke. *Crap. Raymond.*

Just so you know, a nonsmoker can smell smoke a long ways away. Down here where the air is full of moisture, it doesn't dissipate. It holds together, creeps like a slow-moving escalator, and sets fire to your sinuses. And it's just stupid. If you want to stalk someone, wait until you're finished to indulge your addictions. It was a lesson I'd learned the hard way when I was still indulging mine.

I made a sweep of the area, moving a little slower, keeping a little lower. I wasn't sure how far Raymond would go with his intimidation tactics. Out here in these woods with no witnesses, with Detective Robert Raymond telling whatever story he wanted, I wasn't feeling particularly secure.

I got to the tree line and stopped when I saw a figure standing at the mouth of the path. Raymond looked at me, raised his cigarette to his lips. I stepped out of the woods. "Thought I'd hang around and make sure you got out safely," he said as I got closer. I saw his .38 in the holster. The strap was closed and snapped. A good sign. But nothing in his eyes put me at ease.

"You're just a one-man welcome wagon," I said, walking past him toward my car.

He followed me. "Nice wheels." He slapped the palms of his big hands against the hood of my Impala. "Where you headed?"

I felt a string of expletives lining up for their debut. I didn't like being picked on and threatened, and I didn't fucking like him touching my car. And I was hungry. Bad blood sugar goes straight to my mouth. I got in my car, looked up at him. "Offer's still open if you'd like to join me for coffee."

"Nah. But I'll be close by."

drove back into town, past the sheriff's office and the bridge I'd come in on, and followed the blacktop to Highway 441. I went south toward Milledgeville, and fifteen miles of flat road later I found Muskogee Trail thanks to Google Maps—a narrow, cracked paved road with cornfields on one side and single-level brick houses with acreage between them and long, straight driveways on the other. I pulled in just past a chipped green mailbox with shiny, stick-on hardware store numbers that said 826. The 6 had heated up against the metal box in the baking sun and tipped sideways. I saw a woman inside an open freestanding carport. She was leaning over a plywood table with stacked-up cement blocks for legs. I stopped a few feet away and got out. She came out to greet me with a pair of needle-nose pliers in her hand.

"Help you?" She had a sharp twang; long, frizzy bleached-blond hair; and a pair of black stretch pants that told me more than I wanted to know about her body.

"Are you Josey Davidson?"

"Yup. Come on in." She turned back to the carport. We stepped over power cords. A small fan whirred on the workstation. "You buying?" She picked up the pliers and positioned herself on a stool.

I really wasn't sure what I was supposed to be buying. "My name is Keye Street. I'm a consultant to the Hitchiti County Sheriff's Department."

"I guess that's a no, then," she said.

"You're a glassblower?" I saw a torch, mandrels, splitters, hoses. On her table, a plastic bin with thin leather bands and a roll of gold wire, pliers in different sizes.

"Flameworker," she corrected. "And jewelry maker." She reached into a small wicker basket and pulled out a bracelet with a leather strap, a glass triangle on top in a gold wire setting. She handed it to me. A beetle had been preserved inside the glass.

"Wow," I said, handling the bracelet. It was all I could do not to fling it across the carport. I'm not really a bug person.

She picked up a pair of pliers and unwound some gold wire. "What exactly does the sheriff's department have to say for itself?" She was quick with the wire, twisting it into a setting for a glass triangle that held another unfortunate specimen.

I put the bracelet on the plywood tabletop. "I'd like to speak to you about your daughter Tracy."

"My daughter's been dead for eleven years." Her hands kept working, nimble hands that moved from memory. Her daughter had been dead for ten years, not eleven. Tracy had lived for a year after her disappearance. With a sick feeling, I realized Mrs. Davidson hadn't been told about the terrible discoveries made by forensic scientists in Atlanta. "Y'all gonna send me flowers now? I mean that woman on the phone was so warm and comforting when she told me they'd found her."

"I'm sorry," I said quietly.

She glanced up at me with suspicious eyes, tried to read me. "What'd you say your name was?"

"Keye Street."

"What do you want, Keye Street?"

"Was Tracy active? Had she ever had any injuries, broken bones?"

"Goin' down that path again, are we? Y'all still trying to pin it on my husband? My ex was not worth anything and he got rough sometimes. But he didn't have the sense God gave a mule. He couldn't have gotten away with it. And no. He never broke anything on Tracy. But he did hurt all of us at one time or another."

"Where's Mr. Davidson now?"

"He's in jail. Thank the Lord. And so is my son."

I didn't know what to say to this woman. I wondered if she had other family, friends. From where I stood it looked like she'd lost nearly everything. "Tracy have a good relationship with her brother?"

"They were close. My boy wouldn't have hurt her if that's what you're getting at. He wasn't a violent boy. But he did turn out to have an attraction for nice cars." She put down wire and pliers and reached behind her for a thermos. "Unfortunately, they weren't his. Want some coffee?"

"Please," I said to be polite. That's what you're taught in the South. Somebody offers, you accept and you choke it down if you have to.

She poured coffee into a mug that said SIX FLAGS OVER GEORGIA, then filled the plastic top on the thermos and slid it toward me. "Might as well grab that other stool."

I walked past an aquarium full of bugs. Most of them were dead. Some were still moving, trying in vain to scrabble up the walls of their glass coffin. There was a plywood board covering the top, preventing escape. She was trapping them and letting them die, then entombing them in glass. I pulled the stool up to the other side of her plywood table, away from the creepy aquarium. The murky liquid in the thermos cap was a grocery store brand, lukewarm. Snobby Neil would have spit it out.

"It tore Jeffrey up when Tracy disappeared. He and Tracy were two years apart. He was the youngest. They went to and from school together every day on the bus. He was home sick the day she disappeared. He never got over that. Girl just disappeared into thin air. Then that sheriff we had back then comes around with his deputies, and after he finished investigating us, they tried to tell me Tracy ran away. I don't think a one of them ever thought about her again after that."

"I take it you don't think it's possible she ran away with someone she trusted."

"Not Tracy. And that's not just a mother talking. Tracy was real responsible. Her mama and her daddy were drinkin' and fightin' but she cooked the dinner and cleaned house. And took care of me and her brother. Some might say she had good reason to leave. But Tracy wouldn't go running off. I'm sorry to have to say it, but she was the grown-up around here back then."

"Did she have a boyfriend?" I asked.

She looked away from wire and pliers. "I don't even think she'd been kissed." She finished setting the glass triangle with the dead bug inside and began attaching a leather band.

I took another sip of coffee, watched her steady, agile hands work. "How long have you been sober?"

Her fingers stopped for just a second. She looked at me. "Almost eleven years."

Her daughter's disappearance must have made her take a long look at her life, I thought. "Four years for me," I said. I wanted to connect with her. She wasn't going to open up as long as I was just someone else from the sheriff's department who didn't give a shit. "Some days are better than others," I added.

"I know that's right."

"Mrs. Davidson—"

"Call me Josey."

"Was Tracy close to anyone outside the family? Was there an adult she confided in, a counselor, an older friend, maybe? Did anyone give her rides home from school? Anything like that?"

Josey shook her bleached-blond head. "Like I said, Jeffrey and Tracy rode the bus together every day. Tracy was tight-lipped about our business. I think she worried she and Jeff would be taken away if people knew what was going on here. She always had faith in me." Her voice sank, wavered. "She always used to tell me I could quit drinking. She'd hide the booze sometimes or pour it all out, but her father didn't like that much."

"I'm sorry to ask, but do you feel certain Tracy wasn't sexually active?" Something I'd seen in the lab reports was bugging me.

"I'm certain," she said. "Tracy was just a little girl in a lot of ways. Plus, her father didn't give the children a lot of freedom. And my husband never bothered our children that way. For sex, I mean. Thank the Lord for small favors."

We were quiet, Josey remembering and me imagining what their household must have been like back then. "I'd like to know the other little girl's name," Josey said. "They told me Tracy wasn't alone when they found her. I'm sorry for the parents of that child, and I hope God forgives me for sayin' this, but somehow it made me feel better to know my Tracy wasn't alone."

"Her name was Melinda," I said. "She was thirteen too." I didn't tell her Melinda's body had landed there a decade later or that what Tracy had endured she'd probably endured alone at the hands of a violent predator.

I stood up, laid a business card on the table. "My mobile number if you think of anything." I paused on my way to the car, turned. "Thank you for talking to me, Josey. I'm sorry this happened to you. I really am."

The sun was sinking on a long, long summer day. I'd grown up like this in Georgia, long rides with my dad and brother, short ones with cute guys I couldn't wait to kiss—top down on back roads, soft air on my skin. I felt completely exhausted after the visit with Josey Davidson. How badly that woman must want a do-over. The weight from those regrets must be staggering. Sometimes you only get one chance to do right by someone. I thought about Rauser, reached for my phone, then changed my mind.

I could see the lights from downtown Whisper just ahead, and the glowing sign on the diner. I parked in front, saw cobalt-blue booths inside under the long glass wall. A couple of customers sat on metal stools with the same bright blue vinyl seats. A ladle-shaped neon sign lit up the roof, high enough to be seen from the highway. THE SILVER SPOON, it read. HOME COOKING 24 HOURS A DAY. I couldn't remember when I had eaten. God, I absolutely hate it when I hear someone say that. Even worse when someone says they forgot to eat. How the hell do you forget to eat? I hadn't forgotten. The clock had simply outrun me.

I went in and took a stool at the counter. There was a cook behind an oblong opening and one server behind the counter. "What can I do you for, little lady?" He wiped the counter and handed me a laminated menu. He was weathered, twenty years past middle age. A lock of silver hair fell onto his forehead.

"What's good?" I asked.

"Well, it all depends," he said. "If you're in the mood for dinner, the stuffed bass is excellent. Just came out of the lake today. Breakfast, we got some fresh peaches, and Harry back there has been folding them up in some mean pancake thing." He looked side to side like he was about to give up a state secret, said, "Total food porn."

"Ah. Is it legal?" I whispered.

"Barely." He put a glass of water in front of me and a mug and saucer. I thought about the bug woman and her little thermos of coffee. "Harry, the little lady wants to try some of those pancakes you been making."

The cook gave me a nod from the kitchen. The server filled my coffee mug. "Name's Gene," he informed me. "You just passing through?"

"Visiting," I said, and took a sip of rank diner coffee that had been sitting too long.

Gene persisted. Probably had this conversation with everyone new to his counter. "You're a little ways out of the touristy areas, aren't you?"

"Business," I said.

"What kind of business you in?"

"Consulting," I told him, vaguely but politely. I think he took the hint. He polished the counter, then wiped down the booths before the cook called "Order up" from the back. Gene picked up a plate and set it in front of me—a huge pancake folded over like an omelet, peaches and whipped cream oozing from the center. Gene put out individually wrapped pats of butter and a small metal pitcher with maple syrup on the counter. I drizzled syrup over the pancake and cut a piece with my fork. It was dense and cakey and made to absorb the flavors around it—the syrup, the peaches that had been sautéed for just long enough to tease out the natural sugars, the stiff whipped cream with a hint of vanilla. My face must have registered the party in my palate.

Gene grinned. "What'd I tell you? Harry wants to go to some fancy cooking school so he works a lot of shifts to save up. We got people from all over the county coming to eat here now. There's a line for Sunday brunch and fried chicken night."

"Pretty quiet in here now," I observed.

"People around here eat supper early. It's after nine o'clock." Gene put down a small plate. "Applewood-smoked bacon. Local. On the house."

I heard the door open behind me, heard a puff of air escape the seat cover on the stool next to me. A manila folder appeared on the counter.

I glanced over at Detective Robert Raymond. "Oh joy. You going to try to run me out of the diner too? A person has to eat, Detective."

I thought he might smile. "*Try* being the operative word. Medical records." He nodded at the file. "Hey, Gene, how about a cup?"

"How'd you find me?" I took a bite of the thick-sliced bacon.

"That car of yours is easy to spot."

"You go over the medical records?" I asked.

"Your instincts were right. Looks like neither vic had broken bones prior to their disappearance," Raymond said. "Guess that's gonna give you some ideas about who did this?"

I took another sip of burned coffee. "Says something about his psychological requirements. And physical requirements. As in what kind of space he'd need to do what he does."

Gene put a mug in front of Raymond and filled it up. "Hey, Gene," Raymond said. "This is that hotshot investigator from Atlanta I told you the sheriff hired."

Gene gave me a nod. "Nice to meet you, ma'am." He moved quietly around the counter with his coffeepot. I heard him checking on the couple in the booth.

I looked at Raymond. The scarlet veins under the skin on his cheeks looked like tiny explosions under the harsh diner light. I picked up the folder, opened it, took a minute to look it over. My phone jangled on the counter. The display lit up with Kenneth Meltzer's name and mobile number. I picked it up. "Good evening, Sheriff."

Raymond swiveled on his stool and stalked out of the diner.

"Evening, Dr. Street . . . Keye," the sheriff said. "Sorry I had to bail on you today. Had to be in court. Let's meet in the morning. You probably have some things to discuss by now."

After nine hours on the job I hadn't exactly kicked in any doors. But I did have ideas. I told the sheriff that quietly while Gene hovered around the counter and did a bad job of disguising his interest.

"You an early riser? Let's say breakfast at seven-thirty. Silver Spoon makes a good one. You know where it is?"

I didn't mention I was sitting at the diner's counter. "See you then." I clicked off and put my debit card on the counter. Gene collected it. I watched him work the card reader with fingers that looked arthritic. He came back with my ticket. I wrote in the tip and stood up. "Great pancake," I said loud enough for the cook to hear. He gave another nod from the back. I headed for the door.

"Excuse me there, little lady." I stopped and turned. Gene came around the counter. "Rob Raymond was a bully growing up too. Most people around here are scared of him. For good reason, I reckon. I wouldn't get on his bad side."

"Too late." I smiled, thanked him, and pushed through the glass door.

10

The Whispering Pines Inn was part motor lodge, part fake southern mansion. My room was upstairs. I didn't mind the climb. I'd packed light—something I'd gotten good at all those years with the Bureau when I had to be ready to jump on a helicopter or a plane anytime the phone rang.

I set my bag on a chair and pulled the bedspread and mattress pad up at the bottom corners, inspected all the crevasses and seams in the mattress. I put the bottom corners back on, took the pillows off, and repeated this process at the top. Hey, don't judge. The whole bedbug thing is terrifying. The little fuckers are indestructible. If they get in your bags and go home with you, you might as well douse everything you own in gasoline and set fire to it.

I showered and slipped into one of Rauser's T-shirts I'd stuffed in my suitcase on the way out that morning. I'd found it in a pile on the bed he'd left unmade. It was his favorite shirt, navy blue with AT-LANTA POLICE DEPARTMENT embroidered in gold on the edge of the left sleeve. He'd worn it around the house for a couple of days and it smelled like him—shaving cream and aftershave around the collar, his natural scent everywhere else. I pulled it up to my face and closed my eyes. It was the kind of smell that makes you think cognac, something warm and woody and musky. And then I thought about the blouse that had washed up with Melinda Cochran's skin cells trapped in the collar. And Josey Davidson's regrets. And the dead bugs. And Raymond standing too close to me as I looked down into the disposal site, the old server's warnings after dinner. And all my warm fuzzies evaporated.

I glanced at my phone and saw emails from Neil, all of them with attachments, so I pulled the laptop out of my case and found the wireless key for the hotel. He'd sent me the list of the eight registered sex offenders who met the criteria we'd outlined. They lived within a thirty-mile circle we'd drawn around Whisper where Melinda Cochran lived, and the town of Silas where Tracy Davidson lived. They had been in the area when both girls were abducted and when Melinda's body was dumped two months ago, and they had garages, basements, freestanding sheds, or barns on their property. There were a variety of charges. One of them had been busted in an online sting with child pornography. Two had been found guilty of indecent exposure and were considered low risk. I skipped over names and scanned crimes, read the details of the ones that interested me until I narrowed it down to two offenders who had exhibited extreme predatory behaviors, watched and groomed their prey, been convicted of aggravated child molestation, aggravated sexual battery, and aggravated assault with rape or intent to rape, and were designated as sexually violent. Most astounding was that both were classified as midlevel offenders. Their known victims were female and between the ages of eleven and sixteen. The files included statements in which both offenders, Lewis Freeman and Logan Peele, had first denied, then finally owned their crimes, while minimizing the effects of their behaviors on their victims. That should have been a big red flag. These offenders were likely to reoffend, if they hadn't already. They were subject to impromptu visits from law enforcement, but the truth is, this doesn't happen often enough. The department was probably as overwhelmed as most departments are around the country.

I pulled up addresses and zoomed in on satellite. Freeman lived between Whisper and Silas on an isolated piece of farmland dotted with milking barns and equipment sheds. Logan Peele lived in Whisper not a mile from where I was right now, in a redbrick house off the highway with an enclosed freestanding garage and a basement. I could see the garage and the ground-level basement windows when I zoomed in. Both men had the space to hold a captive. Both were known predators. I wondered if their private lives would allow for the practical matters one would have to consider when kidnapping and sexually abusing. How did they explain to family or wives the locked buildings and doors, food and water going into that holding cell, all the extraordinary measures they'd have to take to hold and keep a person alive for so long?

I went back through my photo stream, examined the photos I'd taken in the woods. Then I went back over the lab reports, the sheriff's department records I'd carried out on a flash drive, and I began work on an offender sketch. It was another three hours before I set the alarm and switched off the lamp.

11

He saw her coming, emerging from the shadows in the predawn. It jarred him. He wasn't expecting to see her this way under the streetlights. It was the kind of easy glide that came with practice. He'd seen girls run like that, like butterflies just skimming the surface. He liked her body, small, compact, tight little ass in jogging shorts. And she was probably thinking about him right now, thinking about him every minute, obsessing. Because that's what she did. That was her dysfunction. It wasn't unlike his. He'd read every interview, every recorded word she'd uttered as soon as he'd learned she was coming to Whisper. This woman had dedicated her life to studying people like him.

He sank down low in the front seat as she passed the diner and cut across Main Street. He caught himself smiling, felt a sudden and unexpected affection for her. He wasn't afraid. He wasn't angry. To his great surprise he liked having her here. Though it tempted him in dangerous ways, there was allure in letting her get close, in being understood by a woman.

Careful, he warned himself. But the temptation was too great. He reached in the backseat for his laptop, opened it to a blank document, and began to type. *Dear Keye. I'm thinking about you too.*

Whisper was warm and still as I ran under streetlights past darkened shop windows on Main Street, running shoes barely making a swish on dry sidewalks. I went through downtown and cut over to the lake, where I found a lamp-lit running path that curled around past boat docks with motionless herons and resorts where men in headlighted golf carts whirred around on their predawn maintenance, and lawn mowers busy readying the course for sunrise. The price of real estate took a steady climb the farther I moved away from Whisper. I passed other joggers near nicer hotels—happy joggers who'd slept on good pillows. I looped around a Marriott Resort and headed back for the last couple of miles. My body had returned to running with an easy memory I didn't know it had for anything but booze and sugar.

I heard feet hitting the paved running path behind me and moved to the right to let them pass. "Morning." It was Ken Meltzer's voice. I kept moving but slowed my pace. I glanced over at him. He was smiling. His hair was soaked around the edges, hanging on his neck. "I thought that was you."

"How could you tell? It's not like I'm the only Asian in Whisper. Oh wait. I am the only Asian in Whisper."

Meltzer laughed. I snuck a quick look at his running suit. You can tell a lot about a person by how they get dressed for a workout. He was in long, baggy silk shorts and a goofy oversize tank. His shoulders were tan and rounded. He'd worked on them, and it showed. "I do a lot better being in the office after a run," he said. "Calmer." He was winded. So was I. The sun was up and the temperature had spiked.

"Like a dog," I said. "I mean, they behave better when they're exercised."

"Yeah, like a dog." He laughed again, that easy, generous laugh. "Last one back buys breakfast." He waited for my answer.

"Why are cops so competitive?" I asked.

"You're the analyst. You tell me," he said, and blasted ahead of me like he'd been slingshoted. The back of his shirt was drenched. He grinned over his shoulder. I couldn't resist. I turned on the steam and caught up with him. We ran hard like that all the way back to Main

Street, where we stretched and caught our breath, then cooled down over bottles of water the sheriff took from his SUV. I practically fell into my room at the Whispering Pines Inn, showered and changed, checked my email. Neil had delivered on the social media account for Melinda Cochran. There were 133 people on Melinda's Facebook friends list. Eighty-two of them were local. The list was complete with email and physical addresses. I'd also sent GBI Special Agent Mike McMillan a couple of questions late last night. He'd offered those kinds of favors if I ever needed them after I'd been hired to investigate a crematory operator a few weeks ago. What I had found had the GBI racing to the scene. McMillan had replied last night to say he'd routed my questions to the proper expert. The reply from the forensic scientist was waiting.

I walked into the Silver Spoon diner at seven-thirty on the dot with a case hanging off my shoulder and my hair still damp from the shower. The restaurant was buzzing. The cook from last night was back on duty. He had help this morning. The kitchen was busy. Servers were on the go, and the sound of dishes and forks and the murmur of morning conversations had the place humming. And then I walked through. Conversations trailed off as heads turned and for just a moment a hush as loud as a foghorn settled over the room. Welcome to Whisper.

Kenneth Meltzer was sitting in a booth at the long window, his back to the door, steam rising off a thick white coffee mug. "Morning again, Sheriff," I said, and slid in across from him. I took the case off my shoulder and put it next to me on bright blue imitation leather. A server showed up with a mug and a thermal pot. She asked if I wanted coffee. I certainly did. And I wanted food. Lots of it—scrambled eggs and white cheddar grits, roasted potatoes and an English muffin. The sheriff ordered his over medium with Virginia ham, a tall stack of blueberry pancakes, and a glass of milk. *Milk.* He was a Boy Scout.

"Starving," he said. He was wearing a short-sleeved uniform shirt with the department's logo like the one he wore yesterday, this one newly pressed. "Been a while since I ran with anyone. It's fun. It makes me push a little."

"But not quite enough," I said. "You are the one buying breakfast."

He looked at me. "And here I thought cops were the competitive ones."

"Point taken," I said.

"Doris told me my investigators could have been a little more welcoming yesterday. Guess I should have warned you."

Ya think? I tasted the coffee. Not a lot better than it was last night, but at least it was fresh. "What's up with them?" I asked.

"They're easily threatened." The smile again, dazzling against his tanned skin. "Anything you can't handle?"

"Not so far," I said. "But it would be easier if they were on board."

He nodded. "I'll remind them. They aren't bad cops. They just don't readily warm up to outsiders. They don't like me much either." That much I knew, given Detective Raymond's remarks in the woods. I wanted to ask why he didn't just clean house, rid his department of feet-draggers and the drama that erodes morale. I decided to mind my own business. "So, tell me where you are. I'm interested in knowing your thoughts so far."

"I created a profile based on the current evidence. I want to remind you this is an equivocal analysis. New evidence can always emerge and alter an offender profile. But based on the type of crime, the condition of the victims' bodies, the crime scene, I'm confident it can help with investigative strategy."

The sheriff pulled a digital voice recorder about half the size of a pack of cigarettes from his pocket, put it on the table between us. "You mind?" He switched it on before I could answer.

"I don't," I said. "But I emailed you everything in writing this morning."

"I'm encouraged to see you've been busy earning your exorbitant consulting fee." It wasn't a full smile this time. Just an amused light in his eyes. He left the recorder running. "I don't look at my email until business hours. It tends to ruin my day. Somebody needs me, they can call."

"Noted." I took the file folder Detective Raymond had delivered to me last night out of my case and handed it to the sheriff. The gold wire rims came out of his shirt pocket and he hooked them around his ears, opened the folder. "Neither Melinda nor Tracy had bone breaks prior to their disappearance," I said. "The chips and fractures around the Davidson girl's wrists and feet are consistent with metal restraints. Both victims had bone injuries, but there are some interesting differences. Could be a multitude of reasons for them. His living space, which probably dictates how and where he holds victims, may have changed. He could have moved since Tracy was abducted. This type of offender will attempt to establish control right away, with metal restraints, threats, torture, especially in the early days. If you can break their spirit they're easier to handle. The differences in the level of violence used with the first and second victim tell me he needs a heightened level of victim suffering now to fuel his fantasy life."

"What happened to Melinda?" he asked quietly.

"You didn't read any of the injury reports?"

"We needed cause of death and we needed to confirm homicide and what kind of weapon we're looking for. The rest of it didn't matter."

"It matters to me, Sheriff. It's a way to chart his interaction with the victims. It's a road map into his brain."

"I get that now." He avoided my eyes.

"Melinda had ankle injuries much like Tracy's. A broken wrist, some superficial knife strikes or curiosity marks to her inner arms and face, four broken fingers on her right hand, two on her left."

"What could have done that to her fingers?"

The sheriff wasn't getting it. Not really. It wasn't sinking in. "They weren't broken at the same time, Sheriff," I answered flatly. "He did that. One of the fingers hadn't fully healed at the time of Melinda's death."

Meltzer blew out air like I'd slugged him in the chest. He looked away, found something in the parking lot to stare at. They were his friends, I reminded myself. He might have loved this kid. I decided not to describe the experimental cuts on Melinda's body. It was all in the profile, though—the terrible, bloody curiosity of a killer finding and fulfilling new needs with the point of a knife and a terrified little girl.

"The location of the disposal site indicates familiarity with the area, and according to the interviews no one noticed a stranger in the days leading up to the girls' disappearance," I said. "But he didn't just appear. He watched. He knew when they'd be alone. He's local and it's possible he lived or worked in the Silas area when Tracy disappeared. He might have moved to Whisper later. Or he may work in one town and live in the other. I'd look at real estate, DMV, and voter registration records for anyone moving between the two towns in the last decade. He may also have close friends or family he visits regularly in that area. There's a reason he started in a town twenty miles from here. He's white, middle income, married or divorced, probably has at least one child, a regular guy. And he was able to approach these girls without anyone noticing. He was able to attract them and get them close enough to overpower them. They trusted him. Why? Either because they knew him personally or because they recognized him. They believed they were safe with him. You need to look at everyone in these girls' lives—teachers, coaches, the guy who runs the ice-cream shop, any authority figure. And consider this. He's kept his captives quiet and alive for months. He has to have a property that will accommodate them—a basement, a shed, a garage, a barn, someplace he can lock up, someplace that's just his. Some sacred space even his family wouldn't think of intruding on. It could be a second property."

"I know guys who won't let anyone in their workshops," Meltzer said. "And we have plenty of farmland with abandoned barns and shacks in this county."

I nodded. "Your suspect has had to get at least two victims in and out without detection."

"Understood," Meltzer said tersely.

"Both abductions took place in the middle of the day, which means he could have flexible hours or work at night. He's stable, balanced, shows up for work, and doesn't set off any alarms."

"How about age?"

"Age is tough. Theories have to be evidence-based, and there's just not any evidence to support opinions regarding age. It's risky to speculate."

"You speculated he's white and married or divorced," Sheriff Meltzer argued.

"I deduced based on experience with offenders who are able to evade law enforcement for this long," I answered, and heard the edge in my voice, corrected it. "They generally hunt within their own race. They usually fit in to the community—wife, kids, upstanding citizen, good neighbor, all that."

"Okay. Sure. I get it. Off the record."

"The first abduction took place eleven years ago," I said. "He has to have a vehicle to acquire a victim, a space to hold a prisoner, and enough control over his environment to ensure that his space remains private. You could presume whatever you want from that. But it would be pure speculation."

"This is good work, Keye," Meltzer told me.

"It's better organized in the files I sent you, but it's always good to talk it out."

"First new ideas we've had in a while. I knew a fresh pair of eyes would pay off." The sheriff's words trailed off. The server had arrived with breakfast. "Thanks," he said and looked up at her with soft eyes. "You doing all right today?"

"We're hanging in there," she said sweetly. I saw something familiar in the set of her mouth, the cute snub nose, and realized she was Molly Cochran, the mother of thirteen-year-old Melinda Cochran who'd turned up dead in the woods and who sometimes came to the diner after school when her mother worked the second shift.

"Aren't you supposed to be on afternoons this week, Molly?" Meltzer asked.

"They called me in early today." She spoke with the kind of deep-woods southern accent that told you she'd grown up in the country. "But that just means I get to go home early." The sheriff introduced us. Molly knew who I was. "I heard you were coming, Dr. Street. I hope you can help find out who done this to my little girl."

"I hope so too," I said. "I'm very sorry for your loss."

"From the time she was a little biddy thing I always told her: Melinda, don't talk to strangers. But she loved everyone. She was a real good girl." Molly topped off my coffee and forced another smile. She'd decided a stranger had walked into the community and violated it, sliced into her world, taken her child away from her. Too much faith had been shattered already for Molly Cochran to allow for the possibility that it wasn't a stranger at all who'd abducted and murdered her child. "If you have any questions or anything. I mean if there's anything I can do to help. Me or Bryant. You just call."

I looked into eyes too old and weary for such a young, pretty woman. "I will," I promised. "Thank you."

She patted the top of my hand, then returned to her customers, chatting, filling coffee cups, working for tips while she must have felt like her heart was breaking. The sheriff cut through a thick stack of blueberry pancakes with his fork and didn't look up. I sat there, trying to swallow the lump in my throat, then sprinkled black pepper over my scrambled eggs and pushed them into creamy white cheddar grits. We ate in silence.

"She's young to have a daughter about to start high school," I observed, after a while. I felt eyes on me. It was like having breakfast in the bug lady's aquarium.

"Molly got pregnant when she was sixteen. She and Bryant were high school sweethearts. Happens a lot around here. Pregnancy, I mean. There's not that much to do." Meltzer speared the last piece of ham on his plate and glanced around. He nodded and smiled at a few people. "Seems like you're creating a little bit of a stir, Dr. Street."

"Not my intention, I assure you."

"I'm having a little trouble not staring myself," he said. His eyes landed on me, browner and warmer than I remembered them. My first thought was: *I must have something in my teeth.* And then it hit me. He was flirting. I was completely unprepared for him to swing that door open. I decided ignoring it would be the best strategy. I picked up my phone and found the photograph I wanted to show him, handed it to the sheriff. He stared at it for a while. His long lashes made his eyes seem closed when he looked down. He lifted his head. "Looks like a tree."

"It's the poplar tree you told me to use as a landmark when I walked from the campground to the crime scene," I told him. "Now go to the next couple of shots."

He advanced the screen with his piano player's fingers, graceful and lean but strong and tan like his arms. I liked the square jaw and the leanness in his face, the long, sharp dents in both cheeks, the tuft of hair like a triangle under his bottom lip. He must have felt me admiring him because he looked up at me with knowing eyes, the smile I'd seen a lot this morning beginning to form. The heat hit my brain first, then bungee-jumped through my system. So unwelcome. *So* inappropriate. That's the thing about chemicals. They don't care about proper. They don't care about timing. They don't give a damn if you're talking about how a killer marks his path to dispose of a young body. I reached for the untouched glass of water Molly Cochran had put on the table and took a long, cold drink.

The sheriff went back to the photographs, finally saw what I wanted him to see. It wasn't easy to spot. It was knee-high on the trunk of the tree—slices made in the woody four-inch-thick vines that had severed them perfectly. A section had been removed. "That's a clean cut. That's not natural. A vine will die all the way up when you cut them like that."

I knew this all too well thanks to the volume of information available on the topic. I'd spent some time last night in my hotel room following one link after another on the subject. "Something that thick can live off the tree for months even when it's severed. But eventually it starts to die. And when it does it's the perfect landmark."

"You think the suspect did this," Meltzer said.

I nodded. "I started to wonder why a healthy tree had a dead vine that size. It didn't make sense. See how dry the vine is. It looks like old driftwood. It's been dead for years."

Meltzer was advancing the screen again, looking at all the photos I'd taken in the woods. It occurred to me he might go beyond them and find personal pictures, photos of Rauser, of White Trash and Hank, of Neil, my office, snapshots of my life. "A hunter could have done it."

"It's possible," I conceded. I had no physical evidence to the contrary. "But wouldn't a hunter flag the path, or make a mark on the tree, do something overt? This wasn't that, Sheriff. This was camouflaged." I leaned forward over the table and so did he. "I think he planned Tracy's murder well in advance and scouted out a place to dispose of the body. He knew the embankment was a perfect place to hide her in order to keep the body from turning up in the creek or the lake. So he cut those vines as a landmark. He didn't want it to look like someone had marked it. It was just for him. I bet by the time he walked out there with Tracy, those vines were browning out. He never wanted those bodies discovered. He's a planner, this guy. He's confident, and he's detached. He'd have to be."

The sheriff's eyes moved from the photos to me. He put my phone down. "But there's something else, isn't there?"

I reached across and retrieved my phone. "Both girls had serious enamel defects, according to the forensic odontologist's report." Meltzer turned the ring on his right hand a half revolution, then another, then another. "It's one indicator of poor nutrition. It's not uncommon in cases where the victim has been held for months or years. Could be about control. It's a way to keep them weak and dependent. There may be practical considerations that contributed to their bad health. For example, wherever he's keeping them only allows access at certain times or on certain days without being seen. By the way, my office was able to gain access to Melinda's social media contacts. That would be one of the emails you didn't want messing up your day."

"I can see I'm going to have to up my game," he said, and again let his eyes linger too long.

Molly returned to top off our coffee. We were quiet until she was gone. "Sheriff, I emailed a contact at the GBI last night because I had a question about the lab reports on Tracy. He put me in touch via email with the forensic anthropologist who worked Tracy's case." I pulled the lab reports out, found the one I wanted. "See these measurements and notes right here? Women, and girls once they've been through puberty, are generally wider and shallower than men in the pelvis area. It's one way a scientist can determine gender from bones. But I was curious about these notations." I pointed them out on the report.

"Cartilage damage," Meltzer read.

"I wrote and asked for clarification," I told him. "The scientist responded this morning. That kind of soft bone damage around the pelvis joint most likely occurred during childbirth."

12

Sheriff Ken Meltzer glanced around, kept his voice low. His forearms were on the tabletop and his hands were clasped. "There's nothing in those old interviews with Tracy's friends or her family that says anything about her ever being pregnant."

"There was nothing in her medical reports either," I noted. "And I met Tracy's mother yesterday. She doesn't believe Tracy ever had a boyfriend. I didn't tell her about any of this, naturally."

"That little girl was only thirteen." Meltzer took off the wire-rimmed glasses he'd used to read the lab report and folded them back into his uniform shirt pocket, pushed his longish hair off his forehead with both hands. He turned back to the windows and the full parking lot. He was going to need a minute. I looked away, waited, drank some bad coffee. "We didn't find an infant out there," he said finally. "And we used trained dogs."

"I know."

"So what happened to the baby?"

"We can only speculate," I said quietly.

"Could have died or been sold. Or he could have kept it," Meltzer said. "That's a horrible thought. The child would be about ten now."

"You'll have to consider all those scenarios when you're looking at suspects," I said. Breakfast had taken a decidedly dark turn. "Do you recognize the names Logan Peele and Lewis Freeman?"

He nodded. "We interviewed most of our registered sex offenders when Melinda disappeared and again when we found the bodies. You like one of them for this?"

"Peele and Freeman look interesting. We started with over a hundred offenders in the general area and narrowed it down." I talked to the sheriff about the criteria I'd used to narrow the list. "Also, based on statements to the parole board before release and to their parole officers after release, neither of these men seems capable of comprehending the damage he's done. I think they are highly likely to reoffend. If they haven't already. They're listed as level-two offenders, which means the state thinks there's a thirty-four percent probability they will reoffend. I think it's much more likely than that. They haven't taken any personal responsibility for their actions and from their statements it doesn't appear they've experienced remorse."

"These men have never murdered. That we know of."

"True," I agreed. "And no one mentioned seeing them in the area around the time the girls were abducted. But I think it's important to exclude them before moving forward. They've demonstrated predatory behaviors in the past. The MO fits. They've watched and baited and conned their victims. The known victims are all female and close in age to both your vics."

Meltzer nodded. "We'll circulate their photographs—family, friends, the schools. Registered sex offenders have to submit to a warrantless search here, but the courts can be finicky later. Think I'll cross some t's right now." He punched a number in his phone, spoke with someone he called Dave. He explained the circumstances, asked for search warrants, then made a date to go fishing. He hung up, and looked at me. "Judge friend of mine," he explained. "Lot of friendships built over a fishing pole down here."

"Two terms so far," I said. "You must have made a few friends."

He studied me for a second. I think he was trying to decide if it was a criticism. I remembered Raymond calling him an ass-kisser. Perhaps his criminal investigators' petty jealousies had made him sensitive. He used his thumb to punch in another number. "Major Brolin, we're going to execute warrants on a couple of registered sex offenders this morning. Lewis Freeman and Logan Peele. Meet me at Freeman's in about half an hour. Bring a search team. I'm getting warrants so we can confiscate and examine electronic devices." He listened, answered a couple of questions, hung up, and looked at me. "The major says Freeman isn't allowed to have a computer since it was the primary way he contacted kids and because he doesn't need it to make a living. He's a grease monkey in maintenance at the Swedish chain saw factory up the road. Peele is allowed a computer but he has to bring it in on his quarterly check-ins for examination. Might be time to take a closer look at his machine." He paused. "Listen, Dr. Street . . . Keye, I'm not sure how it usually works after you produce a profile. I assume that's when your job is done?"

"Depends on the job," I said.

"I was hoping you'd stick around. I'd like you to be there when we search these two offenders. And, like I said when we talked on the phone the first time, I really could use another pair of eyes and ears. Brolin and Raymond don't have the luxury of focusing on just these two cases."

"They're not going to like it," I cautioned.

"Brolin's a hater, but she makes up for it by being hard to get along with." We both laughed. "Honestly, neither of them is as bad as they seem. They've both helped develop important programs at the jail. I don't want to just store prisoners. I want to figure out how to make honest-to-God good citizens out of these men. Brolin designed a family program. The prisoners get a few hours without windows or cuffs with their families once a month. Picnic kind of setting. Kids running everywhere. It reminds them what's at stake and makes them want to do better. We've had a lot of them tell us later it was what made them want to turn it around. Brolin's smart. She has ideas. I think she wants to run this department."

I thought about Raymond going off on me in the woods about track records and elections. "You're not planning on running again?"

He picked up the recorder and switched it off. "Not for sheriff."

"Ah." I smiled. "Political aspirations."

"There may be a seat opening up. I've been approached."

"How are you, Ken?" I looked up to see a slim, dark-haired man in jeans and an untucked buttondown.

"Morning," the sheriff replied. "Ethan, this is Dr. Keye Street. Keye, this is Reverend Ethan Hutchins."

"Nice to meet you, Dr. Street." Hutchins's hand was warm and dry when he shook mine.

"Nice to meet you, Reverend. Care to join us?" I asked, and made one of those moves that lets people know you're willing to slide over.

"I'm meeting someone this morning, but if you're still in Whisper on Sunday have the sheriff bring you along to Sunday sermon."

I had visions of lightning striking the church and burning it to the ground. "Couldn't keep me away," I answered.

Ethan Hutchins smiled down at me. He had a gentle face, the kind that made you feel approved of, accepted. Whether it was natural or practiced, it was calming. I had the feeling I could have told him anything.

"Dinner at our place after church, Ken," he said. "You're invited too, Dr. Street. My wife makes the best buttermilk fried chicken in the state and I'm not a bad baker if you like warm biscuits." He smiled again. "See you Sunday, Ken. God bless, Ms. Street."

I watched him being greeted by several people as he passed through the diner. "I hang around their house Sunday afternoons when I can," Ken Meltzer told me. "They love to cook. Nice family. And the pastor's not opposed to a beer and a ball game now and then. They've been good friends to me. And a lot of support to the community through this. Especially Molly and Bryant. They have a daughter too. They understand how difficult it is."

I remembered when Rauser was shot, when he'd gone limp in my arms and I'd watched his blood soaking into the red earth. He'd just said he loved me for the first time. And then a bullet ripped into him. Life can give just that sweetly and in the very next instant take away just that ruthlessly. I think I'd cried out to God that afternoon, maybe for the first time since I was a child. "I guess faith comes in handy when there's a tragedy," I said quietly.

"Yes, it does."

"You a regular at church, Sheriff?"

"My father was Jewish. My mother is a Christian. They decided to educate me in as many religions as they could and let me decide. Naturally, this was not popular with either set of grandparents, but I think it saved their marriage. I never had a desire to go to synagogue or church, though." He paused, thought it over, said, "Then I moved here. Mom was getting worse. I guess I was pretty lonely. And I began to believe in something outside myself. It filled the void. They say faith is the evidence of things unseen. It's not logical. It's something that happens in your heart."

"Actually it happens in your brain," I said. "Like déjà vu. You think you're re-experiencing an event when in fact it's just a neuron misfiring."

A loud laugh came rolling out of him and surprised me. More heads turned. "That's a very clinical view of spirituality. Is that why you're okay with lying to a man of God about coming to church?"

"That obvious?"

"It was to me. But then I'm a trained law enforcement professional." He winked, tossed a tip on the table, and picked up the breakfast tab I'd won fair and square. "Ride with me. Judge's office is in the old courthouse. I'll grab those warrants and we can shake up some sex offenders just for fun."

13

The Hitchiti County courthouse was an ancient granite building with thick mortar between giant, square slabs. Elaborate masonry work curled around windows and doors. A raised gold-letter sign out front announced its spot on the National Register of Historic Places. The lawn was as tended as the golf courses in the tourist areas, and cement pathways led to alcoves with garden benches. I waited in the Ford Police Interceptor, the sheriff's roomy V6 utility. While he went inside, I checked out the driver's cockpit, the equipment on the dash, the controls on the steering wheel, all the bells and whistles a cop needs to do almost everything hands-free except actually drive. The sheriff's department must be doing okay, I decided. I leaned over and checked the mileage. Four thousand. Whatever Raymond's beef with Ken Meltzer, it couldn't have been that the sheriff failed at getting major expenditures approved for the department. I was pretty sure that required a board of supervisors somewhere. I thought again about what Detective Raymond had said in the woods. *You think Meltzer is in a second term because he's a good lawman? It's because he's a charming sonofabitch who knows what asses to kiss.*

I thought about Rauser and his leggy six-foot-two frame in the Crown Vic he loved. He wanted a police car that looked like a police car. He liked it when someone spotted him in the rearview and tapped the brakes.

I sat there a minute, thinking, looking absently at the glove compartment. I glanced up at the courthouse steps. No sheriff. I popped open the glove box. Okay, so I wanted to know a little more about Mr. Clean who'd given up his work in Colorado to come to his mother's rescue, who went to church on Sundays, who looked more like a park ranger than a county sheriff, and who had flirted with me this morning at the Silver Spoon diner.

The glove compartment was neat. The usual stuff—a phone charger, registration, a pair of leather driving gloves, eyedrops, and a small stack of business cards. Local stuff mostly—the hardware store, a landscaper, an auto repair shop, a couple of take-out joints, the Silver Spoon.

I looked up and saw Ken Meltzer jogging down the courthouse steps. Everything went back into the glove compartment as quickly and as neatly as possible. I remembered how the gloves were lying one on top of the other, left hand first, how the business cards were stacked, where the envelope with vehicle documents went. I pushed the glove compartment closed two seconds before the truck door opened.

"Thanks for waiting," Meltzer said cheerfully. He climbed in and snapped on the seatbelt. "Took longer than I thought. They weren't ready. And the judge wanted to talk."

I noticed the morning light catching something on the floorboard. A white business card had fallen out when I'd tried to get everything back into the sheriff's glove compartment. "No problem." I covered the card with my foot.

The sheriff turned toward the highway. "So tell me about Tracy Davidson's mother," he said.

"She traps bugs in a glass aquarium and turns them into jewelry. Can you arrest her for that because it's the stuff of nightmares."

A sideways glance, a grin. "County would be full if I arrested all the weirdos. Guy in the next town covers them in chocolate. Everyone has a story, I guess."

"Except the really boring people. They have a *lot*," I said. I looked out and saw a tractor mowing an open field. A hay baler at the other end was doing its job. The air was sweet with the resiny scent of wheat and cut grass. "To be honest, Josey Davidson is a little bit of a heartbreaker. It's clear she has a lot of regrets. The way she tells it, Tracy was the glue in a violent home. Two alcoholic parents at war with each other. The father was physically and verbally abusive. Sounds like Tracy was the cook and housecleaner and peacemaker. She and her brother were close. Kids cling to one another, they protect one another." I thought about my own brother, Jimmy, about how we'd bonded as children. "Tracy wouldn't have left her little brother. She wasn't planning to run away. She got in the car with her killer because she was conned."

"Looks like the department came down pretty heavy on the father after Tracy disappeared," Meltzer said. "Checked him out up and down. He submitted to a polygraph back then and passed it. He's back in jail. So is Tracy's brother, Jeff. Nice family, huh?"

"Maybe Jeff Davidson has remembered something. Someone he saw Tracy talking to, someone she confided in, a coach, a teacher, a counselor. He might have been afraid to talk at the time, protecting them both from his dad or the authorities. From what Josey said, it sounds like those kids were terrified they'd be removed from their home."

We pulled onto a dirt road. "I'll arrange an interview for you," Ken Meltzer told me. "He's in our jail."

The sheriff slowed and turned right on a dusty lane. We passed unmowed fields, the milking barn I'd seen on satellite in the distance. Another barn that might have been a tractor shed was sun-bleached to light gray with a rusty, sagging roof. This land must have been a working farm at some point in its history. Not now. No animals. Not a chicken or a cow or a dog or a cat in sight. I have a deep and probably irrational mistrust of people who live without animals. Growing up, our house had been a revolving door for foster dogs and cats. It's my normal.

The house in the distance appeared no more cared for than the rest of the property. Drooping gutters were stuffed with debris. Paint chipped off the eaves. There was a filthy white van in the drive. Two cruisers with the sheriff's star on the doors were parked near the house. Major Brolin was leaning against a late-model Crown Vic, a phone to her ear. Two uniformed officers stood in the driveway. Two more were standing on Lewis Freeman's porch, duty belts loaded.

The sheriff got out. I opened my door and reached for the business card I'd dropped. It was from the diner. There was handwriting on the back in big loopy, girlie letters. *Molly 706-555-7367.* I slipped the card back in the glove compartment and closed the truck door.

Major Brolin met us with a nod in my direction so curt I wondered, not for the first time, why she had instantly disliked me. She fired off at the sheriff. No preliminaries. "Is this related to the murders, Sheriff? Because I interviewed this man myself. Twice. Once when Melinda disappeared and again when we found her body."

"Dr. Street believes the two offenders we're visiting this morning are likely to reoffend, Major. I trust her judgment," the sheriff told her. He kept walking. "So let's connect them to the murders or exclude them entirely today. And from now on, we commit to regular inspections of registered sex offenders."

"Exactly how do you propose we do that, Sheriff?" Brolin wanted to know. "Detective Raymond and I have all we can handle already."

"I'm going to get you another investigator, for one," he replied. "And we'll pull a couple of units off the highway to handle rounds once a month. Relax, Tina, it's job security."

He gave her the Meltzer smile and did not get one in return. She didn't appreciate him using her first name in front of me. I was reasonably sure he knew that. Tires on gravel got our attention. I turned to see Robert Raymond driving up. He climbed out of his car and squinted at the day. He looked hungover. I know the look. I've had plenty of mornings like that. Brolin was watching him too. For a second her sour expression turned soft. Or maybe it was just the sun in her eyes.

We stopped a few feet from the front porch. The sheriff motioned for his deputies to gather 'round. Raymond lumbered over smelling of cigarettes. "This man is a registered sex offender," Meltzer began. "If we find anything in there that violates his parole—computers, weapons, child pornography, a joint, a seed or even a stem—we have the opportunity to put him where we don't have to worry about him anymore. That would not break my heart." A quiet ripple of laughter moved over the deputies. Brolin remained stone-faced. The officers responded to Meltzer. How she must resent that. "Additionally, we're looking at Mr. Freeman for the murders of Tracy Davidson and Melinda Cochran. This is Dr. Street. She compiled the criminal profile you'll be issued later." The sheriff looked at me. "Dr. Street, you have anything you'd like to add?"

"We have to think in practical terms about what someone would need in order to abduct, then successfully hold a prisoner for months," I told them. One of the officers flinched. "The lab reports indicate the use of metal restraints. That means anchors, drill holes. Don't forget to look up at ceiling studs. Are there interior rooms with key locks, padlocks, missing doorknobs? Check windows for signs they've been permanently closed or reinforced to prevent escape. Also, he'd have to make sure a meter reader or a UPS driver or friends and family wouldn't hear even the faintest cry. Are there materials that could be used for soundproofing? Doesn't have to be elaborate—drywall, molding around doors, sound panels." I glanced at the van in his driveway. "Is there anything different about his vehicle? Have door handles been removed? Is the back partitioned off from the front? Predators ready their vehicles in case there's an opportunity to reoffend. According to forensics, the murder weapon was heavy with a narrow head, an axe or a similar tool. Soil samples were collected from the crime scene, so you'll want to bag shoes and the floor mats in the van along with any debris."

"Any questions?" the sheriff asked when I finished. No one answered. "Okay, let's get started. Take your time. Be thorough. It's a big place. Detective Raymond, I'll need you to assist in the search." The sheriff walked up the front steps, knocked on a door that had seen better days. It was a cop's knock, loud, official. No answer. The sheriff knocked again. "Lewis Freeman, Hitchiti County Sheriff's Department here."

It took several more knocks before we heard heavy footsteps inside. The smell of bacon and stale cigarette smoke rushed out when the door swung open. Lewis Freeman stared at us through the screen.

He had a jowly face covered in stubble, was 250 pounds, with thinning brown hair and not enough height to pull off that kind of weight. The bags under his eyes, the puffiness, the ruddy complexion, the sheet mark running down his cheek told me he'd been sleeping hard. And he looked like he'd done a little drinking last night. Maybe most nights. "What's wrong? My wife all right?"

"Where is your wife, Mr. Freeman?" Major Brolin asked.

"She took the boys to school and went to work like always. The boys okay?" He scratched his head, tried to blink away some fogginess.

The sheriff opened the screen door and handed Lewis Freeman the search warrant. "My investigators are going to be searching your home, Mr. Freeman. Why don't we all step inside. You look like you could use some coffee. We'll join you."

Freeman looked confused. "What's this about? Listen, I work third shift. I need sleep. I'm not even dressed."

We all glanced down at the navy boxer shorts with big, fleshy white legs sticking out. "I'll go with you to get dressed," Meltzer offered. He wasn't leaving Freeman alone to destroy potential evidence.

Meltzer followed Freeman down a hallway. I heard the sheriff telling him not to worry about his wife and kids. Two deputies came into the house with us. Two of them headed toward the big gray barn. Raymond started walking across the field to the sagging milking barn. Brolin and I stretched on gloves and stepped into a small, cluttered home. The windows were closed and the air-conditioning wasn't running. The house was in the kind of disarray that comes from working parents with children—clothes, books, shoes. A Hot Wheels track ran through the living room and climbed over the couch.

There was a foil-covered plate on the stove and a sink full of dishes. A pot with fresh water spots sat on a cool warmer with a sticky note that said *Ready*. I peeked under the foil and saw biscuits with cheese and eggs and bacon. "Someone loves him," I said.

Brolin flipped the switch on the coffeemaker. Made a little *sseesh* sound. "Takes all kinds, I guess." I realized this was the nicest thing she'd said to me since we'd met less than twenty-four hours ago. She pulled open a drawer, moved utensils around, repeated this until she found the drawer everyone has in their kitchen, the one that holds receipts and menus and owner's manuals and twist-ties. She glanced over at me. "You can't touch anything else," she said. I held up both gloved palms. "I mean you can't participate in the search," she corrected herself.

"Okay," I said mildly. I wanted to tell her I knew things about evidence collection and chain-of-custody her skinny, crabby ass would probably never know. But I wasn't going to let her push my buttons this morning.

Sheriff Meltzer and Lewis Freeman came into the kitchen. Freeman was in jeans: fat-guy jeans that were pulled up around his wide waist and made everything from there down seem small. He was in the same T-shirt he'd worn to answer the door. Small blue-green eyes skirted the kitchen, landed on the brewing coffeepot, then fixed on Brolin, who was still standing at the counter looking through every scrap of paper in the drawer. I figured she knew that if they were going to find anything in Freeman's home today, it would not be in the family kitchen. But it was doing a hell of a job of shaking up Lewis Freeman. Innocent or guilty, people don't like strangers touching their stuff. I could see it unnerving Freeman. I had a feeling Brolin was enjoying it.

Freeman walked past her and took a cup out of the dish drainer. The sheriff started talking about Tracy Davidson, about her good grades, about the way she took care of her little brother, that she was pretty and blond, that she'd disappeared just before Christmas that year.

Freeman poured himself coffee and sat down at the table. "I told y'all last time I'd never even seen the girl in my life." His T-shirt was wet under his armpits. An oniony sweat replaced the smell of bacon in the stuffy kitchen.

"Where were you on December twenty-second, two thousand and three, Lewis?" Meltzer asked.

Freeman gave a dry laugh. "Who the hell knows? You know where you were eleven years ago, Sheriff? Listen, I been married for fifteen years. I was probably sitting right here."

"You were married when you met Rebecca Forsyth online too,"

Major Brolin said. "Remember her? She thought you were a fourteen-year-old boy until you lured her out to meet you in the park." I looked at Brolin. She'd done her homework.

"Yeah. I remember," Lewis Freeman snarled. "There's a big red dot on all those sex offender sites with my name and address because of that bitch." He slurped coffee. In keeping with his refusal to accept responsibility for his actions, he blamed the victim for his offender status. I tried not to think about what it must be like for a young girl to feel this huge man on top of her, grunting, smelling, sweating. Freeman picked up a pack of Kools and a plastic lighter from the counter, lit one, took a drag, coughed on the exhale. He flicked ash into an already full ashtray and glanced at me. "What's your deal?"

"This is Dr. Street," the sheriff answered for me. "Dr. Street is a consultant to my department."

"You're shittin' me." Freeman grinned. "Like on *The Mentalist* or something?"

"That's right," Meltzer said easily. "Dr. Street's going to tell me when you're lying."

The screen door banged closed, footsteps came down the hall. Detective Raymond appeared, carrying a medium-size cardboard box. "Found it in the barn," he told us. "In the goddamn hayloft. Almost busted my ass." He had bits of wheat straw stuck to his clothing and dust on his brown shoes. "Kiddie porn," Raymond went on, and slapped the box on the floor with a thud. "Mr. Freeman enjoys young men too. And there's no door handles in the van except on the driver's side just like you said, Street. And what do ya think's on here?" He held up a flash drive in a plastic evidence bag.

The sheriff looked at Freeman. "Well, that didn't take long. Seems you've violated the terms and conditions of your parole, Lewis. That means we're going to have a lot of time to pick your brain at County."

"I've never seen that box or that thumb drive." Freeman lied badly and pointlessly.

"I have a feeling the lab will tell us a different story," Meltzer said. "Have him taken to County, Major. Dr. Street, we might as well move on and let the team finish here." He took a last look at Freeman. "I'm going to give you a couple of hours to think this over. You know something about these girls, coming clean is the only way to help your-self."

"Bullshit," Freeman spat. Brolin pulled his hands up behind him and clamped on cuffs. I followed the sheriff out the front door and down the steps.

"That was time well spent," he remarked. "Wonder what else we'll find by the end of the day. I hope it's enough to keep him inside a few years."

"I do too," I agreed. "The guy has no remorse. And absolutely no empathy for his victims." I looked at the sheriff. "But he's not our guy. He's morbidly overweight and a smoker. He'd never make that hike to the disposal site. He was winded pouring coffee. And to state the obvious, he's not very good at covering his tracks. That's not con-sistent with your killer."

"I agree." Meltzer was surprisingly cheerful. "But hey, it's still a great day for the people of Hitchiti County. Except his wife and kids. I feel sorry for them."

I thought about the sticky note on the coffeemaker and the foil-covered plate on the stove. I thought about her surviving on one in-come with two children and a property already in disrepair. And I felt sorry for them too, sorry that her husband had put them in that situation, sorry she'd fallen for the guy and married him fifteen years earlier. I was not sorry Freeman was going back to jail. I only hoped he hadn't already sexually abused his own children. "Your people ca-pable of thorough evidence collection, Sheriff?"

Ken Meltzer's eyes softened. That look again, a smile. "We have motorized vehicles and toilets that flush too. Rest assured, my people are as good as you'll find anywhere." We got in his truck. "You just curious or are you thinking I should send a tech to go over that van?"

Meltzer didn't miss a lot. I was beginning to think he was better at this than Raymond gave him credit for. "The door handles were miss-ing," I said. "Freeman works the night shift. Maybe he leaves for work a little early and hunts. I'd get a tech in there with an alternate light source. That van might be a treasure chest of blood evidence and body fluids."

14

"Sorry about the icy reception back there," Meltzer said on the drive from Freeman's house to the next offender's. "Can't be easy to walk into something like that. It was rude even for Brolin. I'll have a chat with her."

"I wish you wouldn't," I said. "It will just make her insecurities worse. Your investigators are concerned my presence here will interfere with Brolin getting credit for solving this case, if it's solved, and hurt her chances at being elected sheriff one day."

"What makes you think that?" Meltzer sounded surprised.

"Besides the obvious resentment? Detective Raymond paid me a visit yesterday when I went back to the crime scene. If you solve these cases with my assistance, he believes it will cement your bid for re-election and hurt Major Brolin's chances at advancement."

"He told you that?"

I nodded. "Maybe if they knew you don't intend to run they'd both settle down and just do their jobs."

"Maybe," Meltzer said. "On the other hand, if solving the case of two murdered girls, however it's solved and by whomever, is less important than their personal agenda—well, let's just say that doesn't put me in the mood to calm their fears."

"Those were Detective Raymond's words. Not hers. And I was paraphrasing," I said.

"We were never friends," Meltzer admitted, and I was struck, not for the first time, by how candid he could be. "They seemed to distrust me as soon as I took the job. I figured it was because I was young to be sheriff. Rob was in uniform and Tina was a detective back then."

"Office romances aren't good for anyone. It turns into an us-against-them mentality."

Meltzer glanced at me. "You mean Brolin and Raymond? They think I don't know. How'd you guess?"

"I didn't guess. I deduced. They're candidates for Co-Dependents Anonymous."

"Tina's married," Meltzer told me. "Nice guy. Too bad."

I thought again about the business card I'd found from the Silver Spoon with Molly Cochran's number on the back, and I wondered if the sheriff was really so innocent about such things.

"Raymond's single," the sheriff added.

"Shocker. He's such a charmer."

Meltzer laughed a quiet laugh. "His wife died. Left him with a toddler. That was before I came."

"Great. Now I feel guilty," I said.

"How about you, Keye? I don't see a wedding ring."

"I'm divorced."

"I ran across a magazine piece about you and the homicide lieutenant you work with at APD," Meltzer said casually, and I knew he'd done his own research on me after I'd been recommended by APD. "It was about hunting serial killers, specifically the Wishbone Killer. Said you were convinced APD had the wrong suspect in custody and kept on it until you broke it."

Warm air that hadn't yet caught fire in the midday sun blew into the cab. Acres of dark green cornstalks with silky tassels rippled like a wave on dry land as we sped past cornfields and white fences and grazing cattle on the two-lane highway.

"Wishbone got away," I remarked, darkly. The friend I'd had since sixth grade was dead. I'd almost lost Rauser too. Bullets had ripped through his temple and chest. I had been badly hurt. We'd both spent Christmas in the hospital. And Wishbone was out there somewhere, reinventing, waiting, and choosing carefully. I had no doubt at all that Wishbone's signature would emerge again someday—the biting and stabbing—and the gory details would once more be splattered all over newspapers and television. It was not a case I viewed as some kind of personal triumph. I'd failed. The killer would kill again.

"You and that lieutenant made a nice couple," Meltzer remarked.

The interview had been done in my living room after Rauser had been released from the hospital. The photographer caught us during a candid moment, the two of us sitting on the couch. It was the largest of four photographs that accompanied the story. We were looking at each other, smiling. And when I remembered that moment and so many more with Rauser, when I thought about the truth and safety in his eyes, in my life with him, I silently cursed myself for what I'd been feeling, for the stupid attraction I'd been playing with. I hadn't shut the sheriff down. I'd let him look at me the way he looked at me, and I'd let him flirt. "We're still a nice couple," I told Meltzer.

"Too bad," he said, without looking away from the road.

By the time we drove down the paved driveway where the second registered sex offender lived, two Interceptor sedans with the sheriff's star were already waiting. I felt like I needed a shower after being inside Lewis Freeman's place. And it wasn't just because it smelled like bacon and sweat and cigarettes. The guy was utterly disgusting. I glanced at the small building thirty feet from Logan Peele's home, about the size of a one-car garage and freshly painted. Plenty of room on this property to hide a lot of secrets. I'd seen closets and garages and basements and cages and dog crates turned into prisons. You never really know what's hiding behind the neighbor's walls or what a human being is capable of until you find something like that.

An aluminum overhang attached to the roof of the building on one end and stretched out over a dark gray F-150 pickup truck. I studied the basement windows on the side of the two-story brick house near ground level. Had Melinda Cochran spent six months in a sunless basement? I noticed the distance between the houses on each side. It was very different from Lewis Freeman's unkempt home and property. I didn't see a trash can or a recycling bin or a piece of lawn equipment. The property was trimmed and landscaped; the garage, the windows on the house, the railing and eaves all looked newly painted. Everything had its place. This was organized. My pulse quickened.

Meltzer parked and we got out. I was introduced to the deputies, and we repeated to Meltzer's uniformed officers what we'd told the first group of deputies at the first sex offender's home—we were there because Logan Peele was a level-two offender who had the space, opportunity, and time, and he was a person of interest in the murders of Melinda Cochran and Tracy Davidson. Peele's wife had left him, I knew from the background material Neil had emailed. He worked from home, which meant he had the flexibility in his schedule needed to abduct two girls in the middle of the day. He'd been in the area at the time both Tracy and Melinda were abducted, and approximately sixty days ago when Melinda Cochran's body had been dumped. I needed to know if he had the other tools necessary—the manipulative skills and demeanor to trick a kid into getting close. Predators are superb at that. They use puppies and kittens and fake injuries to lure their prey. This man had raped his own daughter and then tricked one of her friends into getting in the car with him.

The door opened before we started up the brick steps. Logan Peele stood looking at us. His red hair was short, and he had a closely trimmed carrot-colored Fu Manchu. His eyes were icy blue, emotionless, as flat as a central Georgia blacktop.

"Morning, Mr. Peele," Meltzer said, in the same cocky tone he'd used with Lewis Freeman. "How about inviting us in while my deputies look around?" He opened the warrant and held it up. Peele didn't take it.

"Do I have a choice?" he asked. No concern in his voice. He was a transplant from Pennsylvania, a Georgia State grad. He'd been married right out of college to a southern girl. They'd made their home here. He pointed to the rubber scraper doormat. "Wipe your feet, please." He turned his back and walked inside, left the door standing open. He was wearing faded jeans and sandals, a tight short-sleeved red cotton pullover that showed off the width of his shoulders and the taper at his waist. Logan Peele was clearly as meticulous about caring for his body as he was his property. We followed a long hallway with gleaming hardwood floors and narrow woven runners. I saw smoke and carbon monoxide detectors near the ceiling and a security camera with a blinking motion light disguised to look like a smoke alarm. Classical music was coming from speakers wired into the walls. He led us into his living room. I glanced at the bookcase, at the furniture, modern and pricey, carefully chosen. I looked at the end tables and lamp bases. Not a speck of dust. The bookcase was lined with hardcovers—biographies, memoirs, books about how successful people get that way.

"How about we go to the kitchen where we'll be out of the way for a while? Coffee smells fresh," the sheriff said. "Why don't you make us a cup?"

Peele's fair skin pinkened at the sheriff's suggestion. His jawbone reacted for a split second. Logan Peele didn't like being told what to do and he didn't like us taking over his home. He'd given up any expectation of privacy when he'd agreed to the terms of his parole. It would be difficult for a private man, a man who controlled his environment like Peele did, to live with that. It wasn't sympathy I felt for him. It was simply understanding. He deserved much worse.

We followed him to a kitchen with slate floors and a white marble island with four stools, two on each side, high cream-colored leather backs. There wasn't an orange or an apple or a loaf of bread or a crumb anywhere. Everything was put away. It might as well have been a model home on a realtor's tour. Peele took a glass carafe with milk from the fridge. The cabinets had clear fronts, and the matching onyx mugs and plates were ordered by size. He removed three cups from the cabinet, opened a drawer with a pullout Keurig rack, and took out three K-Cups marked FRENCH ROAST. The sheriff gave me a look that let me know he was enjoying this. We waited in silence while Peele filled our mugs one at a time and set them on the island next to the milk bottle and a bowl of sugar. He placed two spoons on top of a cloth napkin. The sheriff and I were on one side of the island. Peele was on the other with his back to the brushed-steel appliances and sink.

"Want to tell me what this is about?" Peele asked. He sounded bored. He took a sip from his mug, then set it down. I tried my coffee. It was the first decent cup I'd had since arriving in this creepy little town.

"You have a nice place, Logan," Meltzer said breezily, ignoring his question. "You renovated about six months ago, didn't you? Looks good. Work must be going well. You're an IT guy, right? You write software or something?" The sheriff dipped a spoon in the sugar. Some of it spilled on the countertop on the way to his cup. Peele's eyes tracked the spoon, watched the granules land.

"You know what I do for a living, Ken. I design websites." Peele got up, took a sponge from under the sink, dampened it, wiped up the sugar. "It's okay if I call you Ken, right? I mean it seems like we're on a first-name basis now." He rinsed the sponge and placed it in the microwave. He set the timer for one minute and sat back down. "How's your coffee, Dr. Street?" We hadn't been introduced. He'd surprised me by using my name and he knew it. He showed small, straight teeth when he smiled. "Oh come on, Doc. Whisper's Twitter feed is all about it. Amazing how much you can learn on social media. For example, the Internet says you're a runner." He drank from his cup. Intelligent blue eyes regarded me over the rim. "Only interesting thing in this shit town is social media. I don't even buy my groceries here anymore. Not many friends. For some reason the citizenry just isn't all that friendly anymore."

"Because you sexually abused and raped your daughter for most of her life?" I asked in my most clinical and neutral voice. "Or because you stalked and brutalized her best friend? An eighth grader at the time, wasn't she? About thirteen?"

"Touché," Peele said. His eyes moved from mine to the sheriff's. "I assume you're here to ask me again if I killed Tracy Davidson and Melinda Cochran because it's common knowledge that's why you've hired a criminal analyst. For the record, I did not kill them. I did not know them. And now I have work to do. So if you wouldn't mind finishing your coffee and leaving . . ."

He was getting tired of us now, impatient, and I could hear it in his voice. He pushed away from the counter. Meltzer's hand caught his wrist. "Can't let you use the computer," the sheriff said easily. "The computer, that iPhone over there, and whatever else we deem interesting is going with us."

That threw Peele off his smug game for the first time. He blinked. I wasn't sure if he was reacting to the possibility of incriminating evidence on his devices or the prospect of being left without them, which probably felt to a tech guy like standing at the bottom of a staircase in a thigh-high plaster cast.

We heard a thud from somewhere in the house, a book perhaps, something falling but not breaking, then another. Peele's head jerked around. Order had been disturbed in his home and it was undoing him. "Sheriff, will you tell your goons to be careful? I like things neat." Another layer of cool flaked away.

The sheriff and I exchanged a glance. Meltzer seemed amused. "We'll be out of your hair soon. But first, let's talk about where you were on January seventeenth. About two-thirty in the afternoon. That's the last time anyone saw Melinda Cochran alive."

"I was working, Ken. I've gone over this with your people. I was working on a project with a client. My online status was active." Peele's tone had thinned. "My company keeps records. We know who's online, who's not, and who's idle and who's active."

"What we know is that you work remotely and that you were logged in," Sheriff Meltzer said. "That's all we can really be sure of, isn't it?"

Peele laughed. "You think I went out for a little dessert between keystrokes? Maybe snatch some hot little thing and fuck her while—"

Logan Peele didn't get to finish that thought. I hadn't seen the sheriff's body tense. I had not heard a breath come out of him. But Meltzer struck like a rattlesnake and Logan Peele had been jerked off of his stool and thrown against his refrigerator before he could end his sentence. Meltzer's fist dug into Peele's solar plexus. He followed with a quick elbow strike to the side of the face. I heard Peele's teeth clamp together. Blood trickled from the corner of his mouth. Meltzer spun him around, grabbed the back of his neck, and shoved him face-down into the stainless-steel sink. He turned the water on. Peele was coughing, spitting out blood and saliva, blinking away water, trying not to breathe it in. I tensed. A deputy appeared at the kitchen door. Meltzer gave Peele a last shove and walked away from the sink. Peele rose up, angrily jerked a paper towel off a steel holder, filled it with ice. The deputy held up a piece of cut drywall by handles that had been screwed in, the kind you might use on drawers or cabinets. Her eyes moved nervously from the sheriff to Peele to me.

"Is this the kind of thing you were talking about?" she asked.

I got up and examined the square. "Looks like it was cut to slip in and out of a window. The handles make it easy to set up and tear down. It blocks a lot of sound if you cover all the windows."

"There's four of them." The deputy's concerned eyes were still moving from the sheriff to Logan Peele's swelling face.

"Where'd you find them?" Meltzer asked.

"Basement," the deputy answered. "But the windows are too small down there. They don't fit."

"Four windows on the garage," I said.

"Want to tell us what the panels are for, Logan?" Meltzer asked.

Peele took the ice away from his mouth, looked at the bloody paper towel. "You'll find my Stratocaster and an amp in the upstairs guestroom. My wife didn't like the noise." He dabbed the corner of his lips. "Back when I had a wife. Back before I had to submit to this bullshit."

"See if they fit upstairs," Meltzer ordered the deputy.

"They don't fit anywhere," Peele said. He smiled and I saw blood in the grooves of his bottom teeth. "Not anymore. I renovated. Remember? And when the house was done, I even rebuilt that little garage. I lived out there while they were working on my house. Little refrigerator, a nice soft mattress. You could survive out there for a long time." Another bloody smile. He was playing with us.

15

Ken Meltzer was still seething when we left Peele's house. Rage was coming off him like steam. Deputies had worked their way through the house as far as the kitchen. Detective Robert Raymond and Major Tina Brolin had arrived and informed us the first offender we'd visited was now sitting in a jail cell. I wondered if that box of porn Lewis Freeman had hidden was worth it to him.

"Can't arrest him for having sound panels," Meltzer grumbled. We snapped seatbelts into place. "But you better believe if there's anything we can lift off them or anything else, we'll get it."

The sheriff had ordered a scene technician with an alternate light source to go over Peele's house, garage, and basement. Some things can't be washed and polished away, things that can't be seen with the naked eye. If blood or other fluids had spattered there since the renovation, they would fluoresce. What happened in that house before the walls and floorboards were ripped out would probably remain Logan Peele's secret. He wasn't the kind of man who confesses, who needs absolution. Peele's computers, a tablet, and an iPhone were in an evidence box in the back of the sheriff's vehicle.

"I should have held his head underwater a few more seconds," Meltzer fumed. His phone chimed. He looked at the display, dropped the phone into a compartment on the console.

"A few more seconds and I would have stopped you," I told him seriously.

He glanced over at me as he backed out. "I lost it. I'm sorry."

"Quick moves," I observed. "Martial arts?"

"Tae kwon do. I teach a kids' class on Saturdays. If you're still here you have to see these kids. Six to ten years old and so cute it will make your teeth hurt." He seemed to relax a little. "I really am sorry about what happened back there. Reacting to guys who like to push buttons is just playing into their hands. I know that. I was stupid."

"I had a nearly overwhelming urge to slug him and I didn't even know Melinda," I said. "I know you must have thought of her when he started talking like that. He's a sadist. He wanted to hurt you."

"Ever seen anyone tear down a house to hide evidence?" He said it with a light smile and a shake of his head, but he was only half kidding.

"I've seen fires," I said. "Torch the clothing, torch the house, blow up the car. This is my first renovation."

"I think he's our guy," Meltzer insisted. "He has the time and opportunity. He has the history. He has the personality. And his alibi is soft." He looked across the cab. "Here's what I think. Something happened that shook him up. He got paranoid. Maybe he saw somebody out there in the woods too close to his dump site. He knows he's going to be on the suspect list once it's discovered. So he goes forward with this major renovation while Melinda is still in that garage. He said he lived out there, so the contractors expect to see him going in and out, bringing in food and water. The neighbors see it, no big deal. He has the perfect explanation. He keeps it locked when he's not there. Again, it's easily explained. He has electronics. He's a techie. Even the panels in the windows wouldn't seem odd. He works from home. He needs quiet. When the house is ready, he kills Melinda, disposes of her body, moves back in, and renovates the garage. We looked at his financials when Brolin questioned him a few weeks ago. He spent sixty thousand dollars on all this."

"I thought it was interesting he wanted to talk about the garage," I said. "He definitely understood the significance of that. Question is, why did he take us down that path?"

"Ego maybe. You don't have to spend a lot of time with him to see that he thinks he's the smartest guy in the room. He believes he successfully disposed of evidence and outsmarted us."

"Or he's simply read about the cases, knows the details, and wants to intentionally ignite suspicions, waste time."

"You have doubts he's our guy."

"I think he's capable of killing," I answered. "Especially to protect himself. Look at the guy. Control freak, obsessive. Jail would not be his happy place." I looked out the window as we passed the old courthouse and drove through Whisper. It was late morning. The sky was pale blue with long white clouds that looked like jet streamers. The temperature reading on the sheriff's vehicle said it was ninety degrees outside. Georgia was reminding us it was late in August. Our windows were up now, and the air conditioner was blowing cold air into the cab. The sheriff's vehicle drew attention as we drove through town, waves from sidewalks and from other drivers. "He microwaves his sponge," I said. "The guy has some twists."

"I thought his eyes were going to pop out of his head when I spilled the sugar." Meltzer laughed that good, rich laugh.

We stopped on red at one of two traffic signals on Main Street in tiny downtown Whisper, Georgia. I saw Pastor Hutchins talking with someone outside the drugstore. He waved. We waved back—the rituals of a small town. Losing one of their own, someone nearly everyone knew, everyone except Logan Peele and Lewis Freeman, conveniently, must have saddened and frightened them all, reminded everyone how fragile we are, how vulnerable, how unable to protect those we love.

I glanced at shop windows, the square in the center of town with its lush green park, the elementary and middle schools behind it, the same middle school Melinda Cochran had attended. It would have been her last year before moving on to high school. It was a pretty town. Giant oaks leaned over the street to form a canopy and block out some of the sun's stinging rush to midday as we left Whisper for the county seat.

The Hitchiti County Judicial Center sat back off the highway—two circular buildings side by side with a bridge connecting them, tinted glass, and gray stone the color of a thundercloud. The area surrounding the center was pedestrian-only. Stone barricades protected it from car bombs. Lines on parking slots were bright white, and the trees planted or potted around the complex still had tags dangling from young branches.

The sheriff pulled into a slot marked with his name. Parking was fifty feet from the building. Cameras were mounted on light poles, and I was sure there was plenty of electronic surveillance on the building, inside and out. "My whole department is here," the sheriff told me. "Evidence room, archives, lot of the courts are located here, the administrative staff except for Doris, road and marine patrols. The building on the left is our detention facility. We have six hundred and twenty-five beds and about six hundred inmates. Used the urban high-rise detention center model in Arlington. State of the art."

"Why haven't you moved your office?" I asked.

"I do have an office here. The center was completed a year ago and I have to be here a lot. But it's quiet there. I'm interrupted less. And I enjoy walking out the back door and getting on the boat when life gets stressful." He grinned at me. "Plus, I can keep an eye on my investigators."

I smiled. I was willing to bet Major Brolin didn't like that, sharing an office with a detective, even if it was one she was in an intimate relationship with, in a little house five miles away from this sparkling new hub of justice. I was beginning to see that Meltzer kept a closer eye on them than I thought. He punished them for their little betrayals. He robbed them of perks like shiny offices in a spanking-new complex. I thought about him barely slowing his pace to speak to the major as we walked toward Lewis Freeman's house, his icy demeanor. I wasn't sure who he was just yet.

"Of course, Raymond and Brolin are over here every day at some point," Meltzer added as we walked toward the doors. "The labs, court appearances. Be a lot more convenient for them here. But inconvenience builds character. Think I'll keep them in Whisper awhile longer." The smile again, this time with a wink.

We pushed open glass doors and cruised through security, Meltzer stopping to talk to the deputies whose responsibility it is to guard the judicial center. He was light with them, friendly; he appeared to know everyone's name. Ken Meltzer was not a sit-behind-the-desk kind of sheriff. I wondered how that would work for him in Washington if he managed to get elected. He'd like the campaigning, I decided. He was good with people.

I stopped just past the security check and waited for one of the deputies to hand me the plastic bowl with my keys and phone. Carved into the floor in the atrium were the words, "THE OFFICE OF SHERIFF CARRIES WITH IT THE DUTY TO PRESERVE THE PEACE AND PROTECT THE LIVES, PROPERTY, HEALTH, AND MORALS OF THE PEOPLE." —GEORGIA SUPREME COURT. I don't know about you, but I get a little nervous when anyone wants to be in charge of morals.

In the sheriff's tenth-floor office, he gave me access to Jeff Davidson's file and some time to read it in an empty office before I headed for the bridge that connected the two towers and waited alone in an interview room for Jeff Davidson, younger brother to Tracy Davidson, the first victim to disappear and turn up at the bottom of an isolated embankment.

The room looked like a hundred others I'd seen. A box with sage walls, a table, two metal chairs, a camera angled in the corner, recording, broadcasting live to monitors somewhere, an interior window with an invisible observation room behind it. A deputy had delivered a bottle of water. I asked for a second one.

Jeffrey Davidson came in with cuffed wrists hanging in front of him. He had his mother's wide eyes. But the strong bridge of his nose, the dimple on one cheek, the perfectly shaped lips reminded me of the photographs in his sister's file. His hair was dark and needed a cut. The safety-orange jumpsuit hung on him. He sat down across from me. I asked the deputy to uncuff him. Davidson had been in a string of trouble, none of it violent: petty theft, break-ins when homeowners were away, then grand theft auto. He'd never used a weapon, never been aggressive. He had stayed out of trouble in jail too.

The deputy unlocked the cuffs and took them with him. I switched the voice recorder on my phone to the on position and set it on the table between us, bare except for the two water bottles. I looked at Jeff Davidson's thin face. "My name is Keye Street. I'm a consultant to the sheriff's department. I'm here to assist in the investigation of your sister's murder."

"Murder?" Color drained from his face. "They found her?" No one had told him. *Jesus.* It never crossed my mind I would be the bearer of this news. I certainly might have delivered it differently. He'd been in jail when the bodies were discovered. He either didn't have access to news or wasn't interested. I wondered when or if his mother had last visited. I couldn't imagine her not making the drive from Silas to inform him. It was less than ten miles away.

"Yes," I answered quietly. "They found her. I'm sorry."

Davidson clasped bony hands together and looked down at dirty nails. Dark hair fell in front of his eyes. "It's a little late, isn't it?" he asked finally. His voice was even and he'd learned how to disguise some of the accent he'd probably had growing up, the one his mother had. But I could hear that country road and that little house where he'd been raised in every word. I thought about the bug lady again and her weird aquarium, her thick drawl, the too-long, too-blond hair, the regrets. I didn't feel sorry for her this time. I just felt pissed off. Why hadn't she bothered to inform her son about the discovery of his sister's body?

"Yes, it is," I told him. "But we still have a chance to catch the person who did this." I handed him the bottle of water across the table. He took it, uncapped it, and gulped some down.

"Where?" he wanted to know. Of course he wanted to know. They'd been close. Tracy's disappearance was probably the most traumatic event of a childhood chock-full of trauma. Tracy had protected him from a violent father and had given him what a neglectful mother couldn't. I silently cursed his bug-killing mama again for not getting her ass over here. Some people should not have children. I thought about my biological addicts, otherwise known as parents. At least they'd had the good sense to give me up.

"Do you know of a place called Oconee Campground and RV Park?" I asked Jeff.

"Sure. It's in the national forest. Or near it. I used to park there and go fishing sometimes."

"You ever go down there with Tracy?"

Davidson shook his head. "Neither one of us was old enough to drive when she disappeared. And we lived miles away in Silas. That was where she was found?"

"Close to there."

"Do they know how?" he asked. "How she died?"

"Someone hit her very hard," I said. I didn't want to tell him the weapon dug into Tracy's skull and left a pattern of radiating fractures, that she'd been held prisoner, that she'd probably experienced childbirth in captivity. I didn't want to be the one to tell him she'd been discarded in the woods and left to decompose.

"So what are you gonna do now?" he wanted to know.

"Try to understand a little more about Tracy's life," I answered. "Do you remember Tracy having any older friends? Maybe someone she kept a secret? An older boyfriend?"

"We didn't have no kind of life," he said.

I showed him a picture of Logan Peele. "Does this man look familiar at all?"

He stared at the photo for a few seconds. "Yeah. I seen him. He was in here once when I was here. Mean, I heard. I never got close to him."

"But you'd never seen him before that? When you were kids, I mean?"

He shook his head. "You think he did it?"

"Was there anyone she confided in? A teacher, maybe? Any adults who may be able to help us now?"

Once more, he shook his head. "I don't think so, but we were in different grades with different teachers." He looked down at his hands again.

"How about after-school activities?"

Jeff Davidson looked up from his clasped hands. "You shittin' me? What we had was get home and do the chores so you didn't get your ass beat. That was our after-school activity. We went to school and we came right home. And once a week if he felt generous my father would let us leave on Sunday and go to church. And we didn't talk to nobody because we knew what was waiting for us if it ever got back to him. I didn't have no kind of life until that bastard went to jail."

16

en Meltzer was on his desk phone. He waved me in. The office was spacious with a view of downtown Muscogee Creek, the county seat, which sat on the banks of the lake. His desk was covered with papers and sticky notes with little arrows pointing to signature lines without a signature. He was agreeing on the phone, reluctantly it seemed to me, to speak at some function. "This is why I don't like being here," he told me when he finally hung up. "Someone always finds out. And Doris isn't here to protect me. How'd it go?"

"He didn't know about Tracy," I said, and knew instantly my darkening mood was evident. "Don't you notify prisoners when something happens with a family member?"

"Sure," Meltzer said. "We have a system. I'll find out what went wrong."

"He didn't recognize Logan Peele's photograph. Not from eleven years ago anyway. But he recognized his face from lockup. Told me Peele was mean. Had a reputation." I thought about Logan Peele, about his bright, amused, utterly confident eyes. The arrogant prick. "He didn't have a lot of information to offer. But I have a clearer picture of Tracy's home life. Father sounds like a typical abuser. He isolated those kids. They were terrified of him."

"It's discouraging, isn't it." It wasn't a question. It was an *I've been there.*

"Jeff Davidson is twenty-one," I answered. "And he has nothing but a mass of scars from warring parents and violence and kidnapping, and not much chance of turning his life around."

"Eighty percent of the kids around here come from families with incomes below the poverty level, Keye. The only rich people in Hitchiti County are the part-timers with summer homes up around the resorts. What we produce here are service people and support staff. It's got to stop. We have to find a way to give them opportunity. Poverty and hopelessness breed crime."

I didn't know many law enforcement professionals who considered social and economic issues when dealing with criminals. I told him that. "You know why I teach that tae kwon do class on Saturdays?" he asked. "It's about discipline, respect, humility, meditation, funneling your energy and strength. It gives them self-esteem. These kids will need it later in life. Change is coming to this area, but it's going to take time. Years."

"Spoken like a congressman," I said. His eyes stayed on mine. Something about the way he looked at me, something knowing in his gaze, made the moment feel too intimate. I entertained a vivid fantasy of flying out the door and down the long, cold marbled corridors, back to my car, back to Atlanta, back to Rauser. Because everything about those moments when he looked at me like that felt too close, too warm, too familiar, too right.

There was a tap on the door. Meltzer didn't take his eyes off me when he said, "It's open."

A man with thinning hair and a business suit stepped inside. He was very thin with glasses, dark frames. He nodded politely to me. "May I speak with you privately, Sheriff?"

"Sure thing." Meltzer pushed away from his desk, walked out into the corridor. The door closed. I sat there for a moment with just the faint sound of men's voices through the thick door. I got up and walked to the windows, looked out at Meltzer's view. What was I doing? *What was I doing?* I'd had a few flirtations in my life. I knew exactly where those long looks led. The terrible truth that I was as attracted to him as he was to me filled me with guilt. This wasn't me. I'm not a flirter. Not when I'm in a relationship. Or a cheater. But I had a saboteur's heavy hand when it came to relationships, career, success. I wasn't going to do it this time. I wasn't going to let Ken Meltzer's dreamy brown eyes do me in. I loved Rauser, handsome, sexy, kind, funny Rauser. I knew what this was about. Rauser was living in my house and the fucking walls were closing in. It was the first time I'd admitted to myself that I wasn't ready. I was barely pieced back together after my life had totally collapsed. I didn't want to feel married again. I didn't want to feel responsible for someone's happiness. *It's temporary,* I reminded myself. *Rauser's house will be back together in a couple of months and he'll go back home. Fighting to get time together is much better than having too much.* I thought about the silverware drawer I'd labeled. That's why Rauser had been so angry. Because he knew what it meant. Funny how it always seems like you're doing great until someone is standing in front of you, willing and capable and put together, and you realize how broken you are. I find it unbearable.

I noticed the sheriff's iPhone on his desk. For the record, investigators not only have a suspicious nature but are prone to outright, unapologetic nosiness. I stood very still and listened to the muted voices beyond the wood door. I thought this over. One little voice knew it probably wasn't right to look at the sheriff's messages. One little voice wanted to go for it. Three guesses which one won out.

I picked up the phone and hit the message icon. The first name on his list of messages was Molly. Not Molly Cochran. Just Molly. I was going to click on it when the door cracked open. I saw Meltzer's hand holding it partially closed, heard affirmative *yes sir*s. I returned the phone hastily to the homepage and dropped it on the desk.

I was standing at the window looking out at the town edging up against the lake when he came back in. "I'm sorry to keep you waiting." Meltzer's voice was smooth, but I knew as soon as I looked at him that something was wrong. "Come and sit down, Keye," he said. I took my chair across from his desk and he took the other one, faced me. "It's the Davidson kid. He's dead."

"How?" I thought of the way his eyes refused to meet mine, how he kept gazing down at his gritted hands.

"Suicide," he answered quietly. "Six more months and he was out of here."

"Are they sure it was suicide?"

I could see a white square of sky from the window in his dark eyes. He blinked like someone just coming awake, a long, slow blink. "Found him in the kitchen where he worked. Security cameras got the whole thing, apparently. He used a kitchen knife."

"Jesus," I muttered. I thought again about that thin young man sitting across from me in a chilled interview room. *I'm here to assist in the investigation of your sister's murder.* I looked at the sheriff.

"Model prisoner," Meltzer said. "Had a lot of freedom. I talked to Tina Brolin. Mrs. Davidson specifically requested we allow her to notify Jeff that his sister's remains had been identified."

"Well, she never made it," I said. "And I didn't know." I heard an unexpected rush of emotion shake my voice. "I didn't prepare him at all. Shit."

"This isn't your fault, Keye. He had eleven years to prepare. It's absurd to think he hadn't considered the probability."

"Maybe it was about hope. The last flicker of a flame getting snuffed out. His sister must have been his only connection in life. The person he knew loved him."

Meltzer nodded. We were silent for a couple of minutes. "This man who took Tracy and Melinda, he killed Jeff Davidson," Meltzer said. "Maybe he didn't hold the knife but he killed him just the same. I see it with Melinda's parents. Molly and Bryant were happy once. He destroyed them."

I thought again about the text from Molly I hadn't had time to read. "Were they happy? Their marriage, I mean. Before Melinda disappeared?"

"I think they had some stressors," the sheriff replied. "Money. Took a while to get the bowling alley profitable, I think. But they wouldn't have talked to me about that. We're not that kind of friends. And people around here are quiet about their private lives. Why the interest?"

"I'm just looking for something else those girls had in common besides age, gender, and blond hair. He accessed their lives somehow. He spotted them somewhere. We know Tracy's parents had problems. Just wondering if that was true for Melinda."

"Even if it was, how would that give the killer access to their lives?"

"It may not be relevant, Sheriff. I'm searching just like you are. But my experience tells me that selection is rarely truly random in series crimes even with strangers. Maybe it's a physical type, a way these girls carry themselves, speak. Maybe it's something else, something deeper, a circumstance in their life. He saw them somewhere and he decided he wanted them. We need to entertain every possibility."

"I'm going to ask someone from patrol to get you back to your car. I've got to deal with this. I need to handle the notification myself this time. Don't imagine this will be easy for Mrs. Davidson. Maybe she knew Jeff would react this way. Maybe that's why she didn't tell him."

I thought about Josey Davidson sitting in her carport twisting her wires, blowing glass around her bugs, two dead children and a thug for a husband. Some lives are hard to look back on and find a reason to stay sober. "Maybe," I said. "Maybe she's just a shitty mother."

I felt a blast of heat coming up off the baking asphalt as I pushed through doors and stepped outside. A police car eased out of a parking space and came to a stop in front of me. The window came down. "Climb in, Dr. Street. We'll get you over to Whisper. Silver Spoon, right?"

"Right. Thanks." I got in. The officer and I exchanged small talk. He was polite. I asked if he minded if I made a call. He didn't.

I pressed in Neil's number. "How's everything at the office?" I asked. "Any kitchen fires? Lost clients? Injuries?"

"It's all good. Pretty quiet, actually." Neil sounded cheerful. He'd probably used mood-altering substances outside on the docks. This is his idea of not smoking pot at the office. On those rare occasions we have a client come to our business, the one I spent a bazillion dollars redecorating, I'd like for it not to smell like a frat party. "We moved all the DETOUR signs on the street," Neil told me. I heard Latisha laugh in the background. "There were eight of them."

"Moved them? Where?"

"In a three-block circle," he said as if it were a perfectly reasonable answer.

"But why?" I asked.

"Why? Because it was fun, Kiwi." He said it as if I had some deficiency that inhibited my ability to grasp the concept of entertainment. "All that annoying construction traffic is going in circles now. Can you not see the fun in that?"

I glanced at the officer. He was staring ahead through the windshield, politely ignoring my conversation. "I'm speechless," I said into the phone.

"Did you call to say you're coming home? Because people are calling."

"Who's calling?"

"Tyrone's Quikbail has a couple failures to appear. Larry Quinn has a job and about half a dozen attorneys need papers served."

"Put them off," I said. "Don't take anything that has to be done in the next week."

"A week?" Neil repeated. "You were talking a couple of days."

"I may need more time," I told him, and glanced at the cop driving. I wanted to be careful about what I said. I didn't want any rumors seeping out into the general population regarding the investigation. "I don't know how much yet. You can handle it."

"Don't get sucked in down there, Keye," Neil said, and irritation shot through me like a bottle rocket. "You know how you get. And we have an employee now. You bring in the big jobs."

"I can't talk about this right now, Neil. I need you to find some photographs real quick and email them to me."

"Sure. People or locations? You got names?" Neil asked.

I glanced at the officer again. "I'll shoot you a text with the info."

We pulled into the diner a few minutes later and parked behind my Impala. I hadn't told the cop I was driving the old Impala but Whisper was tiny and Meltzer's patrols probably knew every vehicle in town. And my license plate did say FULTON COUNTY. I thanked him for the ride, went to my car, pushed my key into the door. They didn't have key fobs in 1969. No Bluetooth. No GPS. No satellite radios. You had to love a '69 Impala for the sheer beauty of the machine.

I lowered the top and pulled across my body the new seatbelt my dad had put in to replace the original old lap belts. That's when I saw it on my windshield. A piece of white paper folded in half, then folded again so it hung like a parking ticket around the wiper blade. I got back out, plucked it off my windshield, and opened it.

> Dear Keye,
>
> I'm thinking about you too. I thought you would want to know that. I know they hired you to find me. I know all about you. I've wanted someone to talk to.
>
> Listen hard. Can you hear me? More soon.

I held the note by the top corner and called Sheriff Meltzer. I read it to him as I opened my back door, found the aluminum case I use as a scene kit, and pulled out an evidence sleeve. My eyes swept the lot. Four cars. It was a slow midday at the Silver Spoon. I slid the note into the bag and sealed it.

"Is it handwritten?"

"Printed," I answered.

"Sounds like the kind of crap Logan Peele would pull. This morning he was gloating over knowing who you were. But we have his devices. So he'd have to go somewhere else to do it."

"This letter needs to go to your lab. I bagged it. You have a patrol in the area I can hand it off to?"

"Raymond's at the Whisper office. I'll send him over to pick it up."

"He used my first name in this note, Sheriff. I think he feels some kind of connection."

"You need protection," Meltzer said.

"He doesn't want *me*. He wants to *challenge* me. And himself." I looked at the diner window. I saw the backs of a couple of customers at the counter. A woman in a booth was watching me through the window as she ate like she was staring at a television. "The more he communicates, the more we learn about him. This kind of offender wants to insert himself into an investigation, attempt to direct it one way or another, influence investigators. He gets off on the cat-and-mouse. Colin Ireland made calls to Scotland Yard. Zodiac was a letter writer and so was Wishbone. This guy may be special but he's not unique, and judging from the letter he's not terribly sophisticated either."

"You're telling me we have a full-blown serial."

"Unfortunately, I don't think he's full-blown yet. His first victim's injuries were consistent with captivity, struggle, attempts at escape." I had to be careful. The sheriff knew Melinda Cochran. I didn't want it to feel so personal that he couldn't focus. "But the finger breaks in the second victim, her other injuries, that was him dipping his toe in the water. As I said over breakfast, he's evolving, realizing and fulfilling different needs. And now he's engaged us with this letter, issued a challenge. *Figure me out. Catch me if you can. Listen to me.* He just upped the ante. He's not done, Sheriff."

"Then it's time to go public with that information," he snapped. "I'm sworn to protect the people here. They have to be made to understand the threat. I have to release the profile."

"Okay," I said. "But, Ken—" I hadn't used his first name before, and it stopped me for a second or two. "If my name is attached to the profile, Whisper is going to have a media problem and fast."

Silence—Meltzer weighing his options. "Understood."

17

made a quick sweep of the parking lot and the wide street in front of the diner. I could see the sign for my hotel two blocks down, and the shops on Main Street a block over, Whisper Park, the woods skirting it on one side, the middle school and shops and neighborhoods on the others. So many places to hide. Was he watching now? Had he waited to see me read the note, make the call he knew I would to Sheriff Meltzer? I checked the time: 2:12 p.m. How long had the note been sitting on my windshield? My car had been parked at the diner since very early this morning. I hadn't known when I left the hotel to meet the sheriff that I would end up spending half the day in his vehicle tossing sex offenders.

I walked inside the diner. Two guys at the counter turned on stools and stared at me. They had coffee cups. No plates. The woman in the booth who'd been watching me through the window had her eyes on me now, eyes without warmth or welcome. I didn't recognize any of the employees, a server, a cook, a woman behind the cash register clicking the keys on a yellowing old tape calculator. The place was stone-cold quiet except for the sound of her tallying receipts.

"Help you with something?" She stopped adding up tickets long enough to look at me. Normally, when someone walks into a diner, one assumes they'd like a seat, food, coffee. I wasn't getting any offers.

My raised voice, my official voice, the one I'd learned at the FBI, traveled through the nearly empty restaurant. "Did anyone see who left the note on the white Impala in the parking lot?" The counter guys swiveled back around to the counter and said nothing. No one else moved.

I looked at the woman in the booth. "How about you?"

"Nope." That was all she said. It hung in the air, sour as bad milk.

I looked at the cashier. "You?"

She'd gone back to adding up receipts—keys clicking followed by the windup sound old tape calculators make when the tape advances. "Nope." She drew it out so it sounded like *new-ope*.

One of the counter guys glanced back. It reminded me of kids on a playground sneaking a look at whoever's being bullied. We always want to see what that face looks like, don't we? I wondered what mine looked like now as a spark of anger shot through me.

"Have a nice day," I said pleasantly, and walked out.

Raymond was opening the door of his Crown Vic when I stepped into the steamy air. He was probably part of the reason I was receiving this icy reception. Who knew what he'd said, what he and his girlfriend Brolin had told people about me? I thought about the old server last night pulling away when he discovered who I was and warning me not to get on Raymond's bad side. I felt the heat in my cheeks. I was flushed. I didn't even have to look in the mirror to know that. Okay, so maybe I don't always light up a room when I walk in, but I'm not accustomed to the pariah treatment. Sometimes it can get weird in small, lily-white towns where I look so different from the general population. The Chinese heritage I know nothing about is all over my face, and the way I move, talk, dress, laugh—all of it—says I'm not from around here. Whisper felt like it was getting a lot smaller.

"Sheriff said you've got something for the lab." Raymond didn't sound happy about being an errand boy. He'd gotten a haircut, and his receding hairline made it look like his dark hair started on top of his head. He had thick brows and a beefy face, J. Edgar Hoover–style. He was not an easy guy to like.

I handed him the sleeve with the letter I'd found on my windshield. "Probably from the suspect," I told him. "I handled it before I realized what it was. My prints are in the system. They can exclude me quickly."

"Could be someone yanking our chain," he said. "People don't like outsiders around here. Especially if they're connected to the law. And watching us spinning our wheels is always fun for the troublemakers."

"Could be," I admitted. I figured Raymond had a lot to do with people disliking law enforcement. "But the letter and the wording are consistent with the offender profile. We're talking big ego here, Detective. He wants to be heard."

He slipped on gloves and laid the Baggie on the hood of my car, extracted the letter, read it, put it back in the sleeve. "Probably just somebody else thinks you're a pain in the ass." He stared at me, daring me to take the bait.

"Thanks for your support." I opened my driver's door. "This is a creepy little town, by the way. And the coffee is terrible."

"Hey," Raymond said. "Gotta be scary, huh? Getting something like this."

"I'm good," I said. I got in my car.

"Look, maybe we weren't happy about you being here, Street. Maybe we still aren't. But I already said everything I needed to say to you on the subject. So we're square."

"Thanks," I said, and watched him walk back to his car, his big hand holding the evidence at his side. Maybe I was growing on him after all.

I checked my phone and found emails waiting. Neil had delivered the names and photographs I'd requested. I checked the time. Whisper High should be letting out. I wondered if Melinda Cochran's group of friends had stayed together since her disappearance. Loyalties are an ever-shifting thing in the teenage years. They'd made the jump to high school now—ninth graders standing at the edge of the New World. Did the girls still walk home together from school? Did their parents allow it after their friend had vanished? My mother had talked about the atmosphere during the Atlanta Child Murders. I was too young and too shielded to remember. Twenty-nine black children and young men had been murdered. There was terror in the air before Wayne Williams was arrested and convicted. The children had walked together in tight little groups, latched on to one another like they were crossing rushing water. No one knew why children were being hunted or how the killer's selection process worked, but he'd hunted in an area where parents had to work, where they didn't have the luxury of stay-at-home moms or babysitters. So these children stepped out into the world fully aware that someone wanted to kill them. But they held hands and crowded together because there is safety in numbers. Even an offender willing to take some risk acquiring a victim won't pluck them out of a group. That's ex-lover and ex-husband territory. The one who stalks and plans and waits, he's careful. His risk is measured. He has a life. He values it and his freedom.

There was a tangle of traffic leaving the school—cars driven by students packed with kids. A line of buses curled around the front of the building. The parking lot was full of teenagers still hanging out, laughing, leaning against cars, trying to look cool, sneaking drags off cigarettes and attempting to hide plumes of smoke bellowing from young lungs. I pulled in and idled near a group of four, rested my elbow on my lowered window. The green-and-white sign at the edge of the lot said DRUG AND ALCOHOL FREE ZONE. NO SMOKING.

"Anyone know Shannon Davis or Heather Ridge?" I asked, glancing at Neil's email with the photographs of Melinda Cochran's friends. "Or Briana Franklin?"

A lanky boy with curly black hair pointed across the street with the cigarette in his hand. One of the girls slapped his arm. They all laughed. I followed his finger and saw three girls crossing the street, their books in their arms. I parked. It was a steamy-hot afternoon. I was wearing a pair of flared Max C's and my favorite Elie Tahari V-neck button blouse clinging to me under the blazer I desperately wanted to leave in the car. But I needed something to cover the duty holster tucked against the small of my back. No way I was leaving my gun in the car. Maybe the note had shaken me up a little.

I ran across the street. "Shannon!" I called out. All three girls turned, three skirts midthigh, tight tops, sparkly jewelry. "Hi." I walked up, smiling. "And you're Heather and you're Briana." I was so bubbly I could have been the head cheerleader.

"And you're the FBI lady," the brown-haired girl answered. Heather. I had her Facebook profile picture on my phone. Her expression told me she wasn't impressed.

"Former," I said. "I'm consulting with the sheriff's department and I'd like to talk about Melinda Cochran." Heather started walking. The others did too. It was pretty clear who was running this show. I walked with them. "I know it must have been really terrible to lose a friend like that. I'm sorry. I want to find out what happened to Melinda."

"You mean y'all don't know yet?" Heather asked me. "We heard she was held prisoner by some freak that killed her."

Well, there was that. Always one in every crowd. I couldn't tell if she was being the tough kid to cover her emotions or if she simply didn't have them. It had been months since they'd lost their friend. Perhaps she'd just dealt with it and put it away somewhere. "What we know we learned because of forensics," I told them. "What I need to find out is *who* did that to Melinda."

"We don't know who." Briana had dark wavy hair and deep blue eyes, some baby fat, but she was going to be a full-on knockout one day. "We all miss her a lot."

Shannon hugged her books with long, skinny arms and watched the ground as we walked.

"The day Melinda disappeared," I said, "I understand you'd all walked home from school together. Was there anything different about that day?"

"Um. Yeah. Melinda disappeared off the planet. That was different," Heather answered. She began to recite their routine in a voice that told me she'd been through it all before. "We left school, we crossed the park, we bought Cokes from the machine at the hardware store, and then we came straight home."

"It was just a, you know, normal day," Shannon said, quietly. "Before that, I mean. Before Melinda."

Heather pointed ahead. About a hundred feet down I saw brick-columned entrances on either side of the road, each with a subdivision name. "Melinda lived in the neighborhood there. It's not as nice as where we live in Lakeshore Estates."

Shannon jumped in. "But it's not like our parents are rich or anything. Our neighborhood is just newer."

"Newer, better, and we have the lake on our side. But whatev," Heather snarked.

"According to your statements, Melinda turned off toward her neighborhood before you went into yours." I looked up the street to confirm that Melinda's turn would have come before theirs. It did. "And you didn't see or hear anything unusual."

"Right," Heather said. Shannon and Briana nodded.

"No cars on the street?" I followed up. "Looks like you could have seen into her neighborhood as you passed. Nothing comes to mind?"

"We can see the main street but we can't see into the neighborhood. We already told the cops everything," Heather insisted petulantly. This kid was starting to get on my nerves. "Melinda turned left and we turned right. We didn't see anyone and we didn't hear anything. It's not like we knew she would fucking just *vanish*."

"Okay," I said evenly. My mother would have slapped my eyeballs over to my ears if I'd used the F word to an adult at her age. "You remember anyone driving by? Anyone stopping to say hello while you were walking that day?" I looked from Heather to Briana and Shannon. Head shakes all around.

Heather eyed me. "My brother says the sheriff's department is really lame if they have to hire a Chinese chick."

"Oh my God, Heather!" Briana gasped. Giggles rippled through the group.

"What do you think?" I asked.

"I think he's a racist prick first of all. And second, he's threatened by strong women."

"Good call," I said. "When did you realize something happened to Melinda?"

"Her mom and dad started calling everyone after a couple hours," Briana said. "Her mom was off work that day and I guess she thought Melinda came home with one of us at first. But then she got worried."

"And then we all started calling Melinda's phone." Shannon was skinny and pale with wide eyes and heavy lids that made her look like she might need a hospital ward any minute. "And all we got was voice mail. Over and over."

"Did Melinda have a boyfriend?" I pressed. A beat passed.

"She was awkward," Heather answered finally. "Especially with boys. She was, like, one of those girls who was never going to see a dick."

"Nice," I said.

"*God*, Heather," Briana said. "That's so disrespectful."

"It's not like she can hear us," Heather defended herself.

"How about you, Heather?" I asked. "See a lot of dick?" I'd surprised her. It was the first time the superior smirk had faded. "It doesn't take any skill. You know? Pretty much any guy in the world is happy to show it to you. You want to impress people? Start talking about how many A's you're pulling in. Because dick is easy. And bragging about it makes you look desperate and stupid." I shifted my gaze to Heather's friends. "So what was the usual routine? Y'all hang out in the park or the coffee shop or anything after school?"

"What does any of this even matter anymore?" Heather asked quietly. I'd embarrassed her and it was taking her a minute to recover her bravado.

"Sometimes the tiniest things turn out to be really important," I said. I didn't talk about how the smallest shred of information might tell us how he got so close, selected Melinda, accessed her life, then ended it, and sliced into all their childhoods.

"We used the swings in the park sometimes, and sometimes we got ice cream and talked to whoever was in there. Kids mostly," Shannon said.

"Wait," Heather said, as if she'd just remembered. "She had band practice once a week."

"Yeah, that's right," Briana confirmed. "On Wednesdays, I think."

"She played something geeky like clarinet," Heather added. "And Mr. Tray is kind of weird and too touchy-feely." Her bright eyes caught mine. Smart kid. Must give her teachers hell. "And not just with girls either. I mean, he's older than you are and he's not even married or anything." She glanced at my ring finger. "Oh. Sorry."

"What exactly do you mean by *touchy-feely*?" I asked.

"It's more like rumors," Briana said.

Dangerous rumors, if the teacher hadn't earned them. "Are you telling me Mr. Tray behaved inappropriately with his students?"

Briana and Shannon shifted their meek gazes to their friend Heather. "He just, you know, he's creepy."

"Ah," I said. "You do know if a teacher or any adult is behaving inappropriately you need to tell someone immediately, right?"

Heather smirked. "We've had that lecture."

"And I hope you also know that rumors that aren't true about teachers can ruin them," I added.

The girls said nothing. Their eyes said I was being a boring adult.

"Did Melinda walk home alone after band practice?" I asked, and got affirmative nods. If Brolin and Raymond had performed a thorough victimology this information would have been in the files already. I would have known that our victim walked alone one day a week. Her risk goes up. The offender's goes way down.

The sidewalk had sloped down as we neared the entrance to their neighborhood. I caught glimpses of the lake sparkling through the trees over rooftops in their new "nicer" development. On the left I saw the sign for Briarwood Subdivision where Melinda had lived. I could see down the wide main street that ran into the neighborhood. No cars parked against the white curbs. "Did Melinda say anything about having plans that day? Is there a chance she wasn't going straight home?"

Shrugs all around.

"Did she keep a diary that you know of?"

"I don't think she was the diary type," Heather said. "She was more the Twitter and Facebook type."

"Does this man look familiar?" I handed my phone to Heather. She studied the photo of Logan Peele, then passed it from small hand to small hand, hands with plastic rings and nail polish and bright rubber wristbands. They took their time looking at Peele's face, at his piercing eyes. One by one they said they'd never seen him or his gray F-150 in the neighborhood.

"We heard that girl that disappeared a long time ago was found too, where Melinda was found," Heather said. "Is it true?"

"Yes," I said. "Her name was Tracy."

"Is he going to try to get us too?"

I swallowed the ache I felt for them. "Nah. Just be alert," I said with a good deal more calm than I felt. "Stay together when your parents aren't around. Bad guys don't like groups. Don't let anyone talk you into anything that doesn't feel right. Even if it's just a ride home. And if anyone tries, make a lot of noise, scream, run, and call nine-one-one."

Shannon pulled the chain around her neck up out of her shirt. A silver whistle at the end rocked back and forth like a pendulum. "They gave these to everyone at school."

"That's great," I said. But it broke my heart a little. Kids shouldn't have to wear whistles. Kids shouldn't have to worry about being bound and gagged and murdered. "Was anything bothering Melinda? Problems at home, anything?"

"Her parents were poor. They fought about money sometimes," Heather said.

"My parents fight about money and we're not poor," Briana contributed. "I don't think."

"Here's my card. Call my mobile if you think of something." I gave them each a business card. "Just use your head until we get this creep, okay?"

18

drove to the middle school, where the bell rang half an hour later than the high school. I parked and worked my way against the stream of kids blasting through propped-open double doors. The hall was packed. I stuck my head in a door marked TEACHERS' LOUNGE, empty but for one woman lowering herself into a chair. She put a can of Coke and a package of cheese crackers on the table in front of her, and looked exactly like you'd imagine a teacher must feel after a day with eleven-, twelve-, and thirteen-year-old kids. Or as my dad would say, "Shot at and missed. Shit at and hit."

"I'm looking for Mr. Tray's room," I told her.

"It's the band room. Take a right at the end of the hall." She popped the top on the can, leaned back, and blew out enough air to puff her cheeks.

"Thanks." I smiled. "Carry on."

"Oh hey, Mr. Tray leaves early twice a week. I haven't seen him since this morning." She grabbed the crackers off the table and tore the corner with her teeth, spit out cellophane. "I think today was one of his days."

I walked through the emptying halls. The band room door was locked. I returned to my car and found Highway 441, then turned south. Just a couple of hundred yards outside the city limits, I spotted the huge white bowling pin against the sky. Under it, a long red-and-white block building. A bowling-pin-shaped sign hung like a marquee on the front of the building. WHISPER LANES. OPEN LATE. The word COCKTAILS blinked in lavender neon on the front door. The building appeared windowless, a bunker the size of a football field. There were a couple of eighteen-wheelers in a dirt parking lot, a pickup truck, a white van, a Cadillac, and an old Dodge Dart that looked like it might have once been a burgundy color.

I pushed through the door from brilliant sunlight to dimly lit lounge. It took a second for my eyes to adjust. Ahead of me all twenty-four bowling lanes were oiled and gleaming and lit up. But the front of the space was deep in neon shadows like most roadside taverns. I saw the bar to the right with customers on stools. Round tables with chairs were set up like an airport lounge. A silver-haired man in a short-sleeved buttondown and brown dress pants let go of a bright yellow ball. I watched it roll toward the pins, striking them hard. The noise didn't seem to bother anyone. Apparently a bowling alley was as good a place as any to pull off the highway and have a drink in the early afternoon.

I went to the lounge, nodded at the man behind the bar. "You're Keye Street," he said. He was filling a mug from his tap. "My wife said she met you this morning. I'm Bryant Cochran. Give me a second and I'll meet you at a table. Want something to drink?"

Yes, I did. I wanted a big, honking glass of, well, anything. Vodka preferably—coating my throat and loosening up my shoulders and neck. I wanted to feel the heaviness on my tongue. I wanted to forget the way I felt when Meltzer looked at me. I wanted to find out who was taking girls and torturing them and killing them. "I'd love a club soda," I answered. "With lemon."

I waited at a table while Bryant Cochran checked on his customers and poured my soda. I kept thinking about Logan Peele, about the way he'd looked at me in his kitchen, standing there with an ice cube held against his bloodied lip, arrogant and taunting. I thought about the way he knew me. I thought about the note on my windshield.

Two guys at the bar in T-shirts and ball caps drank butter-colored beer from clear glasses and talked about hunting season opening next month and hunting stuff. We don't do a lot of hunting on Peachtree Street. Not that kind anyway.

A woman sitting two stools down drank white wine and listened to them. She was in black skinny jeans, flats, a shoulder-length curly perm. "Why y'all wanna talk about killing all the time?" She spoke to them in a teasing way that said they all knew one another. "Didn't your mamas take you to see *Bambi*?"

Bryant Cochran came to the table in jeans, worn to blue-white, and a red baseball cap. He was a big guy, Rauser's height, but thicker. The jeans were tight around his thighs. He had a close black beard and the kind of chalky complexion you get from living your life inside.

"Is it hard to be in a bar?" he asked. I looked at his face and believed he was absolutely sincere. He set my soda down, flipped a chair around, and straddled it across from me. He'd obviously Googled me. And boy, was there ever a boatload of information out there, both true and outright fiction. So thrilled alcoholism and meltdown were now an official part of my bio. Always instills confidence.

"It is, kind of," I said, and looked into his blue-gray eyes.

"I know," he said. In the background, a slow but steady steam of bowling balls rolled down an alley. I'd never bowled. I'd never even been inside a bowling alley. Not that I was above it. I'd spent plenty of time in bars with a pool cue in my hand. "I had to give it up too." He said it with the matter-of-fact cadence of a country boy. "Drinking, I mean. A couple years ago when the bowling alley business wasn't supporting us, Molly and me had to think long and hard before I applied for a liquor license. It's tempting on bad days."

"And I know you've had some lately," I said. "I'm sorry about Melinda."

His eyes lifted to mine. "It breaks you, Miss Street. It takes a guy like me and snaps him right in half. It was bad enough when we didn't know where she was. But now knowing she'd been held and all." He cleared his throat. "Can you find out who did this? I want to look that bastard in the eye. I want him to know what he did to us."

He thought confronting the monster who had treated his daughter to inexplicable cruelty would give him closure. Family members can't wait for those moments in the courtroom. They want to tell him how he dismantled a family, how he broke their hearts and marriages and lives. But telling a psychopath who wants and needs to make his mark on the lives of others how deeply he wounded you is nothing more than handing him a parting gift. It's another sick memory he can take off to jail with him. I wish judges wouldn't allow it. I wish families understood that the man they were attempting to shame was soaking it in, savoring their pain, and probably fighting a growing erection. These guys don't have a heart you can touch with your pain.

"Mr. Cochran," I began carefully. He stopped me and asked me to call him by his first name. "Bryant," I started again. And I was careful. You can't talk to the family of a victim in the detached way you talk to professionals. You can't describe the psychological characteristics of a crime scene to the grieving father of a murdered girl. You can't break them any more than they've been broken. "Because Melinda was found in this area with another girl who also lived in Hitchiti County, we believe the suspect is local. Especially given the length of time between their disappearances. I think we're looking for someone who has been in this area a long time, someone you or your wife may know." I stopped there. I didn't mention other similarities—broken bones and sexual abuse. I wasn't sure how much the sheriff or his investigators had shared with the parents and I didn't want to drop an emotional bomb for the second time today. I thought again about Jeff Davidson, shaggy and thin and hopeless, staring down at his hands and planning to open his veins with a kitchen knife.

Bryant Cochran glanced at his customers at the bar, the two guys, the woman, then leaned forward and said very quietly, "I . . . we . . . always figured it was a stranger." There was emotion in his voice and it embarrassed him. "Whisper is surrounded by highway. And some of these truckers that come in here are rough guys. *No*." He shook his head. "Nobody that lives around here would do something like that." He blinked watery eyes, sniffed, touched his nose self-consciously with the back of his hand.

I took a sip of my club soda and wished again it were loaded with Absolut. "It's hard to imagine an everyday person could be capable of something so terrible, I know. But one of the things I've learned about this kind of individual is that there's a psychological disconnect between the terrible part-time violence in their life and their real life, the life where they're part of a community. It's the same kind of disconnect that a lot of us have in our everyday lives but it's taken to the extreme. You run a bar. You've seen guys talk to women in a way they'd absolutely hate their mothers or wives or sisters being talked to. Multiply that kind of emotional disconnect between behavior and values by about a hundred."

Cochran was silent.

"Did you or your wife know Tracy Davidson and her family?" I asked. "Is there any connection between you at all? Same church, same anything?"

"That's the girl they found when Melinda was found?" he asked, and I nodded. "Neither one of us knew any of them. And I don't believe we ever ran across them doing anything. Molly and me both grew up around here. I don't know one person in Silas. We only half remember seeing posters of her after she ran away."

"Tracy didn't run away," I said flatly. "She disappeared under circumstances very similar to Melinda's." Another ball rumbled down the alley and cracked into bowling pins. "I want you to think about the people in your life or in Melinda's life, all the relationships. Did she ever have any interaction with someone that didn't feel right to you? Maybe you just felt something in your gut. An adult, a friend who paid too much attention to her. Did she ever mention anyone who bothered her? I know this is tough but it will help."

Bryant Cochran shook his big head. "Nobody in our life that couldn't be trusted with a child." It was a belief held by most people who loved and trusted their friends and family. And it wasn't true.

"Was there anyone Melinda may have confided in if something was bothering her?"

"Just her friends, I guess."

"Did Melinda keep a diary?"

"Not that I know of."

"I understand she was in the school band."

Bryant nodded, smiled a little. "The band got to go to the Rose

Bowl last year. Melinda was so excited. That was just a couple weeks before she disappeared."

"I've heard good things about the band teacher," I lied. I'd heard terrible accusations from Melinda's friends. But I figured it would fly with Cochran. If the teacher got the band to the Rose Bowl he must be pretty good.

"He's all right, I guess. Only met him a few times," Cochran said. "But he does good with the band."

"Doesn't sound like you're crazy about him."

"I think he's gay. Like he-oughta-come-with-track-lighting gay," Cochran said. "It's just uncomfortable for a guy like me, you know? I don't like being around 'em."

What I knew about big burly guys who get uncomfortable with gay men is that they need to turn that spotlight inward. I thought about all the times my brother had been picked on by homophobic creeps. I slid my card onto the table. "Please don't hesitate to call if you think of something."

"Thank you, Miss Street. I heard about how they treated you at the Silver Spoon. Molly wouldn't have let that happen if she'd been there. Somebody put something on your windshield?"

"A note," I said casually. "Did you hear who put it there?"

"Nah, but you know how rumors get started in a small place like this. The sheriff is an eligible bachelor." He said it with a half smile, without bitterness, with something close to admiration. I thought again about the text from Molly Cochran the sheriff had ignored. They were friends, I kept telling myself. He was investigating the murder of her daughter. It was normal. "And some people might have thought y'all looked awful cozy over breakfast."

I smiled. "That's why I'm getting the cold shoulder?"

He shrugged. "Some cops might think you're here to make them look bad. Mostly people aren't used to having an outsider asking questions. Outsiders are usually just tourists. People are private around here."

"So I've heard," I said.

"And, well, you're a woman and, you know, an Oriental."

———

He'd seen her on the periphery, coming out of that little stretch of woods behind the park. Right on time. That's the thing about good girls. You can count on them.

He didn't look up. Not even when he felt her next to him, bending into his raised hood, peering into the engine as he was.

"Whatcha doing over here?" She turned her head and smiled at him. He could smell the grape bubblegum in her mouth. His pulse tapped against his collar. "What's wrong with it?"

"Wish I knew," he said.

She looked back at the engine. "You going to fix it with duct tape?" She giggled at the roll of silver tape sitting on the radiator.

He laughed with her. "Guess I should have learned something about cars." He rubbed engine dirt off his hands onto the shop rag he'd stuffed in his pocket. "I can't find my phone. I need to call somebody."

He watched her reach into the leather bag that hung off her slim shoulders and pull out a phone in a rubbery pink case. Her little pink lifeline. She was going to give it up, just hand it over. And she did.

He keyed in a number, tucked the phone against his shoulder, and leaned back to look at the engine. She leaned in too as if she might be able to help. He jiggled a hose around with the rag, but he was barely aware of his own movements now. His heart was fluttering like a hummingbird. A recorded message that her family had made was playing in his ear, the three of them together taking turns saying their names. *Hi, this is Brooks. And Hayley. And Skylar.* And then all together—*And Luke. You know what to do after the tone.* Yes, he certainly did know what to do.

He talked over the message as if he were giving someone his location. But that was the rehearsed part of him, the part that functioned automatically, the survivor. He listened to their voices while he had his fake conversation, to them pretending to be happy. He got it all out before the beep, before voice mail could record him.

He felt himself pulling in air and letting it out slowly. Something in his body, something carnal and inborn, was preparing him for the moment when everything coiled and waiting would spring savagely to life. He'd waited to feel it again. He lived for it, for her, for this moment, for the scent of that bubblegum in her mouth.

He smiled over at her, put his hand on the back of her neck casually. "Thanks for your help," he said. For someone so smart, she was so fucking clueless.

He slammed her face down hard into his perfectly healthy engine. It stunned her for a few seconds, long enough for him to grab the tape she'd laughed at. He hit the hood brace with his elbow and ducked out of the way, watched the hood crash down, saw her back arch when the latch dug into her. Blood began to seep into her shirt. He jerked her arms back. She was screaming now. And kicking. He knew she would. She wasn't a victim. She was bossy and proud. She had plans. That's what he wanted. Someone with a brain. Someone with something to live for. Or else it just wouldn't be any fun at all.

He wasn't even thinking when he did it. He was just in that moment, that wonderful, crazy, terrifying *moment*. He needed her to shut the fuck up so he could get her in the vehicle and get off the road. He jerked her out from under the hood, spun her around, and swung a fist that landed just over the left cheekbone near the temple. She crumpled like a piece of foil. She'd never been hit. He could tell. Nothing bad like that had ever happened to her.

When he was done, when he'd dragged her around and deposited her limp body in the back like a sandbag, he finished taping her ankles and wrists and mouth. He looked quickly through the purse, wiped down and tossed out a nail file and a compact mirror, then dropped it next to her, pushing blond hair off her forehead. He ran a finger down her face, her neck, into her shirt. She was pretty. He couldn't wait for her to wake up next to him.

He removed the pink case from her phone and used the dirty rag to wipe off his prints. They'd find it. They'd examine it. Maybe the sheriff's hired gun would find it. Maybe her hands would be holding it soon. He smiled at that and tossed the case in the ditch, popped the back off the phone and dropped the battery into his pocket. He wiped down everything carefully, then snapped the phone back together and wedged it in front of one of his back tires.

As he drove away, he lowered the driver's window. He wanted to hear it, remember it, keep one more memory. You hold on to the little things—a warm battery in your pocket next to a swelling cock, the sound of tires crushing plastic and glass, driving it down into the dirt. Because whatever happened between them next, it would never be this new again.

19

I returned to the Whispering Pines Inn and fell across the hard bed. I needed a minute. I didn't know what to make of this day. I didn't even know where to start. But I couldn't forget where the day had begun, with Ken Meltzer jogging beside me, looking into my eyes over breakfast, inquiring about my empty ring finger in a not-so-subtle way as we drove, opening that door, practically kicking it in, the crazy chemistry between us, physical, undeniable. It skipped up and down my skin, up and down my spine, whenever I was near him. *Jesus*. I scrambled up, rubbed my face. What the hell was wrong with me? Mercury must be in Gatorade or something.

A killer had left a message on my windshield today, boldly walked up to my car and left his note with the same invisibility he had enjoyed when Tracy and Melinda disappeared. Nothing is more invisible than the everyday. He was a regular at the weird, cliquish diner. That's why no one gave him two looks in the parking lot. Or had they seen him? Were they protecting him? But why? Perhaps because they knew only a note had been left on my car, not the content, not what he was—a killer. Had he been there when I was there last night, this afternoon? I thought about the guys at the counter, the woman in the booth. I thought about the packed diner this morning over breakfast with the sheriff. Was he watching us even then?

And worst of all, Jeff Davidson had sliced himself open in a prison kitchen today after I'd assumed, wrongly, that he'd been informed his sister's remains had been discovered, and that after over a decade he would be prepared. I should have told someone immediately, a guard, the sheriff. As soon as I realized the news was new to him, he should have been put on suicide watch. I'd underestimated his emotion. Holding out hope that Tracy would come home one day was what had been keeping him alive. I hadn't seen it. And that weight hung heavy on me now. I thought about Josey Davidson and the rubble in her life, the loss. I thought about Bryant Cochran. *It breaks you, Miss Street. It takes a guy like me and snaps him right in half.*

I'd memorized every word of that note I'd found on my windshield today. Now I wrote it on my legal pad and stared at it.

> *Dear Keye,*
>
> *I'm thinking about you too. I thought you would want to know that. I know they hired you to find me. I know all about you. I've wanted someone to talk to.*
>
> *Listen hard. Can you hear me? More soon.*

He was reaching out. That was the good news. He wanted to communicate, to be understood. He was flattered by the attention and probably obsessed by it. My fear and my near certainty was that I would receive his promise of more at yet another crime scene. That's really what the note was about. He wanted us to know he was still out there. And still hunting.

I propped up on the hard bed with hard pillows, which was terrible for sleeping but, as it turns out, pretty good for reading. I did what I always do when in an investigation: read and reread statements, the police reports, every name and every word; go over my notes; write down every step I took today and every piece of information I gathered, what Melinda's friends said, what Jeff told me about Tracy's life. Where did they intersect and who had access to both victims? The answer to that defined the suspect pool—neighbors, coaches, counselors, parents of schoolmates, family members. I thought about the band teacher who had been overlooked, Mr. Tray, and got out my laptop to find his address. If he wasn't at school tomorrow, I was going to have to pay him a visit at home.

My phone rang, a 706 area code, a local call. I answered and heard a familiar voice. "Hey, Rob Raymond here. Figured you'd wanna know that the lab couldn't pull anything off that letter you got. No prints. No trace."

"Too much to hope for, I guess," I said.

"Sheriff's department issued a statement today," he told me. "On our website and on social media with info from your profile so locals know what to look out for. It's getting some attention."

"What kind of attention?"

"Brenda Roberts," he said, and I froze. She was a television journalist in Atlanta with a fascination for my past and for my relationship to APD and Rauser. She'd asked many times for an interview. So far I'd managed to avoid her.

"You spoke with her?"

"Yep. She asked for the detective in charge of the investigation relating to our press release and they sent her call to me. She wanted to know who compiled the profile."

"Shit," I muttered.

"I told her we'd reached out to the Bureau, which is technically true."

"Thanks," I said.

"I didn't do it for you. I did it so your shit doesn't muddy up our investigation."

"Investigation?" I said. I wasn't in the mood for Raymond. "You did it because you don't want any extra scrutiny. Because you know you botched the job. How do you perform an investigation if you can't even compile a victimology, Detective? The information on file about Melinda Cochran's life and habits and family is full of holes."

"We knew her," he insisted. "We didn't need a bunch of extra paperwork."

"Well, that kind of half-assed work ethic is why I'm here. By the way, did you know Melinda walked home by herself one day a week?

Did you know she stayed late for band practice? Did you realize that time after school away from friends and parents might have been her first exposure to her killer? Maybe he got to know her then. Maybe she came to trust him. This offender is a planner. He lays his trap and waits."

I could hear the rasp of his breathing, but he said nothing.

"What do you know about the band teacher?" I asked.

"He's a hero around here. He put us on the map with that band. Our athletic programs suck."

"Thanks for your call, Detective." I stabbed the END CALL button with my finger and cursed.

When my phone bleated again a few minutes later, it wasn't Detective Raymond. "I haven't eaten since breakfast," Kenneth Meltzer informed me. "You hungry?"

"Starved," I said. I didn't add *exhausted, discouraged,* and *pissed off.*

"There's a little place just outside the city limits that makes a great quesadilla. Where are you now?"

I hesitated, and the sheriff caught it. "Come on. We both need dinner and it's been one heck of a day."

"Yes, it has," I agreed.

"You remember the bridge you used to come into Whisper? I'm five minutes from there. I'll wait for you on the other side. You can follow me."

I put my computer to sleep, took it to the hotel safe that was built into the closet wall. It had a digital readout that allowed you to choose the combination. I chose four random numbers and committed them to memory, slipped my computer, my Glock, my camera, and my notes inside, closed the door, and pressed the LOCK button. Metal slid into position with a satisfying click.

Nine minutes later I was crossing the bridge that had first led me into Whisper. The cars in front of me were tapping their brakes. I had a feeling I should be putting on the brakes too. But I wasn't.

His Interceptor was sitting on the shoulder like a speed cop. He swung out in front of me and I followed him a mile to a twisty unmarked road carved out of thick pine forest. After another half a mile, we turned onto a dirt lane. Red dust flew up in front of me. We passed a few cottages, well tended, newish. Some of them had signs in the yard with names. Rentals, I decided.

The road ended at a wide drive and a cluster of log homes on a slightly elevated piece of land. A wooden bench-swing hung off the limb of an old water oak. Giant pecan trees skirted the property. Pebbled paths split off from the driveway to each of the three homes on the hill. I got out. The sheriff came around to my car.

"What's this?" I asked, confused.

"It's where I live." He spread his arms and smiled as if it were perfectly normal to bring your consultant home for dinner. "Mom lives in the center cabin," he told me as we walked up a path toward his home—a three-level cabin with an A-frame center. I glimpsed water in the background, Lake Oconee shimmering in the setting sun. I remembered him telling me the coroner was a real estate agent. I'd made a joke about deals on waterfront property. *Oops.*

"Who lives in that one?" I pointed to the small cabin at the right end of the semicircle.

"Mom's caretaker. Mom needed help and we didn't like the assisted-living facilities around here. So we bought this place together." We stepped up on his porch and he pushed open an unlocked front door. A golden retriever mix let out a yelp and scrambled up on hind legs as if she was coming off a launching pad. Paws hit Meltzer's chest. He rubbed her head and under her ears playfully. "Keye Street, meet Ginger."

She dropped off him and looked at me. The back half of her body moved in the opposite direction of her wagging tail. She had the head and face of a golden retriever, long legs, a chow's bushy tail and lion mane, and I wasn't sure about the rest of her. Apparently there had been a party. Some chows showed up, some golden retrievers, a cocker spaniel. Ginger was what my mother's rescue buddies called a splendid-blended. "Hi, Ginger." I bent and petted her. The wagging speed increased. She handed me her paw. I shook it, said, "Good girl."

Meltzer pushed the door open. "Go do your thing and come back."

Ginger shot through the door and down the steps. "Pulled her out of an Animal Control truck about a year ago. One of the perks of being sheriff." He winked.

We had stepped into an open area with a tall A-slanted roof, a stone fireplace, a kitchen on one side, railed stairs rising to a loft above us. Meltzer went to the kitchen and pulled a pan from a cabinet.

"I always wanted a cabin in the woods. And it means Mom can stay home. Patricia is full-time so I don't have to worry too much when I'm not here." He opened the refrigerator. "I've got white cheddar and baby spinach. How's that?"

"Perfect." My stomach felt like a big, empty cave. I would have eaten the ass-end out of a rag doll about then.

"Bathroom's down the hall if you need it." He pulled out a plastic container. "Downstairs is locked because the steps are steep and Mom could fall. Gym equipment mostly, laundry room. Nice view of the lake on the balcony off my bedroom upstairs, though. Make yourself at home."

The downstairs was neat but lived-in. I looked up at the loft. I wanted to go up there, see what his bedroom looked like, if the bed was made, if it was messy, or if he was one of those guys who used a tube squeezer on the end of the toothpaste. I mean, how much more perfect was this man? He rescued dogs, taught kids on his day off, cared about rehabilitating prisoners, and took care of his mother. I went back to the kitchen. Meltzer was opening a package of flour tortillas. "So what does a county sheriff have to drink?" I opened the fridge, saw tomato juice, two percent milk, an open bottle of Chardonnay with a purple silicone wine stopper. "Interesting," I said, in my best Colonel Klink.

"Uh-oh. Am I being profiled based on my choice in beverages?" He loaded tortillas with spinach, heaped them with cheese, folded them on a dry skillet, and lit the flame on a gas range. His arm brushed against mine as I searched for a glass. He grabbed one out of the cabinet and put it on the counter for me.

"It's the orange juice guys you have to worry about," I told him and took my tomato juice to the table. Pecan trees shaded the thick, green lawn; his mother's cabin was just yards away. I didn't think I'd be able to live so close to my own mother. I took a drink of juice and wished it were a bloody Mary. I looked at Meltzer in his short-sleeved uniform, tanned, muscled arms, blond fuzz like corn silk on his forearms. "Scene techs find anything at Peele's place?" I asked.

He turned our quesadillas with a red spatula, glanced at me. "Little blood in the bathroom sink, but it would be unusual to find a man's sink without a little blood. We know it's Peele's blood type. DNA will come eventually. Digital specialist is looking over his devices. No weapons in the house, and the only pornography was for grown-ups. We did find an axe. He also has a woodpile and a fireplace. No blood evidence on the axe. Not a big surprise, is it? The man tore down his house. I'm convinced that renovation served a dual purpose—new house, destroyed evidence. He's not going to keep a bloody murder weapon around."

"Frustrating," I said. Logan Peele was a sexual sadist. I knew that. I'd seen my share. The nature of his past crimes, the two girls he was convicted of raping, the elements of the crimes, the things he said to them, the things he did to them, the fact that one of them was his own daughter—all confirmed that assessment. Victim suffering heightened his fantasies. I remembered his eyes, the smug way he looked at me while he held that ice cube to his swelling face. "They went over his truck too, right?"

Meltzer nodded. "Every inch. I've pulled one patrol off days and one off nights to keep an eye on him. We have a little gap but he'll be on our radar soon."

I wondered again if it was Logan Peele who had slipped the note under my windshield wiper. There was nothing in the language I could link back to him. But this offender knew every word would be analyzed. He'd be careful. He'd camouflage and manipulate and direct this investigation every chance he got.

The front door rattled and Meltzer left the stove to open it. Ginger rushed through the living room and found me at the table, nudged me with her nose. I petted her. "Does she get a treat or something?" Her ears came up at that, and her head cocked to the side.

"Now you've done it," Meltzer said. He pulled a box from a lower cabinet. Ginger ran to him. He gave her a treat and sent her to the living room. I watched her eat it over her bed, carefully clean up every crumb, then make about eighteen circles before she found the right position to lie down. Meltzer pushed our food from the skillet to a plate, brought plates to the table. He poured himself juice and sat down next to me. *"Bon appétit."*

Our glasses clinked. He held my eyes too long, until I looked down at the browned flour tortilla on my plate. White cheddar oozed out over wilted spinach. I took a bite. It was warm and gooey and comfort-foody. He watched me. "Not bad for a guy who lives with his mom," I told him.

"I tuck myself in too." That look again. The smile.

What was I doing here? I'm not one of those high school girls I talked to today. I know that if some guy is flirting with me and I agree to have dinner with him alone, there will be more flirting. And hopes. What was Ken Meltzer hoping for? A kiss? A beginning? Or just a quickie? Had he fantasized about fucking me in the upstairs loft? I took another bite and looked at him, at that full bottom lip, at his strong, tan hands, the too-long lashes. I thought about watching him pull the boat up to the dock when I first arrived and that long vein popping up in his biceps. I kind of wanted to run my tongue over it right now. I could see myself climbing those steps with him and watching his clothes come off. I could imagine the pressure of his hard body against my thighs, his hands, his mouth. *I could*. I admit it. Okay, so I have a history of outright sabotage. It's like I'd stayed up studying *The Anarchist Cookbook,* then applied it to my life—a poison-tipped dart here, a strategically placed incendiary device there. I thought about Rauser at home. Not boring, not easy, not perfect, wonderful Rauser. The man I loved. And yes, we have those days now, those days when we aren't intimate, when he barely brushes a kiss by me, remote-control days with him on the couch when he's not working, barely moving. But we were settling into something good. We were. So why were the walls closing in? I thought about him fuming over the silverware drawer, questioning me about the bond enforcement job I'd taken to bring in Ronald Coleman. I thought about how I dreaded those moments when he turned into my dad.

Meltzer was watching me. "I don't know if I want to ask what's going on inside your head."

"Probably not. How about your head?" He'd had a prisoner commit suicide inside his jail and he'd had to notify the boy's mother. He hadn't said a word about either. "Must have been a tough day."

"Awful. That woman, Mrs. Davidson, she's just like you said, a hard-luck case. She's worried about how to pay for the funerals of two kids. Tracy's remains are ready to be released." He slid his tortilla on the plate, reached for his glass. "Sometimes I'm glad I never had kids. I think the heartache might outweigh the rewards. Watching Molly and Bryant go through losing Melinda . . . I don't know how you get through something like that. How about you? You ever want that life?"

"Stay-at-home mom sounds kind of good. Only without the children." Meltzer chuckled. We ate quietly for a minute. "I talked to Bryant today and to Melinda's friends, the three girls she walked home with the day she disappeared."

"Anything interesting?"

"A music teacher named Tray." I didn't mention Cochran's homophobic comment about track lighting, that he'd told me the sheriff was *the* bachelor to catch, or that he'd listed the reasons everyone hated me—stranger, female, Asian. "Melinda had band practice once a week," I told him. "Tray's name isn't in the original reports. I went by the school but I missed him."

"We didn't talk to him at all?" He got up and came back with a bag of chips, poured some out on our plates.

I shook my head. "Would have been easy to miss without a thorough victimology. One of the hazards of knowing the victim. I'll give you a report in the morning with a list of everyone I've spoken to and what I've learned. Just so we're all on the same page. And I want to follow up on the band teacher tomorrow. You know anything about him?"

Meltzer ate a potato chip, shook his head. "Not anything personal. Tray really turned our band into something. Brings in a lot of support for the school. You like him for this?"

"I like him until he's excluded." I decided not to tell the sheriff what the girls had told me—rumors about the teacher's inappropriate behavior with the kids. Something about those girls felt off to me. I wasn't sure why they'd lie, and maybe they hadn't, but I wasn't ready to throw a man and his career under the bus. Not yet. "I need a background on him, residences, employment history, credit, criminal, whatever we can find. You want my office to run it?"

"We'll run it first thing. I'm not sure I can afford your office."

I took the last bite of my quesadilla, felt the string of cooling cheddar hit my chin. Ken Meltzer leaned over. I swallowed. He touched my chin with his napkin and looked into my eyes. Lightning shot through my body. He was going to kiss me, I realized. And I wasn't moving away.

The front door swung open. "Harold, I have been looking everywhere for you." It was a small woman with short gray hair. Her voice was scolding and age-dried. Ginger jumped up and ran to her. "Hello, Red," the woman said, and patted the dog.

Meltzer looked at me helplessly. "She thinks I'm Dad again. I'm sorry." He raised his voice. "It's okay, Mom. I'll be right there."

"Harold, who is that woman?" his mother demanded. Ginger was weaving around all our legs, panting, tail wagging.

"I'm Keye Street, Mrs. Meltzer." I went to her and held out my hand. She took it. "I'm working with the sheriff's department."

"Is that what you're calling it these days?" she said. She'd seen the almost-kiss. I froze.

Meltzer laughed. He took both her hands and looked at her. "Did you ditch Patricia again?" His voice was soft with his mother, patient.

She frowned. "I don't want to see that woman. She's a pain in the ass. Is *Castle* on? I think I'm missing *Castle*."

Meltzer picked up the remote control and handed it to me. "DVR," he said. "I have to check on Patricia."

"Can I watch with you?" I asked Mrs. Meltzer. She looked at me with the wide brown eyes she'd passed on to her son. I clicked the remote and sat down on the couch, patted the place next to me. In the background Meltzer was talking to the caretaker. Mrs. Meltzer sighed and sat down. Ginger jumped up next to her. I found the saved programs menu. Twenty-three episodes of *Castle*. I grinned up at Meltzer and got a shrug. I hit PLAY and we both leaned back into the couch. Mrs. Meltzer put the balls of small, bare feet against a leather storage square that doubled as a coffee table. I kicked off my shoes and did the same thing. She nodded her approval.

Meltzer hung up the phone. "Mom, Patricia says you were taking a nap while she was taking a shower."

"I tricked her." She was staring at the screen as the opening segment played. "Oh, I love this part. We need popcorn, Ken."

"Right." He went to the kitchen. I heard cabinets opening and closing, the microwave coming on.

"You know," Mrs. Meltzer confided to me in a whisper, her eyes fixed on the screen. "I can't remember one storyline in this show. I just want to see if they're going to make out."

"I hear ya," I said. She sent an elbow my way, a soft jab that meant we'd connected, shared a joke.

A few minutes later the cabin smelled like popcorn. I glanced over the back of the couch at Ken Meltzer awkwardly pulling a hot bag out of the microwave, throwing it on the counter like it was on fire. He caught me looking at him and mouthed, *Thank you*.

A minute later he sat down on the other side of his mother—Hitchiti County's sheriff, his rescued dog Ginger, his mother, and me on a couch watching network television and eating popcorn. It couldn't have gotten any weirder. I mean, I never watch network. But it was a welcome and strangely wonderful end to an otherwise dark day. I didn't know then that the day and the darkness were just beginning.

20

Meltzer's phone rang as I was preparing to leave. I'd just made it through my first-ever episode of *Castle*. I watched him check the display, answer while I talked to Mrs. Meltzer. He plugged one ear with his finger and walked quickly into the hallway. His body language had changed. Whatever news he was getting wasn't what he wanted to hear. I saw him click off a couple of minutes later and make another call. His voice stayed low. He returned and looked at me. "We have to go," he said. Then to his mother, "Mom, Patricia's coming over to watch TV with you, okay?"

The door opened and a heavyset woman walked in wearing knee-length shorts and flip-flops, a man's T-shirt. Her face was round and very plain but you had the feeling she was about to laugh. Brown bangs squared off over her eyebrows. She smiled at me. The sheriff didn't bother to introduce us. He had other things on his mind. He slipped into his harness and checked the S&W 40 he carried.

"Will you feed Ginger?" he asked the woman. "And make sure she gets out again before you leave?"

"You betcha," she answered and sat next to Mrs. Meltzer. "Want to watch some TV, Virginia?" Mrs. Meltzer's hand came across and patted her caretaker's knee.

We were out the door a second later. "We have a girl missing,"

Meltzer told me. His tone was curt. "Her name's Skylar Barbour. Wasn't home when her parents got off work. They called teachers, then they called her friends, and then they called us. We're taking it seriously. I have a bad feeling."

"Was she in school today?" I asked as we walked quickly down the pebbled path.

"All day. She appeared normal and not upset. Friends say they *saw* her walking toward home."

"So she disappeared between school and home. How far is that?"

"Not far, but she would have had to take a trail through those woods on the southeast edge of the park." There was a little jiggle in his voice because we were moving fast. "Here's what we have so far. Patrols took preliminary statements from the parents, who told them their daughter always takes the bus home. Tina Brolin was able to contact a couple of the girl's friends, who said she always walks home with them."

"So the parents are lying," I said. "Or their daughter was."

"Like I said, I have a bad feeling."

"Skylar's Caucasian?" I asked. "And blond?"

"Affirmative."

"Age?"

"Eighth grader," Ken Meltzer answered, grimly. "Thirteen. Same school where Melinda went." We stopped at our vehicles.

"But there's no evidence she was abducted," I reminded him. I was having trouble selling it. I had a bad feeling too. I was thinking about Logan Peele and the band teacher who'd flown under the radar and the greeting on my windshield, a warning, a promise. "Your offender, if this turns out to be his work, he hasn't had time to do what he does, Ken. He holds them. If he has Skylar, she's still alive."

"Jump in," Meltzer said, as if he hadn't heard me. "We're meeting Brolin and Raymond at the parents' place."

"I'll follow you." I got in my car and waited for him to pull out. I wasn't going to drive up with the sheriff after nine in the evening. I'd had enough trouble with Brolin and Raymond. Why feed them? And I was feeling guilty. To borrow from Jimmy Carter, I'd lusted in my heart. They'd smell it.

We wound back through Whisper, quiet and quaint and lamp-lit, and hiding so many secrets. The sheriff cut through a neighborhood off Main Street and we came out on a dirt road half a mile later. The marker said COTTONWOOD ROAD. It was pitch dark. No moon. No streetlights on country roads. I followed the sheriff's taillights through the dust, our headlights touching the fringes of a field with tall, blowing grass, rippling and rolling like a black sea in the dark night.

I saw the sheriff's vehicle turn past a mailbox; headlights hit white fences, a long ranch house at the end of the lane. Skylar Barbour had gotten dressed for school there this morning. And she hadn't come home.

Raymond and Tina Brolin were leaning against Brolin's Crown Vic. Raymond was smoking. Both looked grim. We joined them.

"Major Brolin," I said, and nodded. "Detective Raymond."

"The Barbours are waiting," Brolin said. She didn't look thrilled to see me. No doubt Raymond had shared our conversation with her. I'd scolded him for conducting a very sloppy investigation. It would be hard for her not to take that personally. I didn't care. How they handled it going forward would determine what kind of cops they really were.

"We're going to start at the beginning," Meltzer told us. "They came home from work to an empty house. Let's play it close. No need to alarm these people unnecessarily. And if there's something else going on here, we don't want them to clam up. Understood? We treat them like suspects, they'll dive for cover."

"With all due respect, Sheriff," Major Brolin said, "it's not our first rodeo."

I glanced at Meltzer, saw the muscle ripple across his jawline. "I'm well aware of that, Tina." He'd lowered his voice, but it had an edge I hadn't heard before. He'd also dropped her designation and used her first name. "I'm also aware that your last rodeo ended with the missing girl found dead in the woods eight months later. I'm going to make sure this doesn't end that way."

We followed the sheriff up the steps to a long railed porch. A German shepherd stood on the other side of a glass storm door. A low growl came through the glass. Meltzer pressed the doorbell, and the dog started to bark and show teeth.

"It's okay, Luke." A man in a business suit came to the door. He was late thirties with thinning brown hair. "Brooks Barbour," he told Meltzer, pushing open the door. They shook hands. "Thanks for coming."

"I'm Sheriff Ken Meltzer, and these are my investigators." He introduced us. Barbour invited us inside. Luke sniffed the air as we passed.

We found Mrs. Barbour sitting at an oblong table in the kitchen clutching a mug of something, shivering on this hot August night in Georgia, used Kleenex balled up around her. Luke sat down next to her chair. Hayley Barbour had the hollow, shocked eyes you see in hospital emergency rooms, seeing and not seeing. We all sat down at the table.

"We're anxious to get Skylar home, and I know you are too." Meltzer spoke gently. "Most of the time these things are just a matter of somebody getting their signals crossed, someone made plans and forgot to call." He was right. Kids don't come home all the time. Almost none of them have been abducted. "But that doesn't mean we're not taking this seriously. We know you're worried and we're here to help. We may have to repeat questions my deputies already asked but bear with us."

The Barbours nodded. "When was the last time you saw your daughter?" the sheriff asked.

"This morning." Hayley Barbour spoke for the first time. "I took her to school." She answered almost mechanically, like a sleepwalker.

"Did you speak to her during the day at all?"

She shook her head. "I didn't. Brooks, did you?"

"No. But that's normal," Brooks Barbour said. "We don't usually talk until I get home."

"What time is that, sir?" I asked. I was trying to put a time on her disappearance.

"I get home around six-thirty or seven," Brooks Barbour said. "But Hayley is home by five-thirty." Hayley nodded her agreement. Skylar was last seen around three o'clock. Which meant she had vanished sometime between three and five-thirty. A large window of opportunity. My heart sank.

"Was anything disturbed when you got home? Are any of Skylar's things missing?" I asked.

Hayley shook her head. "The deputies asked us to check for missing items but we didn't find anything." Her hand reached for Luke, her fingers disappeared in his thick fur.

"Can't you see what they're doing?" Brooks Barbour asked his wife. His voice was sharp and angry and shot through the room in accusing spirals. Luke leaned in closer to Hayley. "You're trying to figure out if she ran away, aren't you?" he asked Meltzer gruffly. "Our daughter would not run away. Something happened to her and you need to be out there. Right now. Looking for her."

Hayley didn't look at her husband. "I heard Luke whining through the door when I got home," she told us. "I knew right away something was wrong." One side of her mouth twitched. She bit back a sob. "He bounded out when I opened the door and ran up the driveway. He still hasn't settled down."

"What usually happens when you get home?" I asked.

"Skylar and Luke are in the den where she does homework," she told me. "Luke barely looks up when I come home. He's Skylar's dog." She covered her mouth and squeezed her eyes closed. "Oh God," she moaned. The icemaker buzzed, cubes dropped into a freezer tray. I glanced at Brooks. He'd looked away. Some people pull in close during a crisis. Some people curl up in a little ball. Or was his response more than that?

Detective Raymond took a notepad from his shirt pocket and put it on the table. He looked dead tired. The weight of his jowls and the bags under his eyes made him look like a cartoon dog. "I know you're worried to death," he said, in a voice I hadn't heard before. "I just need to verify some information we got from the responding officers. Skylar was wearing khaki-colored pants and a sleeveless green blouse. Is that correct?"

"Yes," Mrs. Barbour answered. "And a Nine West purse from Macy's. Small, oblong, tan with a wide black band and a square buckle. And pink Nikes."

Detective Raymond verified other details—birth date, names of teachers, friends—then asked for a photograph of Skylar. Brooks Barbour got up, disappeared somewhere in the house. Luke stayed with Mrs. Barbour.

"Does Skylar have a phone?" I asked.

Hayley nodded. "We've been calling it for hours." Tears filled her eyes and spilled down the pale skin of her cheeks. She pulled a fresh tissue from the box, clutched it. "It was her birthday present."

"Can you describe the phone?"

"It's an iPhone," Brooks told us. "In a pink OtterBox." He'd returned with a framed photograph, a five-by-seven with the swirly gray-blue backdrop of a school picture. I studied the face of a smiling blond girl with her father's brown eyes, a navy sweater vest over a white collared shirt.

"Would you mind writing down Skylar's cell phone number for us?" Meltzer asked.

Hayley found a notepad and scribbled down a number. "We've called the provider already," she told us. "There's an app that finds it when it's lost, but there's no signal." Her voice wobbled. So did her hands.

"Did the mobile provider tell you where the GPS went out?" I asked.

"No," Hayley answered. "I . . . I didn't think to ask. I don't understand any of this. I talked to her friends. I called her teachers. Skylar was at school all day. She wasn't sick. She was *fine*. She wasn't talking about doing anything but going home. And the bus drops her right at the end of the driveway. Her friend Pam told me she walked home today. I don't understand that . . ."

"Skylar walked home every day," Major Brolin said flatly. Meltzer's head jerked in Brolin's direction. The total lack of empathy in her tone made even Raymond's head turn. "Her friend didn't tell you that?"

"What are you talking about?" Brooks Barbour lowered himself into a chair.

Brolin took her time. She had a notepad in her hand. She flipped one page, then another. "I spoke with the bus driver." Another page turned. She squinted. "One Vicki Bello. Said Skylar's been on the bus only one day since the school year began. That was the first day of school."

"That can't be right," Hayley insisted. "Skylar *was* riding the bus this year. We made her. Because those girls were found in the woods just before school started. Brooks . . ." She looked beseechingly at her husband.

"Are you telling us you really don't know how your daughter gets home in the afternoons?" Brolin's tone stayed accusing. "Or are you deliberately omitting information?"

"Just exactly what are you trying to say?" Brolin was pushing Brooks's buttons and we were all discovering he had a hair trigger. "Is this how your department treats *victims,* Sheriff? Because we're not the bad guys. We're the ones that called you to help us find our daughter!"

"Was Skylar upset about anything this morning? Maybe you noticed something was bothering her recently?" I suggested, and kept my voice even, hoping some of the tension would dissipate.

"So now you're on the runaway thing again?" Mr. Barbour jumped up, his cheeks flushed. "What the hell is going on here? Get out there and *find my daughter*."

"We have an active and organized search going on right now, Mr. Barbour," the sheriff assured him. "Patrol units are on it. They have Skylar's description and all the information you've already supplied. We'll get her photo out right away too. But we have to collect as much information from you as we can. Your cooperation will make this process go faster."

"The questions may be upsetting to you, Mr. Barbour," Brolin added. "But it's what we must do in order to help Skylar." It was the first decent thing out of her mouth since we'd arrived. I was starting to hate her even more than I did yesterday. Meltzer told me at breakfast she was smart. I wasn't getting that.

"Mr. Barbour," Meltzer said calmly. "If your daughter was upset about something, say, a boy, she might go to a friend, want to talk to someone. See where we're going? Maybe just a new place to look."

"I don't know," Mr. Barbour answered impatiently. His fuse had been lit and he was having trouble putting it out. "We made a list already for the deputies. And Hayley talked to most of her friends. We've called everyone."

"We had a fight." Mrs. Barbour admitted it so quietly I almost didn't hear her.

"*Hayley,*" her husband warned, but she kept going.

"It was nothing." She wouldn't look at us. "I mean, she just turned thirteen. She wants to do things we don't think she's ready for."

"What things, exactly?" I asked, gently.

"She wanted to ride with friends to a dance Saturday," Hayley answered. "I don't want her in a car with a bunch of teenagers. And she doesn't want to be dropped off by her parents. It's the kind of arguments we have now."

"Can't you get an Amber Alert out or something?" Brooks asked.

"Not until we're certain Skylar has been abducted," Major Brolin announced with characteristic sensitivity. She was mad at me and maybe at the sheriff and she was taking it out on the family of a missing girl.

"Abducted?" Hayley gasped. Of all the ugly possibilities swirling in her brain, this one clearly hadn't occured to her. Mr. Barbour paced to the end of his kitchen, rested hands on the sink, stared out the window at the darkness. Meltzer stirred. I wondered how long he was going to let Brolin hammer at them.

"Mrs. Barbour," Brolin continued, "do you know the whereabouts of your daughter?"

"*No,*" Hayley answered with a frantic whimper.

Brooks came back to the table fast. Rage seemed to be the only emotion he was good at. And he was really good at it. "Please fucking tell me you are not delaying looking for our daughter because we're *suspects*. It's *bullshit* about patrols, isn't it? Goddamnit, what do you want us to *do*?"

"Brooks," his wife begged. "Please." She looked at Brolin with wet eyes. "She just wasn't here when I got home. Luke was crying. I told you. I knew she hadn't been here to let him out. The door was locked. Skylar's so bad at remembering to lock doors . . ." She faltered.

"So you're willing to take polygraph tests?" Brolin persisted. "Tonight?"

"Jesus," Mr. Barbour rasped. "Whatever. Right now. We'll both fucking go right now if it means you start doing your jobs."

Meltzer had had enough. "Would you excuse us? Major Brolin, would you mind stepping outside with me?" He stood and so did Brolin. Meltzer looked down at Hayley Barbour, who was destroying another Kleenex with her fingers. "Every unit we have available is looking for Skylar right now. And if she's not home soon, we will have feet on the ground checking every inch of this town. No bullshit. You have my word."

21

Meltzer and Brolin left the kitchen. Raymond sat forward, clasped his big hands on the table. "I have a teenage boy," he said. "I do the best I can. But sometimes our kids, they hide things from us. They want their own life. You can't blame yourself for not knowing where they are every second."

Brooks Barbour drooped down into a chair. With Brolin out of the room, it no longer felt like a combat zone. Mrs. Barbour wrapped her hands around her mug. "Skylar complained about the bus," Hayley said softly. "She had to ride the entire route before it dropped her off. Ninety minutes. She could walk home in fifteen. Brooks and I both work. I'm only able to pick her up at school once a week. We told her about those girls they found in the woods. We talked to her about stranger danger. She took it seriously. I know she did."

Detective Raymond used his phone to copy the photograph of Skylar, then tapped at it with beefy fingers. The photo would go to headquarters, and soon, I knew, every patrol on the street would have a picture of Skylar Barbour's face. My phone vibrated and lit up a few seconds later. Raymond had copied me.

"Did Skylar ever mention talking to anyone on the way home?" I asked.

"No." Hayley shook her head.

"How about other family members? Grandparents, aunts, uncles? Does Skylar ever go anywhere else after school?"

"No." Again it was Hayley who answered. "To Pam's house sometimes, but only with permission. We don't have family here. We've only been here two years. Brooks was transferred. He's in the hotel business."

"Did she have a favorite place?" I asked. "Some of the kids hang out around that Coke machine over on Main Street and the ice-cream shop."

"I don't know." Hayley's voice was full of frustration and fear. She was starting to realize she really didn't know what her child was doing. Her eyes met mine, wide and panicked as the unflinching tsunami of doubt rushed at her. "You think someone did something to her, that man who killed those girls." It wasn't a question.

"If someone saw Skylar today, it might help us," I said evenly. "That's all."

She picked up the framed photograph of her daughter. A fingertip passed over the navy sweater, the collar of Skylar's white shirt, then traced the young, pretty face. "I don't know . . ."

"I don't know either," Mr. Barbour said. Some of the red had washed out of his face. But his skin was splotchy. And he was thoroughly annoyed by our questions. "Again, we didn't realize she wasn't taking the bus."

"But she walked home from school last year, correct?" Raymond asked. "What was her routine then?"

"Her friends would know," Hayley answered as Luke's attention shifted and Sheriff Meltzer walked back in. Brolin wasn't with him. "Do we really need to come to the station tonight?" Hayley asked him. "I'd like to be here . . . in case Skylar comes home." Luke whined, pushed his muzzle into her hand.

"Of course not," the sheriff said. "Wait for your daughter here. Try not to worry. It's still early. She could be at a movie or something." He sat down next to her. Luke watched him; so did Brooks. Neither looked friendly.

"Skylar would never do that without permission," Brooks said, then threw up his arms. "Oh hell, what am I saying? I guess I don't know what she'd do without permission, do I?" He rubbed his face like it itched. "It's actually comforting to think she might have just said fuck the rules, fuck my parents, and she's off somewhere with some boy I'd hate. That would actually be a relief."

"Well, the odds are on that kind of scenario," Meltzer told them in a voice that made you believe him. "I wouldn't worry too much."

"We'd like to have something of Skylar's if you don't mind," Raymond said. "Her hairbrush, something like that. And an unwashed garment from the laundry basket." He was trying to make it sound like a casual request, trying hard not to disturb the thin veneer of calm in the room. But the look the parents exchanged said they understood.

"I'll get them," Brooks said.

"Do you mind if I go with you?" I asked. "I'd like to see Skylar's bedroom."

Mr. Barbour hesitated. "Show her, Brooks," Mrs. Barbour told him. "They want to help."

I followed him through the family room to a carpeted hallway. A handmade sign on a door at the end of the hall read KNOCK!!! The three exclamation points were each a different bold color to reflect the gravity of her command. I imagined Skylar dressing for school with all the concerns of a kid of thirteen. She was mad at her mom. I was willing to bet that she would give up all her resentments, even that dance on Saturday they'd argued about, to be home again now.

Brooks stopped at the bathroom door and flipped on the lights. He turned and looked at me. "If she walks in right now, we're in deep shit. This is Skylar's space."

"Ah," I said, and smiled. "Privacy issues. I had them too." I stood watching him from the hallway as he pulled a couple of drawers open. "I promise to take the blame if we get caught," I said.

He glanced up at me. And I saw it in his eyes. He knew Skylar wasn't going to walk in. He yanked open another drawer. "Her hairbrush must be in her purse. Or in her bedroom." He slammed the drawer shut.

"No worries. We'll find something. Hey, you look like you could use some fresh air."

He rubbed his face and eyes again, shook his head. "I'm okay."

"Is it all right if I check out her room now?"

"Do what you need to do," he said. "Her laundry basket is in the closet."

"Does Skylar keep a diary?" I asked.

For about half a second, I thought he was going to smile. "She has a diary. Hayley read some of it last year. So Skylar bought one with a lock."

"I'd like your permission to take it with me," I told him. "I'll return it."

"Just don't mention it. It will upset Hayley."

"Does she have a computer?"

"The one in the den. There's nothing personal on there except it's logged in to her social media." He started to walk away then turned back. "We should have never gotten her that damn iPhone. It was Hayley's idea. As soon as we handed it to her, we forfeited the ability to fully monitor her. What if she met some creep online?"

"You can't blame yourself or your wife because your daughter isn't home right now," I said. "Give it a little time. She'll get home."

"Alive?" he pressed. "Can you promise me that?"

"That's why we're all here." I met his furious gaze evenly. "To make sure Skylar gets home safely."

I watched him go back down the hall. Then I pulled on gloves. You don't know where a case will lead. Or where you might find a crime scene. Being careful to not corrupt potential evidence along the way is always a good idea.

I pushed open the closed door with the handwritten sign and stepped carefully over scattered clothing, books, and shoes. I wouldn't need the laundry basket. There was a teen magazine on the bed table, a TV remote. The remains of a glass of juice sat on top of a chest of drawers next to a half-eaten toaster pastry. I stood there looking at it. It was past dinnertime now.

A single shelf held up by L-brackets was loaded with books. I ran a gloved finger along the slick, unused spines of hardcovers—book-club editions of the classics. At the far end, the Harry Potter series and the *Hunger Games* trilogy were well worn.

There was a desk under the double windows, antique white like the bedroom suite. It was a simple writing desk with one center drawer. I pulled it open and exposed plastic heart-shaped paper clips, rubber bands, glue, scissors, pencils and erasers, a few pieces of copy paper, and a three-hole punch.

I heard a voice from the hall. Raymond appeared in the doorway. He held up a plastic bag with a toothbrush. "Barbour told me he couldn't find the hairbrush so I got this," he said. I reached deep into the drawer and felt around. "Got the last location on her phone," he said, and I stopped, looked up at him. "Maybe a sixteenth of a mile from the end of the driveway up Cottonwood Road. Near the walking path."

"So if she was abducted," I said, keeping my voice low, "he parked on the road and waited for her to come off the trail. It makes sense. He'd want her near his vehicle. He wouldn't want to overpower her in the woods and then have to drag her out."

Raymond checked the hallway, then stepped in and closed the door. His eyes swept over the mess that was Skylar's bedroom and saw what mine had seen: a teenager's room, not a crime scene. He picked a blouse off the floor and rolled it up. "Almost no traffic out here," he remarked. "It's mostly open land. This place and a few small farms farther down the road. That's about it. Nobody woulda seen him."

"Precautionary acts like surveillance—learning routines, knowing where to wait, disabling GPS—it's exactly the offender's MO in acquiring the other victims," I said, and ran my hand up under the desk along the bottom of the drawer. "You get her call log too?"

"Yeah. And get this: Her last call was to the landline in this house."

I pulled the drawer all the way out. "Why would she do that? She knew her parents weren't home. She would have called one of their cell phones."

"Million-dollar question right there," he said.

"Well, is there a message on voice mail here?"

"Nothing. Looks like she hung up before the introduction finished playing."

"That doesn't make sense," I said.

"No shit. Maybe it was a butt dial."

"Anything else jump out on her call log?"

"Haven't had a hell of a lot of time with it yet."

"You get me a copy once you know the numbers?"

"Sure thing," Raymond said. "You find anything?"

I peeled a piece of clear tape away from the drawer and held up the tiny aluminum key stuck to it. "Spare diary key. No diary yet."

"Those things have a two-dollar lock anyway," Raymond said. "I used to pick them all the time in order to invade my kid's privacy."

"Any guesses on where this kid hid her diary?"

"My boy hides everything in the bathroom," he said, opening the door. "Because he's such a friggin' genius."

"Want to have a look?" I picked up a silver cross that was lying on the chest of drawers. I slid open a drawer on a blue jewelry box that played a Disney theme song I recognized but couldn't name. There were a couple of silver bracelets and a leather wristband. I heard cabinets opening in Skylar's bathroom. I opened the second drawer and found birthday cards signed by Skylar's grandparents. Each had a crisp new fifty-dollar bill inside.

"Bingo," Raymond said, and came around the door. The diary was pink. "'Dreams, thoughts, and secrets,'" Raymond read the front, and held it up for me to see. A tiny pink padlock hung off the latch. "It was in an industrial-size tampon box."

"Well done," I said. I walked over to him and reached for the diary. He jerked it back. He had the reflexes of someone who'd been working twelve hours and started the day with a hangover. I was pretty sure I could take him. But I knew he'd resist more if I pushed for it. That's the kind of sweetheart he was. "Might be something in here we need," he said.

"Personally, I'd rather read Cyndi Lauper's memoir than stay up all night reading deep thoughts by a thirteen-year-old," I told him. "But you have to hand it over, Detective. And you know the sheriff would agree that I'm the one who needs to read it first."

His eyes narrowed. "All right. Okay." We both knew the sheriff would back me up. "But keep me informed. I am still officially the detective in charge of this investigation. And believe it or not, I give a shit."

I plucked the pink volume from his hand. "Thank you."

We walked out and I closed Skylar's door. We followed the hall, crossed the den. In the kitchen, Hayley Barbour was writing something on a sheet of paper. Raymond and I sat down; the diary I'd wedged in the back of my waistband cut into me. Skylar's rolled-up shirt was stuffed under Raymond's big arm.

"Mrs. Barbour is making a list of Skylar's after-school activities as well as friends and passwords to social media accounts," Meltzer told us.

Her tears had started again, falling on the thin paper on the tabletop. She squeezed the pen so tight, her index finger was deep red at the tip. Meltzer did what Hayley's shuttered-up husband seemed incapable of doing. He reached for her hand. It was a completely natural response, the desire to comfort. Luke let out another plaintive whine. "I'm going to use every resource we have to bring Skylar home," Ken Meltzer promised her. He looked at Brooks but didn't let go of Hayley's hand. "If you need anything, if you think of anything, no matter how small, call one of us. Doesn't matter what time."

We left cards with our private numbers on the table and walked through a hardwood foyer to the front door. I glanced into the living room, a long formal room, the kind families never use unless they have company. Then I stopped. Meltzer followed my eyes to a metal music stand with an open practice book. Advanced alto flute. Next to it a gunmetal-gray instrument case.

Skylar Barbour played flute in the school band, Brooks Barbour told us in the foyer, while sobs from the kitchen came down behind us like hard fists. She had band practice once a week. It was the day she was out of school late enough for Hayley to pick her up on her way home from work.

I checked the time. Ten p.m. Seven hours since Skylar stepped on a walking trail and disappeared into the woods.

22

We stood by our cars in the Barbours' driveway, Raymond, Meltzer, and I. Brolin's Crown Vic was gone. We didn't ask where she had gone. We didn't have to. Brolin had acted like an ass and Meltzer had given her a time-out.

"Hayley said Luke was going nuts when she got home," I told them. "Maybe the dog heard something. GPS went out up there on the road. Stands to reason that's our crime scene."

"If there is a crime scene," Raymond pointed out.

I shook my head. "The runaway theory really doesn't play for me. No clothes or other personal items are missing, except a hairbrush she probably carries with her every day. There's cash in her jewelry box. We found her diary. She'd never leave that for her parents to find. Add to that the locked door Skylar never remembers, Luke's behavior, the fact that we have witnesses who saw her step onto the path for home. She hadn't talked about having plans. She hadn't seemed troubled or preoccupied. Something bad happened after she stepped into those woods." I wished I had talked to Skylar's friends myself. Because if Brolin had come down like the hammer she was, the girls might have retreated, withheld the way kids do when they think they're in trouble. I thought about the three girls I'd talked to earlier, Melinda's closest friends. Something about that conversation was still bugging me.

"Maybe Barbour got carried away," Meltzer suggested. "The man is obviously a pressure cooker."

I nodded. "The only thing completely implausible at this point is that this girl killed her phone and ran away from home."

"Brooks Barbour is tripping my switches," Raymond said. "Seems like the kind of guy who could lose his shit. We'll check his alibi in the morning, talk with his employer."

"Get their phone records," Meltzer told him. "Let's make sure they've been calling Skylar's number and the provider like they said. And schedule polygraphs for first thing tomorrow. Right now, let's get some deputies. We'll come in from the park side of that trail. Rob, you start on this end of the woods. Keye, you take the road. And Rob—get that shirt wrapped up. Keep her scent fresh. We may have to get some dogs out here. Dark night."

As if on cue we all looked up at the sky. No moon. We followed the sheriff up the driveway and onto Cottonwood Road. Raymond pulled to the side. I parked behind him. Meltzer kept going. I took a super-bright LED flashlight from the glove compartment and felt under the seat for my Glock. It was in the safe at the hotel, I remembered. I hadn't taken it to dinner with the sheriff.

Raymond got out, looked back at me. "Happy hunting," he said, and clicked on his flashlight and headed into the woods.

I opened the back door of my car, tucked Skylar's diary into my scene case, got out a fresh package of gloves, and stretched them on. A tight glove on a hot night in Georgia is no fun. They don't breathe. It's uncomfortable. I stood there for a second getting my bearings in the starless night, then began crisscrossing the wide, rocky road. Out here away from the city and traffic all I could hear was the swampy buzz of insects and night birds rustling the leaves. I saw Raymond's flashlight weaving side to side as he stepped in the tree line on a beaten-earth path and began his search. What we found tonight and where we found it would speak volumes about what had happened to Skylar Barbour. And how it had happened. Every chilling, screaming detail. Brooks Barbour said she'd carried a purse. Had it been dumped in a struggle? Had someone tossed it aside and left us with prints, trace evidence, DNA?

There was a ditch on the right edge of the road. I followed it, slowly sweeping my light around the area, then crossed the road again, taking short steps, trying to illuminate as much ground as I could. It wasn't enough. A flashlight didn't have a chance against a country night. I went back to my car, turned it around. My headlights lit up the road. And I was looking at Brooks Barbour and Luke. My breath caught. I threw the car in park and got out. "Mr. Barbour, what can I do for you?"

"I saw your light from the house. If you think she's out here somewhere, I want to help."

"I'm sorry," I said. "I'm going to have to ask you to leave."

"I get it. I'm a suspect. You think I'll mess with evidence or something but—"

I interrupted him. "This area has to be protected until it can be thoroughly searched. Please leave now."

"Look," Barbour insisted. "I'm not the most demonstrative guy in the world. I admit it. But I love my daughter. I would never hurt her."

"You'll have a chance to say whatever you need to say in the morning at your interview and polygraphs. I'm sorry," I repeated.

"You haven't met Skylar." He wasn't leaving. "If you had, you'd remember her smile, her great big wide smile . . ." His voice trailed off. I waited. It was the first time I'd heard emotion from him that hadn't instantly turned to anger. "We won't survive this, me and Hayley. Our marriage, I mean. Skylar's our glue. And now we're in that house together. And I realize I can't even stand to look at her without our daughter in the room."

"Go home, Mr. Barbour," I said. "Be kind to your wife. And wait."

"At least take Luke," he said. "He's Skylar's dog. He can help."

I wasn't sure if Luke would like that idea, but it sounded good to me. I held my hand out. Barbour dropped the leash. Luke came forward, sniffed my fingers, then leaned against my leg—the big dog hug. I rubbed his shoulders and back. He sat down next to me. "Good boy," I told him as Barbour's footsteps crunched away from me. Luke made no move to follow him.

I watched until he was a dim shadow in the light from my headlights, then picked up Luke's leash. "He's not the most touchy-feely guy, is he, fella?" Luke looked up at me. "I guess it's just you and me." He stood up with a dog's intuition. He knew he had a job to do.

We started to walk, Luke putting his nose alternately in the air to catch a scent too faint for a human's blunt senses, then to the road as he led me until my headlights were too far away to provide enough light and I had to switch on the flashlight again.

The dog's pace suddenly picked up. He was pulling me and he was strong. I was trying hard not to slide on gravel. He stopped, made a few circles in the middle of the road, whined, then strained his leash and tugged me toward the ditch. I felt that rush every investigator gets when they know something's about to happen, something hidden is about to be revealed—excitement tinged with dread and fear.

Luke pulled me to the edge of the ditch. I made him sit while I swept my light over tangled grass. The ditch was dry from weeks without rain, and the sandy bottom was smooth from the runoff of storms past. I caught a glimpse of something in clumps of weeds on the side of the bank. "Stay, Luke," I commanded. He shifted nervously on his haunches but obeyed while I climbed down awkwardly into the ditch and pushed through a mound of broad-leaved weeds with gloved hands. I felt it, and then went in for a closer view with my flashlight, carefully separating the grass. A pink case with a bitten apple on the back that said OTTERBOX. My light picked up something glistening on the case, a tiny smudge. I said a silent prayer for ridge detail, pulled out my phone, snapped a picture, then called Ken Meltzer.

"I found something," I told him. "It fits the description of the case on Skylar's phone. We need lights out here, Ken. Before whatever else we have is lost or contaminated. Can you send Raymond back with evidence tags and bags? I don't want to move until we can collect the evidence and mark this spot. And I need to turn off my headlights before my battery dies."

I knelt next to Luke, put my arm around him. I heard his tail thumping against the road. That's the thing about dogs. They have this beautiful way of experiencing joy on even the darkest days.

Ten minutes later, I saw a light bobbing through the woods. Raymond went to his car first, then walked over to mine and cut the lights. "What's he doing here?" Raymond eyed Luke cautiously.

"Long story," I replied.

"I don't like dogs," he grouched. "Sheriff said you found something."

I shone my light on the spikey grass and weeds. Raymond stepped down into the trench and leaned in with his light. "Well, look at that," he murmured.

"I thought it would be better if you bagged it in case evidence is challenged later."

"Good thinking," Raymond said.

"There's something in the road too. Luke smelled something."

Raymond snapped a couple of pictures, then zip-tied a manila tag to the spot where the phone case had lain and climbed back out with the phone case in an evidence bag. We stood there, Luke leaning against my leg, panting, Raymond and I staring down into the ditch.

"I was thinking about the evidence in the Melinda Cochran case," I told him.

"Yeah," Raymond answered. "That's right. A phone. The battery was gone. No prints on the pieces we found. It was busted up in the middle of the road."

We exchanged a look. I put Luke on my left and let him lead the way. He did, his nose to the ground. He found a spot just left of the center of the road and began working in circles. Raymond and I swept our flashlights around the area.

"I've got something," I said after a few minutes. My light swept over a crushed glass screen, tiny dusty shards. My heart sank. It had been an iPhone. We'd probably run over it ourselves.

I took a picture, and Raymond pulled an ink pen from his pocket, squatted next to the flattened phone, used the pen to flip it over. Glass fell out of the shattered frame onto the road. Raymond looked up at me.

"No battery," he said.

23

The floodlights arrived, clusters of them mounted on tall tripods and set up on the road like a movie crew was at work. Meltzer's team moved carefully around the taped-off spot we'd determined was our crime scene, the point where I knew Skylar Barbour had lost control of her young life. A generator rumbled. A dozen deputies and a K-9 unit had been briefed before they spread out over the area. Temporary road posts were set up so scene tape could be attached and a perimeter could be built. The road had been blocked and closed. Raymond had taken photographs and left markers where he'd bagged evidence. He now paced slowly inside the big square, eyes on the ground. A crime-scene technician had taken charge of the evidence he'd bagged, marked and organized and stored it, then knelt on the road collecting samples from dirt and glass. I stood watching her, Luke at my side.

"I know you," the technician said. She glanced up at me. A strand of hair fell on her forehead. She blew it back. "We studied a case you worked on in school. The Marshland Murders. Master class in nailing an offender with trace."

It had been my first case with BAU-2. I'd produced a profile that differed from the working profile at the Bureau. I didn't believe the offender was someone who cruised I-95 in Florida waiting for an opportunity. I was convinced he made his own opportunities and that he wasn't a stranger to his victims. I took a lot of heat for arguing my theory against more experienced agents and behavioral analysts. But I had known I was right. I *knew* him. Some cases, it's like the stars align. Everything makes sense. That's what happened for me with the Marshland Murders. In the end, I'd fingered a suspect and shadowed him on my own time. One blazing Florida afternoon I'd followed him out of the city and watched him back his truck into what I would later discover was his dump site. I watched him roll a barrel off his truck. I surprised him that day. He didn't fight. He could see my hand trembling on the Glock and the sweat from my hairline. He knew I'd fire and he was right. The FBI pulled nine bodies from the marsh fifteen yards away, each of them in a fifty-five-gallon steel drum—a bobbing, shifting, floating graveyard. The killer was a landscaper and handyman, the kind of guy who'd volunteer to clean a neighbor's gutters, an all-around great guy, a husband, father, friend, who had been slitting the throats of boys and women and stuffing them in metal barrels and dumping them in the glades for years. Scientists were able to connect him to all the murders with tiny particles from the cypress mulch he used in his business. It was on his clothing and shoes and in his vehicle and on the victims and inside the barrels. And the steel drums he was using left more trace evidence: Tiny, nearly invisible flecks of paint had chipped off the drums when he'd loaded them or when a drum tipped over and rolled on his truck bed. They sealed the killer's fate in the trial phase as tightly as if they'd closed the lid of one of his steel drums. Good old-fashioned police work, as Rauser would say, is usually what leads you to your suspect. It was the case that sent my career and my reputation soaring.

"I remember it," I told the tech.

"I'd shake your hand if I could," she said. "I'm Sam."

"Nice to meet you, Sam. Listen, that phone case you tagged into evidence—I noticed a smudge of some kind on it." I handed her my phone and she studied the picture I'd snapped of the case and the shiny smudge. "It's some kind of oily substance. Really interested in what it is."

"Sure thing," she said. She had the kind of southern accent that made *thing* sound like *thang*.

"I want to have Melinda Cochran's phone pulled from evidence and rechecked as well," I told her.

Sam nodded. "Will do."

The sheriff joined us. Sam stood up holding an evidence bag full of glass in one gloved hand and tweezers with a tiny piece of black glass in the other. She slipped the tiny piece of glass into a separate small bag and laid it on top of something that looked like a toolbox, hit it with bright light. We leaned in to have a look. "I think we have a serial number." She read off the number. The sheriff jotted it down, then walked over to where his detective was still walking the area with his eyes locked on the road. I saw Raymond get on his phone immediately, and I knew he was contacting the manufacturer—the advantages of a 24/7 world.

Sam returned to the place in the road where she'd been collecting evidence. Luke whined at my left leg. "We've got blood evidence," Sam announced a moment later. I followed her light to a single spot in the dirt, smaller than a dime, rusty brown under the artificial light. She took pictures of the stain with a bright flash.

"What can you tell about the stain?" I asked.

She looked up at me. "I'm not a spatter analyst but it's a drip stain. Edge characteristics and directionality says it came straight down. Careful where you walk, Dr. Street. Maybe we got the offender here too. Whatever happened, it didn't involve a lot of blood. I'd say he probably hit her here, though."

Luke whined again, stuck his nose to the ground. He could smell the blood on the road. He'd gone around in circles at something I couldn't see. His owner's blood. Skylar's scent. I decided to walk him home. He'd had enough, and I needed to clear out while the scene was being processed.

I kept thinking about that school picture, the smiling, brown-eyed girl in a sweater vest. I didn't want her to be on a hard floor in some dark basement. I didn't want to think about those bright eyes growing dark and hollow. But the similarities with the other cases were too great to ignore—the MO, the missing battery, the crushed phone, the time of day, the age, race, gender, hair color.

I started down the road. I felt Luke's tail hitting my leg, heard him panting, felt his pace quickening. He was excited to be going home.

Fast footfalls on the pebbly road caused both Luke and me to turn. Luke growled. "It's okay, boy," Meltzer crooned. He held out a hand for Luke to sniff. "It's just me. Thought I'd walk you. Good idea using the dog, by the way. Gave us a jump on finding that phone case."

"He found the blood too. But it wasn't my idea. Brooks Barbour showed up with Luke."

"Barbour walked up there?" the sheriff asked.

"Made my antenna go up too," I said. Luke stayed close to my leg.

"What did he want?"

"Wanted me to know how much he loved his daughter. Said he wanted to help."

"Interesting." Meltzer was frowning. "You buy it?"

"He confirmed he can't stand his wife. I believed that part. Jury's still out on the rest."

Meltzer's phone rang. He answered and listened, then said, "Okay, thanks. First thing tomorrow, cross-check all the teachers at Skylar's school with the school in Silas that Tracy Davidson attended. Run home addresses too. Let's see if any of them made the move from one area to the other. Start with Daniel Tray, the music teacher. Keye's going to talk to him tomorrow. I want her to have whatever we can get first." He disconnected. "Using your investigative strategy, Dr. Street." I saw his white teeth in the dark and heard the grin in his voice.

"Hence the exorbitant consulting fee," I reminded him.

"That was Rob," he said. His deep, fireside voice grew serious again. "It confirmed the serial number is one of three active devices registered to Brooks Barbour's account. We'll check the Barbours' phones but I think there's little doubt it was Skylar's."

We walked for a couple of minutes. I could hear the rustle of his uniform, his breathing, feel his hips lightly bump into me as we walked. And I felt all those dueling emotions too—exhaustion, excitement at new evidence, sadness at what the evidence meant, guilt at my attraction to a small-town sheriff, and astonishment that the physical pull of his body so close to mine was enough to stir me even in the middle of an investigation. Nothing an addict's brain enjoys more than a little inner chaos. It's like jet fuel. Those pathways had been carved out years ago, and they opened up wide for just about any emotional roller-coaster ride I wanted to take. But what rose to the top was sorrow. I felt sick over Skylar, worried, bombarded with images of other victims, dozens of other children in dozens of other cases. I didn't even know this child and I couldn't bear to think about her suffering. Life isn't always kind to the most fragile among us. It's the hardest injustice to contemplate.

I tapped on the door and Mrs. Barbour opened it. Luke ran inside, positioned himself immediately at her ankles. She patted him, still looking at us, then at the road behind us ablaze in light, lamps weaving through the woods behind the scene like skiers on a downhill course.

"Did you find anything?" I saw again the stunned, shattered look in her eyes I'd seen when she was huddled in her kitchen.

"No," we lied in unison. Tomorrow at the judicial center, after their polygraph tests, they would be brought up to date. But not tonight. Too much was uncertain tonight. Hayley looked again at the road and the lights, then back at us. She'd registered our withholding with the built-in lie detector of a mother. Tears and betrayal filled her eyes again. She might even have understood the significance of our lie—that we'd found something and the news was not good, and for all those mystical reasons law enforcement uses in lieu of full disclosure, she wasn't being told the truth. But the world is full of suspects. Even glistening-eyed mothers were not free from suspicion. We had to be careful.

"For our records," the sheriff asked casually, "do you know Skylar's blood type?"

"B-positive," she answered, faintly.

He smiled at her, and his voice stayed calm and smooth and reassuring. "There's a message in that, Mrs. Barbour. Stay positive. She could walk in any minute."

We left her standing at the door with her missing daughter's dog, in the home she shared with a husband who couldn't stand the sight of her.

"It's going to be a long night in that house," Meltzer remarked as we walked back toward the road. "You think they're for real?"

"Grief-stricken and guilt-stricken look a lot alike. Too soon to tell."

"Listen, Keye, I wanted to thank you for tonight, for just going with the flow."

"With your mom, you mean?"

"Yeah. She has a tendency lately to ditch Patricia and barge in."

I laughed. "I for one am grateful for her timing."

"I was going to kiss you," he said, and I felt my heartbeat catch in my throat. "And you were going to let me."

Shadowy figures performed their strange rituals behind scene tape under the lights ahead. We walked toward the scene—a desolate, weeping movie set.

"Can I be really honest, Ken?"

"Please," he said.

"This chemistry thing—it's going to be a distraction. And it's not simple for me. You know that. I'm just not ready to set off a stick of dynamite in my life right now."

"I understand," he said quietly.

"I need to think about what happened on that road up there," I told him. "I need to think about digging this creep out of his filthy hole and bringing Skylar home."

Our shoes cracked down on dirt and pebbles. Insects screamed from trees, deputies' voices called for Skylar from the woods beyond and reminded me of the way it sounds to search a house and hear "clear" after each room is secured. I saw a deputy moving slowly through the ditch where Luke found the phone case.

"Mom liked you, by the way," Ken said. "I'm told she may not remember me for much longer. So I'm just trying to enjoy these moments with her. It gets crazy sometimes. She thinks Ginger is a dog I had growing up. Half the time she thinks I'm my father. It makes some people uncomfortable. You seemed okay with it."

"Well, my business partner is a pot smoker. So I'm used to it."

Meltzer laughed, that big, rumbly laugh, probably the first laugh on this road today. He stopped and looked at me. "Christ, how can you make me laugh in the middle of all this?"

The sheriff of Hitchiti County was a romantic, I realized, the kind of guy who'd fall for you because you're nice to his mom and his dog.

Deputies were piling out of the woods and moving into a field on the other side of the road as we neared the scene. We knew Skylar wasn't out there. But the search had to be done. I squinted at the floodlights. I had to raise my voice over the generator.

"Interesting he removes the battery," I said.

"He wants to disable GPS," Meltzer said.

"But GPS told us exactly where the phone was disabled," I argued. "He'd know that. Plus, he's leaving the device behind. It's no threat. He's wiped it down. So why take the batteries? If he needs to disassemble the phone why not just toss the battery in the ditch too?"

Raymond had lumbered up and pulled a cigarette out of his pocket. He didn't light it. "He has a thing for batteries?" he suggested sarcastically.

"That's insightful for you, Detective," I answered, not taking the bait. "I think it's a trophy. A memory. He likes this part." I swept my hand in the direction of the road. "The part where he overpowers his victim. He's all jacked up on chemicals then. It's probably the only time in all his interaction with the victim he's able to get that rush. He wants to commemorate it."

Raymond blinked heavy lids at me. "And you think we're the creepy ones?"

"You find anything else?" the sheriff asked him, before I could reply.

"Found a few more drops of blood," Raymond reported. "Drag marks too. Although we fucked them up with our cars. If I had to guess from the marks and the blood, he hits her there." He pointed to where Sam was photographing the ground. "Lot of displaced rock and dirt there, like maybe he was trying to get control of her. There's some kind of disabling blow, first blood hits the ground, then he drags her back around to his vehicle."

Meltzer nodded his agreement. "Sounds right."

"Good news is, there's not much blood," Raymond added. "He wasn't trying to kill her. He just wanted to disable her."

"And take her to his hole," I said thickly.

Raymond threw up his hands and walked away.

24

It was a silent ride to the hotel, curling through Whisper's back streets. I'd left the sheriff conferring with his deputies. Another scene tech had arrived to help process that square of road and the ditch. They'd asked us politely to leave. No one had to twist my arm. I wasn't doing anyone any good standing there.

I climbed the outside steps up to my hotel room. My key card was in my hand when I reached to push it in the door and realized I was staring into a blank space, a darkened room, a door already cracked open.

I stepped back, heard the growing *thump, thump, thump* in my ears. Fight or flight. There it was. What was it going to be? My gun was inside. I had no flashlight. No anything.

I spun around and hit the door with the side of my foot, kept moving. The door swung open hard and slammed into the wall. *Adrenaline and cortisol.* I could taste it in the back of my throat. I waited. No sound. No movement inside. I reached one arm inside and found the light switch.

Empty room. Dresser drawers pulled out. The contents of my suitcase dumped on the bed. I went quickly to the closet and checked the safe. The readout said it was locked. I keyed in the four-digit code, popped open the safe, grabbed my Glock and shoved in a clip. The bathroom door was closed. And I wasn't the one who'd closed it.

I turned the knob with my left hand, gave it a little push, then swung in with my Glock. Nothing. I snatched open the shower curtain and saw an empty square.

I let myself breathe. I'm an emergency person. I have an inexplicably cool head for the unexpected. It's the aftershocks that wreck me. I felt them now in my knees.

I inspected the door. Whoever had broken into my room had used some kind of pry bar and torn the heck out of it. It was bent and scarred. Definitely not a professional job. The lock wouldn't slide into place. I attached the chain to hold it closed while I cleaned up the room and assessed the damage. My clothes were there. The shaving kit I use as a makeup bag sat on the bathroom counter. My toothbrush was where I'd left it in a plastic hotel cup. Good bet I'd never use that toothbrush again. I went back to the safe. My Mac, my digital camera, my notes—everything was still there. There were no marks on the safe to indicate someone had tried to open it without the code. Someone had gone to a lot of trouble to take nothing. Was this another message? Or was it something else entirely? According to Bryant Cochran, there were a whole lot of folks who didn't like having me around. I thought about Logan Peele, then glanced back at the door. I'd ruffled some feathers in the thirty-six hours I'd been in town. One sex offender was sitting in jail, another had had his devices confiscated. Tina Brolin hadn't even tried to disguise her venom. And when she had misdirected it at the family of a missing girl tonight, Meltzer had ordered her away. Where had she gone? But why would Brolin do this? Why would Peele? Why not take something? Or leave something? Could this be random, some teenage prank or a thug looking for credit cards and cash? Why was the safe untouched?

I repacked my suitcase. The weight of the day made my shoulders and head ache. I slipped the lip of my duty holster in the back of the navy slacks I'd been in all day and walked outside with my computer bag hanging off my left shoulder and my suitcase in my left hand. I wanted my right hand free. I wasn't feeling the love in Whisper at the moment.

A dozing clerk, roused by the bell on the door, blinked when I walked into the lobby, wiped the back of his hand across his mouth. I put my key card on the counter in front of him. "Checking out?" He got out of the desk chair he'd been sleeping in behind the counter.

"Someone broke into my room." I gave him the room number. "So yeah. I'm checking out. Door was jimmied and it won't lock now. You see anyone?"

"Did they take anything?" He seemed to brighten up. He'd probably hoped for a good robbery. "We never have break-ins here."

"Right," I said. "So did you see anything?"

"No!" He came around from behind the counter and peered out the doors into the parking lot as if he could see something helpful now. "Want me to call the cops?"

"Sure," I said. "Tell them what you just told me. Be a lot of help."

I lugged my things out and loaded my car. Yellow streetlamps softly lit the shops and the narrow lanes of Main Street as I drove out of Whisper. It was a postcard town. Everything about Whisper and the surrounding area—the thick forests, the rolling farmland, the vast, icy-blue water, the manicured resorts—all of it beckoned, invited. It was one big fucking WELCOME sign. But to me it whispered locked basements and eyes in windows, and secrets. And murder.

I drove toward the resort area I'd jogged through a couple of miles out of town. I found a Fairfield Inn with a room. It wasn't exactly the Ritz, but when does a PI get the Ritz? The room was clean. The door hadn't been pried open, and it wasn't in downtown Whisper. I performed the bedbug check, turned corners back on all the bedding, checked the seams and crevasses in the mattress. There are few things that can fill my heart with dread like a bedbug. They're sneaky. And they bite. I shivered at the thought.

I took a shower and toweled my hair, brushed my teeth with a hard toothbrush I'd bought in the lobby, fell into bed with my stomach rumbling. The sheriff's spinach quesadilla had worn off hours ago. I considered the hotel vending machine again. I would have paid ten bucks for a package of Hostess Ding Dongs—chocolate cupcakes stuffed with cream. Well, they call it cream. Lord knows what it is. My mother would have slapped it out of my hand.

I used the key I'd found taped under Skylar's desk drawer and opened the tiny pink padlock hanging off her diary. Notes of varying size torn from lined school paper tumbled out on the bed. Skylar must have opened it carefully, kept it flat, knowing special memories were stuffed inside the cover. I thought about Skylar handling this diary, sitting down to record secrets and dreams. I thought about Raymond not wanting me to have it.

I unfolded one of the notes, a torn-off scrap bent in half with ragged edges. *My brother says Robbie says he likes you.* I opened another one. *They totally made out.* And another. *OMG! Did you see her shoes?* I read on through each bitchy, hormonal, funny, childish, innocent note; some of them had clearly been passed around and contained two or three styles of handwriting.

A photo among the notes got my attention, Skylar and a girlfriend hamming it up in an old-fashioned photo booth. Did they still make them? Four frames. Girls smiling self-consciously, giggling as they grinned. Earrings dangling. The department would access her photo stream online. I'd make sure of that. No one used paper anymore, at least not a teenager. Everyone's lives, mine included, passed through our smartphones into a storage cloud somewhere. Raymond might have thought about online storage already and gotten the ball rolling. The detective had some thug in him, but he wasn't stupid. I'd watched him at the scene tonight and with Skylar's parents. His reconstruction of the abduction based on drag marks and blood spatter was careful and thoughtful.

I flipped through the diary, went to the last entry, dated yesterday. One line. *I HATE my parents!!!!!*

She wrote about her fears that her arguments with her parents contributed to the tension between them. She regretted the fights later but held stubbornly to her belief in the utter injustices perpetrated against her by Hayley and Brooks Barbour. Based solely on Skylar's complaints in her journal, they appeared to be protective parents, not abusive ones. Skylar was interested in music but bored with band practice and scathingly critical of the "lame" music teacher. I learned that her primary interest since the new school year began was in a boy named Robbie. *Saw Robbie. He's so gorgeous. Saw Robbie. He's so smart.* The entries ran from a line one day to a crowded page another, from the flippant and shallow and self-absorbed to the dark and shallow and self-absorbed, which was exactly where she was supposed to be emotionally at thirteen. That thought—the protected unworldliness with which she approached life, the pure innocence of inexperience—wedged in my throat like a cotton ball.

I read back a couple of months before my eyes burned and I was no longer absorbing anything. I switched out the light and lay there in the dark. I thought about that smiling girl with caramel-colored eyes. Where was she tonight? Chained to a pipe in some barn or shed, shivering with cold and fear? Was she hungry? We knew from the lab reports that Tracy and Melinda had been fed just enough to be kept alive until they'd served their purpose. Offenders don't take prisoners and cook them balanced meals. These people can get up from a steak dinner upstairs, clean their plates off in the trash, and walk down basement steps with a two-month-old package of cookies from the vending machine at work and toss it at their captives without a thought. Look at Ariel Castro and the hellhole he'd created for three women and a child in Cleveland. Look at Brian David Mitchell, who took fourteen-year-old Elizabeth Smart and chained her to a tree, starved and raped her, and held her for nine months. I'd seen predators' lairs, their filthy dungeons littered with Frito bags and plastic water bottles, excrement and shackles and ropes and knives and dildos and pornography. The victims' only value is in what needs they satisfy in the offenders. Age, innocence, suffering, starving, the terrible sin of breaking a child—none of it matters.

I flipped over on my side, stared at a parking lot light through a separation in the heavy curtains. I took a shaky breath. God, I wanted to find that kid. I wanted to find her and watch Luke slobber her face with kisses. I wanted to find the sonofabitch who was holding her and put a bullet in him before those light brown eyes of hers grew dark and vacant.

I reached for my phone to call Rauser, to say good night, to tell him I loved him, to hear the voice that had steadied me for years, as both friend and lover, the man I'd nearly betrayed. Or had I already betrayed him by letting the sheriff get so near? I'd enjoyed it, after all— the fantasies, the flirting. And if that weren't enough, here I was parsing the definitions of sex and betrayal like Bill Clinton at a deposition. How would Rauser define cheating? I reviewed every moment I'd spent with Ken Meltzer. The almost-kiss would have hurt Rauser far less than the walk on the dark road tonight with Meltzer next to me, sharing the tension and heartache and fear and exhilaration of an investigation like this. That connection, that intimacy, those moments, I knew exactly what that would feel like to Rauser. I dropped the phone back on the bed table.

At six a.m. I stood in front of the mirror looking at the tiny creases at the corners of my eyes, the ones that hadn't been there a couple of years ago. Some foundation, blush, a little pencil under the corners of my bottom lashes and I was beginning to look human. I searched for my mascara. And then I searched again. I poured everything out of the makeup bag. What the hell? It was Lancôme Ôscillation Intensity. Power mascara. Thirty-six bucks a tube and it had probably ended up on the floor of that hotel bathroom after my room was tossed. *Shit.* So far central Georgia was about as much fun as Gordon Ramsay at a redneck picnic.

I headed downstairs. The smell of bacon hit me as soon as the elevator doors parted. I followed it to a room off the lobby with tables and chairs and a television. Sunken trays, steaming at the seams, were filled with scrambled eggs and grits, bacon and sausage. There were bagels and waffles and syrup and jelly. And tall dispensers that squirted OJ or thin brown coffee into cups. I ate breakfast alone at a small table and watched the hotel guests move in and out, some piling up plates and heading back to their rooms with puffy eyes and bed head. Some stayed, slurping the hot, tasteless coffee and pouring watery syrup on toaster waffles. A guy came in wearing a Krispy Kreme uniform and carrying a crate full of green-and-white boxes. I watched him slide the boxes into a rack on the counter. I waited for my chance to move in. Here's the thing about Krispy Kreme's original glazed doughnuts: They are flat-out awful cold and hard. But if you pop them in the microwave for a few seconds, the glaze melts and they get soft and pliable and they are almost as good as when they come off the conveyor in Midtown. I grabbed a fresh plate and two doughnuts, then nuked them for ten seconds. The day was looking up. I took

Skylar's diary from my bag and read while I washed Krispy Kremes down with weak coffee. I missed Neil and his espresso maker.

She wrote about the last school year and summer days, about friends who had gossiped behind her back, and her ongoing efforts to dump the school band. She'd been in the band for a couple of years, which meant Skylar and Melinda were in the band at the same time. Skylar's parents and her music teacher pressed for her to stay in the band for the year. She wasn't pleased. It wasn't the kind of music she wanted to play. She'd had band practice twice this year and she'd ditched it once to watch Robbie and his garage band rehearse. She obsessed about Robbie, drew hearts around his name. He'd walked her back to school in time to meet her mom the day she'd skipped practice. They held hands. A kiss. The summer had been all about her BFF, rides to the mall down I-20, Coke floats, going to movies when they could catch a ride. Whisper was too small for a theater, and Skylar cut into town on that path on summer nights and walked the neighborhoods, sometimes with her friend after their parents were asleep. Sometimes she was alone, full of bored, pubescent restlessness and desire. Too young to drive, she felt marooned in the ranch house over the summer while her parents worked and her best friend was away on a family vacation. She chronicled walks around town with her dog. She walked past the church and stopped to talk to the pastor and his wife gardening at the rectory next door. She wrote about pulling weeds and taking tomatoes home to her mother, having lunch with the minister's family and baking cookies with Mrs. Hutchins and their daughter, Robin. There were other mentions of Robin. Things like *played with Robin* or *she still likes dolls*. Robin was younger and a fill-in friend, I decided, but Skylar liked her. She went to the drugstore and the coffee shop and the diner. She bought Cokes from the machine and lay on her back in the park with her head on Luke like a pillow. It was the diary of a sweet, wandering, lonely kid. Those long hours alone had put her at risk. The Barbours, it appeared, did their very best when they were home—movies and books and pizza night, board games. But their daughter had begun to withdraw: She dreaded the dinners and wrote *sigh* and *boring* and *ugh* when she recorded them.

I looked again at the photo booth picture, then tucked it back into the diary, locked it so nothing would tumble out, and put it in my bag. On the television in the bland breakfast room, there was a lot of talk about how much the royal baby would be worth if everyone else in the family died, and Miley Cyrus had made everyone's list of celebs most likely to freak the fuck out this year. If Skylar Barbour was still alive, she was learning just how cruel life could be. But the world, it just kept on turning.

I was on my way out when they broke for local news and I heard: *The bodies of two young women found murdered in the woods near Lake Oconee have been linked to the disappearance of a third girl. Is there a serial killer in Hitchiti County? The full report from Brenda Roberts at six.*

25

The Hitchiti County Judicial Center jutted up out of the landscape, big and modern. Every one of those beds taken by the state was revenue. Sheriff Ken Meltzer seemed to be good at the business of being sheriff. He'd grown his department. He'd lowered the crime rate, which was miraculous considering what I'd seen of his investigators, and he'd taken care of his own, made deals over a fishing pole, and gotten himself reelected. But this hulking charcoal-stone and glass center surrounded by barricades and asphalt seemed an abomination so near lakeshore architecture and ancient oaks and scented, climbing jasmine. And was it at odds, too, with the guy who liked to hike and watched *Castle* with his mom? I thought about being in his home last night, standing in the kitchen with him at my elbow, those cabin stairs I'd fantasized about climbing.

"How'd you sleep?" a voice behind me asked as I passed through the first set of metal detectors at the complex entrance.

"Shitty," I grumped. I didn't mention I'd changed hotels in the middle of the night.

"Me too," Meltzer said. His hair was damp and I saw the light shadow of a beard. "The Barbours' polygraphs are scheduled for seven. They should be upstairs now. Brolin and Raymond will interview them. You can watch from the observation room if you'd like."

"I'd like to, yes," I told him. "I've been thinking about them. I hope they didn't see the news. It's not the way you want to be told."

Meltzer's face told me he had no idea what I was talking about. He'd probably grabbed a few hours of sleep, then come straight to the complex. He tunes out in the morning, he'd already informed me. He doesn't check messages or emails before business hours and if someone wants him they can call. I guess no one had called.

"They reported that forensics had linked Skylar's disappearance to Melinda and Tracy," I told him. "I hope that's true. MO and signature certainly have. But ideally your investigators and the family get that news before the public."

"Lot of deputies on the scene last night." He was frowning. "It could have gotten out. Guess that reporter kept digging until she found a crack." He nodded at the elevator. "Come upstairs with me. We might have something from Freeman's van." We stepped into an elevator. Meltzer pressed the button for the fourth floor. "That flash drive Raymond found in Freeman's vehicle was loaded with child porn. Enough to keep him locked up awhile."

"How about Peele's devices?" I asked.

"Clean, according to the digital specialist. There's a chance he could have scrubbed them without the expert detecting it, but it's a slim chance. He'd need to have access to the kind of programs the Feds use. He's coming to pick them up."

"You plan on talking to him while he's here?"

"You bet. Don't you want to know what he did yesterday? Remember that gap in coverage I mentioned? An hour between the time the scene techs left and the patrol arrived on the street. Peele's truck wasn't there. He didn't show up until almost nine last night."

The elevator opened. "By the way, they found a nail file and a makeup compact near the ditch last night. It hadn't been there long."

"No purse?" I asked.

"Nope. That's it. The crushed phone, the phone case, a nail file, a compact, and the blood evidence."

"He dumped everything out of the purse she might use as a weapon." I thought about that as we stood outside a glass wall looking into an oblong room lined with a desk-high counter, three work-stations, three rolling chairs, computers, and more equipment.

"Firearms and tool marks are down the hall," Meltzer told me, and I detected a hint of pride in his voice. Cabinets with glass fronts lined the top section of the room. They were neatly stacked with white envelope-size boxes labeled with handwritten information. Microscopes sat on a wide stainless-steel table in the center, a latent print development chamber, alternate light sources, fume extractors, machines for evidence drying, centrifuges, and a whole lot of new technology I didn't recognize. It had been more than four years since I'd had reason to visit forensic laboratories. Science had zoomed past me.

"I'm impressed."

"We take work from other agencies to support the center. And it helps relieve the logjam. One day, when the money and expertise is available, we'll add mitochondrial DNA typing. I hope that will happen early next year."

"More impressed," I said, and smiled.

"So what kept you up?" Meltzer asked.

I looked over at him, then back at the window. "I read Skylar's diary. Sad, sweet kid. Just a regular kid."

"Tough to read, huh? No revelations?"

"She was lonely, happy when school started. She did mention your friend the pastor and his wife. And their daughter. Thought maybe I'd talk to them. Skylar liked being with them. I think she missed having happy parents. She had a crush on a boy. I'm going to see what I can find out about him. And she was trying to quit the band, but her parents and her instructor wanted her to stay."

"Daniel Tray," Meltzer said. "The one we missed. We ran him. Looks clean. Not even a speeding ticket. He grew up in Whisper, went to college, taught for a year in Boston, then came back here. He's forty-five. He's been back here for twenty years."

"Anything interesting happen while he was in Boston?"

Meltzer shook his head. "No missing or murdered students, if that's what you mean." He pushed open the door. There were two techs in the lab. I recognized both. Sam leaned away from a microscope and looked at us.

"I don't think you've had a proper introduction," Sheriff Meltzer said. "Keye, this is Samantha Petri. Sam, this is Keye Street."

"We met last night," she told the sheriff, and peeled off a glove to shake my hand.

"Sam has aspirations," Meltzer remarked drily. "She has the FBI in her sights. We'd like to keep her around here for a while. But the grass is always greener." He winked at her.

"It's not greener," I warned her. "And the money isn't that great either."

"Ah, but they get all the new toys," she said.

"Tell us about the Freeman van," Meltzer said. "Then I want to talk about what we got off Cottonwood Road."

"Mori did the van," Sam answered, and nodded in the direction of the other technician.

He touched a screen and a fingerprint came up. He expanded the detail. "One of three in the van," he told us, gesturing to the screen. "They don't match samples from Freeman's children or wife. Two of them aren't in the system at all." He stared at his screen. "Lifted them on gel. With any luck we'll be able to isolate chemical composition. We've also sent samples to the GBI from the van along with the toothbrush from the Barbour house." If Skylar's body turned up somewhere someday too damaged for identification, her DNA profile would be in a database. "I'm Mori Payne, by the way," the tech told me. He was thirty, clean-shaven, round-faced.

"Nice to meet you," I said. "You mentioned a third set of prints in Freeman's van. You have a match on them?" We knew Freeman wasn't responsible for Skylar's disappearance. He had been sitting next door in a holding cell at the jail by the time Skylar left school. And he wasn't right for the murders. But he was a danger to children, probably even to his own children. And the guy was utterly disgusting. I'd support incarceration based solely on smell.

"We lifted the third set from several areas in the back of the van," Mori said.

"Where there's no door handles," I told Meltzer.

"Fingerprints belong to Damian Howard," Mori told us. "He's fifteen. Got his thumb printed for a temporary learner's permit a couple of months ago, which is the only reason he's in the system."

"I'll have somebody talk to him," Meltzer said. "Quietly. Boys don't report these things. Poor kid."

Girls don't report either, I wanted to say. The shame of molestation and rape is genderless.

"You have something from the scene last night?" I asked Sam instead.

"First of all, I was able to type the blood on the road. B-positive," she told us.

"Skylar's blood type," Meltzer said.

"Right," she confirmed. "The nail file and the compact were wiped clean. There will be skin cells in the file. Probably the victim's since it was her file, but there's a chance we've picked up some from the offender. I've sent the sample in for DNA typing." She looked at me. "Remember that little smudge on the phone case?"

I nodded.

"It's motor oil. Got it out with a solvent extractor. Very common ten-w-thirty. I went back into evidence and checked the phone from the Cochran scene. I found minuscule amounts. Nothing visible to the naked eye, but I was able to establish the viscosity. We're looking at the same oil."

"How about the nail file and the compact?" I asked. "Oil on those too?"

She shook her head. "But he used the same cloth, because I found fibers on the phone case that matched fibers in the file. Check this out." She walked us to a microscope she'd been peering through when we arrived. I looked at the screen and saw three fibers on a clear surface. They looked more like thick wires at this magnification. "They're tinted," I said. "Pinkish red."

"I'd say they came from an industrial maintenance cloth," she told us.

"Like a shop rag?" I asked.

"Exactly. Manufactured for maximum absorbency and minimum shedding. A red one. Not a lot of pilling in a material like this, but if you rub it on something that can grab trace like that rubber phone case or a nail file, it's going to leave fiber evidence."

"He used it to wipe his prints off everything," I said.

Sam nodded. "Looks that way."

"Anything else about the fibers? Anything to pinpoint the store that sold the cloth?" the sheriff wanted to know.

"Doubtful," Sam said. "They come in packages at just about any auto parts and hardware store in the country. Interesting, though. There was a heavy concentration of oil on the phone case. And dirt. So the place on the rag he used to wipe down the phone had a lot of dirt and oil on it. And it was deep in the rubber pores. Like he pressed hard."

"What about the dirt in the sample?" I asked. "Different from what you'd get on Cottonwood Road?"

"Engine dirt, metal filings, grease," Sam answered. "Probably unscrewed caps with it, something like that. We also have trace amounts of other fluids, like coolant and brake fluid. What you'd typically get from working on an automobile engine."

We were silent. Meltzer said, "He's a mechanic?"

I turned to him. "He's faking a breakdown." A door had flown open and I was dashing toward the light. "He has his hood up and he's pretending to work on his engine. That's why the drag marks curved around in a half-moon on the road. They started at the hood, where he disabled the victim. He pulled her back to the car door in a semi-circle."

"And he uses her phone to make a fake call for help." Meltzer was staring at me.

"There's the con," I said.

"And that's why the last call on Skylar's phone was to the stationary line inside her own house," he added.

I nodded. "Because he knows the number. And he knows no one is home. And he has to pretend he's making a call. He wants her phone. He wants her convinced and relaxed and in just the right position so he can blitz her."

"Maybe he's called that number before. Maybe he knew voice mail would answer and exactly how long he had." Ken Meltzer had the same expression I must have had—excitement, that back-and-forth that can give flight to an investigation, the complete rush of hope that comes with understanding a scene.

"I think he pushed the rag into his engine and pressed it into that phone because he wants us to know how he does it," I told them. "That was the message of the note. *Listen hard . . . More soon.* He's leaving bread crumbs. He wants us to know how smart he is."

26

"We heard on the news that Skylar was taken by the same person who killed those girls," Hayley Barbour said, sitting in the interview room. Brolin and Raymond shifted in the metal chairs across from Skylar's parents. "Is it true?"

"The physical evidence left behind is very similar," Raymond said carefully.

"But you know she was taken," Brooks insisted. "You *know*."

"I'm afraid it looks like that, Mr. Barbour. I'm very sorry," Brolin said. "And that's why it's so important for us to have your help. We believe Skylar knew this person, trusted him. Or at the very least recognized him. We believe he pretended to be having car trouble and she first saw him after she came off the walking trail."

"So he was parked on our road *waiting*?" Brooks's tone was disbelieving.

"We think so," Raymond answered.

Hayley made a sound like a small puppy. Her eyes were swollen and red. How many tears did she have left in her? The investigators questioned them about landscapers and handymen and wrote down names. They asked about their automobiles and who made the repairs. They inquired about their friends. They gathered leads and made lists. That's what detective work is. It's the meticulous task of sorting through lives and schedules, spending habits and half-truths. Because people lie, even good people, for a million intimate reasons. Raymond and Brolin were thorough and professional and empathetic, and I liked them a lot more when the interview concluded than when it began.

I opened the observation room door and watched Skylar's parents as they left. They moved with the downtrodden posture of street people. I remembered Barbour's words. *We won't survive this, me and Hayley. Our marriage, I mean. Skylar's our glue.* That was a lot of pressure for a kid. She felt it. She worried in her diary that her blow-ups were causing the problems between her parents.

Brolin and Raymond stepped out of the interview room talking. Their conversation cut off sharply when they saw me. "Well done," I said.

Brolin's top teeth pressed into the dent in her bottom lip. I thought she might smile. Maybe that *was* a smile. I think I shivered a little. "You hear that, Rob?" she asked. "Dr. Street thinks we did a good job."

"Oh yeah? I guess we can retire now," he said.

"Yeah, I feel all warm inside," Brolin said.

They turned and headed toward the elevators. "You think she'll put in a good word for us?" Raymond asked, loud enough for me to hear. "With the sheriff, I mean."

"I hear they have a *rapport,*" Brolin sneered.

"Hilarious," I called out behind them. They didn't stop. I checked the time. Eight a.m. Skylar had been missing for seventeen hours and Meltzer's team was still shutting me out.

I sent a text message to the sheriff and asked when Peele was due. My phone rang nine seconds later. "He's in an interview room now," Ken Meltzer told me. "Thinks he's waiting for his things to be released. Where are you?"

"Observation room two."

"Stay put," he told me. "He's a couple of doors down. I need a few minutes. There's a little cubbyhole with espresso if you walk past the elevators. You have time. And you look like the latte type. That's what they drink in the city, right?"

"Sure," I said. "It's the official drink. What type are you?"

"Latte," he said, and I heard his smile.

I clicked off and pushed in Rauser's number. I hadn't even called to say good night last night.

"Streeeet," he answered. "Highlight of the morning right here. How's it going down there?"

"Another girl disappeared yesterday afternoon. It's our guy. We caught a break on some physical evidence, though," I said. "The sheriff's team is icing me out. Two investigators. Total dicks. I may have to go rogue."

"That's your specialty," he said, and we were quiet for a few seconds. I paced the empty corridor with the phone to my ear. Light streamed in a row of windows lining the corridor. I looked down at the asphalt parking lot and the newly planted saplings that edged up against it. "Listen, Keye," Rauser said. "I know we're new at this. Maybe you feel like you gotta report in or whatever. Maybe you've been with the kind of guy who needs that. Me, I'm not an insecure man."

"Where's this coming from?" I asked.

"You give me room when I'm working. The favor extends both ways, that's all. That's why we're good together, you and me. So just, you know, find the kid. I'm good. White Trash is being totally sadistic to Hank but I think he's starting to like it."

Rauser was not only a secure man, he was an instinctive one. He knows me. And he knows what to do when he feels me slipping. He lets go. I leaned my back against the cold marble wall, closed my eyes. "You have any idea how much I love you?"

"Yeah, I know," he said, and I heard the flint on his old Zippo catch on the third strike. "You left me with your cat."

He'd stopped smoking last Thanksgiving. And now it seemed he was again. I didn't question him. I understand all the ways addiction can rise up and pull you back under.

We said good-bye and less than ten minutes later, I was standing in an observation room with Sheriff Meltzer, watching Logan Peele drum his fingers against a gray metal tabletop in an interview room devoid of natural light. We were each holding a latte. I'd bought three.

The third for Peele. Meltzer pulled the plastic cap off his cup and blew into steamed milk and coffee. The judicial center didn't know it was August outside. Icy air blasted through new ductwork.

Peele got up and paced the room. He had the fluid movements of someone completely at ease with his body, the gym body he'd probably developed in prison. But that body had the coiled energy of a cheetah. Irritation was getting the best of him. He didn't seem to be aware of being watched, but I knew that he was certain he was.

Meltzer chuckled. "He doesn't like waiting. Or is it confined spaces?"

"He doesn't like anything he can't control," I answered. "How long's he been there?"

"An hour. I wanted to wait for my deputies to give his property a good going-over while he was gone."

"Nothing?" I asked.

"Nothing," Meltzer said. "And you don't seem surprised."

"Acquiring a victim right after your people left his property would have been brazen. Bringing her back to that same property, even more so."

Meltzer glanced at me. "He's arrogant enough."

"True." I nodded. "But I don't think he's stupid enough. I guarantee he hasn't stopped the behaviors that put him in jail the first time. He's just gotten smarter."

"He could be holding Skylar somewhere else."

"True again."

He opened the door for me and we stepped into the corridor, then into the interview room where Peele waited. "Welcome back to the Hitchiti County Judicial Center, Mr. Peele," Sheriff Meltzer said as we walked in carrying our coffees. "Have a seat." Meltzer set a cup down in front of Peele.

Peele eyed the coffee, took it in his hand, a coating of red hair on his knuckles. He didn't sit. "I should have known you were the reason I had to wait."

"Just a couple of questions before you collect your things, then you're free to go."

"Where are my things?"

"Downstairs," Meltzer told him. "Property room. You sign for them and you're free to go."

Peele pried the top off the latte and sipped. "Not bad," he remarked. "And since you obviously didn't find what you were looking for on my stuff, I'll just enjoy this on the way home."

Meltzer's hand closed down on Peele's wrist, fast like a trap closing. "Sit," he demanded.

Peele stared at him. Then he lowered himself back down and found his smirk.

"You didn't fuck up my day enough yesterday?" Color was coming up in the fair skin on his neck. "I have to make a living, Sheriff Meltzer. You're not supposed to interfere with that."

"Tell us about yesterday," I said. "After the sheriff's team left your house. What did you do?"

"Well, Dr. Street, I fucking cleaned my house. The *team* made a mess. I might as well have invited in a bunch of baboons."

"After that," I pressed. "Between three and four?"

"I drove to Conyers, where I could find a decent place to shop. And where nobody knows me. God, I need to move out of this hick town."

"What kind of store?"

"Food, Sheriff. A man's got to eat."

"You have your receipt?" I asked.

"I don't know." Peele smirked. "Maybe."

"A guy like you knows where his receipts are," I said. "You know where everything is."

Peele showed me the straight row of small white teeth. "Perceptive," he said.

"Where's the receipt, Logan?" Meltzer asked. He wasn't amused.

"I probably threw it away," Peele answered. His index finger picked at the cardboard sleeve on his latte.

"You must have thrown it away somewhere other than home," Meltzer said. "Because we've been through everything in that house, including the trash, while you were sitting here."

Peele didn't blink.

"What's the name of the store?" Meltzer asked.

Peele was silent.

"Did you use a credit or debit card?"

"Cash," Peele said.

"I don't think you fully understand the situation you're in." The sheriff leaned forward and looked into Peele's blue eyes. "We just searched everything you own. In fact, my deputies probably spilled trash all over your shiny floors. You know, because they're *baboons*."

Peele smiled.

"A very serious crime has been committed," Meltzer pushed. "And you don't seem to have an alibi."

Our coffee jumped. The flat of Peele's hand had slammed the table-top. The dam had broken. "And you don't seem to have a missing fucking girl. Or anything else. So fuck off."

Meltzer sat back, glanced at me. "Did I mention a girl, Dr. Street?"

"No, Sheriff. I don't think you did," I replied.

He'd stumbled for the first time. "I'm speaking in generalities." His eyes blazed at us. "I figure it's something like that or you wouldn't be fucking with me."

Posters had not even begun to hit telephone poles and bulletin boards, neighborhood searches hadn't even had time to organize. "How does a man who says he has no friends in town and who doesn't have devices to monitor the Whisper gossip feed hear about a missing girl?" I asked.

"I never said I didn't have a television," Peele's blue eyes danced with energy and nerves and the delight of confrontation. "Look, I had a meeting here at seven last night. That should be easy enough to check."

"What kind of meeting?"

"Sex offender treatment program. Sheriff, you should keep up with these things. I was right downstairs. It's a lot of fun. Guys like to re-live their freaky shit on the pretense of expressing remorse. Remorse is a big theme. You should drop in sometime, Dr. Street. Everyone leaves with a hard-on."

The hand Meltzer had on the table closed into a fist. His forearm flexed. I shot him a look. *Chill*. Interview rooms have cameras.

Peele had seen what I had seen. He'd have learned to read aggression in jail. He rocked back in his chair, folded arms over his chest.

Meltzer put Skylar's picture on his phone and pushed it across the table. Peele didn't look at it. "She lives about a mile from you," Meltzer said.

"It's Whisper," Peele said. "Everyone lives a mile from me."

"She attends the junior high," Meltzer continued. "She didn't come home yesterday afternoon."

"I'm not allowed to hang out around schools, Sheriff. Remember?"

"You have another piece of property somewhere, Logan? A little getaway maybe?"

"I'm sure you've already double-checked those records and found out I do not." Peele looked down at Meltzer's phone, touched the screen with a manicured fingertip to bring it back to life. "Nice-looking kid. Never had the pleasure."

"If anything happens to this girl because of something you've done or withheld, everything you've built since you got out, that clean house, all your nice electronics, all the things you control, it's all gone," Meltzer threatened. "Have a great day."

Peele stood up, put one finger on the top of the coffee cup we'd brought him, and pushed. It tipped over. Coffee slowly gurgled out the plastic spout onto the table. He walked out.

"Great guy," Meltzer grumbled when the door slammed behind Peele. It felt like the air had been sucked out of the room. He righted the cup and we stared at the milky pool on the table.

"Three dollars in latte right there," I remarked.

"So how do I cover this bastard?" Meltzer wanted to know. "I can't afford to lose him."

"Give him room," I said. "Because if he's the one, he's hidden Skylar somewhere else."

"She'll need food and water—"

"He wouldn't care what she'd need, Ken. If he supplies her with anything it's to use it as a bargaining chip. Not because he cares if she's hungry and thirsty. He'd let her die to keep from exposing himself. And the only regret he'd have is that he didn't get enough time with her. Never forget that."

27

ictoria Pope rose from her chair and came around her desk to greet me. She was slim, African American, with straight shoulder-length hair. "You must be Dr. Street." She extended a thin hand. Short mauve-colored nails precisely matched the color of her blouse. "Please." She gestured me to the corner of the office where there were two chairs with a small walnut table between them. It was an interior room in the judicial center complex. No windows. But bookcases and vases of dried flowers, a couple of paintings, and walls of deep saffron warmed the office. She took one of the chairs, crossed long brown legs that looked like they spent some time at the gym. "Ken Meltzer asked me to speak with you about the participants in our sex offender counseling and treatment program."

"Thank you for seeing me so quickly," I said.

"Normally, only a review committee would be privy to information regarding our sessions." Her voice was tentative. Almond-shaped eyes studied my face.

"I understand," I said. "It's also my understanding that given your position as an in-house psychologist with the state, the privacy that normally exists between doctor and patient is forfeited in a criminal investigation. There's also a clear-and-present-danger exception. And I wouldn't disturb you if I didn't believe that exception applies here."

"I am compelled to provide certain information, yes," she conceded.

"A thirteen-year-old girl was abducted yesterday just a few miles from here. She was last seen walking home from Whisper Middle School at three o'clock. We believe her disappearance is connected to the unsolved murders of Tracy Davidson and Melinda Cochran."

"The bodies that were found in the woods." She said it without emotion.

"Yes. The suspect is using a lure to attract the victim. Physical evidence tells us he's pretending his vehicle has broken down. After he overpowers the girls, he disassembles their phones and GPS, wipes his fingerprints. That sound like any of your guys?"

She thought for a moment before replying, her eyes on one of the paintings, a landscape of a river. "The purpose of treatment is to break the chain of behaviors that lead to sexual reoffending, Dr. Street. With work, it provides skill sets to live productive, prosocial lives without the offending behaviors. That's what we're trying to do here. We've had good results."

"Uh-huh. So are any of your guys right for this?" I pressed.

"They are not unlike addicts. Most of them are one bad decision away from a relapse and—"

"Let's talk about the ones you think are making bad decisions right now," I interrupted.

"I have the feeling you're not particularly interested in the work we're doing here." She spoke in that polite, nonreactive tone every counselor I've ever known uses.

"I don't mean to be disrespectful." I matched her polite and raised her some of my southern mama. "I just don't have time to care about your program, Dr. Pope, or whatever it is you're trying so hard to protect. What interests me is narrowing the suspect pool as quickly as possible in order to get this child home alive, and with the minimum physical and psychological damage."

"I understand but—"

I interrupted again and saw her surprise. "Every hour that ticks by increases the likelihood that a thirteen-year-old child will be brutalized and raped by a sexual sadist. The two murder victims found in the woods were that age. Before they died, they had suffered significant malnutrition." I saw Victoria Pope's lips twitch. "He starved them before he killed them. They had bone injuries. They had been tortured. I'm not here to cast a shadow on your treatment program. I fully understand the value of counseling in breaking destructive chains of behavior." I decided not to tell her just how intimately I comprehended destructive chains of behavior.

"What makes you think one of my group is involved?" Again her tone was devoid of resentment or anything that resembled emotion.

"In an interview this morning, Logan Peele mentioned a girl disappearing before we'd given him that information. He claimed he'd seen it on the news. Maybe he did. But it has to be explored. His alibi is soft for the time the girl disappeared. He says he was here later."

"Logan was the first one here last night," she said. "I found him alone in the conference room where we meet."

"How did you find his demeanor?"

That mouth twitch again. If we were playing poker I'd watch for that. And maybe we were. She didn't answer my question. "Have you met Logan Peele?" she asked me instead.

"Yes, I have."

"He can be quite aggressive and arrogant. He made sexual remarks to me before group. He wants to believe—and he wants me to believe—that he is attracted to adult women. And he wants to frighten me. But I didn't notice anything different about him last night."

"He have any friends in the group?"

"My patients aren't supposed to have any contact with one another outside our sessions. Or with any other convicted felon. To my knowledge, they don't communicate outside group."

"Three victims have been abducted sometime after leaving their school. As I said, the physical evidence suggests the con is probably engine trouble. Anything familiar about that scenario? Maybe something someone talked about in group?"

"No. I'm sorry."

"How about the names? Tracy, Melinda, Skylar."

"No," she said again. "I require my patients not to use real names here. We have to consider the victims' privacy and safety."

I thought about Peele saying they used therapy as a way to brag about their crimes and get a sexual charge. "Logan Peele told us that some of your members talk about their offenses in some detail during these sessions," I said.

"That's true. But I monitor this extremely closely. I pay attention to the details and how they are delivered. I stop it immediately if it begins to sound like anything but contrition."

"What do you think about Mr. Peele?" I asked her.

"One of the ways we measure progress is how willing a sexual offender is to acknowledge and accept responsibility for his behaviors and for the repercussions of his behaviors," she responded. "I have three members of my group who have a long ways to go in that regard. Logan is one of them."

I agreed. "Peele blamed his ex-wife for turning him in."

"Exactly. Some offenders can learn to take responsibility for their actions and control sexually abusive behaviors. But Logan was grossly underclassified as a medium-risk offender," Victoria Pope told me. It was exactly what I'd thought when I'd read his file. "If he was upgraded to high risk he could be electronically monitored. I've made that recommendation for three of these men. Logan only comes to group because it's part of his contract to stay out of jail. The same was true with Lewis Freeman. But the system is overwhelmed. Some offenders slip through the cracks." She paused. "I'm glad Lewis is back in jail, Dr. Street. I've talked to his parole officer twice in six months with concerns about his likelihood of reoffending and the unlikelihood he can be rehabilitated. I would never put the success of the program above the lives of children."

"Who else besides Peele and Freeman was in the group you thought should be reevaluated?"

She hesitated again, then gave me the name Lamar Bailey. I'd seen it on the final list of eight registered sex offenders Neil had compiled. I had read Bailey's statements to the parole board, and unlike with the cases of Peele and Freeman, I'd detected an acceptance of his actions and their impact on his life and others. I'd thought I'd heard remorse and a desire to change. But Dr. Pope had the opportunity to observe him in life. Perhaps she was privy to information she wasn't disclosing now.

"Did anyone fail to report for group last night?" I asked.

Her tiny black pupils widened, then returned to pinpoints. She went to her desk, tapped at her keyboard, took up a notepad, and wrote something down. She brought the note back to me.

"Lamar Bailey," I read aloud. She'd also written Bailey's DOB, address, phone, and the name of his parole officer.

I said good-bye to Victoria Pope, then stood in the corridor outside her office and pulled out my phone. "Good morning again, Detective Raymond," I said with maximum team spirit.

Raymond, however, skipped the pleasantries. "You get something at the shrink's office?" Obviously the sheriff had briefed him.

"A registered offender named Lamar Bailey didn't show for group last night. He's on the doc's most-likely-to-reoffend list. Need to check with his parole officer and see if he called in the absence. And check his alibi for yesterday afternoon."

"Sure," Raymond said. "It's not like I have anything else to do."

So much for team spirit. I disconnected.

The heat was blasting off the baking parking lot in pungent, petroleum-based fumes. By midafternoon on a cloudless day, the asphalt gets so hot it feels soft under your shoes. The tar bubbles up out of it in shiny, sticky black patches. Kids poke at it in the road on summer days. They'd twirl it around the tips of sticks and sword fight with them, leaving black smears on their clothes and skin. I remembered racing home with blackened hands that smelled like a road repair crew.

What would Skylar be doing now if she hadn't been plucked out of her life? She'd be in morning classes, looking forward to the lunch hour, social time in the cafeteria, writing notes, dreaming about Robbie and his garage band.

The hungry fingers of a headache reached for my temples just as my eye caught movement, a vehicle crossing over the bright yellow lines in the parking lot. It was a dark gray F-150. Peele's truck. Was he waiting for me? I felt myself stiffen. His window was open, and the sun had turned the red hairs on the arm resting there into glistening steel wool. He pulled into a parking space two slots away. He stared at me, gave me a nod. That's when I heard shoes hitting the paved lot behind me.

"Dr. Street, do you have a minute?"

I turned, squinted against the bright morning. Brenda Roberts was headed for me, cameraman in tow. Cameras used to scare the shit out of me. So did Brenda Roberts. But I've learned from experience that if you look scared on camera, your friends will make fun of you later. And what people need to see on television from the investigators charged with bringing them justice is confidence. So I choke it back.

"Dr. Street, you've been asked to consult on the murders of two thirteen-year-old females in Hitchiti County and the disappearance of another. Is this the work of a serial killer?" Brenda had latte skin and the bearing of a lioness. An Armani silk blouse I'd admired and hadn't been able to afford at Phipps Plaza hung off her this morning like it had been stitched only for her. She pushed the microphone at me.

"I'm sorry. I'm not at liberty," I told her. "Statements regarding investigations come only from the Hitchiti County Sheriff's Department." I kept moving.

"The department released your profile of the killer online. And now there is a third victim." The mike came back at me.

"I'd like to remind you that the incident yesterday in Whisper was an *abduction*."

"You're a freelance analyst, Dr. Street. Your specialty is violent serial offenders. One would infer your presence here means there *is* a serial murderer at large."

"Infer?" I repeated, incredulous. This is why police departments have spokespeople with cool heads to handle the press. "I'm sure you'd prefer facts. And I'm sure they're forthcoming."

My phone went off—the wailing of an Amber Alert, different from any other alert on my phone and unmistakable. Brenda Roberts's phone followed. "Stop tape," Roberts told her cameraman, her honeyed television voice sharpened by irritation. We both looked at our phones. *Amber Alert: Abduction. Whisper, GA. 13 yr old WF. Hr: Blond. Eyes: Brn. Cottonwood Rd 3pm. Name: Skylar Barbour.*

Roberts looked up from her phone. "They're just getting an alert out?"

"There's criteria," I told her. "The system normally requires a description of the offender or the offender's vehicle."

"So a witness hasn't been located?"

"No comment," I said.

"But they ran the alert anyway, which means there has to be evidence the child is in imminent danger." Roberts didn't miss much. "So it is the same suspect. What's the evidence?"

"No comment," I said again. I opened my car door. Heat rolled out like I'd broken the window on a house fire. Roberts hovered around me as I lowered the top.

"What gives, Keye? We talked about a feature last month on the phone. You seemed open to the possibility." Her voice dropped to a near whisper. She was holding the mike at her side. "Listen, this could be all about you investigating with the clock ticking on the third victim. The anatomy of an investigation, getting into the mind of a killer, that kind of thing." I got in my car. The steering wheel felt like a hot coal. "Any viable suspects among the registered sex offenders you've been questioning?"

I looked at Logan Peele, sitting in his truck. He gave me a little salute. "No comment," I told Brenda Roberts.

28

kept an eye on the rearview mirror on the way back to Whisper. I didn't want any more surprises. Peele had waited in the parking lot after his interview, while I met with Dr. Pope. Why? The nod, was that supposed to intimidate me? Or was he waiting for something else as well? Or someone? Could Peele have given Brenda Roberts information? She'd be the journalist most likely to nibble at a tip that included my name. Peele would relish doing anything that might muddy an investigation, because it entertained him, or because he was in fact the killer Meltzer wanted him to be. Sensational headlines could hurt Skylar's parents even more than they'd been hurt already. And Peele liked hurting people.

The air was full of wild mint and sweetgrass and baled hay, and smelled like a basket weaver's shop. I checked the time. Almost ten. Almost nineteen hours since Skylar had last been seen alive. She'd probably had her last decent meal at school yesterday. She'd been mad at her mom when she was dropped off yesterday morning, and all her pubescent misery had propelled her out of that car. Hayley Barbour had probably replayed that argument in her mind a million times.

I pulled over on the shoulder. I needed a minute, one minute to draw the clean air into my lungs and push out the images, the terrible images. Because they were only useful when I summoned them, controlled them, when I could scrutinize them for evidence, what they told me about *him,* the man who could break a little girl's bones for his own pleasure.

I leaned against the car, looked down the empty highway. As soon as Peele pulled out of the justice center today, someone would be on his tail. Meltzer wanted Peele as badly as he wanted to find Skylar. Where was she? In what windowless room, what hole in the ground, what basement, what barn? And where were we? Not far enough. Detective Raymond was getting the skinny on Lamar Bailey, the sex offender who hadn't shown up for group. Raymond and Brolin would be following other leads and reinterviewing witnesses. Had anyone noticed a man with a broken-down car? Someone changing a flat tire? Having the right question was sometimes the key to jogging the flawed human memory.

I got in my car and wished for an iced coffee, one of Neil's treats for scorching days. I was heading back to Whisper to see what I could shake loose. It felt like I was chipping away at a stone wall with a toothpick.

I drove down Main Street and parked. I left the tiny key and padlock that fit Skylar's diary in the glove compartment and took the journal with me.

I exited across the park under a jasmine-smothered arbor and walked to the middle school Melinda and Skylar had attended, a long one-story building, unremarkable and institutional. I pulled open a double door and walked into a corridor lined with display cases—trophies, photographs, ribbons—not for athletics, but for the school band. An article from *The Atlanta Journal-Constitution* about Whisper Middle School's invitation and subsequent performance at the Rose Bowl was framed and displayed. Skylar's parents had wanted her to stay in the band.

I walked down the empty hall on sound-absorbent commercial tiles in three colors—pale yellow, navy blue, and gold, the school colors. I slipped by the principal's office and then the admin office, unnoticed.

I didn't want anyone alerted to my visit. I wanted to find Daniel Tray on my own. I drew bored stares as I passed open classroom doors, from kids who wanted to look at anything but what they were supposed to be looking at. I thought about that, and about how easy it was to walk into the school.

The hall was T-shaped. I followed it to the end as I had yesterday and turned right, passed another bank of lockers and a couple of classrooms. I stood there watching him, average height, average frame, not skinny, not fat. His hair was brown and short, thinning in the crown so that a bare spot the size of a half dollar showed white scalp. He was the kind of guy who looked better straight-on than in profile because his chin was short and pulled down into a skinny neck. He had a bulging Adam's apple. He was humming to himself, absorbed in his task, putting instruments back in cases, breaking down music stands, folding chairs and stacking them.

"Daniel Tray?" I said.

He jolted the way people do when they're thinking hard and unaware of the world. He crossed the room wiping his hands on a chamois polishing cloth, an unsure smile on his face. "Can I help you?"

"My name's Keye Street. I'm a consulting investigator with the sheriff's department."

Tray wiped his right hand again and shook mine. I was thinking about polishing cloths and oil and Skylar's phone. "I heard the sheriff had hired an outside investigator to help with Melinda Cochran's murder. And that other girl." He had the fringes of an accent that had once been southern.

"Tracy Davidson," I said. No one seemed to know her name and it bothered me. "You have a second to talk?"

"Sure." He said it enthusiastically, like he'd wanted someone to talk to. He hurried to the back and grabbed two chairs off the stack, unfolded one for each of us. "You know Melinda was a student of mine. It's terribly sad what happened to her. It was such a shock. Nothing like that happens in Whisper."

The room had the fatty smell of slide grease and woodwind swabs and valve oil. And it hit me the way scents do that connect to memories—Jimmy deciding he'd have a go at the trumpet when we were kids, his plastic bottle of valve oil tucked in a corner pocket of the velvet-lined case.

"Did you know Melinda well?" I asked.

"I like to think so." He glanced at the diary I'd put in my lap. "I try to develop relationships with my kids. We have more fun that way."

I thought about Bryant Cochran's comments, which implied Daniel Tray was overtly and stereotypically gay. What I saw was a thin guy in his forties with a quiet voice who was losing his hair and probably stayed in on Friday nights. I thought about what Melinda's friends had told me, the dangerous rumors about Tray behaving inappropriately with children. I'd run across pedophiles in my career. They'd all identified as heterosexual.

"Melinda confided in you?" I asked.

"As much as children that age are willing to confide in a teacher or parent. And teachers are not high on their list of confidants."

"You think Melinda was hiding something?"

"No. Not really. But I had noticed she seemed . . . less focused. She started wanting to leave as soon as practice was over. She seemed less involved with the band outside practice." He shrugged. "It's natural. It's about the age we begin to lose them."

Skylar had been less interested too. She'd written about wanting to quit. It wasn't much, just a scrap to file away. "You talk to Melinda about this?"

"I asked her if anything was wrong. She said there wasn't."

"You had this discussion with Melinda after school?"

He nodded. "One afternoon after practice. We have one after-school practice a week on the field, so we can work on our routines. And we meet two days a week in the classroom." Tray's eyes moved to the diary and back again. I heard the rush of air through the HVAC system in the silence between us.

"Did you consider telling the police Melinda had been disengaging?"

He looked surprised. I couldn't tell if his eyes were green or brown or both. "No. I only saw Melinda for forty-five minutes three times a week. I guess that's why they didn't talk to me. All the teachers were brokenhearted for her family. Melinda was special. We all cared about her. And I think we all felt she'd ace a scholarship one day and contribute something to the world."

"I was told she was a little awkward," I said, thinking again about the conversation I'd had with her friends.

"Melinda Cochran?" Tray asked and again looked surprised. "Hardly. Very smart, confident young woman."

"With boys?"

"Again, not awkward," Tray said. It was another small thing, something that didn't fit. Someone was lying—Tray or Melinda's friends. Why?

I pulled up Logan Peele's photograph. "You recognize this man?"

"Never seen him."

"Were you surprised to hear Melinda's body was discovered?"

"Oh no. We all thought the child was dead," he said. "I just don't think we understood what she'd fallen victim to."

"What was that, in your opinion?"

"Well, there was that other girl out there who'd been killed too, so . . ."

"Tracy Davidson."

"So this clearly wasn't some random thing. This was someone who kills kids." He swallowed and the knot that was his Adam's apple slid up and back again. "Never thought I'd be talking about murdered kids, kids who were ours."

"You ever see Melinda out of school?"

"I suppose I've run into most of the kids at some point at the grocery store or the pizza place. But specifically to meet her? Or any student. No. Even if she'd wanted to talk I would have insisted on it being here at school." His forehead was glistening.

"But the band travels," I said. "You travel with them. So you do see the students off campus."

"Well, yes, but—"

"In fact you have a lot of time with them outside the classroom, right? Airplanes, buses, hotels."

Sweat let go of his hairline and trickled down his temple. He dabbed at it with the chamois cloth. "I'm not sure what you're implying, Miss Street, but I can assure you that our trips are chaperoned. We always have at least two parents along. And I don't spend any time alone with the children. Not ever."

"How about Skylar Barbour? She travel to California with the band last year?"

"Yes."

"Is she a good student? Smart like Melinda, talented?"

"They actually have a lot in common—bright, outgoing, grown up for their age. But why are we talking about Skylar?"

"When was the last time you saw Skylar, Mr. Tray?"

He didn't hesitate. "Yesterday, in the hall. Today was her day for music class but she wasn't present." The trickle of sweat had turned to a stream. It made it all the way to his jawline before he swiped it away. "Has something happened to Skylar?"

"No one's told you? Her parents made several calls to teachers and friends last night. The detectives spoke to some of her friends, the bus driver."

"*No*. My God. What's happened?"

"She didn't make it home from school yesterday."

"What do you mean she didn't make it home?"

"Vanished." I said it bluntly.

"Oh God." He was getting breathy and twitchy as if he might fly up out of his chair. "I come in after second period on Friday. I haven't spoken to anyone today."

"No one called you last night at home? You're not friends with the other teachers?"

"No. No one called me. And no, we're not really friends outside work." His eyes had darkened. I saw more brown than green now.

I opened the diary, glanced down at a random page. "Says here Skylar talked to you about wanting to leave the band."

"What is that? Is that her diary or something? So something awful happened to her too?"

"It appears she was abducted. Perhaps by the same person who murdered Melinda and Tracy."

He touched his forehead, rubbed his eyebrows. "Okay, wow. Yeah. She wanted to leave band."

I remembered the music stand and flute book I'd seen at the Barbours' house. "She's what, alto flute?"

"One of only two in the band. And good. Would have been a big loss. I kept hoping she'd rediscover her passion for it if she just stuck with it a little longer."

"Like Melinda?"

"Yes," he agreed quietly. "I really can't believe this is happening." He paced to the door and back. His hands pushed through thin hair. "Her parents must be frantic. The whole school will be frantic."

"Skylar wrote about a boy named Robbie," I said. "What's Robbie's last name?"

He shook his head. "I'm not sure. I've only taught two that went by Robbie, one is in the sixth grade and one moved on to Whisper High a few years ago. Eighth-grade girls don't get crushes on sixth-grade boys. And Melinda and Skylar were in-girls."

That didn't fit with the awkward girl her friend Heather had described. "You know Melinda's friends well? Briana, Shannon, and Heather?"

"No," Tray said. He was forcing himself to calm down a little but his face was still flushed. "None of them took band. But I've seen them. And you know the teachers talk in the lounge. We kind of know what's going on with the kids. Melinda's group was inseparable. I mean, they walked home together." He sat back down. "That's why we were all surprised Melinda could be abducted after school. I mean, how can that happen?"

"How do you think it happened, Mr. Tray?"

"I . . . I don't know. I heard that Melinda lived in a different neighborhood and he got her when she was alone on her street."

"So you never went to her home."

"No. Of course not. Why would I?"

"Do you know all the kids who walk home from Whisper Middle School?"

"Of course not. It's just that we've had a lot of time to talk about Melinda."

"Of course," I agreed sweetly. "Do you know if one of the boys you taught named Robbie has a band?"

"Robbie Raymond. He would be a senior now. He's quite a talented guitar player."

"Where were you yesterday afternoon, Mr. Tray?"

"Me?" Astonishment and panic crossed his face.

"Just routine," I assured him.

"I was here until four. And then I went home."

"Really?" He was lying. "You have someone who can verify that?"

"I don't have to ask permission to leave. I just leave."

"Uh-huh. How about after that?"

"I went home. I practiced. Then I made dinner and watched television."

"Practiced?"

"I play violin."

"Wife?"

"I'm not married."

"Partner?"

"I live alone."

"Anyone else see you?"

"I don't know."

"A neighbor?"

"I don't know." I saw the moment he realized his voice had gotten too loud again. He'd nearly shouted at me. I watched him reel himself in. "My neighbors work. They're not usually home in the afternoon."

"And you got home sometime after four?" I asked.

"That's right."

"So that leaves a gap, doesn't it? Skylar disappeared a little after three. I was here at about three yesterday, by the way. Your classroom was locked. And you were gone. In fact, I was told you'd left much earlier."

His pupils expanded like I'd just hit him with a bucket of epinephrine. "I must have gotten the times wrong," he explained. He was a bad liar, the kind of guy who'd never be able to ace a polygraph. His body had betrayed him repeatedly since I'd walked into his classroom and begun to push. He looked at me. "I can't really be a suspect."

"What kind of vehicle do you drive, Mr. Tray?"

"A Honda. Why? It's an Accord, a two thousand two."

I got up and put one of my cards on the chair. "No plans to leave town, right?"

"No." He said it quietly. He was staring down at his shoes.

"Have a nice weekend."

He blinked up at me.

29

I closed the band room door behind me. School was in session, students and teachers tucked away in classrooms. I stood there for a second in the empty hall, then reached for my phone. "Sam," I said when Meltzer's lab tech answered. "Keye here. Listen, that oil you found on the phones. No question at all it's engine oil? Could it be instrument oil?"

"No way," she said. "You'll remember in addition to the oil the sample was full of engine dirt and metal filings. All consistent with the scenario we discussed."

"How about the cloth? Could it have been a piece of chamois?"

"Totally different fiber," she told me. "What's up?"

"I'm not sure. I'm just trying to make the pieces fit, I guess." I walked down the hall and turned toward the administrative offices. "You been able to determine anything else about the vehicle?"

"About all I can tell you right now is that it's not a new car. Not with all the gunk in that sample."

"Thanks, Sam." I disconnected and turned at the plaque that said KATHY HILLYER—ADMINISTRATIVE ASSISTANT. Kathy Hillyer smiled like I was an old friend when I stepped into her office. Sun was streaming through blinds that were tilted down, the long slats shadowed on the floor. "Hi," she said. *High-eye.* "And what can I do for you today?" She was southern, my mama's kind of southern. Sugary. I didn't trust it, and that probably had little to do with Kathy Hillyer, administrative assistant, and much to do with Emily Street, mother.

"My name is Keye Street. I'm working as a consulting detective with the Hitchiti County Sheriff's Department."

"Well bless your heart. Aren't you cute? I am so glad they let women do that now," she added.

Life on Planet Kathy must be interesting. They had salons there, that was for sure. Her hair and nails told me that. And she was so 1960—the heavy lipstick, the hair twisted on top of her head, the square-neck dress cut almost a shade too low for school—as if she'd just dropped by after a day on the set of *Mad Men*. "Would you like to sit down, honey?"

"Thank you." I took a chair across from her desk. "Ms. Hillyer," I began.

"Kathy," she corrected me.

"Kathy. Do you keep the attendance records?"

"Why, yes. I do. Right here in my computer."

I'm so glad they *let women use computers,* I wanted to say. I bit it back. "Would you mind going back to last school year, January seventeenth to be exact, and tell me if any teacher was absent that day?"

She hit a few keys, then stopped abruptly, as if she'd remembered something important. "I may have to get permission from Principal Olsen to do this."

Everything Kathy said sounded like it ended in a question mark. I didn't want the principal or any other paper pusher who might put the brakes on involved. Someone would start demanding subpoenas. "Official business," I said confidently. "Would you like to speak with the sheriff?"

"Who wouldn't?" Kathy cooed. "Mr. Dreamy."

"I have Mr. Dreamy right here on speed dial." I held up my phone and smiled.

She blushed a violent pink. "Oh Lord, I don't want to bother him! Everyone knows how busy he gets. I don't actually have to turn the records over to you, correct?"

"Correct." I nodded. "It's just routine. All I need is the information."

A few keystrokes later she looked up. "The music coach had an excused absence that day." She searched my face for a hint of what this news meant to me. "Dan Tray."

I pretended to jot down his name like it was no big deal. "Is Mr. Tray usually here every day?"

"Oh yes. Dan's here every day. But only thirty hours a week. Even with students being bused in from other areas, we still don't have enough interested in music to warrant a forty-hour week. So he works half a day twice a week."

"I saw a lot of press and trophies in the display cases. Looks like the band program is huge."

"The band is a source of pride for us all and *very* accomplished," Kathy assured me. "But let's be frank: Unless you're teaching classes in smoking, cheating, and where to buy beer and condoms when you're underage, most of these kids couldn't care less."

"January seventeenth last year is the day Melinda Cochran disappeared," I said.

"Poor Melinda!" she gasped. "That poor, poor little thing."

"Did you ever see Melinda leaving school with anyone?"

If Kathy Hillyer looked to her right she could have seen the view of the front of the school. *If* she looked to her right. And if she'd bothered to tilt her blinds up. "I never saw Melinda take one wrong step. Sweet, smart thing. I was devastated to hear they'd found her."

"Was she awkward and shy in your opinion?"

"Heavens no."

She visibly recoiled when I showed her Peele's picture. She recognized him because she'd followed the court case, she told me. She'd known one of his victims, the daughter of a close friend. Peele had never been near the school, she assured me. Not that she would have known through closed blinds. "Did you know Melinda well?"

"No. But we get a sense of the kids and who they are. Some of them are special."

"So they're not all beer-swilling, rubber-buying vandals?"

Her painted lips curved. "Ten percent. Maybe."

"How about Skylar Barbour?"

"So it's true," she whispered. Her face went white. "Principal Olsen told me this morning that Skylar didn't go home."

"She tried to get home," I said, and got up, took the plastic rod on the side of the window, and twisted it to tilt the blinds up. Kathy swiveled her chair around but didn't rise. "She walked right through there." I pointed at the park. "And through that line of trees and then she disappeared. She had a crush on a boy named Robbie. Do you know him?"

"Oh, well, I wouldn't take that too seriously. I bet half the girls in town are fantasizing about him. His little band plays almost all the dances."

"You're telling me he's a heartthrob?"

Her smile came back. "He must have gotten that from his mother." She lowered her voice into something like a whisper, the way southern women do when they're about to slander someone. "The mother passed away when he was little and Mr. Raymond never remarried. Maybe that's why he's such a grouch. We had to deal with him once on a behavior issue with Robbie. Just boys being boys, but Mr. Raymond made it *very* difficult. For us and for his son."

Detective Raymond hadn't been a big help to me either. "Ms. Hillyer . . . Kathy, did you happen to notice what time Dan Tray left yesterday?"

"Two o'clock," she said without hesitation. "I remember the time because Principal Olsen had an appointment with a vendor who was waiting in my office and I had to step out in the hall. I'm sure it was two o'clock. He had his violin case."

I put my card on her desk. "Thank you for your time."

I walked out of Hillyer's office and pressed the metal bar on one of the double doors, pushed it open. A hot wind hit my face. The bell rang. I glanced back inside and saw the halls filling with a rush of students. Twenty-four hours ago Skylar had been one of them.

30

One of the double doors in front of the school pushed open. From my seat on the park bench, I raised my binoculars and zoomed in. Daniel Tray was moving fast. He was carrying his violin case and fishing around in his front pocket. He pulled out a mobile phone, dropped his keys on the school steps. He balanced the phone between his chin and shoulder and picked up the keys. I could see his face, see him talking, see his hands moving. He was upset. I watched him disappear around the corner where faculty parked, and headed quickly to my car.

Five minutes later, his silver Honda pulled out of the school and turned left. Behind the wheel of my car, I pulled out and followed him.

A '69 convertible is a terrible choice for a tail. I might as well pipe music out through a loudspeaker and put a snow cone on my antenna. Tray turned at a granite sign etched with a cross-and-flame symbol. Whisper Methodist Church. The letter board had a message about making God the director in your personal movie. HE KNOWS HOW THE STORY ENDS.

"Catchy," I muttered. I don't like thinking about how the story ends. Not my story.

I pulled onto a drive that split into two massive parking areas, one below the church, one to the side. The lawn was shaded by giant water oaks and magnolias. The church rose up to an arch in the center, granite and stately, enormous. A window, stained glass and alive with color, depicted Jesus with his shepherd's staff, cradling a simpering lamb. I could see the parsonage to the right. In front of it, a sign said WHISPER COMMUNITY GARDEN—HELP US FEED THE HUNGRY.

Skylar had written about helping with the garden, going inside for cookies, the Hutchinses' daughter, Robin, younger but still fun. She'd written about walking home with her dog, Luke, and a bag of home-grown tomatoes. The rectory was six, maybe seven blocks from the school and not much farther to the Barbour home off Cottonwood Road—an easy walk for a kid with a dog on a summer day.

I watched Tray park, run up the church steps, and pull open one of the heavy wooden doors. I followed. The room I'd entered was long and narrow with stairs on each end, carpeted in deep red. Floor-to-ceiling curtains blocked my view into the church. I heard the quiet murmurs of male voices. I parted a curtain. Daniel Tray was on his knees. Pastor Hutchins stood before him, holding both his hands.

"It's going to be all right, Daniel," I heard Ethan Hutchins tell Daniel Tray. "But you have decisions to make. Listen to God. Remember He always works things out for our good."

I stepped through the curtains into the church. Ethan Hutchins's head turned. Daniel Tray rose to his feet, his eyes never leaving mine as I walked past rows of polished wooden pews toward them.

"This is outrageous!" Daniel Tray blasted me as soon as I got near. "Is nothing sacred? Did I forget that I forfeited some right to privacy?"

"Daniel, please," Ethan Hutchins said gently.

"I'm surprised to see you here, Mr. Tray," I said. It probably wasn't the only lie I was willing to tell in church. "I was just coming to speak with the minister."

Tray pushed past me and stalked up the aisle, swept curtains out of his way with an annoyed flourish. I looked at Hutchins. "I'm sorry to interrupt, Reverend Hutchins." Lie number two.

"This is God's house. You're not interrupting. We are always open."

"Is that right," I said.

His smile widened. "Not big on the God stuff, huh?"

"I'm a little rusty," I admitted.

"Ah. Well, come to my study. It's not very church-like." We walked around the platform with the lectern, and rows for a choir, and stepped through a doorway into a hall. "Ken says you've been enormously valuable to him," Hutchins told me as we walked. "This community needs a break, Ms. Street. We've had too many tragedies. I hope you're here to tell me Skylar's been found."

We stepped into his office—heavy furniture, tall bookcases, no windows, but it was lamp-lit and comfortable. I took one of two chairs on the other side of a wide antique desk. He took the other chair and faced me. "Skylar's still missing. That's why I'm here, to talk about her." It wasn't really lie number three. I *had* wanted to speak with him. I simply failed to mention that I'd shadowed the music teacher here and eavesdropped while they prayed together. If lightning was going to strike, it would be about now.

"Skylar and her parents are members of our congregation. But they're more than that. They're part of a big family. I know you haven't seen the best side of this community, but believe me, there are a lot of good people. Skylar and her parents helped us build the community garden. Hayley and Skylar worked every growing season and bagged produce for hungry families. Several members of the community have shown up today to pray for Skylar."

"Is that why Daniel Tray was here?"

"All of them have the expectation of privacy. Including Dan Tray."

"I spoke with him earlier. He seemed very troubled."

Ethan Hutchins said nothing.

"Do you think he knows something about Skylar?" I asked.

"Heavens no. Daniel is an emotional man, but he's not a bad man."

"Would you tell me if you believed otherwise?"

He leaned forward a little, hands clasped, looked into my eyes. "Sometimes the ethical goal of protecting the community clashes with the duties of the ministry, Dr. Street. People have to trust this is a safe place to unburden themselves. It's a responsibility I take very seriously. But I can assure you that if someone was confessing to a crime against a little girl—and I believe that's what you're alluding to—that confidentiality would have to be broken. Not protecting my neighbors is inconsistent with building a healthy faith-based community. Methodists don't see confession as sacramental." He shrugged. "God doesn't want us to protect murderers and child molesters."

I always get nervous when men start to talk about what God wants. "I find it interesting Daniel Tray would rush here immediately after our chat. One might think he had something to get off his chest."

I saw the tiniest crinkling at the corners of Minister Hutchins's eyes. "Coming to a house of God to pray or to be ministered to in times of grief and confusion is perfectly normal to millions of people, Dr. Street."

"Skylar liked coming here," I said. "She wrote about it in her diary. I think she liked the family atmosphere. Did she ever talk to you about something bothering her? Or someone?"

He shook his head. "But I think she was lonely over the summer. She and my daughter, Robin, played sometimes. And we all ate a lot of lunches together in the parsonage, me, Bernadette, Sky, and Robin. I always called her Sky. It fit her."

His mobile phone lit up and vibrated on his desk. "Pardon me." He got up and looked at it. "Bern has lunch ready. She was at the judicial center all morning. Apparently she's the only lip-reader in Hitchiti County. How about having lunch with us. We'd love it."

I stood. "I can't. But thank you. Your wife is a lip-reader?"

He chuckled. "You have any idea what it's like living with a lip-reader? I can't get away with anything. Yes—she's deaf. As a result she has a superior understanding of communication. Which means she reads your lips, your body language, and your facial expressions. Bern's my Geiger counter. Always steers me right."

"Wow," I said. "Can I borrow her for Vegas?"

He laughed again. "We don't really do a lot of gambling. It's a Methodist thing." We walked back through the sanctuary. "Change your mind about lunch?"

"I wish I could," I told him. "Ken says it's the best place in town."

"Bachelors are easy to please." We parted the long curtains, pushed through heavy doors, and stepped out into the full blaze of Georgia's midday sun. "And here she is now. The head of our family," Ethan Hutchins said with a smile.

A woman came up the steps, smiling. She had honey-brown skin, the kind of striking face that said *Southern Asia*. I saw his navy tie swing forward when he leaned to kiss her cheek. Using sign language, he spoke the introductions.

"Keye Street, meet my wife, Bernadette. Sweetheart, Dr. Street came to talk about Skylar."

"It's terrible," she signed while Hutchins spoke for her. "I can't even imagine what Hayley and Brooks are going through. If something ever happened to Robin . . ."

I was invited again to have lunch and when I declined, Bernadette invited me to dinner on Sunday. I watched them walk across the lush lawn between the church and their home. She reached for his waist. He draped his arm over her shoulder. They moved with the kind of rhythm that told you they'd done some walking together. It shouldn't be surprising to see a married couple still in love, but I stood there, watching them. Meltzer liked to hang out in the Hutchinses' home. Skylar, too, was drawn to them. Was it because of the love missing in their own homes?

31

My phone vibrated with a 706 area code, a local number I didn't recognize. "Keye Street."

"This is Heather," a young voice said. "'Member me? Melinda Cochran's friend."

"Of course," I said. "What's up?"

"That lady officer called us all today. Me, Briana, and Shannon. The one that interviewed us before. The bitchy one. You know who I mean?"

"I think I know the one."

"She was asking if we'd seen anyone with a broken-down car or something. And then we heard about the stuff on the news at school. And you were nice so we thought we could ask you if you know who did it yet, because Melinda was our friend."

"The awkward friend," I said, a little cruelly. "Bad with boys, right?" She was silent. "I know that's not who Melinda was. Look, Heather, if there's something I should know, it's time to let me help. There's another girl missing from the middle school. You won't get in trouble. All anyone cares about is getting Skylar home so she doesn't end up where Melinda did."

I could hear her breathing. I pressed harder. "Why did you deliberately mislead me about Melinda?"

"Our parents don't want us talking to you or anyone. They think something bad will happen."

"Did you see anyone that day, Heather? Was there someone with car trouble you saw on your way home from school?"

"I'm going to get in trouble. I gotta go."

I heard the click and headed to Meltzer's new war room. "Good afternoon," I said. Brolin, Raymond, and Meltzer were lined up like birds on a clothesline looking at the board they'd created—columns labeled VICTIMS, SUSPECTS, EVIDENCE, WITNESSES. Magnetic binder clips were stuck to the board under the appropriate columns, each headed with a photo of victim or suspect. Everything was movable, erasable, as changeable as a fledging investigation.

"Afternoon, Doc," Meltzer nodded. "Okay, here's where I am. I've pulled Deputy Ferrell into Criminal Investigations. She applied a while back, as you know, Tina," he said to Major Brolin. "And it is abundantly clear to me that we need more bodies in this unit right away. For now, Ferrell is home base. This is to ensure we have a steady flow of information available to us all. You'll contact Ferrell by mobile phone. No radios. We have media in town now. Let's assume they have scanners. Ferrell will relay new information via group text message. And I'm encouraged to see we have four names in the suspect column. Let's start there."

I glanced at the board. Logan Peele's icy gaze locked on me from the suspect column. *Reg offender no alibi.* Below his photo was Daniel Tray's. *Middle school teacher for Cochran/Barbour—No alibi.* Below Tray's photo was the sex offender who hadn't showed up for his group treatment program. The note next to Lamar Bailey's picture said *Reg offender—unexcused absence—AWOL.* Below that was a face I recognized from the diner. It was the man who had served me the first night I was in town, the one who'd withdrawn once he learned who I was. *Gene Johnson—reg offender—tipped Peele.*

"Gene from the diner is a sex offender?" I asked. He was not on the list Neil had given me, which meant he didn't fit the original criteria we'd used to narrow the suspect pool.

"Level one," Raymond said. A clock with three hands ticked off seconds loudly at the end of the room. "He got too drunk one night and flashed some people in the park. Gene thought it was funny as hell. Turned out to be a bunch of high school kids."

"So why is he on the board?" I wanted to know.

"He's in Dr. Pope's treatment program," Brolin answered. I put my things down and stepped closer to the board. "And he imparted some real interesting information to Peele last night after their group session. We have it from the surveillance cameras. We enhanced the video. Let's see it, Rob."

"This was gathered from five different cameras last night around the time Victoria Pope was having her group session," Raymond told us. The security footage showed the F-150 pulling up, Logan Peele getting out and walking the same walkway I'd just used to get to the judicial center. Next we saw him inside at the elevator, then getting off the elevator and disappearing into the office Dr. Pope used for group. "Now watch this."

The door opened and the corridor filled with men, men in jeans, men in business suits, average-looking men, men who might have been leaving a sales meeting. Twelve of them. Raymond reached for the mouse as we watched Logan Peele come through the door. Behind him, Gene Johnson put a hand on Peele's arm, stopped him. Raymond slowed the video. Johnson's lips moved. *"Somebody took a girl."* Raymond spoke the words for him. Now I understood why the minister's lip-reading wife had been asked to come to the complex. Brolin and Raymond had aggressively followed up. It was good work.

"He might have also said somebody took *the* girl." Raymond froze the image on the screen. "It's kinda hard to distinguish that one word, but we're solid on the rest of it."

"You know how Peele responded?" I asked.

"Couldn't get it." Meltzer was frowning. "He never turned toward the camera."

"As if he knew it was there. What time did your deputies take the first call from Skylar's parents?" I asked.

"That's the problem," Brolin told me. "This was recorded half an hour before. That's how Peele knew about a missing girl in your interview this morning. Not because he'd seen the news."

"We know Peele went home after this. We had eyes on him. And we checked his financials. Debit card charge to Pizza Hut for sixteen dollars," Raymond said.

"Alibi Hut," Brolin muttered, miserably. "How many creeps have we had alibi out with a pizza delivery?"

"Have we picked up Gene Johnson yet?" Meltzer asked.

"Got him," Raymond said. "Set up a temporary interview room next door."

"We have audio and video in the room," Brolin added. "No window, obviously."

Raymond pulled up the feed on the monitor and we saw the old server sitting at a bare table, probably smelling, as the diner smelled, of bacon and caramelized onions and oil. "Go find out how he knew about Skylar before we did," Meltzer told them.

Brolin walked into the interview room with a manila folder. Raymond lumbered in behind her. He put his phone on the table. They sat and faced Gene Johnson. Johnson straightened in his metal chair. The sheriff sat next to me.

Raymond spoke first. "How you doing, Gene? Do you know why you're here?"

"No. I don't. You know me, Rob. I don't get into trouble. Not since I quit drinking."

"Logan Peele your buddy or something?" Raymond asked.

"He's in that program they make us go to. That's all. I toe the line, Rob. I don't hang around with those guys."

Brolin opened the folder and looked down at it, a tactic meant to imply she had information she wasn't sharing. She lifted her eyes to him. "That's curious, Gene. Because we have you on video telling him, and I quote, 'Somebody took a girl.'"

"Yeah," Raymond said roughly. "Curious." He clicked his phone on and slid it across the table to Johnson.

Johnson stared miserably at Raymond's phone screen. "There's no sound," he said finally.

"We have it on the house security," Brolin lied effortlessly. "Want to tell us how you knew Skylar Barbour was missing?"

"I don't know nothing about it," Johnson insisted. "I swear."

"Bullshit." Raymond's big, puffy face was grim and impatient. He looked bone-tired. This investigation had been hard on all of us. "You got off easy on your first offense. We figured you just got drunk and acted up. But now it's starting to look like you're one of them. That disappoints me, Gene."

Johnson shuddered but stayed silent. He looked as if he was going to cry.

Brolin leaned forward. "Where's the girl you warned Peele about?"

"How would I know?" Gene shot back.

"You said somebody took a girl. So where is she?" Brolin pressed. *Who has Skylar?*"

"I don't *know*!"

"You warned Logan Peele before we received the missing persons report," Brolin told him. "How'd you know?"

Johnson looked confused, but he was silent.

Brolin scraped back her chair and stood. "You will be held accountable if something happens to this young woman," she threatened. "And I'll make it a priority to see that your status is reviewed. I'm starting to think you're a danger to the community living on the outside."

Johnson cracked. "My wife, okay?" he said. "It was innocent. Her best friend is a bus driver for the middle school, that's all. Somebody called her and said that girl had disappeared. She told my wife. That's how I knew."

"Then why not just say that right off, for fuck's sake?" Raymond snapped in disgust. "'Cause this just makes it seem like you're lying your ass off now."

"She was really upset," Johnson said. "I didn't want to get her in trouble 'cause she wasn't supposed to tell anyone yet."

"Damnit," the sheriff spat, beside me. This wasn't going where we wanted it to.

"And you gotta run and tell Peele about it?" Raymond asked Johnson. "Why?"

"'Cause I knew if something bad happened to her you'd start rounding us up." Johnson's face knotted. "And you did. I just wanted to warn him, that's all. Some of us are trying to live normal lives, but that's not easy when deputies show up every damn time something bad happens."

"What's the driver's name?" Brolin asked. "The one who called your wife."

"Vicki," he said. "Um . . . Vicki Bello. Lives over on Maple. Look, don't get her in trouble, okay? They were just talking. Vicki said the parents were calling everyone. Even the kids."

"That's the bus driver's name," Meltzer murmured. "In Hayley Barbour's statement. She called the bus driver Mrs. Bello. And Major Brolin spoke to her too."

Tina Brolin was standing now, looking at Johnson in disbelief. I knew exactly how she felt. She'd thought she finally had it within her grasp—the answer to Skylar's disappearance, the killer or someone who could lead us to the killer. "You're free to go for now," she told Johnson.

"Call the driver and see if she'll admit to calling Johnson's wife," the sheriff ordered when they returned.

We listened as Raymond made the call, disconnected, nodded. "Checks out," he reported.

Major Brolin plucked Gene Johnson's photo out of the suspect column. Her front teeth pressed hard into her bottom lip and her eyes were as feral and unpredictable as a Siamese cat's. She flung the photo across the room like a Frisbee. It fluttered and failed. The clock sounded hollow and loud. Skylar's photograph looked down at us from the board, beckoning, pleading.

32

Missing, it said in the wide, uneven strokes of a black marker. Skylar's photo hung alone in the open center of the board, away from the evidence column, away from the witness and suspect columns. Simple notes chronicled what we knew of the last day anyone had seen her: *School, leaves school, walks home. 3 p.m. School out. 3:17 Skylar's mobile/Cottonwood Rd to Barbour landline.* Those last hours, those last moments before the crime, they always boil down to a few bare lines. You have to remind yourself they're more than that. Someone was in those moments, experiencing them, living their life, thinking their thoughts.

"Parole officer's trying to track him down," Raymond was updating us on the sex offender Lamar Bailey. He wasn't home and hadn't shown up for work. My eyes drifted to the suspect column and Bailey's photograph.

I moved Daniel Tray's photo to a clean section on the board. "I dropped in to see the band teacher who taught both Melinda and Skylar. His reaction to the news Skylar had disappeared was more stress than grief. He was actually sweating. And he lied to me." I made a list next to his photo with a squeaking marker that sounded like wet sneakers on tile. *Leaves early 2X a week. Excused absence 1/17/M Cochran abduction. Lied about time. 2 p.m. No alibi.* "He told me he left at four yesterday. He didn't know I'd been by the school to see him at three o'clock." I'd been inside that school while Skylar crossed the park for the last time and walked into the woods and vanished. Perhaps she was one of the throng rushing through the double doors when the bell rang. Perhaps we'd rubbed elbows at the door. My life had crossed paths with her in those last precious moments before she became a victim. "The admin assistant said she saw Daniel Tray leaving at two," I told them. "He also works a thirty-hour week, which makes him free at midafternoon twice a week."

Brolin picked up a marker and scrawled *opportunity* next to Tray's photo. "We ran him again yesterday and he was clean," she said. I noticed the *again*. "We didn't consider him a person of interest when Melinda disappeared." Brolin was trying to cover. She was telling us they were aware of Tray and had excluded him. But the files reflected a different story. They'd let their familiarity with the victim prevent them from compiling a complete victimology, which would have rooted out Tray and everyone else Melinda had contact with in her life, and now Brolin was trying to save face, and maybe save her ass. I knew the sheriff wasn't happy with his team.

"Deputy Ferrell is canvassing Mr. Tray's street," Meltzer told us. "Tray told Keye he went straight home from school. We need someone in the neighborhood who can corroborate."

"He was shaken up when I interviewed him," I told them. "Ten minutes later he comes out of the school, obviously distraught. He's talking fast into his phone. Then he drives straight to the church. By the time I get inside, he's huddled with the minister. In prayer. Anyone else find that suspicious?"

"Very," Brolin said grimly.

"I spoke with Ethan Hutchins," I told them. "He said a lot of people had come to pray since the news broke about Skylar. He assured me he doesn't protect violent offenders."

"But you didn't buy it?" Brolin said.

"Something's going on with Tray," I answered. "We need to know why he lied. His time is currently unaccounted for after two o'clock, and that coincides with Skylar's abduction. And there's the excused absence on the day the second vic disappeared."

"Fucker looks like Mister Rogers," Raymond rasped. "Hard to trust that. And it's not like we haven't seen the God thing before with crazies."

"If no one supports his alibi, we'll have a closer look," Meltzer said, like he was checking off his list.

"Couple of other interesting items," I added. I pointed to the names on the board under the witness section—Shannon Davis, Briana Franklin, and Heather Ridge. "When I interviewed these girls, Heather referred to Melinda as awkward."

"Not the Melinda I knew from the diner," Brolin said, and the sheriff agreed.

"Apparently not the Melinda anyone knew," I said. "So Heather intentionally misled me. Why? She called me a few minutes before I got here. She was fishing. She wanted to know what we had."

Raymond chuckled. "Probably trying to cover some kid shit. They're always guilty of some kind of crap at that age. And believe you me, you never know what they're thinking."

"Maybe," I agreed, and looked back at the board. "Or maybe those girls know something. I walked down the street with them yesterday. You can see right into Melinda's neighborhood. Y'all know those neighborhoods. If someone was waiting for her, how is it they didn't see him?"

Shannon Davis. Briana Franklin. Heather Ridge. Brolin put a big question mark next to their names.

"I'm not trying to shoot your theory down or anything." Raymond shifted his big body, stuffed some of his shirttail back under his belt. "But as a parent to a teenager, let me tell you they're self-absorbed as hell and they lie their asses off for the fun of it. Robbie hasn't told me the truth in three years. Melinda's address is on a side street that runs off the one into the neighborhood. We found her phone at an intersection. That view would have been partially obstructed."

"I got a call from an attorney this morning. After Tina spoke to the girls, the parents contacted him," the sheriff said. "Upsets the girls to keep talking about it, I was told. Any more questions will have to be scheduled with attorneys present."

Raymond muttered something. Meltzer flashed him a look.

"A couple of things are bothering me," I told them. "It's not unusual for there to be an interval between serial crimes. The offender uses the time to emotionally distance himself from an offense, compartmentalize, detach from his violent behaviors. He tries to psychologically reintegrate into society, and into his own life. The ten-year gap between murders we have with Melinda and Tracy could mean the killer was out of the area for that period of time or he was incarcerated. It could also have to do with the level of fulfillment achieved with the last victim. Some of these guys get married and lead a normal life for long periods of time. It's not always understood what triggers a dormant period or a violent period. But we've got significant differences in behaviors before and after that long cooling-off period. Tracy's injuries were much less severe, even though she was held for a longer time. That's inconsistent with the sadist who tortured Melinda." *You broke her fingers and nearly severed her head*, I thought. *Why?*

"You saying this monster's schizophrenic or something? Or just getting worse? Because there are significant similarities," Raymond argued. He ticked them off on his fingers. "Time of day. Age of the vics. Disposal site. And they were both blondes."

"The disposal site establishes case linkage. It's indisputable, I know," I said. Raymond wasn't a stupid man. But he was rude and lazy. And he'd dropped the ball on the investigation into Melinda's disappearance. Because of that, Skylar was now in terrible jeopardy. I felt my temper flare. "And yes, he's significantly more violent now, more sadistic. But I think our guy's come to enjoy the act of ending a life as much as he enjoys controlling his victims. Tracy was killed with a blunt object, perhaps the flat side of an axe. Her back was turned. He didn't want to look at her. He just wanted to get it done. Fast-forward ten years and he decides to use the sharp side of the axe. He wants bigger, bloodier, something more satisfying. It's likely he was attempting to decapitate her and simply didn't do it correctly. Offenders without a medical background have to experiment, use trial and error. He's new to decapitation. He needed the force of a downward swing. He's learned that now. Melinda probably fell into the embankment when he hit her the first time. Positioning of the bodies supports that. Tracy was thrown. Her body was near the center of the crater. But Melinda rolled off the side."

They were staring at me as if I'd just clucked the national anthem. "What?" I asked.

Raymond shifted, muttered something that sounded like *Geesshh*. Brolin turned back to the board. "So he's more violent," Meltzer agreed. "And he wants attention. Bad combination, in my experience. Skylar may have less time than the others."

"He's not as careful," I said. "Maybe his illness is progressing. He's leaving evidence and messages for us to find. Risky behaviors. Look at Zodiac and all his coded, bragging letters to the media and to police. David Berkowitz with his rambling *I am Son of Sam. I'm a little brat* letter. Wishbone did it with APD last year in Atlanta. But for this killer, it's a new behavior."

"Zodiac got away," Brolin said flatly. "So did Wishbone." She held my eyes for a moment, then looked away. I'd worked the Wishbone case. Rarely a day passed that I didn't expect to see Wishbone's venom and torture in the headlines again.

"Well, this one's not getting away," Meltzer said. "I think his ego is bigger than his brain. Which brings me back to Peele." He turned to Brolin. "What's the latest?"

"He sat in the parking lot for an hour before he left this morning," Brolin reported. "Then he went straight home. He's been there all morning."

"I saw him in the parking lot," I said. "He made sure I noticed him. He watched while Brenda Roberts interviewed me. I wouldn't be at all surprised if he tipped her I was in the building."

"He's a bastard," Raymond growled, impatient. "Turns out we made good use of that reporter, though. Getting the word out and all." That was a matter of opinion. Generally the less the media knows about an investigation, the faster it can move. Raymond grinned at me. "Who knew you came with your own camera crew? I gotta remember to wear my makeup from now on. Maybe you can get me an interview."

"Lay off, Rob," Brolin warned.

"No harm done. Just a little friendly fun." He scraped his chair back, smoothed the front of his shirt. "Gotta hit the head."

"Hurry up," Brolin told him, as he left the room. She slipped into a tan blazer, which fell nicely over the duty holster on her hip. "There are a few farmhouses down on Cottonwood Road. Maybe someone saw a vehicle. We had a robbery this morning and we're late getting started. And I want Skylar's friends on the record as soon as school's out before their parents intervene too. Everyone was upset last night. Hard to get clear information."

"What can I do?" I asked. "Anyone canvass the shops on Main Street?"

"We had a patrol unit check in with everyone," Brolin said.

"I could speak with Skylar's friends," I offered. I didn't want Brolin to scare them to death.

"We got that," Brolin said. "Rob's good with kids."

"Sure," I said. Hard to imagine Raymond was good with anyone. But I had seen a different side of him when he spoke with Hayley Barbour at their home. He was a father, after all, and none of us were. Or was Brolin a parent too? I hadn't asked. I tried to visualize her as a nurturer of children, a sacrificer, a listener, a giggler, a chauffeur. "Then I'm free to talk to the teacher again," I said decisively. I grabbed my bag. "Hey, Raymond," I called. "Got a sec?"

Detective Rob Raymond gave me a curious look when I caught up to him and pulled the pink diary from my bag. "I promised I'd get this back to you."

He looked at it, then lifted heavy lids to me. He was part Raymond Burr, part J. Edgar Hoover, big, dark, all attitude. I knew a bully when I saw one.

"Your son and Skylar were having a flirtation," I told him. "I thought you'd like to know before you turn the diary in."

"What are you talking about, Street?"

"Some kissing. She cut band practice to see him. Pretty tame stuff."

Raymond took the diary. The pink journal looked odd in his meaty hands. A photo tumbled out and hit the floor faceup, Skylar in a photo booth—four frames, two happy girls. Raymond bent down and picked it up. He looked at it for a minute. "I'll be damned," he muttered. "I thought the little fucker was gay."

"He never mentioned her?" I asked.

"Kid's seventeen. He doesn't tell me shit."

"Your son may have information about Skylar we need. The Skylar he knew had a crush on an older boy and cut classes to see him. Did she have other behaviors that put her at risk? Maybe he knows something else about her."

"You read the diary, you tell me about her behaviors," Raymond said. "And you stay the fuck away from my kid."

"You know how honest she was with her diary?" I shot back. "She didn't even mention Robbie was in high school. It would be a big deal to a middle school girl, a seventeen-year-old boy giving her attention. Barbour told me his wife read Skylar's diary last year. Skylar found out. She didn't trust they wouldn't find it again. She was editing."

"I'll talk to him," Raymond rasped. "And I'll check this into evidence." He walked away.

"You're welcome," I called. He didn't turn.

I returned to the war room and told Meltzer and Brolin why I'd left to speak with Raymond.

"Robbie's a good kid," Meltzer said. "Rob should be the one to talk to him first. This has got to be hard on all the kids."

Raymond came back in. He was still holding the diary. Meltzer picked up a marker and wrote on the board. "This is Deputy Ferrell's number. Put it in your devices. And answer when she calls, please. She'll forward credible tips from the tip lines and keep us up to date. Let's communicate with her hourly. Everyone checks in with a progress report."

We all keyed in the deputy's number. Raymond's phone played a minuet, not the ringtone choice I'd imagine for him. He listened, said, "Okay, thanks," and disconnected. "Another goddamn dead end. That was Lamar Bailey's parole officer. He wasn't at group last night because he's been in the hospital since yesterday morning."

33

Her chains heaved and clanged behind her. She groped out into the blackness like a mime. For a moment, he watched the frantic, ghostly image through his goggles. He closed his eyes, remembered the hood slamming down on her, her back arching under the weight and pain, the latch slicing through fabric and biting into skin and tissue. He'd practiced hitting that brace with his elbow and getting out of the way. If he had thought of that with the Cochran girl, he wouldn't have had to punch her in the throat. He'd almost killed her before he got her in the car.

"Skylar," he said playfully. "I can see you. Hey, I brought you some food. My favorite. Bologna and mustard. And water. You want some water?"

She pressed against the wall, drew her knees up to her chest. The chains attached to her ankle cuffs pulled taut. He saw her flinch when her bloody back touched the wall, and he felt the warm, primitive stirrings of an erection.

"Stay away from me!"

The stained twin mattress on the floor reeked of urine and mold. He pushed the goggles to the top of his head, struck the wheel on a Bic lighter, and lit a kerosene lantern. It filled the room with sharp, acrid fumes.

She squinted up through the light she'd been deprived of for hours. *"Why are you doing this to me?"*

He lifted the orange bucket next to the mattress. He was wearing thin surgical gloves. He always wore them in this room. "Use this. I don't want to have to clean up after you."

"Let me go, you freak!"

"Just for that I should take the sandwich back," he told her calmly, and watched her for a minute before he reached in the bag he'd brought the food in for a spiral notebook and a pen. "But since you're new here, I'm going to give you a second chance because I know you're hungry."

"Fuck you," she spat. Strands of golden hair stuck to her face. She'd started to cry again. She'd been crying a lot. It was annoying. But her eyes didn't let him down. They were angry and defiant. He liked that.

"I want you to do something for me, Skylar." He picked up an axe and carried it in one hand, dropped the notebook and pen on the stinking mattress in front of her. "Write exactly what I tell you to write. Go off script even once and I'll cut your fucking head off."

Ken Meltzer rubbed his forehead as if he was getting my headache. We were driving toward Daniel Tray's house. "I'm going to stop and grab us something to eat," he told me. "I'm running on empty. How about you?"

"Yes. Hotel breakfast was awful." Except for the Krispy Kremes I didn't mention.

"They have breakfast over there? I thought breakfast was walking down the street to the diner."

"I changed hotels," I said. "I haven't had time to tell you. When I got back last night, my room had been broken into."

"What was missing? Did you call anyone? Did anyone make a report? Why the hell didn't you call me?"

"I'd left you standing on the road at the scene. It seemed a little more important than my missing mascara," I told him. "My valuables were in the safe, which was undisturbed. They either didn't know it was there or they were interrupted."

"No more notes?" he asked. His voice was sharp.

"No."

He started to say something. My phone bleated. Neil. Meltzer got out of the SUV, headed into the diner.

"I need you to run Daniel Tray's background for me, financials if you can get them, and medical," I told him. People could hide a lot, but a psychiatric history has a way of stripping off the varnish. "I want to know if he owns the house or any other properties. See if you can get a floor plan from the deed records. Any expenses on hardware, renovations, stuff like that."

"Will do," Neil said.

"Also, expenses leading up to January seventeenth of this year and yesterday when the third victim disappeared," I told him. "Anything that looks different, even a spike in his grocery bill." Melinda and Tracy had suffered malnutrition but he'd have to feed them something. He needed to keep them hydrated. Bottled water cost money. "See if you can zoom in on satellite now and tell me about his place."

I waited while Neil found Tray's address. "Looks like a frame house, two, maybe three bedrooms," he said. "I'll have the deed in a sec. One level. Might have a crawl space or a cellar. I don't see basement windows. Shed out back. Pretty small. Insecure. Aluminum. Any reason the sheriff's department isn't running him?"

"They did," I said. "Tray has no criminal record. But his alibi is soft and he freaked out when I interviewed him. The kids I talked to called him *touchy-feely*. But these kids were also lying to me and I don't know why. He taught the second and third victim. Melinda and Skylar were pulling away from the band and his classes. I want to know if it's because their band teacher is creepy. The team here didn't find any obvious ties to the town of Silas where the first victim lived. Look again, Neil. Maybe Tray has family or friends there."

"Eleven years ago she disappeared, right?" Neil said. "You sound totally stressed, by the way."

"Ya think? Skylar's been in some hole and it's only going to get worse for her. We need to cross this teacher off our list if he's innocent and move on. I need it, like, *now*."

I clicked off and sat there for a couple of minutes thinking about the office, about what was waiting for me when I returned, feeling that churning dread in the pit of my stomach. Meltzer got in with two take-out cartons and two Styrofoam cups with straws. He handed me one of each, put his cup between his legs in the driver's seat and his carton on the flat console between the seats. "Not the healthiest thing on the menu, but I've become a connoisseur of foods that can be eaten with one hand while driving."

"I've never known a cop that didn't eat fast and one-handed," I said. He smiled.

Most times, it's just basic manners not to speak with food in your mouth. But there are occasions when you need to talk and eat and keep moving.

"Both Melinda and Skylar were disengaging from band and, according to Mr. Tray, from outside activities with classmates. Why?"

"I don't remember Bryant and Molly saying anything about problems with Melinda other than normal teenage stuff. Little fights about where she could go and for how long. Nothing huge. That reminds me. I got a text from Molly this morning. It's in my phone. Have a look."

I washed a bite of fish down with sweet tea, wiped my fingers on a paper napkin, and picked up the sheriff's iPhone. He didn't know I'd held it in my hand once before and ached to read his messages from Molly. I'd been suspicious. It's in my nature. I clicked on the message icon. *We know you're trying as hard as you can and we love you for it. Come by the lanes for a bite and a beer if you need a pick-me-up. Bring the new partner.* I read the two messages above it. Same vein.

I swallowed down some guilt with the tea. "Molly seemed really nice."

He nodded. "She helped take care of Mom while we were looking for a full-time caretaker. That's how I got to know them."

"Bryant was nice too, despite the fact that he called me an Oriental and made a remark about gay men making him uncomfortable." I put the sheriff's phone down and grabbed a potato wedge from the box in my lap.

"Bryant's a product of his upbringing. Poor. No formal education, a macho, country-boy culture. Probably never crossed the state line. If you're not growing hair on your knuckles, Bryant thinks you're gay." Meltzer chuckled. "If he actually knew a gay man, or knew that he knew a gay man, his opinion would change. He's thick sometimes but he has a good heart."

"He says Tray's gay," I said. "Not that it matters for our purposes."

"Except that your average serial is usually heterosexual."

"You stay up reading the serial handbook last night?" I smiled at him. My phone jiggled and lit up. I looked at the message. "It's from my partner. Says Tray's on an antidepressant called Zoloft. It's for mild depression. I think half my family has been on it at some point in their life."

"Really?" Meltzer asked. He picked up a potato from his box. "Depressed family?"

"Clinically," I answered. "Fortunately, I'm adopted." I looked at my phone. "My partner says no spikes in Tray's spending around the abduction dates. Neil's looking at social media and possible contacts to Silas. Tray owns his house, no other properties. Pays his bills online, gives about ten percent of his income to a couple of ministries, your pastor's church, for one, and a television ministry."

"Well, that explains him going to the church," Meltzer said. "He's a religious guy."

"Zoning and deeds aren't showing any renovations or additions to the property since he's owned it," I read. "The house was built in nineteen thirty. Two small closets. No basement. No receipts yesterday. Whatever he was doing, he wasn't using his debit card. Same on January seventeenth. Nothing to alibi him out. He was divorced seven years ago. And he has a ten-year-old daughter."

Meltzer's head shot up. We both thought of Tracy Davidson, of the baby she'd given birth to ten years ago.

"Welcome to the dark side," I told Meltzer.

34

"**M**r. Tray, Hitchiti County Sheriff." Meltzer raised his voice and let go of the second round of loud cop-knocks. My headache skirted across the ridgeline over my eyes, but the fist in my temple had relented with lunch. The silver Honda was parked in a driveway that had been poured with cement years ago and since broken away, exposing dirt tire trenches. The house was olive green, the kind of house a thirty-hour-a-week music teacher's salary could buy. Fat white oaks shaded its shingled roof.

The sheriff banged again. "Mr. Tray, please open the door. It's important I speak with you."

"I'll check the back." I went down the wooden porch steps, rounded the corner of the house—and slammed into Daniel Tray.

Tray staggered back. His right palm flew to his heart. "Good grief. Ms. Street!" He was wearing snug knee-length shorts that made his hips seem wider and his legs thinner, army green like his house. The golf shirt was cobalt. The collar curled at the tips from the dryer.

"Doing some yard work?" I asked. He was holding a shovel.

"Are you going to accuse me of burying bodies in the backyard?" He jammed the edge of the spade in the dirt with one swift, hard movement. He was stronger than he looked and he was definitely more comfortable on home turf. "Because you already practically accused me of, let's see, meeting my students inappropriately. Do you have any idea what even the suggestion of that could do to me? I happen to like teaching music to kids, Ms. Street. I don't do it because I'm sexually attracted to children. I do it because it's fulfilling, okay?"

"Nice," I said. "I can see you've given this some thought. We just need to clear up a few things, Mr. Tray, and we'll be out of your hair. I know you'd want us to do the same if it were your daughter."

Tray's greenish eyes darkened and drifted over my shoulder. Meltzer joined us. "I don't want my neighbors to think—" Tray said.

"We parked a couple of doors down," Meltzer told him.

"Look, I was upset when I found out about Skylar," Tray told us. His left hand was still on the shovel, stuck in the earth. "And I know I must have looked suspicious to you. It was just such a shock. Skylar was a sweet kid."

My heart hit my stomach. *Was*. She *was* a sweet kid. The condensing unit a foot away buzzed and clicked on. Hot air from the rusty fan inside rustled our clothes and made a row of tall iris stems shimmy against the side of the house.

"Is there somewhere we could sit and talk?" Meltzer asked. His voice was friendly, a daddy voice, a bedtime-story voice, a voice that made you forget he was wondering if you were a killer of girls. Tray gave another glance at the street. Meltzer pressed a little harder. "We don't have time to spare right now, Mr. Tray."

Tray's shoulders slumped. He pulled the shovel out of the dirt and leaned it against the house. He led us around back to a small stone patio. I saw a four-foot Japanese maple sitting in fresh dirt. A tag still hung on one branch limb. The aluminum shed Neil had seen on satellite was open to a lawn mower and neatly stacked garden tools. We sat down at a metal table, a bright orange umbrella overhead. I looked at the row of woods behind the house. You can hide a lot in the woods.

"You lied about what time you left school yesterday," I said. "Why?"

"I don't even know for sure what time I left, okay?" Tray's long, bony arms were propped on the gritty tabletop. "I came straight home."

"Did you talk to anyone or see anyone?" Meltzer was leaning back in the metal chair, long body relaxed. "Skylar was abducted just a little after three. We have a witness who saw you leave the school at two, but we can't find anyone who saw you after that."

"I didn't know I'd need a story." Tray's eyes were watering, as if he were looking into the sun.

"You remember where you were when Melinda Cochran disappeared?" I asked.

"I was at school when I heard about Melinda."

"But you don't remember where you were that day? January seventeenth?"

"I was at work."

"The attendance records show you as absent that day."

His right hand opened and closed. Fear blazed in his eyes. "I only used two sick days during the last school year. And if one of them was the day Melinda disappeared, I swear to God it was just some freak coincidence—"

"Okay, so here's what's going to happen," Meltzer interposed, before I could speak again. His voice stayed even but I felt the coiled energy coming off him. "I'm going to cuff you like a common criminal and bring you in for questioning as a person of interest in the kidnap and murders of Tracy Davidson and Melinda Cochran, and in Skylar Barbour's abduction. I'm going to haul you in the back of that plainly marked vehicle through town with all the windows down. That's going to create a lot of buzz. We may even tip that reporter hanging around town. And then we're going to pick apart every infinitesimal piece of your private life until we understand why you're lying about where you were yesterday at three—"

"Whoa!" Tray held up both palms. "Just whoa. Okay, listen." His fist clenched again. His gaze skittered away from us. He was deciding what to tell, figuring out what to let go of, what to color. "I'll tell you but you can't tell anyone."

Meltzer's eyebrow came up. We exchanged a glance.

"Let me get this straight." Meltzer leaned forward. "You want to cut a deal or you'll withhold information in a homicide investigation? Is that what you're saying?"

"I'm seeing someone. Okay? She's married." Tray's words came out in a panicked torrent.

"This *she* have a name?" Meltzer asked.

"Yes," Tray answered quietly. And I suddenly knew why he'd run to church today. His lover was an adulterer, and he'd lied to me to cover their deception. A big deal for a guy who gives a good chunk of his income to Christian ministries.

"Good Lord," I muttered quietly. I'd sensed deception and rooted out an affair, not a killer. I pinched the bridge of my nose, closed my eyes for a second, as the sheriff took the name of Tray's afternoon booty call. Daniel Tray wasn't our guy.

The breeze spun the umbrella sticking through the hole in the table like a pinwheel and brought us the smell of fermenting apples from a tree next door. I saw them on the ground, brown and rotting, saw the yellow jackets buzzing greedily around them.

Small towns, I thought.

35

A poster with Skylar's face was taped to a telephone pole. The word MISSING over the photo. We sat there looking at it. RAISE AWARENESS AND HELP BRING SKYLAR HOME! CANDLELIGHT PRAYER—FRIDAY 8:30 P.M.—WHISPER PARK. The minister's wife came out of the hardware store where we were parked. She put a stack of posters on the sidewalk, then taped another poster to the front door. She saw us and waved. We waved back. She wasn't smiling either.

"Let me talk to the florist," I told Meltzer. "I think she's more likely to talk about her private life off the record."

"Right." He nodded. "I'll speak to Bernadette and hit the coffee shop. Are you opposed to more caffeine?"

"Never," I said fervently.

I signed hello to Bernadette Hutchins, then crossed the street and walked three stores up. The door was stenciled in white. PACE FLORAL DESIGN. MON–SAT 9:00–5:00. CLOSED FOR LUNCH 12:00–1:00. Below that, someone had taped another MISSING poster.

Inside, roses in cheap white vases and carnations stuffed into wet green foam with baby's breath and other greenery chilled behind glass doors. It all looked and smelled like a funeral to me. The bell had jangled when I opened the door and she'd looked up from a pile of long-stem roses on the counter, clippers in her right hand. She was brown-eyed and pretty in a simple way. Plain, my mother would have labeled her after a *Bless her heart* or two.

"May I help you?" she asked, but I saw her lips tighten. She knew who I was and why I was there. Tray had warned her. It had probably sounded something like: *She's Chinese.*

"Mrs. Pace?"

She snipped a leaf off a rose stem, then cut the end at an angle and put it in a different pile. "The driver will be back soon," she told me, keeping her eyes and hands on her work. I had a feeling she wasn't very happy with her boyfriend at the moment.

"My name is Keye Street. I'm working with the sheriff's department. I think you already know that. And why I'm here. This won't take but a minute," I said.

She clipped another stem. She still wasn't looking at me. "I've been seeing Dan for over two years. I know it's wrong. But I've been so unhappy—do you have to tell my husband?" she asked quietly. "He thinks I have Jazzercise."

Five minutes later, I walked out of the floral chill into the searing sun. Meltzer was crossing the street with two tall plastic cups. Bernadette Hutchins was several doors up with her posters, Skylar's face plastered all over. "Latte, frozen. For the city girl. How'd it go?" As Meltzer handed it to me, I saw two women staring out the drugstore window across the street.

"They've been meeting for two years twice a month," I said. "Ferrell verified the reservation at the Marriott in the resort area."

"That leaves one suspect on our board," he said grimly. "He's been in his cave since he left us this morning. And you don't like him for this. So where does that leave us?"

I glanced at the coffee shop next to the drugstore. More curious eyes peering out. "I could be wrong but I simply don't think it's possible for Peele *not* to be noticed. I mean, come on, he has a red Fu Manchu and arms like a weight lifter. And as far as we can tell, Peele is a stranger to all three girls. Besides, no one will ever know about the crimes Peele is or isn't committing. He doesn't want to go back to jail. He's not going to send me letters."

"So why doesn't he just alibi out of yesterday and end this?" Meltzer answered his own question. "You think he has an alibi that he's not using. Because he likes stringing us along."

"It does cost you time and resources," I told him. "And he probably is hiding something."

I saw a flash in the window across the street, a reflection, and turned to see what it was. Brenda Roberts's cameraman leaned against a lamppost twenty feet away. His camera was pointed our way. I didn't see the reporter. Meltzer followed my eyes. We started walking toward his vehicle, our backs to the camera. "I'd love to bring Peele in," he said. "I could hold him for a while without charging him. But if he is our man, you know he's not going to tell us where Skylar is. And who knows if . . ." He stopped.

"He'd let her die," I said, finishing his thought. "Which is another reason we can't rule him out. That's exactly the kind of man we're looking for."

We got in the truck. Meltzer looked back at the street. "Camera's still on us," he grumbled.

"Must be getting stock footage. I don't see Roberts."

Meltzer sighed. "They've got me coming out of a coffee shop. The only thing that could make that more clichéd would be if I had a doughnut in my hand."

"And a beer belly," I said.

A single bell tolled on the sheriff's phone. He tucked his cup between his legs and pressed the phone against his left temple. "Meltzer," he said. He listened. "How long was he gone?" His right thumb turned the small ruby on his ring finger in tiny, uneasy half circles. "Stand by, Major." He put the phone against his leg. "Plainclothes unit on Peele said he jogged by them thirteen minutes ago. Hooded sweatshirt, shorts, sweaty. He was going *home*. Which means he slipped out and we don't know how long he was unaccounted for."

"He's jogging? This time of day? In a hooded sweatshirt? I don't think so," I said. "He knows he's under surveillance. He knows he was missing for an undetermined amount of time. He understands the implications of that. And he understands that you will have to respond to this. He's playing with you, Ken. Why else would he make sure they saw him?"

"Because he's arrogant enough to believe we can't catch him." He lifted the phone and gave Brolin orders. "Let's see who we can pull off patrol and get them out there. We're going to have to cover every inch within a mile of that place. Look at everything, talk to everyone. Rob checked one of Skylar's shirts into evidence. Have him give it to the K-nine unit and let's get them moving. And the unit that lost Peele—I want them back in uniform within the hour sitting in their squad on the highway. In the sun. For a week."

He clicked off, said *damn* under his breath. The muscles flexed in his jaw. "I gotta get a new job." He threw the Interceptor in gear, then hit his brakes hard enough that I almost lost my frozen latte. The florist, Nora Pace, appeared at my window. She was holding one of those white vases I'd seen in the cooler. It held a single pink carnation. A note card was stabbed into a fork-shaped plastic stem.

She thrust the vase at me. "I recognized your name and realized this was for you. We were supposed to deliver it to your hotel, but since you're here . . ."

I didn't take the vase. "Where'd this come from?" I asked her.

"There was a note under the door when I got back from lunch with some cash and the card that's on here, with instructions to deliver it to you at Whispering Pines Inn," she said. "I threw in the carnation and the vase since we're a florist, not a courier service."

"A secret admirer," Meltzer said, and almost as the words were coming out of his mouth he seemed to realize what Nora Pace might be holding. He reached in the back and opened the latches on his scene kit, handed me gloves and an evidence pouch.

"He doesn't know I've changed hotels," I said, as I stretched on the gloves.

"Interesting Mr. Fu Manchu was conveniently AWOL when this arrived," he remarked.

"Yes, it is." I lifted the card off the plastic pitchfork and slid it into a paper evidence pouch. Plastic looks good on TV but condensation can corrupt evidence. I turned to Nora. "You got back at one o'clock?" I remembered the CLOSED FOR LUNCH sign on the door.

She was starting to look nervous. She glanced back at her shop, then at the cameraman easing across the street. "A few minutes before."

"You still have those instructions? And the cash?"

"In the trash," she said, standing there in the sun with her little white vase. "The note, I mean. The cash is in the register. It was a twenty. It would be on top."

"I'll take the florist. You take the cameraman," Meltzer said. He was out of the vehicle with his scene kit held by its handle like a businessman with a briefcase. "I'm calling Ferrell to pick up that card and whatever else we have inside."

I pushed open the door, and Nora Pace stepped out of the way. She looked scared. "You can keep the flower," I told her. "And not a word of this to anyone. Please." She nodded. She didn't have to be reminded we were keeping some secrets for her too.

The sheriff disappeared inside the shop. Daniel Tray's married lover followed him, holding the vase out in front of her like it had been contaminated. I headed for the cameraman. "How long have you been here?"

I saw his finger hit a switch on the camera. He lowered it to his side. "I got here when you got here," he answered. Which probably meant he'd been tailing us from a distance and definitely meant he hadn't gotten the offender on tape. "They're preparing the park for a candlelight vigil tonight. I'm supposed to get some video."

"The park is back there," I told him, and watched him walk away. He pulled out his phone and glanced over his shoulder.

I looked at Main Street, quaint and tidy, cars parked in angled slots in front of the storefronts. Was he out there, looking out of one of those windows, watching us trying to figure out what we had and how to keep a lid on it? Behind Main Street, Whisper Park prepared for the prayer service. Was he playing the concerned neighbor, helping out? Or had Logan Peele delivered that card while he was out on his jog?

I heard the bell jingle on the florist's door. The sheriff crossed the street and handed me his case. We got back in the truck. I checked to make sure the camera guy wasn't hovering, then released the metal latches on the hard-sided case. I lifted the manila envelope lying flat on the top and opened it, peered down inside to see a lined piece of paper, hole-punched, with ragged edges.

> Please deliver this card to Keye Street
> at the Whispering Pines Inn.

I stared at it, felt it plucking at nerves already stretched as tight as guitar strings, felt its silky fingers slipping around my neck. "Ken," I said, "it's Skylar's handwriting."

36

Nothing is more accustomed to the ordinary, more tuned to the predictable footfalls of its regulars, than a main street in small-town America. We notice the extraordinary—orange running shoes, blue hair, tats, a stranger hovering, dark sunglasses, a car creeping behind a bicycle. Main Street was on alert today. Whisper was full of posters and dark speculation, and still I hadn't found one person who'd noticed someone slipping a card under the florist's door.

The hard, jagged truth that someone was targeting children in this honeysuckle town had engulfed the population like the hot fangs of a fire. Reality was setting in for everyone.

I'd glimpsed the sheriff coming out of one store across the street and going into another. A shake of his head told me he hadn't scored yet either. How long had it taken—two, three seconds—to slip an envelope under a door? Bernadette Hutchins had been on the street half an hour before we arrived, and the florist had been open when she papered its door with Skylar's photo. The shops that faced the florist—the hardware store, the coffee shop, the drugstore—all had a view that was partially obstructed by the cars parked in front. And Whisper wasn't the kind of town that needed traffic cameras and sidewalk monitors on every block like downtown Atlanta, which was as wired and closely watched as a high-stakes poker game.

I had begun at the top of the street and worked my way back down to Smith's Hardware, near Meltzer's vehicle. I checked the time. Another half an hour had been chewed up, thirty more minutes ticking away like a detonator.

I saw the sheriff on the other end of the street. He was about to go into the Italian restaurant. I looked over the shops. I could see a slice of the park from here and beyond that the middle school. I could hear voices, young voices, in the park.

Mr. Smith came out of his store and stood beside me, a big, barrel-chested guy in his seventies with liver spots on white fleshy hands. He pulled a pipe from his pocket and tapped it. Ash and burned-black tobacco drifted down to the sidewalk. From the other pocket came a pouch of new tobacco. The cherry scent roused a memory of my dad in his shop tinkering and smoking the pipe my mother wouldn't let him have in the house.

"It's a damn shame something so bad could happen in a town like this." Smith lit his pipe with short puffs, stared out at the street.

"It's a shame anywhere," I said.

"What happened here today?" he wanted to know. "Why all the questions?"

"We have reason to believe the man responsible for the murders and abductions was here," I answered. I wasn't going to share the evidence with him.

"I didn't see anything. Me and my only employee have been in the back most of the day."

"You know your customers, Mr. Smith? You know what projects they're working on, they consult you for advice?"

"Some of them." He nodded. "Although we're getting new folks from the city around here now that would rather use the building supply place up the road. But it's mostly lumber. People gotta come here for some things. You looking for anything specific?"

"Soundproofing materials, someone reinforcing or adding on small spaces. Let's say for a music studio or a game room. You remember someone buying things like that? Heavy lengths of chain?"

Smith rocked on his heels like a wave had slammed into him. He looked at me, removed the pipe from his mouth. It scraped his teeth like a fork. "These girls are being chained up?"

"We know he's using metal cuffs. Stands to reason he's welded on chains." I thought for a moment. "How does he do it? How does he hold them? That's what I need you to think about—your community, their habits, their property, their personalities, and what they're buying. You, the grocer, the barista, the drugstore owner, all of you. That young girl." I pointed to the poster on the pole next to us—pretty, blond Skylar with the world in front of her. "She needs her neighbors to think that way right now and help us find her. The killer, he's close. He knows the neighborhood. He fits in. He could be your next-door neighbor."

Bushy gray eyebrows wrinkled. "What makes a pretty young lady want to do this kind of work?"

I wasn't quite half his age, which made me young to him. I smiled. "It's a living," I said, and saw Meltzer coming out of the restaurant up the street. "Thank you for your time, Mr. Smith."

I met the sheriff at his truck. "Any luck?" he asked as we got in. He started the engine and cranked up the fan.

"Nothing," I said.

"Me either." Meltzer backed out of the parking space and pointed the SUV in the right direction up Main Street, then tapped his brakes and rolled his window down. I saw him smile. "Hey, Robbie," he called out his window. "What's up, kiddo? Aren't you supposed to be in school?" He glanced over at me. "Rob's boy," he explained.

Robbie Raymond was coming out of the smoothie shop with a sweaty plastic cup in his hand. He grinned and came over to the truck. "Hey, Sheriff." He was tall and very lanky, a blue-eyed blond boy with thick hair, a happy wide smile, and faded acne scars near his jawline. "They let us out half an hour early to help in the park. You know, for Skylar." I saw his father's cheekbones and tall frame, but apart from that he had none of Detective Raymond's blunt, ham-handed features. "My dad came by a little while ago. He says y'all don't know who did it yet. It's gettin' pretty weird around here right now. Nothing feels the same. Bunch of us guys, we want to go looking for her."

"My deputies have been organizing search teams. We could use you and your friends. Get a sign-up sheet," Meltzer told him.

"Cool," Robbie said, and peered into the cab at me. He had to lean down to do it. "You must be Ms. Street." He switched the smoothie to his left hand and jabbed the right one in front of the sheriff. I leaned across the cab. We laughed awkwardly as we shook hands.

"Listen, Robbie, I know you knew Skylar," the sheriff said gently. "Anything you can tell us that might help?"

"I didn't even know her until this school year. So, like, a couple, three weeks."

"She confide anything at all to you?"

"Nah, not really." Robbie frowned, thinking about it. "I mean, she wouldn't ride the bus home because everyone on the bus is lame and she wanted to talk to her friends and mess around after school and stuff. I guess that was a secret."

"Anything else?" I asked.

His attention was drawn to a couple of boys about his age and height coming out of the smoothie shop. "I'll meet you over there," he yelled to them, then leaned in the cab a little, lowered his voice. "Skylar came to watch us practice a couple times. Girls do that. It's no big deal. But the guys gave me a hard time, you know? 'Cause she was crushing on me and she's in the eighth grade. I walked her back to the school once. But she was all about the dance this weekend and wanting to be with me and stuff. Like a date."

"When was the last time you saw her?" I asked.

"Wednesday, I think," he said, and I remembered her last diary entry. *I HATE my parents!!!* She was pushing them to let her go to the dance unchaperoned. "She walked over to the high school and watched baseball practice. I acted like I didn't see her." His mouth pulled tight. He looked around self-consciously, used the back of his hand to wipe the corner of his eye. "I'm sorry. I didn't know. If I'd been nice maybe she woulda been watching us practice or something instead of—"

Meltzer squeezed his arm at the biceps. "Not your fault, buddy. None of this is anyone's fault."

"Yeah, I guess so," the teenager said uncertainly. "Look, I gotta go, okay?"

"Take off. I'll see you tonight," Meltzer said.

"Nice to meet you, Ms. Street," Robbie called with a wave back at us as he ran across the street.

"You two seem close," I remarked.

"He studied tae kwon do under me at the dojang. Four years. I got to know him. Poor kid. All these kids, they'll never forget any of this," he said, and I knew he was right. "Kids always blame themselves."

"What happened to his mom?" I asked.

"Boating accident." He turned off Main Street. "Before I got here. The way I hear it Rob took it pretty hard. Did some heavy drinking for a while. And he didn't make any friends. Mean drunk. Robbie was still a baby. His aunt took care of him until Rob pulled it together. He ended up raising a good boy."

I knew what it was like to lose something, to try and drink it away. "What's Brolin's story?"

"Got married right out of high school. Stayed married. Most folks around here stay married regardless of whether they're happy. I can't decide if that's a good thing or if it's just depressing." He looked over at me. "They make an unlikely couple, don't they, Tina and Rob?"

"Nora Pace told me she finds the band teacher irresistible, so anything is possible," I said.

Meltzer's phone went off. He looked at the display, then switched to the Bluetooth device in the vehicle. "Go ahead, Sam. I'm here with Dr. Street. What do you have for us?"

"I think y'all are going to want to see this," she said in the twangy accent that made me think Ozarks and curvy mountain towns. "There was a note and a photograph in the card."

We pulled onto Logan Peele's road and passed deputies moving up it, through the field across from the houses, and through Peele's neighbors' yards. Peele had messed with them, and they were making sure his neighbors knew it. "Read us the letter," Meltzer told Sam.

Sam cleared her throat. " 'Dear Keye, I've started hurting her. I *thought you'd want to know. She's weak. She won't last. Don't you hate it when you find out they're not who you thought they were?'"* She'd read it like an old telegraph, adding the words *comma* and *period* and *question mark*. She'd read it without anything at all in her voice. She'd read it like a scientist.

An officer with a German shepherd on a body harness stalked alongside the ditch. One of Peele's neighbors stood on her porch with a phone to her ear. Brolin and Raymond stood near Brolin's Crown Vic. They turned their heads and stared as we approached. Meltzer slowed, then braked in the middle of the road.

"He's telling us about his selection process and why he kills them," I said. "He's shifting responsibility, blaming them, as if they've deceived him, and us because we haven't captured him. This is part of his compartmentalization process. Shifting blame allows him to emotionally detach from his violent behaviors."

*D*ear Keye, I've started hurting her. I thought you'd want to know. She's weak. She won't last. Don't you hate it when you find out they're not who you thought they were?

"So who did he think they were?" I asked. "How did they appear? To him, to the world? And why does that attract him?"

"Melinda was smart and outgoing just like Skylar," Meltzer said.

I thought about Melinda's friends. "They were both the leaders in their packs. Confident, pretty, blond. Tracy fits the type physically. But she wasn't outgoing. She wasn't an alpha. She wasn't even allowed relationships outside of school." The differences in the offender's selection and behavior with the first victim bugged me. "He requires a stronger personality now. It makes his time with them more interesting. Until he strips away their confidence and makes them afraid and timid and ugly. Then they aren't what he wants anymore."

"Sam, you get any evidence off that stuff?" Meltzer asked.

"Dirt and a few fibers. Still working. The note was sealed inside the envelope so it's the evidence least likely to have been corrupted.

The soil sample and what's in the dirt along with the fibers may help ascertain location. We lifted several prints off the note inside. They belong to Skylar. ALS picked up fluids on the note. It's not blood. Judging by the spatter pattern, it's tear fluid." She left it there while that vivid picture played in our minds. "The prints on the envelope belong to Nora Pace, the florist," Sam continued. "The twenty-dollar bill is embedded with years of gunk. I don't expect much help there. As I said, there's a photograph. It came off a color printer. We'll work on the paper and ink and see if we can identify the machine. The print is average, not photo quality, which makes it more common, unfortunately. The handwriting is confirmed as Skylar's but the final sample tells us the victim was under extreme duress."

"What final sample, Sam?" Meltzer said.

"Hitting SEND on the images now, Sheriff," Sam said. She didn't want to read it to us. She wanted us to see it.

Our phones went off, Meltzer's first, mine a heartbeat slower. I opened the first picture, a shot of the letter Sam had read to us. I saw Skylar's loopy handwriting, widened the screen and studied it. "Sam, it looks like there's a couple of punctures. That from the pen?"

"Definitely written on a soft surface," she answered. "Once we process the evidence, we might be able to tell you what the surface is."

A sound came out of Ken Meltzer, something flayed and aching. His lips, usually red and full of blood, had drained to chalk. He held up the image on his phone—a picture of a right hand, a girl's mutilated hand. *NINE MORE*, it said at the bottom in a shaky, ragged print. He'd made her write it after he'd broken her finger. I imagined him cracking her fine bones, the throbbing, burning agony of that.

NINE MORE.

"He's put us on his timetable," I said.

37

He opened the door shirtless with a thick white cotton towel around his neck. He was wearing jeans, cut low below his navel. His stomach was rippled with muscle. The full veins in his arms rose up under his skin. He stepped out on the porch. The German shepherd sat next to its handler, panting in the heat, but alert. Bright eyes rolled up at Logan Peele. "I've been expecting you, Sheriff," Peele said, pleasantly. "Nice to see you, Dr. Street."

"We could waste a lot of time talking about where you went today," Meltzer snapped. "Or you can let us in with the dog so we can get this over with. Let me remind you I don't have to ask."

Peele tossed his short red hair with the towel, dried an ear. "You know I really don't want that animal in my house. But wait." He held up an index finger, reached inside the door, pulled out a plastic bag, and dropped it in front of us. "Figured you'd want them. My jogging clothes."

Peele looked from Meltzer to me, gauging our reaction. He'd thought about this. Every detail. He'd entertained himself and cost us precious time. "Get out of the way, Logan," Meltzer said.

Peele smiled, stepped to the side with a sweeping welcome gesture. "Tick-tock," he said, as the sheriff stalked past him into the house.

I walked down the steps to the cement driveway. It looked pressure-washed. Big surprise. The entire property was immaculate.

"So how's Whisper so far, Dr. Street?"

I looked up at Peele. I didn't answer.

"Why don't we go out for a drink sometime?" he said. "I'll tell you what I'm thinking right now and you can tell me what it means."

"You're trying too hard, Mr. Peele," I said. "To be interesting, I mean."

Raymond's Crown Vic eased down the driveway. Brolin had left for Whisper to interview Skylar's closest friends. Meltzer had separated them in order to cover more territory. Plus, he had been furious with them for not starting the dog and the handler at Peele's house before the suspect had a chance to shower and destroy evidence.

Raymond got out and glared at Peele, still standing on his porch. Then he motioned me over. He smelled like sweat and cigarettes. He'd just had his ass handed to him by the sheriff and he didn't look happy.

"Tell me what the letter said."

I pulled up the image of the letter on my phone and handed it to him. I watched him read it. "Christ oh mighty," he muttered.

"The photo is on the next screen," I told him. I glanced down into his car and saw cigarette boxes and fast-food wrappers and what looked like it had been an iced coffee, with some milky, melting ice. And the shirt we'd taken from the Barbours' laundry, Skylar's shirt. It was on the passenger's seat in a heap.

"Fuck." Raymond wailed the word like he'd been hurt. His hand was on his stomach. He bent forward and thrust out my phone. I grabbed it and backed away. "Fuck," he said again, then bent at the waist and threw up.

"Hey! What the hell?" Peele yelped as chunky yellow-brown vomit splattered his driveway.

The front door opened and Meltzer came out followed by the dog and the deputy. He walked past Peele without a word or glance, came down the steps, looked at me, then at Raymond, then at the driveway. He frowned. The sun caught the lines around his eyes. The dog started to bark. He pulled past me, dragging his handler toward Raymond.

"Get that fucking thing away from me," Raymond ordered. He was backing up as the barking dog continued to alert on him. Peele started to laugh.

"Deputy, get control of your dog!" Meltzer shouted.

The dog ran his nose up and down Raymond's pant leg while Raymond stood there stiff and pale. The dog sat and barked up at his handler. "What the fuck?"

"You brought the victim's shirt for K-nine?" Meltzer asked.

"Brolin told me to," Raymond said defensely. He looked like he was going to toss his cookies again.

"Where is it now?" Meltzer asked.

Raymond reached in his car and grabbed the shirt. The dog started to bark again. The handler gave him a good-dog pat. "No evidence bag, Rob?" Meltzer said. "Really? It's like working with Barney Fife sometimes."

Peele howled and applauded. "Well done," he said. He was holding up his phone, recording us. "Another fine job by the Hitchiti County Sheriff's Department."

Raymond wiped his mouth again, spat. "Fucking dumbass dog . . ."

"Pull the deputies out of here," Meltzer told him quietly, keeping his back to Peele and his video. "Then go into town and find me a witness to something in this damn place."

We headed for his truck. "Hey," Peele yelled behind us. "Clean this shit up." Neither of us looked back.

We were quiet at first, both of us trying to digest the letter, the photograph, the time spent on interviews and searches that went nowhere, the scene at Logan Peele's house and in his driveway, Raymond's horror at the photo of Skylar's broken finger. Both of us were painfully aware of the time display on Meltzer's dashboard. Twenty-four hours since Skylar had tried to help her kidnapper with a breakdown and found herself battered and bound instead. There was dirt on the letter. Whatever it had come in contact with had a fine layer of dirt and dust. I looked at the image of the letter on my phone, read it again.

"Gotta be a dirt floor," I said, more to myself than to the sheriff. We were on the highway heading back to Meltzer's cop shop, where I could retrieve my car. He was expected to speak tonight, to reassure Whisper. "A barn or shed, a basement or crawl space," I said. "An abandoned farmhouse."

"Plenty of those around here. Broken down enough to have a lot of dirt too," Meltzer said, following my line of thought. He hit the Bluetooth button on his steering wheel and called Deputy Ferrell. "Deputy, reach out to the captain at uniformed patrols. Let's get some units out to inspect all abandoned structures in the county—sheds, barns, houses, businesses. Start with the Whisper area. And remind him we're radio silent on this. Coordinate with the search teams. We don't have time to cover the same ground." The voice that usually radiated comfort sounded tired and beat by frustration. "What about the time line?" he asked me, when he'd disconnected. "When that little girl doesn't have any healthy fingers left, she's out of time? What do we have? Nine days? Nine hours?"

"He wants us to think nine, nine days, nine minutes, nine fingers, whatever. But he's a psychopath, Ken, which makes him a good liar. He could kill her anytime if the mood strikes."

Meltzer was silent.

"This phrase," I said. "He's used it in both notes. *I thought you'd want to know*. It must be a regular part of his vocabulary. And he's buddying up, giving us little trinkets, letting us know he's doing us a favor. He's not just thinking about Skylar now. He's thinking about us thinking about him. It's feeding his illness. Makes him unpredictable. He needs to insinuate himself into the investigation. That's the thing about violent serial offenders: They're good at lying and good at raping and killing, but they're impulsive and childish and incapable of self-reflection. And this craving to be recognized, it's usually their undoing. So keep the cards and letters coming, you creep."

"He's thinking about *you* thinking about him," Meltzer reminded me. "The letters are addressed to you."

"He wants to be understood. He thinks I can. It's a kind of transference. Happens in therapy. Patients fixate, sometimes even eroticize the person they think accepts their actions without judgment. He probably believes I have the empathy for him he lacks for his victims." I thought for a minute while Meltzer sped up the two-lane.

"He's come full circle. He very carefully and quietly captured, held captive, and murdered Tracy Davidson. Her body lies there for a decade and he doesn't need attention, doesn't even need to reoffend, as far as we can tell. Then something triggered him and he took Melinda Cochran. There was an escalation in violence, evidence of torture. Melinda's death was bloodier, more fantastic, an attempted decapitation. Now Skylar. And the letters. Leaving the card today was clever, but he's not brilliant. He simply knows the routines of the town."

"I keep thinking about the people I know here in this county," Meltzer said. "You know, the person who could walk down Main Street talking to people or whatever after he put that card under the door with a picture like that. And I can't seem to put the pieces together. To think someone around here is responsible boggles the mind. We have some characters. And we have some troublemakers. But none of them could do this."

"Yeah, well, back to the liar thing," I said as we pulled onto the side road to the judicial center. "This ability to compartmentalize, to brutalize a victim without guilt, then be kind to the family and the neighbors, it's just a magnified extension of the way we separate from events and behaviors every day. Cops compartmentalize. You have to. That's what allows a psychopath to fit in to his surroundings. Look at Ariel Castro, just a guy in the neighborhood. He liked music. He was quiet. His friends liked him. At trial he said he was a good person, that he wasn't a monster."

"Back to the self-reflection thing," Meltzer said.

"Who was on Main Street today that absolutely no one would think twice about?"

"Shopkeepers," Meltzer replied. "Regular customers."

"The minister's wife," I said, and Meltzer's head whipped around. I held up palms. "Hey, just an example. Everyone saw Mrs. Hutchins but no one mentioned her because they knew the questioning related to the kidnapped and murdered girls." I sat there staring down at the letter on my phone. An idea crossed my mind. "You said a lot of hunters use those woods around the crime scene, right?"

Meltzer nodded, and pulled into the slot on the side of the building marked with his title. "Why?"

"When I was at Whisper Lanes, some guys at the bar were talking about hunting. One of them said something about his cams."

"Cameras," he said. "Trail cameras. Sure. You know who the guys were?"

"No."

"I've never seen any cameras out there," he said, and called Raymond. "Rob, you see any hunters' cameras out there in the woods where we found the bodies?"

"Wasn't looking," Raymond's breath sounded labored. Hot day. Sunny park. Sour stomach. I almost smiled. "Not that easy to see anyway. Hunters camouflage them."

"You know anyone that uses cameras?" Meltzer asked.

"No, but Bryant's place gets packed with hunters in season," Raymond answered. "He might know. Why you thinking trail cams?"

Meltzer explained what I'd heard.

"Want me to follow it?" Raymond asked. "Not much of a lead, but maybe we'll get lucky."

And you can get out of the sun and into a nice, cool bar for a beer, I thought. Meltzer said, "Stay in town. Things don't happen in a vacuum. Somebody saw something. I want Skylar home, Detective. Alive."

38

I passed the city limits sign on 441 and saw the white bowling pin on the front of the building, glowing white in the sun as if it had been dipped in bleach. I parked in front of the red-and-white oblong building and saw the lavender neon on the door—COCKTAILS. I took a long drink from bottled water that had lost its chill in my car and thought about vodka and soda, a tall glass, lots of ice, a twist. A hand-written sign on the entrance said: FRIDAY NIGHT WESTERN NIGHT CANCELED. COME PRAY FOR OUR CHILDREN IN WHISPER PARK.

The air inside was dry and cold and lit for a lounge. The lanes stretched out empty today, like gleaming runways, abandoned and polished and waiting. No balls rumbling down the alley and cracking into pins, just the croon of country music coming softly through speakers and the inconstant murmur of voices from the bar.

I tried to remember the men I'd seen when I was here. Two men with caps and T-shirts, redneck-looking guys with some bulk and scruff. I couldn't have picked either out of a lineup right now, and that irritated me. But I remembered the woman in skinny jeans and a curly perm. I spotted her now at the bar with a glass of white wine in front of her. The fingers on her left hand were busy flicking at her nails. She missed having a cigarette in her hand, I thought, and immediately remembered Rauser's nicotine cravings blasting over him.

I took the stool beside her, nodded when she glanced at me. Bryant Cochran saw me and came over. His hair was combed and his beard was trimmed. "Ms. Street, how can I help you?"

Movement caught my eye. Molly Cochran came out of the back. She was in western boots and a skirt. She was pretty and curvy, a small-town Miranda Lambert. "What is it? Did they find the girl? Did they get him?"

"No. I'm sorry," I said. Curly Perm leaned in closer. "But we're very close," I lied. Bryant moved on, to serve someone at the end of the bar. "I just had a couple of questions for your husband when he's free. About a customer." I smiled. "You doing double duty?"

"I'm always here on Friday, darlin'." She spoke with the same open friendliness she'd shown me at the diner. "It's his busy night. Nothing to do in Whisper on a Friday night except come here for dancing and drinking and bowling. Parking lot's usually packed by seven. And the kids fill up the alleys." She ran a soft white towel around the inside of a beer glass, held it to the light, saw a spot, and used the towel again. "Not tonight, though."

"This must be hard," I told her. "It's so fresh. I know it brings up a lot of emotion."

"Every ache those parents are feeling while they wait for their little girl to come home, we've ached," Molly said. "Whisper supported us, we want to be there for it. You coming?"

Yes, I wanted to say, *because he'll be there. Because he'll have to be there. He has to appear normal.* "Wouldn't miss it," I said.

Bryant set a club soda in front of me, a twisty bit of lemon attached to the rim, lots of ice. A good bartender always remembers. I thanked him and took it gratefully. "There were a couple of customers here yesterday," I told him, then glanced at Curly Perm. "They were talking about hunting. Both had ball caps, scruffy beards."

"That's about half our customers," Bryant said. Molly slid the polished glass in the rack and picked up another one.

"I heard you talking to them," I said to Curly Perm.

"Could be Tom and Will," she said. She was trying to be careful with her tongue but she was overcompensating, like a drunk walking down the sidewalk. "'Member what they were talking about?"

"Trail cameras," I said. "Hunters' cams."

"It does sound like Tom Watson and Will Rawlins," Bryant said. "They were here a couple of times this week. Big-time hunters."

"You know how to get in touch with them?" The club soda felt good in my hand, natural. I took a drink and let the soda burn my throat.

Curly Perm giggled and slid her empty glass to the edge of the bar. I figured it was her third. "I didn't even know their last names."

Bryant pulled a clean glass from the hanging rack and poured from an uncorked bottle of white wine. "Tom lives in Whisper. Has some land on the other side of the bridge out there near the national forest." His voice faltered. That wasn't far from where his daughter's body had been found in a crater in the woods. "You think a camera got something?"

"Just following every angle," I said noncommittally. "Is that common knowledge? This trail camera thing? Lot of hunters use them?"

"I didn't know about them until Tom mentioned he'd set some up last year so he could see where the deer hang out. I thought it was stupid," Bryant told me. "Like cheating. Like fishing with firecrackers. Tom says his wife and kids really like watching the footage too, 'cause the deer are so beautiful and all. And he can track their patterns."

I slid my card onto the bar. Molly picked it up as fast as a dirty glass. "If he happens to stop by, give him my card. See y'all tonight."

I took another gulp of cold soda, then walked out into the blasting heat. I had Neil on the phone before I reached my car. "I need an address and phone number in Whisper for Tom Watson, probably Thomas. Mobile number, if you can get it. Text it to me."

"About how old is this guy?" Neil wanted to know. "That's a common name."

"Late twenties. Thirty at most. And it's Whisper, Neil. There's like only two thousand permanent residents here."

"Just want to make sure I don't hook you up with his dad. I'll text. And don't look at your phone until you're stopped. That boat you drive will end up in a ditch."

I called Tom Watson's home number as soon as the text came and got a recording. I tried the mobile number and got voice mail there too. "Mr. Watson, my name is Keye Street. I'm a consulting detective to the Hitchiti County Sheriff's Department. You may have information that would be helpful in an investigation. Would you call me back as soon as possible?" I left my number as I pulled into Whisper and cruised around until I found an empty parking space behind the hardware store.

The park was full of kids and teachers and parents. A long folding table displayed clear plastic bags filled with new tea lights. A plywood stage had been set up. Another plywood base had been covered with red velvet. Two girls about Skylar's age knelt there, each of them with a bag of tea lights. They set them in the base and squeezed glue on the bottom, placing them carefully in a pattern I couldn't make out. I saw Brolin and Raymond talking to two kids. Robbie and one of the boys I'd seen come out of the smoothie shop were setting up a lectern on the stage. A photo of Skylar was taped to the front. Over the heads of strangers, I saw Pastor Hutchins and his wife. Bernadette had her arm around the shoulder of a young girl. Her hair was blond and long. Their daughter, Robin, I presumed, whom Skylar had mentioned in her diary—Skylar's perfect family.

I crossed to the school, stood at the double doors, and checked the time. Four-oh-five. I walked at a leisurely pace down the steps, across the schoolyard, and through the park, feeling the sun on my back as Skylar would have just yesterday, which felt like a thousand years ago. The cool shade dropped down around me when I stepped onto the path. It was well marked and well used. I imagined Skylar using this path every day, walking home, thinking about school, her friends, her crushes, getting home to Luke.

Light flickered between the trees. When I stepped out of the tree line and reached the center of Cottonwood Road it was four-seventeen. Twenty-five hours to the minute since the call was placed from her mobile to the landline inside the house. It would have taken Skylar twelve minutes to get from the school to the point where the offender acquired her. It had taken another five minutes for the offender to get her phone and make the call. They'd talked for a couple of minutes, I realized. He'd been biding his time, running his con, probably messing with his engine, building his courage, waiting for that moment, hoping it would be as terrible, as spectacular, as he'd fantasized.

I crossed through the tangle of people preparing the park for the vigil to get my car. Mr. Smith stood outside his hardware store talking to a couple I recognized from their Main Street shops, the antiques dealer, the pharmacist. All grew quiet as I neared. We exchanged a nod.

Six minutes later I was on Cottonwood Road looking at the mouth of the trail I'd just used to retrace Skylar's steps. The killer could have watched Skylar leave school from just about anywhere in downtown Whisper, beat her here, and set up his fake breakdown with minutes to spare. He would have wanted to do it that way, I thought. He'd want his timing to be spot-on in order to minimize his time on the road and the possibility of a witness. He had a coyote's mind for gauging his risk.

I got out of my car and gazed down at the Barbours' white-fenced home. Red dust from the road drifted by. There were cars in the Barbours' driveway, family and friends, no doubt, huddling in close for comfort. Then I heard my phone buzzing on my seat and reached in for it, hoping it would be a return call from the hunter Tom Watson. It wasn't. It was the deputy Meltzer had assigned to chart progress and relay developments.

"Good afternoon, Dr. Street. Wanted to let you know we now have access to the Internet storage with Skylar Barbour's saved photos."

"Can you email me something?"

"There are hundreds of photographs," she told me.

"How about a link?"

"Not my area. I'll see what tech can do," Ferrell answered.

"Tell me what you see," I said. "Any photographs of adults?"

She was quiet for a minute. I envisioned her scrolling through Skylar's photo stream on the war room monitor, row after row of Skylar's friends, Luke, places the girl had been. "Mostly kids. Mostly girls being goofy, her dog, a couple boys. Band trips. Adults in those pictures we're attempting to identify. Probably chaperones. Couple pictures of her parents," she told me. "And there are a few with the minister and his family standing in front of the community garden."

Skylar had snapped the picture of the family she wished she had.

I hung up just feet from where Skylar had been abducted. Yellow spray paint marked the areas where evidence was found on the road last night—Skylar's blood, the smashed phone, the case and compact and nail file.

I looked up at the Barbours' ranch house on the hill, shadowed by black walnut trees, the afternoon sun turning the filigreed, breeze-ruffled leaves bright.

I got back in my hot car. Heat and irritation prickled my skin. Nothing had panned out. I felt like pounding my fists on the dashboard. Meanwhile, that little girl was perched on some demented tightrope. Not one lead had taken us anywhere, not Skylar's diary or call log or photos, not one witness, the sex offenders—Lewis Freeman and Logan Peele, or the old offender who'd whispered to him in an empty corridor on video—not Lamar Bailey who hadn't shown for his mandatory group therapy because he was in the hospital. Not Daniel Tray who'd alibied out because he fucked a married woman twice a month.

It's not like television. Not everything works out in the end. That possibility rocked up at me now, muscular and choking and rolling black like the sea at night. I looked at the house and thought again about that caramel-eyed kid in the photo booth.

39

This case was growing cold. I felt the chill coming off it as I waited to hear from a hunter who may or may not have trail cameras in the area. I knew that unless one of us—me, Raymond, Brolin, Meltzer, Sam—dug some new lead out of the frustrating rubble we'd unearthed so far, Skylar's next hours or days or weeks would be cruel and long. How long? That was the question. How long would it take him to grow tired of her? To feel the need to escalate the situation because he'd constructed a chess game with law enforcement. How long until she went from a prize that had obsessed him to everything that was wrong and inconvenient in his life? Because once she fulfilled her purpose, or couldn't fulfill her purpose, as he'd alluded to in the letter, the psychological disconnect would be immediate and complete. He would be sick to death of the burden of her. He'd blame her for the hassle and the pressure, and he'd want her ripped out of his life. His world, his normal life would call him, as it always does with this kind of offender after they offend, and he would crave the emotional cooling-down, the process by which he reintegrated himself back into life and separated himself from Skylar and the other murders. And when he was done with her, it wouldn't be a regretful, bittersweet good-bye like it had been with Tracy, but a quick, blunt good-bye. He'd broadcasted his intentions when he turned the sharp side of that axe on Melinda. I knew exactly what he planned for Skylar, and every tick of the clock felt like an axe blow. Investigations have one thing in common. They each hand you a basket brimming with half-truths and partial facts. Extrapolating some meaning from a thousand tiny strands of yarn is the challenge.

I had to find that calm, flat space and shut out the muddled, dark distractions, the time, the wrong turns. Everything depended on clarity now. Driving always helps me get there.

I lowered the top on my Impala and hit the two-lane. The lake was rippled and muddy blue in the late-afternoon sun as I turned my car loose to do what it does best. I curved around the point, smelling all the mossy, breeding, algae-tangled things that feed off its waters.

A couple of miles in, I saw the first signs for the national forest. Dirt roads wound into the acreage on my left and led to hiking trails. On the right just past a bridge railing, I turned into the campground entrance.

I got out and looked up at the trail a killer had used to walk his victims to their own murder scene.

My phone went off. It was the hunter's number. "Mr. Watson, thank you for calling me back."

"What's this about?" Tom Watson wanted to know.

"There's an area off the point of the lake near the national forest. Catawba Creek runs through it. About a thousand acres. You know it?"

"Sure," Watson said. "I grew up around here."

"I understand you use trail cameras."

"Nothing illegal about trail cams," he said.

"Mr. Watson, I'm sure you are aware the bodies of two murdered girls were found on that land. If you or anyone has cameras in that area, they may contain valuable evidence."

"I only used a trail cam out there last season. This year, some asshole vandalized it. I hadn't even activated it yet," Watson said, and my hopes sputtered, then pinwheeled down.

"When was your camera vandalized?"

"June, thereabouts."

Melinda Cochran had been murdered late in June, perhaps early July. "Where was the camera mounted?"

"Hmm. Be hard to explain if you don't know the area—"

"I've been there several times," I interrupted. "I'm here now. At the campground."

"Okay, if you walk straight up that path a couple hundred yards and veer away from the lake, there's a big poplar tree with brown vines all over it just before it gets hilly. That's my landmark. That's where I had my camera."

It was someone else's landmark too, that tree with those thick vines that had sucked at it, lived off it, until they were deliberately severed. "How about video from last season?" I asked.

"Nah. Sorry. Didn't see a reason to keep it."

Somehow, the killer had known about Watson's cameras. Had he heard Watson bragging about them at the diner, the bar? Or had he seen something in the woods, something out of place? He wanted to put Melinda's body with Tracy's in that hole. He wanted to kill her where he'd murdered Tracy. And so he destroyed the camera so he could complete his fantasy undetected. "You remember anything about the video? Did you see anyone?" I asked.

"Nothin' human. Nobody's gonna go out there at night unless they're up to no good," he said as I peered up at the dark woods and felt tension crawling up my neck, the headache creeping back around the base of my skull. What would happen to Skylar when the killer was done with her? His dump site had been discovered. Would he risk trying to put her where he'd put the others? Was that important to him now? He'd taken full advantage of all the creeping, natural things of the earth to cover his crimes, the parasites and bacteria, the scavenging animals, all the enemies of DNA. And he hid his victims well in a natural crater choked with leaves and branches and debris. I didn't think he'd come back here. He'd have no way of knowing if the area was being watched, electronically surveilled, if he was safe. He'd find a new place for Skylar. And if we didn't find her alive soon, we might never find her.

"I sure hope y'all get that guy," Watson said.

"Me too," I agreed and disconnected. I could smell the Impala's hot engine. I thought about a killer with a shop rag, a fake breakdown, what his dirty hands must have smelled like, felt like. I had to re-group. I had to consider every possibility and at the moment only one came to mind. I called Neil. "Do me a favor, would you?"

"It's like you only call when you need something," Neil said with the usual amount of snark in his voice.

"That's our deal. Remember? Listen, I need some birth records." I gave him the information and got back in my car. "And I need them fast. Lot of people in the park right now and out of their houses. I want to take advantage of it."

"Which means you want to go snooping in someone's stuff?"

"Exactly."

"You seriously suspect the *minister*?" I thought he was going to laugh. Neil has a delightful, inappropriate appreciation for real-life drama. I heard his fingers hitting the keys.

"Our killer's melting into the community. Those girls trusted him. So, yes, at this point even Pastor Hutchins is fair game." I remembered the voice recording I'd made of the interview with Tracy Davidson's brother, Jeff, before he'd killed himself. *We went to school and we came right home. And once a week if we were good my father would let us leave on Sunday and go to church . . .* "And find out where Hutchins was before he took over this church," I told Neil. Look for connections to the town of Silas where the first victim lived."

"Be a great cover," Neil said. "A preacher. Hears all your secrets."

"A guy you'd stop to help on the road," I said, and spun out of the dirt lot onto the highway. "Ethan Hutchins knew both girls. One of them hung out at his house with his daughter over the summer. His daughter happens to be the age Tracy's child would have been if that child had lived. And I'd just seen Hutchins and his wife in the park with a blond girl who looked nothing like her dark-eyed, dark-haired parents. And the minister's wife was in town when I received a message from the offender."

"Oh my God," Neil said. "You suspect the wife too?"

"Call me back."

I pulled into the empty church parking lot, followed it around to the back, where the hulking new addition came out on each side of the original granite chapel. I remembered watching the minister's wife walking up the church steps, her smile, their kiss, them walking away with their arms around each other. I'd liked Ethan Hutchins. I'd liked them through Skylar's diary, and through Ken's eyes. But Hutchins had opportunity. There was a connection between him and two of the victims. I had to know. Before I went to that prayer vigil tonight and looked into the minister's eyes I had to make sure that his family was what it appeared.

I took the driveway that dipped down out of the church parking lot. I could see tomatoes on vines in the garden when I got out of my car, red and fat and ready to be picked. Wire baskets were filled with compost, and an old Ford truck sat in the grass at the back corner of the garden, the bed full of mulch and bags of garden soil. I thought about Skylar's diary entries, the time she'd spent here, the tomatoes she carried home on lonely summer days after she'd come here to play with Robin Hutchins.

The house was granite like the church, with the look of an English cottage. Lavender had been planted in front and the fragrant shoots fanned out against the nearly ash-white stone. English ivy twisted up the stone walls. I parked behind the house. The lawn there was mowed and green and shaded. A tree house had been built around the trunk of an old white oak, a hanging ladder swayed in a hot breeze. The perfect home for the perfect family.

I moved around shrubs and garden hoses, peered in windows with my hands cupped against glass and saw an open, unfinished basement with a couple of picnic tables. Potted Christmas cactuses set in the dim basement light inside waiting to come out and bloom for the holidays, a washer and dryer and a fiberglass folding table.

I picked the lock on the basement door, inspected every corner of the basement, found boxes of clothes labeled CHARITY and all the normal things humans can't part with—children's books Robin had outgrown, a high chair, a tricycle. I searched around a push mower and a gas can, looked inside a tool kit for red shop rags.

I found the stairs leading up to the kitchen, took them quietly. The kitchen held the vague smell of cooked food and coffee. It was clean.

The house was narrow and long, low-ceilinged, neat, lived-in. I moved through their rooms like a prowler, quietly sliding open drawers and peering into closets. I wasn't thinking about their privacy. I was thinking about Skylar. And that made me righteous. It blurred moral borders, and I was very aware it was exactly the kind of compartmentalization I'd described to Ken earlier.

I found a sleeping cat. No locked cupboard doors. No big secrets. I went down the basement steps and out the back door, aware of the ticking clock, the dimming light, thinking people may want to come home and shower and change after being in the sun all day before the big event tonight.

My phone vibrated in the back pocket of my jeans. It was a group text from Deputy Ferrell to Meltzer, me, Brolin, and Raymond. *Fibers—cotton, rayon, steel, polyurethane, kerosene & urine present. Soil samples and mold indicate moist environment. Possibly an underground structure or one dilapidated enough to be exposed to earth. Search team criteria have been refined.*

I quickly replied to the group: *Has to be a mattress. An old one. She's not in some hole. The space is large enough for a mattress.*

I thought about the second note and remembered the shaky hand, the tiny puncture from the pen. Skylar had composed the note he'd made her write sitting on a dirt floor using a filthy old mattress as a table.

And then I saw it, a lone extension cord running from the house. I followed it thirty feet and saw it dive down into the earth. The door to the storm cellar was painted a greenish tan that blended nicely into the landscape. I lifted it and saw thick padding on the underside. Light flooded concrete steps, five of them going straight down. I felt the cold fingertips of a shiver caressing up my spine.

I ran down the steps and called out for Skylar. I found a string attached to a bare bulb and clicked it on, taking in every corner of the small, cool room—crates of bottled water, canned goods, boxes neatly stacked, batteries and pens and pencils, a soccer ball, a few books. There were pillows and blankets protected in plastic and folding director's chairs. No mattress. No Skylar. This was a tornado shelter, not a prison. My heart was hammering.

My phone went off. "Robin Mae Hutchins," Neil said. His voice was garbled. I moved closer to the open hatch door. "Licensed private adoption agency in Atlanta. It was a legal adoption. And I couldn't find any connection to Silas or any connection to the victims via social media sites. I think your preacher's clean."

"Yeah," I said, swallowing disappointment. "I'm starting to get that. Thanks, Neil."

I clicked off and stood there for a minute, my heart still fluttering like a spooked bird. A moment of hope. Gone. I had wanted her waiting down here for me. I wanted to get her up those steps and into my car and to a hospital. I wanted the world to give her back.

Frustration and tears felt hot on my face. *Another dead end,* I kept thinking.

"Shit." I slammed my foot into the soccer ball, watched it careen against the concrete block wall. "Shit, shit, shit."

I climbed the steps and called Sam for clarification on one point. I looked again at the extension cord running inside the shelter, and sent one more message to the group.

The kerosene. It's residual. A lantern. That means no elec & confirms vacant or abandoned property. He has to leave home or work to get to her. And he probably smells like kerosene. Someone knows him.

Brolin answered a moment later. *Adding patrols to the search teams with more concentration in outlying areas. They're on until dark. Back at first light.*

Meltzer: *Will announce new evidence tonight.*

Me: *He's going to feel the pressure when you make that announcement. He's going to realize the world is shrinking. He'll try to move her.*

40

The sheriff's department is urgently seeking information on the missing girl, Skylar Barbour, who is in a very dangerous situation. Her kidnapper has been tied to two other murders in the area.

An Atlanta news station led with "a developing story in Georgia's Lake Oconee region" as I towel-dried my hair in my hotel room and prepared for the service.

The anchor desk directed us to Brenda Roberts live at Whisper Park, where residents prepared for a candlelight vigil. As she recapped the story, the screen switched to the footage from earlier today. I saw myself standing on Main Street with the sheriff. Meltzer's sunny hair was sun-streaked in the midday light. He was taut and narrow-hipped and looked good with a badge at his belt and his S&W 40 under his arm.

Atlanta resident and former FBI profiler Keye Street, seen here with the Hitchiti County sheriff, consulted with Atlanta police on the Wishbone Killer cases and the cases known as the Birthday Murders. She is working closely on this tragic situation.

I lowered myself onto the bed with the towel still in my hand. We were standing too near, Meltzer and I. It was innocent. We'd seen the cameraman and pulled in close. We weren't thinking about anything at that moment beyond the case and Skylar. But there was something about our body language, about our interaction, about his bare arm brushing against me, the comfort and familiarity in our eyes. We had neither comfort nor familiarity, of course. What we had was chemistry and the kind of case that keeps you jacked up. It's like being in a hurricane sometimes. Rauser knew it. We'd had all those crazy, charged-up emotions. And if he saw this footage, he'd see exactly what I was seeing now.

I watched the screen as the sheriff came out of the florist with his scene kit, handed it to me. We got in his truck.

The suspect is reportedly attempting to communicate with the sheriff's department, and Dr. Street, who was trained in the analysis of serial crimes, is attempting to piece together the clues.

I opened a tube of drugstore mascara I'd picked up to replace the one I was missing, and stood in front of the bathroom mirror trying to erase the drain of the day from my face. My phone rang and I saw my brother's number. "Hey, Jimmy."

"I can't believe you answered. You never answer when you're working." My brother had picked up my mother's swampy Carolina accent just as if he'd been raised on the banks of Albemarle Sound. He'd lost some of it while living out west, but a southern gentlemen still lurked in his voice.

"I'm on a forced break," I told him, and dabbed a little foundation under puffy eyes. "I'm getting ready for a thing."

"While it's always a thrill to see my sister on the news, I do have to make an observation," he said. I braced myself. "That sheriff is smokin'."

"He is that." I smiled, leaned in near the mirror, and brushed my lashes with cheap mascara. "It's a problem."

"I thought so," Jimmy said. He had seen what I'd seen, what I hoped Rauser wouldn't. I was already making my excuses, building my defense. Not because I'd done anything. I hadn't. And no matter how many times I told myself that, I knew this was different. Because I wanted it, because I wanted him, because I knew how easy it would be to bring those fantasies to life.

"I want them both. Okay? There, I said it. I'm a terrible person."

"Despicable," Jimmy agreed, but I heard his smile. "So what are you going to do? About this hot sheriff, I mean."

"I'm going to get dressed and go to work, Jimmy. And keep showing up for work until we find that little girl. That's my only plan right now."

"How's the case going?"

"Well, we have no viable suspects," I admitted. Everything I thought I knew about this case had turned to a spinning dust cloud. I didn't tell him I'd searched a minister's home or cried and kicked things like a petulant child. "But we have new evidence. And it's going to get us closer to him."

"The news says he's communicating."

"He is, which is why we have new evidence. So much for the serial mastermind."

"Do you think he'll kill her?" Jimmy asked quietly.

"I know he will," I said.

I dressed and packed a light bag, threw it in my car. Old habits. I'd learned it at the Bureau when analysts had to jump a plane at all hours. You had to have decent clothes for law enforcement briefings. And you had to have clothes for all the dirty, inconvenient places killers hide their victims.

I found dinner a couple of doors down. I ate without interest. I ate because my body needed fuel. I ordered coffee, scrolled through my notes. What was I missing? What wasn't I seeing? He was standing right in front of all of us. He was casually walking streets and parks a free man while Skylar was locked up in some filthy shack, some ratty cellar. He was looking into the eyes of his friends and neighbors and coworkers and feigning concern. That he'd go to her later, take what he wanted from her, hurt her because he liked to hurt, was not a moral dilemma.

I pulled into Whisper at dusk. Candles glowed in the park. The edges had been lined with luminaries that reminded me of the way runways look at night from airplane windows. Police cars surrounded the park. The parking spaces were full. Whisper was bursting at the seams. I parked in a loading zone behind the school cafeteria, and headed for the candles and the crowd. A television news van was parked on the fringes with the logo of the local Atlanta ABC affiliate. Music mixed with the hum of voices; a Kimberly Perry song was playing on some kind of loop. The song must have meant something to Skylar. And so I walked into the park with a lump in my throat, which was not the way I'd wanted the evening to begin.

I wandered through the crowd—people arm-in-arm, weeping, embracing. I saw Hayley and Brooks Barbour near the lectern. A cameraman was hoisting a camera to his shoulder. Reverend Hutchins patted Hayley's hand as he bent his head to hers. The platform I'd seen the schoolgirls working on earlier had been tilted up on one end. Candles flickered in the shape of Skylar's name. I glimpsed Bryant and Molly Cochran, each with an arm around the other, both holding candles. I moved through the crowd, searching shocked faces. *One of you isn't grieving,* I kept thinking. *One of you knows where she is.*

The music faded and Ethan Hutchins stepped to the lectern. The minister began with a prayer, and then he talked to the hushed crowd. "We lift our voices tonight and our candles, their flames as fragile as life itself, in support of community." His voice was serene. It carried smoothly over the jagged edges of terror and grief that crowded the park. "There is fear here tonight. There is rage and sorrow. We hold one another close . . ."

I eased through the throng of candlelit faces as the minister quoted scripture and talked about the power of many voices in prayer. I saw Daniel Tray standing near a cluster of kids. I saw Tina Brolin standing next to Ken Meltzer. Both were in full uniform. Robert Raymond stood in the background, also in uniform, solemn-faced, staring down at the ground. Teenagers sat cross-legged on the grass. A banner stretched across the lawn in front of them read: WHISPER MIDDLE SCHOOL. WE MISS YOU, SKYLAR! Skylar's brown-haired girlfriend from the picture in the photo booth held her candle, cupping the flame with her free hand, wet-eyed and shell-shocked, struggling to make sense of the incomprehensible.

I saw Melinda's friends, the girls I'd walked with as they tried to remember the day Melinda disappeared, the girls who'd told me about their music teacher, the girls who'd told me Melinda was awkward, the girls who had tried to mislead me.

I moved to the front row and listened to the minister. Bernadette Hutchins reached for my arm. She squeezed a little when I looked at her and didn't let go. We stood there side by side as her husband spoke, the town behind us, shaken numb and holding their flames. Bernadette had no idea I'd been through her house, looked in her drawers, searched the storm cellar, violated her trust and privacy. And I was okay with it. I was.

The minister talked about the value of faith in trying times. I wasn't even sure what that meant. Faith that Skylar would come home? Faith that bad things don't happen to innocent people? Because they do. He finished with another prayer, and Ken Meltzer stepped in front of the microphone. Pastor Hutchins touched my shoulder as he passed and slipped in next to his wife. Someone handed us candles. Bernadette let go of my arm for the first time.

Meltzer was brief and professional. He seemed comfortable behind a lectern, commanding, reassuring. He repeated the information from the Amber Alert, and added new information we'd obtained from forensic evidence. The kidnapper—he was careful not to say *killer*—is likely to be holding his captive in an abandoned or vacant property without electricity, he told the people of Whisper. He might keep odd hours, be secretive about why he leaves work or home. Someone may have detected a kerosene scent about him or his clothes. Meltzer appealed to everyone to search his or her memories. Were you on Cottonwood Road around three-fifteen yesterday? Had you noticed any broken-down vehicles or vehicles out of place? Did you know anyone who was in the area of the abduction? He reminded everyone that the tip line number was on flyers all over town and that sign-up sheets were available for volunteers who wanted to help. He then spoke briefly about the oath he's taken twice, and what the community means to him and to his mother, who had traveled back to her roots a decade ago. I spotted her for the first time when he gestured to her. She sat in a folding chair, her caretaker sitting next to her, and Ginger the golden retriever mix at her feet.

Hayley and Brooks Barbour followed the sheriff to the microphone. Hayley's voice wobbled and broke as she said Skylar's name. Brooks bit his lip and stared straight into the night. I had to look away. Feel it, push it aside. Feel it, push it aside. That's what you do. That's what you *must* do. Save it. Stuff it in your pocket and pull it out on your own time. Have a complete, magnificent fucking breakdown only when the case is closed. Think about the victim and the killer, I reminded myself. Forget the collateral damage.

I said good-bye to the minister and his wife, set my burning candle on a folding table with other burning candles, and worked my way back through the crowd. I wondered if his eyes were on me now. He had the advantage of knowing who I was.

I saw the playground as I pushed out of the packed crowd, the wooden fort and the swing set, a few kids playing, parents hovering and talking. A boy was sitting on top of the fort, watching over the heads of the crowd, as Hayley Barbour's frail, breaking voice followed me out of the swarm. Robbie Raymond lifted his hand shyly in a half wave.

"How you doing?" I stopped at the base of the fort, looked up at him. His long legs dangled off the side.

"I don't want to be here. But I couldn't stay home either. You know?"

"I know," I reassured him. He pushed himself off and landed on his feet next to me. When his face came out of the shadows, I saw the bruise around his eye and cheekbone.

"Robbie—what happened?"

"Ran into a door," he said, and smiled a little.

"Ah," I said. "Door must have had a big old fist attached."

Robbie was silent.

"You sure you're okay? You need to talk about anything?"

I saw his eyes drift past me, saw them widen. He took a step back. I felt a heavy hand on my arm, spinning me around. I looked up into Detective's Raymond's sour face. I grabbed the hand and jerked it away. "What the hell, Raymond?"

"I told you to stay the fuck away from my kid." His tongue was thick, and I smelled booze.

"Dad," Robbie said. "Stop. Okay? Just stop."

"You shut the fuck up," Raymond ordered. He was a mean drunk, the sheriff had told me.

"Detective," I said firmly. "You smell like a brewery. You're in a public place representing the sheriff's department and you're making a scene. This is such a bad idea." We already had the attention of the parents at the playground. "Go home," I told him quietly. "Robbie, can you drive him?"

"Fuck you," Raymond snarled. "Fuck you. Fuck both of you." He stalked off, wavering just a little when he turned but doing a good job of not appearing like a drunk.

I looked at Robbie. "He do that to you?" I reached up and touched his cheek. He winced away.

"It's okay. I'm okay. He's under a lot of pressure."

I looked back at Raymond lumbering out of the park. "You have someplace to go tonight?" I asked, and Robbie nodded. "Stay here, okay?"

I sent the sheriff a text. Brooks Barbour was at the lectern when I saw the sheriff emerge from the crowd. I told him about Raymond, about Robbie's black eye. Meltzer was furious. "I'm going to kill him," he fumed quietly as we walked. "But first I'm going to have a deputy follow him home. And when he's sober, I'm going to fire his ass. The only reason I haven't fired him around a million times is because I was worried about how he would support his kid. I happen to like the boy."

"I don't think Robbie should go home until Raymond's sober."

Robbie was still standing near the wooden fort. I saw Meltzer tense when he stepped into the light. "That's quite a shiner," he said playfully, and put his arm around Robbie's shoulders. His expression, his voice, didn't betray what I knew he was feeling. "How about you go home with me when this thing is over tonight. We'll grill a steak and put some ice on that eye."

"Sounds good." Robbie nodded.

"Dr. Street, care to join us?"

I shook my head. "Sounds like a guy thing."

"Well, we all need a good night's sleep. That means you too,

Dr. Street. That's an order," Meltzer said. "Been a tough day for everyone."

"Sheriff Meltzer! Dr. Street!" Brenda Roberts was running at us. She moved on three-inch heels like they were cleats. Her cameraman had his camera out. Robbie stepped back into the shadows. Meltzer sighed.

"And it just got tougher," I said.

41

spread my notes out over the double bed, every thought I'd put down on paper since Sheriff Ken Meltzer had called my office at the first of the week. It seemed like a decade ago. There were more notes in my phone I'd made when there wasn't time to find pen and paper. I rolled a chair over, sat next to the bed, and started organizing. The entire day had been spent reacting to new information. He liked it that way, I thought. He'd thrown us some scraps to keep us busy.

The entire blanket was covered with lined yellow sheets I'd pulled from my legal pad. I looked at them all, read them, made checkmarks on the ideas that had been explored and exhausted. I made new notes about the dirt and fibers Sam had found on the letter. Meltzer had done a good job of getting the information out tonight, and he'd given an interview to Brenda Roberts to further that agenda while I slipped away with Raymond's battered son to find Mrs. Meltzer, her care-taker, and Ken's dog, Ginger.

I pushed in the flash drive Brolin had given me and clicked through a page at a time, rereading witness statements, the lab reports. It was after one when I turned off the light. We were starting early, meeting in the war room at five a.m. and then fanning out. The search teams would begin again at daybreak. It was a small county. Eventually they would find his lair.

The room was icy. I pulled the sheet over me, thought about the day—Daniel Tray and his lover, the girl in the park staring down into the flame she held, praying for her friend's safe return. Raymond seeing the photo of Skylar's broken finger, the dog, Peele laughing and heckling, Sam's emotionless twang reciting the letter. *Dear Keye, I've started hurting her. I thought you'd want to know.*

A thought crossed my mind, then grabbed me by the throat. I sent Sam a text. *I'm sorry. I know it's late. Just a quick question. The first letter, the one I found on my windshield, what prints did you find?*

I reopened my Mac and pulled up the software we use for background checks while I waited for Sam to hear her phone and respond. Neil could have done this faster. Neil could have done it with his eyes closed. But his eyes probably *were* closed right now.

Sam's text came back. *No prints. No fibers.*

One-thirty in the morning, more than thirty-four hours into Skylar's abduction, and something was finally making sense.

By two, I'd found our man's connection to Silas, Georgia, where Tracy Davidson had lived until that day after school when she had been lured away. I'd always wondered how he'd done that. Now I knew. And I learned a few other things that ignited my hopes, sent them soaring, and cemented the suspect in my mind.

I got dressed—field clothes—and left my hotel again. I'd wrestled with whether to notify the sheriff's department. But I couldn't. Not yet. I needed more than flimsy connections. I needed evidence. In the end I'd decided to keep my eye on him until morning, make sure he was home or at work, not somewhere tormenting Skylar. And then I'd lay it all out for the department and hope they'd run with it, start the quiet process of investigating, building their case, surveillance, GPS tracking. He would lead us to her if we were careful.

I coasted past the house, followed the street to its end, and turned around at a tangle of kudzu-wrapped pine trees. Then I cut my lights, eased back up the street. I parked along the curb a few houses down.

A streetlight buzzed, blinked, made popping sounds, dimmed like headlights in a fog by the heavy, moist air that settles in on hot August nights. My windows were down. I heard the roar of air conditioners wedged in windows and the whirling fans in condensing units alongside the houses.

I reached around to the back floorboard and found my travel pillow. It's the kind of thing you keep in your car when you spend a lot of time parked on streets watching people. I stuck the pillow behind me and leaned my back against the driver's door with my binoculars in my hand. I studied the house, the front door with no deadbolt, the darkened single-pane windows. No security. No need.

His vehicle was here. He was home, probably sleeping just fine. That meant he wasn't with Skylar. I'd rather she be alone and hungry and scared than dealing with this monster. I had him now, or thought I did. But I only had one chance. If I confronted him with circumstantial evidence, Skylar was dead. He'd never go back to her. He'd never risk it. If I stayed cool and laid out a good case in the war room in a few hours, we could start closing in. He knew the county was being searched building by building and shack by shack. Old storm cellars and wells were being pried open. It was all out there now, practically every piece of information law enforcement had. He'd have to clean the scene, remove anything that was suspicious so some deputy's antennae didn't go up. And he'd have to move Skylar. He'd kill her. It was the only conclusion, the only way to protect himself now.

I lowered my binoculars and leaned into the pillow against my door. My eyes ached and I let them close, but my mind was doing 110, racing back over every moment since I'd arrived, questioning myself, the sheriff's department, seeing all those candlelit faces in the park, probing Whisper's darkest corners. Every investigator in the world has had those cases where they'd have bet the bank on a suspect and found out later they had it all wrong. Investigations are twisty, changing things, as thin and ephemeral as August mist. They remind you of your own humanness and that at the height of all your perceptive rectitude, you could be as wrong as hard desert rain. And I'd been wrong too many times in the past thirty-six hours.

I think it was the sound of the screen door banging. Or maybe it was the scrape of the key in the ignition that roused me out of a drifting sleep. The car was backing out of the driveway, the fog blurring his brake lights. My heart thumped against my rib cage. He was on the move. He'd set his clock to slip out early, when the streets and highways were empty.

I waited for his taillights to disappear off the street, then started my car. The moon was a ringed crescent. A bad moon, my mother would have called it. August fogs and moon rings meant dark days in winter.

I kept my distance as he curved through Whisper for the highway. One glimpse of my white Impala in his rearview and he'd pull off, change plans, perhaps even lead me somewhere to do to me what he'd done to them. I felt for the Glock next to me on the seat.

His headlights touched the tasseled edges of a cornfield as I followed him down a dark two-lane, my own lights off. My right knee had a tremor when I pressed the accelerator. My body was generating the hyperaroused cascade of hormones that prepares you for danger. I could taste them, feel them coursing through me, terrifying and addictive. It must have been close to what he feels in those moments when he's talking to them but not hearing, when norepinephrine is blasting through his system, when he's getting an erection and his snake's brain is telling him the exact moment to strike.

He touched his brake lights and slowed, almost stopped. He'd seen me, I thought. He turned onto a narrow one-lane dirt road. I waited, then followed, kept his brake lights in front of me for a mile, red dust rising up off the road and clinging to the haze. I tensed with every curve, expecting to see him waiting for me around each bend.

He turned again. South this time. I saw tall grass and weeds in his headlights. I stopped and picked up my binoculars, watched his car creeping through a field.

I pulled up location services on my phone. I'd completely lost a sense of where I was.

His brake lights glowed crimson. He'd stopped, the arc of a small structure illuminated briefly before he cut his lights.

"Skylar," I whispered, and thought about the panic and terror she must feel at hearing that engine. I pressed in Meltzer's number, picked up my gun, and started through tall, wet grass that rippled like water as I ran, soaking my legs. "I need backup now, and an ambulance." My voice shook.

The lake was near. I could smell it—a thousand pungent, intoxicating scents hanging in the heavy air. The woods edging the field looked like a ragged black wall. Everything alive in Georgia on a late-summer night buzzed and bit and scampered as I ran. My heart was ricocheting off my eardrums. I looked up at a thin web of light emitting from the structure ahead. The lantern, the kerosene residue on the note. My foot hit a rock and I went down; dirt and pebbles tore into my palms.

And then I heard it, and the world tipped up on its axis—Skylar's scream, hoarse and jagged, like breaking glass in the night.

"Let her go. Let her go!" I screamed, and ran hard and fast in that swaying, disorienting blackness toward the building ahead. I fired my gun. I had to distract him.

A bullet kicked up the earth in front of me. The *pop* of his service weapon registered in my brain a moment after. I kept moving. He fired again. I felt the dirt spray my cheek, and dove into the grass. A third shot nearly hit its target.

"Let the girl go!" I yelled. "It's over, Raymond."

42

could make it out now. It was small, a ramshackle woodshed, a smokehouse. Raymond was standing at the corner of the shack. The lantern was burning on the ground behind him, making him darker, bigger, bulkier. He fired again. Nowhere close. He'd lost me.

I inched slowly toward him through reedy grass, felt the dry ground burning my elbows raw. I found my keys, wrapped a firm fist around them so they wouldn't jangle, then hurled them with all my might. I heard them hit the ground, heard his weapon discharge again. I scrambled up and fired.

Raymond howled, grabbed his leg, nearly crumpled. His gun hit the ground. *"Don't move,"* I yelled as I ran toward him, the Glock in front of me. My own voice sounded foreign, packed with adrenaline and fury. I scooped up his gun and wedged it in my pants, saw his shredded pant leg and the blood spreading over his thigh. "Give me your cuffs and your keys, asshole."

Raymond made a move toward his belt, winced. I took a step closer and aimed at his forehead. "Keys and cuffs. Now." I looked at the shack, shouted out. "Skylar, honey. You're safe. It's going to be okay, sweetheart. I'm coming in to get you."

"How'd you know?" Raymond asked.

"The note you took to the lab. My prints weren't on it. I handled it without gloves, which means you wiped it clean. You had to make double sure you hadn't left anything on it. And the iced coffee in your car. You'd been in town. Robbie said so too. No one would have noticed you leaving the note."

His legs were stretched out in front of him awkwardly. He dropped the cuffs. "Put them on," I ordered, and called out to Skylar again. I heard no cries for help. No screams.

"So now you think you're gonna get to be the big shot," Raymond growled, not moving. "You have no idea—"

"I did some checking on you. Your sister lives in Silas. She's a teacher where Tracy went to school. You were around there a lot back then since Robbie lost his mom in the lake and all. Funny thing about your wife." I bent and snapped the cuffs on him. He didn't move. "She was a pretty blond, wasn't she? Found out she was a good swimmer in high school."

Raymond grimaced. His pant leg looked slippery and dark in the lamplight. "None of it matters now," he said.

"You move while I'm gone and I'll kill you when I come back." I grabbed his keys. "You even look at her when I bring her out, I'll shoot you."

I took the lantern. Thirty-seven hours into her nightmare, I was finally going to dig her out.

The stench of urine and mildew and worse slapped me in the face when I pushed the door open. "Skylar, honey. I'm here. It's going to be okay."

I held the lantern in front of me and saw that smiling girl in the photos looking up at me. Her mouth was stretched wide and silent, eyes fixed with the terror and betrayal she'd taken to death. The axe lay next to her head, gleaming with blood and tissue. He'd killed her like he'd killed Tracy, as if it were just a necessary task. He'd used the axe because he didn't want to discharge his weapon. Not when the whole county was watching and listening.

I knelt down next to her, smelled her blood and excrement and her dirty hair. I saw a single mattress, stained and reeking. I saw the Nine West handbag he'd let her keep. Skylar was on her back with her legs straight out in front of her, ankles rubbed raw and bruised. Chains had been secured around an old engine block and stretched out four feet, rusty ankle cuffs attached to them. He was dragging her out when he'd heard me running and screaming, running and screaming, then firing my gun. It was too late. I was too late. I hadn't screamed loud enough. I hadn't fired fast enough. I'd let the world have her. I'd let it crush her and break her parents' hearts.

I put her head in my lap, touched her warm forehead, pushed blond hair out of her eyes. "I'm so sorry," I told her. I choked on the words. Even they were too late.

I put her head down gently, staggered outside, furious and heartsick, sucked clean air into my lungs. Raymond watched me, my bullet burning in his leg, his cuffed wrists in his lap. He was sweating.

"You fucker!" I cried. He stared up at me in the lantern light. "You could have let her live. You knew this was almost over. You knew we were closing in."

"I had to end this my way," Raymond said. "You don't understand, Street—"

"Oh I understand," I snarled. "Remember, I'm the one who gets you."

I heard that panicked scream again, raw and sharp—I heard it shooting across the fields to the lake, ripped open and full of terror. I thought about Hayley and Brooks Barbour. This sunrise was going to feel to them like the swing of that axe. I thought about Bryant and Molly Cochran holding their candles in the park for the little girl he'd taken and tortured and dumped like trash. I thought about him standing over that hole with me, grinding his cigarette into the dirt and leaves, threatening me. I thought about Josey Davidson, childless, twisting her wires.

Sirens screamed through the night. Rack lights flashed in the distance and lit up low pockets of sky like a lightning storm.

I lifted my Glock, and I shot him again.

43

I didn't go back inside that stinking, broken-down prison. Meltzer and Brolin were inside now. They had walked past Raymond without a word after I'd briefed them at their vehicles. Brolin had nearly broken down when she looked at him. She'd made a tiny sound like a sick cat. Meltzer had reached for her arm to steady her, to keep her moving.

The path to the shack was alive with squad cars and deputies and light in the fog, and the squawking of police scanners. Sam and Mori had arrived in the crime-scene van. Lights had been erected as they had the night we'd searched for evidence on Cottonwood Road. Sam had swabbed Raymond's hands for gunshot residue and other evidence, had photographed his clothes before they went in to process the crime scene. She'd instructed the deputies to bag his clothes at the hospital. Under the bright lights I saw now that the front of his shirt was speckled with blood spatter.

I turned Raymond's weapon in to evidence, then walked out in the field alone to search for the keys I'd thrown, the keys that had bought me time, and maybe saved my life.

Sometimes it ends this way, I reminded myself. Sometimes things don't work out.

I heard Brolin's voice behind me. "Was the second shot just for fun? Or was that self-defense too?"

An ambulance howled up the path. I turned. "My weapon accidentally discharged."

"Mine would have accidentally discharged in his *face*," she spat. She wasn't kidding. She helped me look for my keys. The sheriff came out and we all watched Raymond loaded onto a gurney. Two deputies piled into the ambulance behind him. An EMT slammed the doors.

"What am I going to tell Robbie?" Meltzer asked quietly. "He's at my house sleeping."

"I just can't believe it," Brolin said, not for the first time. "How could he do something like this?"

"Let's find Raymond's sister," Meltzer said. "Robbie's going to need her."

"She's in Silas," Brolin and I said simultaneously. She looked at me, and I saw it in her eyes. She'd realized all the ways she'd looked right past him, ignored the connections. "He used me," she said. "He kept me close to protect himself."

"He used us all," the sheriff told her. "Nobody's getting out of this clean."

"I have to go to the hospital and get his statement," she said. "We can't give him time to think."

"I'll send Ferrell and the tech guy with video," Meltzer told her. "I think you should sit this one out, Major."

"Ferrell's a rookie," Brolin argued. "He'll lawyer up on her."

"I'll go," I said. "He told me he wanted to end this his way. He's ready to talk. He didn't even put up a decent fight. Funny how it goes like that. In the end, they're just cowards. They just put their fucking hands up."

"You can't go," Meltzer said. "You shot the man, Keye. I'm sure the evidence will support you, but if you were one of my people, you'd be on paid leave right now and nowhere close to the case. You're done. You're a witness now. Meet us back at the judicial center so we can get your statement. Come on, Tina, ride with me. We have to wake up Skylar's parents." He looked at me before he got in his truck. *You okay?* he mouthed.

The coroner's van zoomed past. I gave him a thumbs-up. But as I walked back through the field to my car, I knew I'd lied.

44

The statement I gave to Meltzer and Brolin in an interview room at the judicial center was long and detailed. It had to be told, then written and signed. I started with the notes in my hotel room, the memory of Raymond's messy car, the melted iced coffee inside, remembering Robbie mentioning his father being in town, the dog from the K-9 unit tweaking to Raymond. We'd thought it was because he'd mishandled evidence, but it was because he'd been near Skylar. I told them about the first note, which had been wiped clean. I'd run a check and discovered Raymond's wife was a strong swimmer, that she was small and blond just like Tracy and Melinda and Skylar. That's why he punished them. He was trying to punish his wife. And that's why he'd gotten drunk then and why he'd gotten drunk last night. Because he knew how close we were and he knew he had to kill Skylar and clean up his dungeon. I told them how I'd found his sister had taught at Tracy's school. He was in uniform then, and Tracy probably knew him as the police officer brother of a teacher. And even as cautious as she was about upsetting her abusive father, she might have accepted a ride from him. I told them I'd gone to his neighborhood, slept on his street, and woke to his brake lights backing out. I told them I hadn't notified them before we arrived at that field because I wasn't sure, and because he was one of theirs. I wanted a smoking gun. I didn't know I'd find a dead girl. No one said it, but I knew we all thought it. Might the ending have been different if I hadn't acted alone? Would Skylar have lived? How would we have acted as a unit if I'd called them from the hotel when my suspicions first piqued? We'd never know. And the weight of that fell hard on my shoulders.

I looked through the glass at Robbie Raymond in the next room. His fair skin was splotched with red, his blue eyes were puffy and watery. A bruise covered his cheekbone and circled one swollen eye. A woman stood with her arms around him, tall and dark-haired like Raymond, but with softer features. His sister, I realized, Robbie's aunt. The woman who'd cared for him after his father had murdered his mother in Lake Oconee. She held him. I saw the tremors shake his big body. Meltzer followed my eyes.

"Both his parents are gone now."

"He have a clue at all?" I asked.

"No," Meltzer said. "Said his dad didn't talk much. He went out a lot and Robbie never knew where. But it scared him when he heard about the kerosene last night. He'd smelled it on Rob. He was trying not to believe it."

Ferrell returned from the hospital and we all watched the video—me, Meltzer, Brolin, Ferrell, and the tech guy who had cued it up. We saw Raymond in a hospital bed, propped up, given enough pain meds to take the edge off. He wanted to talk.

"When did you first meet Tracy Davidson?" Ferrell asked him.

"The day I took her," Raymond said. Beside me, I heard Brolin suck in air. Any doubt she was harboring had been torn away from her. "But I'd seen her at my sister's school. And I don't know what happened. I swear to God, I don't know what happened. Something just snapped in my brain. And then I had her. I couldn't do anything but keep her or kill her. I couldn't let her identify me. I had Robbie to take care of—"

"Yeah, you're a real hero, Raymond," I muttered.

Ferrell's voice was calm, steady, no judgment. "Did you kill Tracy Davison, Mr. Raymond?"

I smiled. She wouldn't refer to him as detective. Not now, not with the dishonor he'd shown the department.

"Yes." Raymond's big head drooped from pain or shame or exhaustion. "I couldn't do it anymore. I couldn't take care of her."

"Did Tracy Davidson become pregnant and give birth while you held her?"

"Yes," Raymond said.

"What happened to the baby?"

"It died," Raymond answered quietly. "I dropped it down an old well."

"Did you kill Melinda Cochran and Skylar Barbour?"

"Yes."

"Did you kill your wife?"

"Yes," he said. Nothing but resignation in his voice. He was ready to send himself to death row. "I caught her with someone, another man. I was just going to scare her . . ."

"God," Meltzer muttered. Brolin covered her mouth and walked out. I didn't move. I'd heard too many statements. *Something just snapped. I don't know what happened.*

"I don't get something," I said, watching the screen. "Why did he look at the picture of Skylar's broken finger and throw up?"

"You said it yourself. He's a psychopath. He's whatever he needs to be." Meltzer said it grimly.

Fluorescent lights buzzed above us, the room still and cold as a cathedral.

"And Luke," I said. "Why didn't he spark to Raymond that night?"

"Keye," Meltzer said gently. "We have him. It's the only good thing that came out of this. We have him red-handed and he can't hurt anyone else. We have his confession. And when the scene is processed, you know as well as I do that it's going to lock in the case against him. Come on, look at you. You're exhausted. Go home."

I looked down at my torn-up hands and knees, the blood on my shirt and pants. I hadn't even known it was there. I'd lifted Skylar's sweet head into my lap and I'd apologized to her. Too late.

"Go," Meltzer said. "Sleep. You did your job. This is the part we know how to do."

I went back to the hotel and stood under a hot shower, raw skin stinging from the fall I'd taken in the field. I stood there until the water ran cold, twisted my hair in a towel, and climbed into bed. It was noon. Brooks and Hayley's daughter's body was in Atlanta now, probably already on an autopsy table at GBI. I thought about Skylar's eyes, her blood and tissue clinging to the axe. I thought about the last thirty-seven hours of her life. And I forced myself to close my own eyes.

I didn't open them again until six. I made a terrible cup of coffee from a tiny pot that poured water over a bag, and switched on the television. It was all there, the sensational news that a local police detective who had worked on the cases had been arrested for three murders.

"According to the Hitchiti County sheriff," Brenda Roberts reported, *"the suspect in custody would have been a uniformed deputy at the time of the first abduction and murder. Local townspeople are in shock. The detective was a longtime resident . . ."*

I saw a clip with the sheriff, scruffy and unshaven the way he was when I'd last seen him. Meltzer gave me full credit for identifying the killer. He didn't share any other details regarding the capture or the hours Skylar had endured at the hands of a killer. The victims were lost in the news reports. They were all about Raymond and his sick subterfuge, not Skylar, who loved movies and reading and dogs and boys. Not Melinda, who loved music and art. Not Tracy, who cared for her brother and mother, protected them. Tracy, who was probably too polite and too cowed by authority not to climb into his car that day.

I brushed my teeth, splashed some water on my face, and got dressed. My phone trembled on its charger at the bed table. I saw Meltzer's name and reached for it.

"So I'm just thinking, you're probably leaving soon," he said. "And I'd like one chance to have dinner with you when I'm not the sheriff and you're not the consultant."

I sat down on the bed. "I don't think that's a good idea."

"Because you're afraid," he said.

"Yes," I told him. "I'm scared to death of turning my life upside down. And if I ever decide to do that, I'm not going to do it this way. He's a good man, Ken."

"I understand," he said.

"How's Robbie doing?"

"He's with his aunt now. Poor kid. We went through Raymond's house today and confiscated the electronics. We matched the printer to the photograph. Haven't located the original image. Or any other images. No online storage. Probably deleted whatever he had. But the case is rock-solid, right down to his prints on the axe handle. And we recovered evidence from the well."

I was silent. I couldn't think of that newborn and Tracy's suffering.

"You still worried about something?" Meltzer asked.

"Rough week," I answered. "I keep seeing Skylar. I'll get there."

"Want to come outside and say good-bye face-to-face?"

I parted the curtain. He was leaning against his truck. No uniform. A clay-colored T-shirt and faded jeans, boots. Good Lord, he was gorgeous. He smiled. Held up his phone, ended the call and dropped it in his back pocket, then waited.

His eyes were that soft brown I'd seen over dinner at his house. A slow smile, a blink, long lashes, lips full of color. He'd gotten a shave, and the triangle under his lip was perfect again. "Why'd you have to come here?" I asked as I walked toward him.

"How could I not? It's one of those 'what if' things, you know? I don't want that on my shoulders." He bent and pressed his lips against mine. I felt his hand come around me, felt him step closer, his body relaxing into me, pulling me nearer. His mouth was wet and soft and every taste, every movement, every shiver, told me how much he wanted me. And I knew what my body, my lips, my fingertips, were saying to him.

"People don't kiss like that if there's nothing there, Keye," he whispered. He'd pulled back, touched my face lightly with his fingertip.

"I know," I said.

He smiled and nodded. "Good-bye, Dr. Street. For now. You have to come back for the court case, don't forget."

I watched him get in his Interceptor. "Good-bye, Sheriff," I said quietly as his taillights disappeared in the distance.

45

had dinner alone. I packed my things, bagged the clothing with Skylar's blood, and tossed the bag in the hotel dumpster. And then I slumped down on the bed. I wasn't ready to go back to my life and my business and my love affair. I wasn't ready to be touched by the lover waiting at home. Meltzer's hands, his mouth, felt burned into me.

I thought about Skylar in cold storage at the crime lab, and her piercing, sorrowful scream clawed through my heart.

I curled up and squeezed my eyes shut. Because that's what I do now when alcohol isn't waiting for me on the other side, when the depression settles in and the only thing that feels right in a dark hotel room is a good cognac warming my throat. It's the work. It's trying as hard as you can and knowing sometimes your best isn't good enough. It's the death. I'd spent four years drinking my way through it. This is how I do it sober.

And so I slept off the cravings, showered, packed my car, and ate halved figs with Gorgonzola and balsamic and Greek yogurt as the sun came up at a restaurant on the lake. I took my time. Nothing to hurry for now. A Sunday morning. The lake was still and quiet, the mist rising up off it like a spirit. Another sunrise for Hayley and Brooks Barbour without Skylar, without the routines. I thought about her diary, the family rituals. The little things, it's what you miss most.

I looked back at the lake and drank my coffee, ignored the Atlanta paper a waiter had put on the table for me. I was thinking about driving, just getting in the car and heading for the coast, for Jekyll Island, for salt air and twisted-up old oaks with black, sea-smoothed limbs.

My phone vibrated and growled on the table. I glanced at the display. *Heather*, it said. Melinda Cochran's friend. I'd locked in her number when she'd called me at the justice complex. I let it ring. I was ready to leave Whisper, leave Melinda and Tracy and Skylar. The display lit up again a minute later. "Shit," I growled, and hit ANSWER. "This is Keye Street. What's up, Heather?"

"I didn't tell you the truth about something," she said. I looked back at the lake and listened as it came pouring out of her like an exorcism. I thought about Meltzer saying, "Nobody comes out clean." She'd given Melinda to him. They all had. She'd let him have her as I had, as Meltzer had. She hadn't meant to. They didn't know the thing they were protecting was the thing that would kill her.

"No one knew, Heather. It's not your fault." I gathered up my keys and left money for the check.

"I was glad at first when she was gone," she confessed, and started to sob again.

I got in my car and mapped out my route, found the highway and headed south. Thirty minutes later I parked in front of a blue split-level and walked up the sidewalk past red geraniums and gerbera daisies. I picked up the newspaper on the sidewalk and carried it to the door, knocked lightly.

"Ms. Raymond," I said. "I'm sorry to disturb you so early. I'm Keye Street."

"I know who you are," she said evenly. She'd awoken to a hard truth this morning. She'd lost a brother. And all the terrible things he'd done had pulled at her mouth and eyes and aged her.

"Do you think it would be okay if I talked to Robbie for a few minutes?"

She hesitated. "He's been through so much . . ."

"Just a few minutes," I pressed, and she stepped aside and gestured for me to come in.

"He just woke up," she said. "I'll let him know you're here. Would you like something? Coffee?"

"No. Thank you. I'll wait here."

I stood in the foyer looking through a glass storm door at the manicured lawn, the neighborhood, middle income and cared for. "Dr. Street." I turned and looked up at Robbie's face. Some of the swelling had gone down and that bruised eye was open now and clear and blue. "What's going on?"

"I'm headed out of town. But I wanted to check on you. Feel like taking a walk?"

"Okay, sure." He slipped long, sockless feet into Nikes. We crossed the lawn together and walked down the sidewalk, Robbie watching the ground, hands dug into his pockets. "My dad okay?" he asked, after a while.

"Still in the hospital," I said. "They'll move him today. I've been thinking a lot about him."

"Me too," Robbie said. "I miss him. You never think about losing your dad."

"He told me he just wanted to end it his way." We walked under the water oaks lining a street warmed with morning light. "He told me that's why he killed Skylar. Because he just wanted it to be over."

"Do we have to talk about this?" The teenager's voice was distant and aching.

"You remember Tracy, don't you?" I asked. I stopped and looked at him. He wore jeans and an untucked blue shirt. He had that slumpy teenage-boy posture. He didn't take his hands out of his pockets. It took him a long moment to answer.

"I heard him open the trunk," he said darkly. "I was sleeping in the car. He didn't know I got out and followed him."

"So you saw her. Did you see him kill her?"

"Yes. Oh God." He put his hand in front of his mouth. Robbie started to cry. "I couldn't tell. He's my dad. Are they going to keep him a long time?"

"He murdered three women. I think he'll be convicted on two of them. There's a lot of evidence."

"They told me he killed my mom. So that's four."

"But you killed Melinda, Robbie," I said. His chin came up. No more sadness. No more grief. His eyes dried almost as quick as he'd whipped up the tears. He said good morning to a woman who passed us with a yipping, tail-wagging Yorkie. We started to walk again. "You know, when I got the first note and handed it to your dad, he wiped it down before he took it to the lab. I realized this morning that wasn't at all what it looked like. He was protecting you. Same with Skylar. In his fucked-up logic your father decided to kill her, to clean up your mess. That's why he hit you, isn't it? He was furious about the photograph. The guy puked when he saw it. And the notes. You very skillfully planted the seed in my head that your dad had been in town when the letter was delivered. You took Melinda and Skylar. That's why there was an escalation in violence, that's why Melinda's body was rolled and not thrown. Because you didn't know what you were doing. She fell when you hit her, didn't she? Was she dead or did you leave her to die?"

"Very interesting theories, Dr. Street. Honestly, I'm totally blown away right now."

"He must have realized when the bodies were found, because you screwed up and dropped evidence, that he'd raised a killer," I said. "He made you promise not to do it again, didn't he? And then I came to town, and the rumors and the gossip started, and you knew it was your chance to grab Skylar and throw him under the bus."

I thought he might smile. His lips quirked. "Crazy talk."

"Oh come on, Robbie. Like I could sell this to Ken Meltzer. With all the evidence pointing at your dad. Ken adores you. Besides, you know I'm not a cop. You want to frisk me or something? You think I'm wearing a wire? You want to check my phone? Maybe the FBI has a recording device in it. Maybe a big black helicopter will swoop down. That would be a fitting end, wouldn't it? Lot of drama and attention. I'm sorry I couldn't arrange it for you. This is for me, for closure." I took my Glock out of the holster, held up my arms, my phone in one hand, my Glock in the other, made a circle. "Go ahead," I challenged him. "But make a move for the gun and I will shoot you."

Robbie didn't touch me. He watched with something that looked like amusement. His dry eyes were lit with the new fire and fear and delight of being seen for what he was, what he truly was. In the end, I knew his ego would win. The thing he believed in most of all was his ability to con the world. He watched me with his clever predator's eyes, sizing me up, judging his risk, my weaknesses.

"Lot of things weren't adding up," I said, lowering my arms, returning the Glock to the holster. "And then one of Melinda's friends called me. The girls knew you and Melinda were flirting or whatever you were doing, and they were hiding it, protecting her, because they knew her parents wouldn't approve. And when they heard about your dad, they thought that by continuing to protect Melinda's secrets, they'd exposed Melinda to him, through you. They still haven't put it together. Because you're the cute guy with the guitar, right? I realized you were the reason Melinda and Skylar were pulling away from school activities. Because the adorable little psychopath in the neighborhood was seducing them."

"A psychopath," he said. "Is that what I am?"

"We both know you are."

"Because I like them when they first get tits?"

"No. Because you can't feel their pain. Your dad, he's a thug and a killer too. But he's different. He doesn't crave it. He feels remorse. He could stop."

"He's an idiot," Robbie said. "So easy to get him all torqued up. When he found the phone on the road he was so mad I'd done it again. Especially with you here. He said the searches were starting. I told him I wanted to fuck with her like he fucked with that Tracy girl. I was in the car that day he talked her into getting in, in the front seat. He told me Tracy was lying down because she got sick. But I knew he hit her."

"So you got your dad all worked up. You knew he'd go out there to clean up the scene and make Skylar disappear. You set him up. Just like you set me up. You knew I'd spark to him with your black eye and his finger in my face at the park, the clever hint you dropped on Main Street. Well played."

"I have to admit it was easier than I thought. I'm learning a lot about human nature. I'm smarter than you think I am."

"Maybe," I said. I started walking back to my car. He followed me. Of course he would: I was feeding his ravenous ego. "There is one thing I'm curious about, though. I think I understand, but I want to be sure. These girls liked you. Melinda and Skylar would have gotten in your car. So why con them with the breakdown? Why risk doing it in the open?"

"Because not doing it is riskier." He said it matter-of-factly.

"You want to get control right away. Is that it?"

"Gotta show 'em who's boss," he said. "Get them in the car and they get squirmy and start worrying about their mommies and daddies and where you're taking them. They can spook and bail."

"Ah. You tried it before," I said. "And screwed it up. Did she report you?"

"Seriously? I'm the cop's kid. Who'd believe some weepy teenage girl? And I'm a heck of a nice guy." He took a deep, exaggerated breath and blew it out. "You think we could talk sometimes? I like talking to you."

"Enjoy it while you can," I said, and opened my car door.

He looked down at me with those innocent blue eyes. "She looked so pretty in your mascara, Keye. I thought you'd want to know."

I took a last look at him as I pulled away, skinny and sweet and battered and not at all like the monster he really was. I switched off the voice memo app on my phone, hit PLAY, and listened. I heard my voice and Robbie's. I praised the smartphone gods, touched the SHARE button, and emailed the entire conversation to the Hitchiti County Sheriff's Department.

Epilogue

drove the way I'd fantasized over breakfast. I drove like I'd stolen the car, top down, hair flying behind me. I drove toward the thing that always grounds me, sets the world right after it's tipped up on its end, connects me again, mends what's broken and numb. I drove toward the marsh and sand and gnarled live oaks until the scent of Jekyll's briny, seductive coast rose up over the hood of my Impala, musky and voluptuous and ripe. A Low Country girl had raised me. My mother had fished and played and come of age on the banks of the Albemarle Sound, and she wove gorgeous, vivid, harrowing, romantic tales about the geography that had shaped her. And in doing so it had shaped her children. Jimmy and I both are terrified of the sea while being irresistibly pulled to it.

I saw my phone lighting up on the seat next to me as I crossed the causeway bridge. First Rauser's ringtone sang out, then Meltzer's. No designated ringtone for the sheriff. Not yet. I didn't answer for either of them. I needed to think. I needed bare feet on the hard-packed sand. I needed salt air. And miles between us. Just for a minute, an hour, a day. I needed to be alone. I needed to make decisions.

When I heard the default ring a second time, I reached to silence the ringer. I had expected to see the sheriff's name again, but I saw a

954 area code instead. I thought about Robbie talking about learning human nature. Curiosity got me.

"Keye Street," I answered.

"My name is Ching Lan Lin," she said. Her voice was smooth, unaccented. "Do you recognize my name? I'm your mother."

Acknowledgments

One of the many things I didn't realize when I began the Keye Street series is what a collaborative process book writing is and that it takes an army of people to help a writer get it right. I've been fortunate to be surrounded by exceptionally smart and generous professionals.

Huge thanks to my amazingly dedicated team at Random House who believed in a new voice and nurtured this series. I have tons of starry-eyed adoration for you all.

Thank you Special Agent Dawn Diedrich from the Georgia Bureau of Investigation and Dr. Jamie Downs, Coastal Regional Medical Examiner, Georgia Bureau of Investigation.

Thanks to the gang at Victoria Sanders & Associates, to Chandler Crawford and Angela Cheng Caplan for everything you do. And a special thanks to Victoria Sanders, who made this possible.

Benee Knauer, friend, best research assistant ever, straight shooter, what would I do without you talking me down a couple of times a year? Thank you.

And to Ken Meltzer, animal lover and high-bidder in the character name giveaway to benefit homeless animals and the Lifeline Animal Project, who graciously agreed to let me have my way with his name and reputation. Ken, I hope your wife approves.

Can't get enough of Keye Street?
Keep reading for an extract from the very first
in this thrilling series

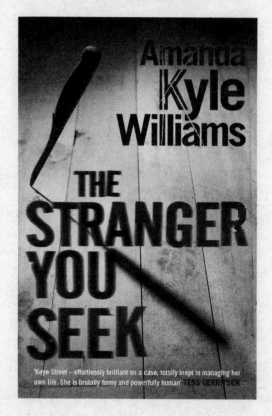

Out now

Prologue

The sun had not even burned dew off the grass under the live oaks, but the air was thick and soupy already, air you could swim around in, and it was dead-summer hot.

Inside the car she had not yet noticed parked on her street, a patient hunter dabbed at a trickle of perspiration and watched as Westmore Drive began a sleepy jog toward midweek.

The white-trimmed windows in the small brick house were flung open around seven, and she first appeared as a faint image behind the kitchen window, nearly abstract behind glass and screen, but no less an object of desire. The smell of cooking food drifted from her screened windows – frying bacon and toast and coffee – and Lei Koto's killer felt the first stab of hunger this placid summer morning.

A little before ten the street was silent. The last neighbor had left for work, 9:50 on the dot as always. The smells from Lei Koto's kitchen had shifted from breakfast to something else, something green and cabbagy and rank.

The car door opened, then footsteps on the concrete walk, a briefcase, good shoes, a white smile, a business card.

They always open the door.

Chapter One

My name is Keye Street. First name from my Asian grandfather; my adoptive parents awarded me the second. By trade I am a detective, private, that is, a process server and bail recovery agent. In life, I am a dry alcoholic, a passionate believer in Krystal cheeseburgers and Krispy Kreme doughnuts, and a former behavioral analyst for the FBI. How I ended up here in the South, where I have the distinction of looking like what they still call a damn foreigner in most parts of Georgia and sounding like a hick everywhere else in the world, is a mystery Emily and Howard Street have never fully unraveled for me. I know they had wanted a child so badly they adopted a scrawny Chinese American with questionable genes from an orphanage. My grandparents and guardians had been murdered and my biological parents consisted of two drug addicts and one exotic dancer. I have no memory of them. They took flight shortly after my birth. I can only manage a word or two in Chinese, but my mother, Emily Street, who is as proficient in innuendo as anyone I've ever known, taught me a lot about the subtle and passive-aggressive language of southern women. They had tried for a cute little white kid, but something in my father's past, something they have for my entire life flat-out refused to share with me, got them rejected. It didn't take me long to understand that southerners are deeply secretive.

I embraced the South as a child, loved it passionately and love it still. You learn to forgive it for its narrow mind and growing pains because it has a huge heart. You forgive the stifling summers because spring is lush and pastel sprinkled, because November is astonishing in flame and crimson and gold, because winter is merciful and brief, because corn bread and sweet tea and fried chicken are every bit as vital to a Sunday as getting dressed up for church, and because any southerner worth their salt says please and thank you. It's soft air and summer vines, pine woods and fat home-grown tomatoes. It's pulling the fruit right off a peach tree and letting the juice run down your chin. It's a closeted and profound appreciation for our neighbors in Alabama who bear the brunt of the Bubba jokes. The South gets in your blood and nose and skin bone-deep. I am less a part of the South than it is a part of me. It's a romantic notion, being overcome by geography. But we are all a little starry eyed down here. We're Rhett Butler and Scarlett O'Hara and Rosa Parks all at once.

My African American brother, Jimmy, whom my parents adopted two years after I moved in, had a different experience entirely. Not being white, we were both subjected to ignorance and stereotyping, but even that seemed to work in my favor and against Jimmy. People were often surprised that I spoke English and charmed that I spoke it with a southern accent. They also assumed my Asian heritage made me above average. I was expected and encouraged to excel. The same people would have crossed the street at night to avoid sharing a sidewalk with my brother, assuming that being both black and male he was also dangerous. He'd picked up our mother's coastal Carolina accent, the type usually reserved for southern whites in a primarily white neighborhood at a time when diversity was not necessarily something to be celebrated.

He couldn't seem to find a comfortable slot for himself in any community, and he spent high school applying to West Coast universities and carefully plotting his escape. Jimmy's a planner. And careful with everything. Never screwed up his credit, never got fired, never had addiction issues, and never rode down Fifth Avenue in New York City after a few too many with his head sticking through the sunroof of a limo yelling 'Hey, y'all' like I did. Jimmy's the well-behaved child. He now lives in Seattle with his lover, Paul, and not even the promise of Mother's blackberry cobbler is an attractive enough offer to bring him home to Georgia.

How I came to be here this night, edging my way along an old frame porch, double-clutching my 10mm Glock, body pressed flat against the house, peeling paint sticking to the back of my black T-shirt and drifting onto cracked wood, is another story entirely.

I had once been called Special Agent Street. It has a nice ring, doesn't it? I was superbly trained for this kind of work, had done my time in the field before transferring to the National Center for the Analysis of Violent Crime (NCAVC) at Quantico as a criminal investigative analyst, a profiler. A few years later, the FBI took away my security pass and my gun, and handed me a separation notice.

'You have the brains and the talent, Dr Street. You merely lack focus.'

I remember thinking at that moment that the only thing I really lacked was a drink, which was, of course, part of the problem.

I was escorted that day to the FBI garage, where my old convertible, a '69 Impala, white-on-white and about half a mile long, was parked at an angle over the line between two spaces. Fire one Special Agent, get back two parking spots. Sweet deal.

Now, four years later, I passed under the curtained front window and congratulated myself on accomplishing this soundlessly. Then the rotting porch creaked. The strobe from a television danced across the windows, volume so low I could barely make it out. I waited, still, listening for any movement inside, then stuck my head round and tried to peek between the curtains. I could see the outline of a man. *Whoa!* A big outline.

Jobs like this can be tricky. Bail jumpers move fast. You've got to go in when you can and take your chances. No time to learn the neighborhood, the routines, the visitors. I was here without the benefit of surveillance, without backup, going in cold with my heart thundering against my chest and adrenaline surging like water through a fire hose. I could taste it. *Almonds and saccharin*. I was scared shitless and I liked it.

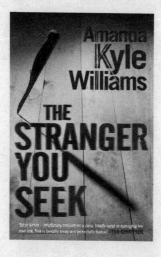

The second in the gripping Keye Street series
By Amanda Kyle Williams

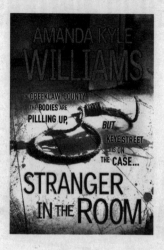

Keye Street is looking forward to a romantic weekend away with her on-off flame Lieutenant Aaron Rauser. But amidst the Fourth of July celebrations, a killer hits the sweltering streets of Atlanta.

Leaving hauntingly festive clues on each of his victims, Keye's cousin Miki is next on the killer's list to be gift wrapped for the Atlanta Police Department. As the heat racks up, so do the bodies . . .

Out now

headline